ENTERING TENEBREA

BOOK ONE OF THE TENEBREA TRILOGY

ROXANN DAWSON and DANIEL GRAHAM

POCKET BOOKS
New York London Toronto Sydney Singapore

An *Original* Publication of POCKET BOOKS

POCKET BOOKS, a division of Simon & Schuster, Inc.
1230 Avenue of the Americas, New York, NY 10020

ISBN: 0-671-03607-6

First Pocket Books printing March 2001

10 9 8 7 6 5 4 3 2 1

POCKET and colophon are registered trademarks of Simon & Schuster, Inc.

Cover design and illustration by Dan Curry

Printed in the U.S.A.

Tenebrea: (Latin) shadow darkness—the liturgical office of matins and lauds sung on the last three days of the Holy Week, with a ceremony of candles.

chapter 1

Andrea took a sip of coffee, then hiked up her skirt as much as modesty allowed to let some sun on her pale legs. She'd faded during winter, her olive skin now looked ivory in contrast to her raven black hair. But the sun could restore a warm tone to soften her high cheekbones and give proportion to her wide-set brown eyes. She looked over the rim of her white porcelain cup to see her husband shepherd their young daughter, who toddled aimlessly among the crush of people milling about the waterfront.

Saturday morning on a vital spring day at Baltimore Harbor—Andrea had taken this tonic each of the twenty-two years of her life: as an infant buckled into a stroller, as a child dangling her feet from the pier, as a tomboy eyeing the cadets from the nearby Space Academy. As a young single woman she toured the old relics from the Federalist Era: monuments, ancient military forts; and their hardware. Her favorite was a black sailing ship as old as the harbor itself: The *Constitution*, a ship famous for her thick oaken hide and for fighting unfairly. She had too many guns according to her adversaries, most of whom she sank.

In recent years the harbor provided a new fascination for Andrea—different species. Baltimore had in the past twenty years grown in importance as an intergalactic port of call for the Alliance. Earth had recently become a hot property because the Alliance discovered a second space-faring human civilization living in the Chelle's quadrant of the galaxy. This new collection of humans was known only as the Cor Ordinate, and they fostered a reputation as independent, distrustful, and possibly aggressive. Although Andrea did not appreciate political nuances, she knew that Earth, heretofore the poor relation in the Alliance, suddenly had clout, as the other members presumed that the Cor Ordinate and Terrans would stick together, upsetting the balance within the Alliance comprised of the Jod, the Chelle, and the Artrix.

She saw a trio of Chelle—on Earth the Chelle never traveled alone. She watched with amusement as they clustered about the ornate espresso machine that ground black beans, then hissed and spit steam in a great show of force to produce tiny cups of beverage. The diminutive Chelle were pale gray, with delicate gangly limbs on squat torsos. They wore uniforms without insignia that looked more like lab coats: loose beige knee-length smocks with long sleeves. Skinny gray legs protruded down to narrow shoes with no buckles, ties, or straps. The Chelle stood on tiptoes to look over the brass rail that kept them from touching the espresso machine. They stared with wide dewy eyes, pointing and criticizing the bad design of the machine—as always hypercritical and suspicious. Terrans simply accepted as fact that the Chelle disliked all things that smacked of Earth.

Andrea noticed a lone Artrix sitting on the concrete steps, a mature male judging by the size and color of his fur. The Artrix had a dense short coat of fur, ranging in color from a creamy yellow to a burnt orange, some mottled, some snow-white with age. Females tended to have lighter fur, plus they typically wore gaudy earrings and flashier pantaloons. He studied a slender stalk of chickweed that managed a toehold in a crack in the cement. *Just a bunch of hairy farmers*, Andrea thought. The Artrix boasted the best agri-science in the galaxy.

His face was beautiful: deep-set eyes over a short snout, not at all like a dog or cat, but round and soft with a herbivore's flat teeth. Around his eyes, the facial hair turned pale, almost the reverse of a raccoon's mask. His body was well proportioned by human standards: a muscular creature used to physical labor.

Andrea surveyed the crowd looking for the formidable Jod with their military bearing, thick bodies, and hairless scalps, but she saw none.

Settling back in her chair, she watched the morning sunshine reflect off the tall buildings of steel and glass that ringed the old harbor, casting dappled light. Even the water seemed active today. An old screw-propeller tug pushed a heavy liquid-hydrogen barge. Bass horns bellowed a warning to clear the deep channel. The cluster of acrylic sails scattered. Hover-taxis veered behind to cross the wake of the precocious tug and her bulbous cargo.

Beyond this nautical free-for-all, stood a grassy hill terraced by ancient earthen works, once populated by cannon, now dotted with gray and white grave markers. Among them rose an obsidian mausoleum, a gigantic black gem. Two years ago, she interred her father's ashes there. She obeyed her father's will and put his ashes with her mother's; it seemed artificial at the time—a great deal of ceremony, flags, rifle reports, drums, bugles, crisp military orders. Two hours of dramatic flair for a simple transaction: she recovered her mother's urn, added the contents from a silver box engraved with her father's name, then returned the urn into a locked drawer—much like an old-fashioned bank vault. Andrea was eight months pregnant with Glendon at the time. Her husband Steve stood silently at her side. Hordes of sympathetic people pressed their hands onto hers and looked into her eyes, yet all she remembered was how lonely the day was.

Andrea forced her gaze off Federal Hill and the shiny black mausoleum, efficiently dispatching that unhappy day to the past. She looked farther into the harbor to a cluster of bristling, glistening spires. There stood the Space Academy, a ghost town on Saturdays, all the cadets gone except for the few miscreants in blue spacesuits pounding the quad, marching off demerits. The academy stood at the mouth of the harbor flaunting her beauty, an architectural composite of tradition and technology—seemingly layered. Thick granite walls speckled with moss marked the periphery and bound the institution in a traditional fortress. A few quaint halls and monuments of weathered stone and tarnished brass clung to the past. Then soaring above tradition stood five towers of clear graphite, each crystal edifice catching and refracting light, ever changing, one moment an orange flash of fire, the next the blue reflection of ice.

Her father, Commodore Flores, had so often pointed to those spires with pride: *Someday you'll be a cadet. Someday, you'll command a starcruiser.*

The stars. Andrea found herself gazing at the academy's launchpad. She studied the shuttlecraft that sat there—a squat cone, not an Earth design. She squinted to make out the hull markings, a set of concentric rings in random colors and widths: Jod markings. She smiled with self-satisfaction. She would have graduated from the academy this year if . . . if she'd followed her first set of dreams.

But her dreams got sidetracked as she fell in love with Steve Dewinter, a mechanical engineer and weekend sailor. She married young to the bitter disappointment of her father. His terse rebuke still rang in her ears. *You are throwing your life away! Wasting yourself!* She remembered the sudden regret that swept his face, but she also remembered his stunning lack of retraction. She chose Steve, and the easy affection she shared with her father withered in mutual disappointment. Steve's foster parents also objected to the match, or more candidly, to Andrea's family connection to the military. Steve shrugged off the Dewinters' nervous pacifism as an annoying, if not culpable, bit of ignorance about the nature of the universe. They reluctantly attended the wedding but excused themselves from the reception at the Officers' Club. Steve still tried to patch the strained relationship. Today was a case in point. He'd wanted to take Glennie to see the reclusive grandparents. She adamantly refused, taunting Steve: *If they want to see their granddaughter—which they don't—they can just crawl out of their Nabbs Creek bungalow and meet us at the harbor for brunch.* Andrea knew her word was final. Steve cajoled but never contradicted Andrea on matters involving their daughter. The Dewinters could wait.

Her father, on the other hand, would have melted at the prospect of a grandchild. This speculation pinched her natural smile into stoic resignation. *Throwing my life away? Had you lived to hold your granddaughter in your lap, your hyperbolic wrath might have changed to joy. Dad, you were as rash and passionate as you were disciplined and forgiving, and almost randomly so . . .*

"Andi." The sound jerked her back from her daydream. Her husband Steve patiently led their daughter Glendon up the terra-cotta steps, one step at a time, to the cafe, both faces wreathed in smiles. Steve continued speaking, assuming he had Andrea's complete attention, "Did you see that street vendor pestering us? Gee, they're getting pushy."

"No." She took her eyeshades off. "Where?"

Steve pointed in the general direction. "The purple hair."

Andrea looked through the collection of street performers. An Artrix juggler levitated four silver orbs. A pale Lavorian woman danced with iridescent hoops around her body before a wall of enthusiastic merchant marines. She sang on the pentatonic scale as her hoops obeyed her exotic movements, each hoop emitting a tone that bent and stretched with her.

"Mommy . . ." Glendon vied for attention, as if the two adults were merely momentarily distracted from her presence. Andrea reached down—almost a reflex—and hoisted the pleading child into her lap. The little girl buried her face into her mother's chest, her head nuzzled beneath Andrea's chin, playing a little game of mock shyness.

"Mommy. Fee' d' bir's." Glendon's request fell on deaf ears. *Purple hair?* Finally Andrea spotted a clown, a bit stocky, even grotesque in costume—a thick shank of dirty purple hair, white face paint, and a red ear-to-ear grin painted on. The clown disappeared behind a cafe, leaving the crowd.

Andrea snapped, "Was he human? These Alliance imports ought to be quarantined."

"A *she*. The clown's a woman, I think. She slapped this stupid tattoo on my wrist, then tries to hustle me for two slips."

Andrea laughed out loud. "And you gave her the money, didn't you?"

Steve had a soft heart, especially for strangers. No hard-luck story was outrageous enough; although she loved his generosity, Andrea felt it her duty to modify this overdeveloped virtue of his. "Well, there she goes with your money. Don't complain about pushy street people when you reward their behavior."

"I couldn't let Glendon see me get into an argument with a clown."

With raised eyebrow, she said, "Afraid she'd see you lose the argument?" she teased. "Let's see this work of art." Glendon peaked sideways through her mother's curtain of hair to see.

Steve showed her the back of his left hand—just above the wrist, a bright yellow disk with blue halo. "That's it? That's all you get for two slips? Steve, sweetheart, you've been had again."

"I didn't get much of a choice. She grabs my hand and . . ."

"Excuses."

Steve picked at the yellow. "It won't come off—must be acrylic." He changed the subject. "Glennie wants to feed the birds. You coming?"

"No. I've scrubbed enough stuff off the deck of your boat—I won't help you refuel the gulls." Spoken like a true waterman. She thought Steve too sentimental, always gushing about the bay, the harbor, the puling gulls, and his sloop, *The Deeper Well*. Andrea, on the other hand, cherished everything about the bay, but without the sentimentality—just practical affection.

She fished a small tube from her purse, then began anointing Glendon with sunblock, ending with their ritual, "And here's a kiss on your head." Andrea gave her a squeeze as she kissed the delicate curls. She sent her off with Steve to buy popcorn with a warning, "You keep Glennie away from the edge of the dock. I won't have her falling into the water again."

"Don't worry." Steve grinned.

"I wone fall'n, Mommy." Glendon grabbed Steve by the leg.

"That's right, Glennie. You hold onto Daddy." Andrea softened, and her natural smile broke through the stern front she pasted on for Steve's benefit. "Okay, at least you'll both go together."

Andrea watched the brazen seagulls swoop down around her husband and daughter. They gleefully tossed popcorn over the water to those mewing, feathered scavengers who moments before might have been pecking a fish carcass or some belly-up blue crab or a rank scrap of garbage. *Gulls don't deserve popcorn.* Andrea purposefully stayed aloof at her cafe table and looked over the crowd beyond the frenetic atmosphere to the water.

Then, a sixth sense warned her something was wrong—a mother's instinct beyond explanation. She quickly spotted a congregation of gulls and in their midst, her daughter: toes at the edge of the seawall. Andrea rose and yelled, "Steve!" *If she falls in, I'll . . .*

Steve couldn't hear over the commotion of frenzied birds and squealing daughter. Or perhaps he simply ignored Andrea's maternal complaints about the water. He grew up on the bay (Andrea said with authority that he'd never really grown up). His daughter would grow up loving the bay. Glendon would grow up savoring the carnival of smells from the waterfront: bay seasoning, cotton candy, coffee, and popcorn—all blended with fishing-boat smells: oysters, crabs, diesel, and pipe tobacco. Steve would teach her to sail; infuse in her the awe of a September squall—sixty knots of pure fury blowing up the bay! He'd show her the breathtaking pinks and reds of a Chesapeake dawn, and he'd share the grace of the magical calm found during a midnight dinghy ride under a canopy of stars. All very grand, and didn't she love Steve for his grand hold on life? But Andrea punctured Steve's inflated agenda reminding him from time to time, *First, we've got to teach Glendon how to swim.*

Andrea waved. Steve paid no attention. He bent over their child, laughing as she kicked at an aggressive gull who'd made a grab for her tiny paper sack of popcorn. Tentative kicks. The child's pluck made Andrea smile. *Good for you, darling!* The offended seagull squawked, wings raised in outrage—in Andrea's mind a threatening gesture.

"Steve!" She raised her voice a half pitch, but with no effect. Now, she'd have to be the *spoilsport*, snatch Glendon from the dock's edge. But that was her duty.

She swallowed her last sip of coffee and put on her eyeshades. She dropped a handful of brass coins on the table, then stepped out from the cafe awning into the sunlight, weaving through the Saturday morning crowd coaxed onto the docks by the ubiquitous street vendors hawking crafts from exotic worlds. Odd, seemingly useless electronic gadgets from the Chelle system; Jodic crystal, and Artrix leather goods filled flimsy stalls. *If he lets Glennie fall into that cold water . . .* In her haste, she jostled the juggler, now mounted on a unicycle, causing him to lose the magnetic levitation and spill the silver orbs.

She paused for a perfunctory apology, then pressed into the crowd. She heard firecrackers—*pop! pop!* The loud noise turned heads. Andrea looked around for the culprit. *Punk kids—they ought to fine the parents.*

Somebody screeched—*laughter? screams?*—then more firecrackers. *There are laws . . .* The old red and gold popcorn wagon toppled to its side. *This is getting out of hand!* Andrea thought. *A few rowdy kids are going to spoil everybody's day.* The gray-haired popcorn vendor staggered back and collapsed as if the earth shook his legs out from under him. Others fell. The crowd lurched. The Lavorian dancer dropped to one knee, then the other, snared in her hoops. Her long hair whipped about her face. The dancer sat up, confusion and shock in her eyes as she looked down at herself: she clutched her chest and a wet indigo poured through her fingers like ink. The crowd scattered, knocking each other down as they scrambled up the steps. Others leapt into the water.

Not firecrackers! The reality stunned her. *Gunfire!* Andrea stood in the chaos and strained to see the pier, but the crowd blocked her view. *Run Steve, run Glennie!* People began to fall around her. The noise of shrieks and gunfire deafened. A half-dozen men wearing plain gray overalls bullied their way into the crowd—all of them intimidatingly large, each brandishing a large-caliber pistol, firing with seeming randomness into the crowd. Andrea found her voice, "Steve! Glennie!"

Then she felt herself knocked off balance, backwards. She spun to the left as she hit the terra-cotta steps. Another body fell at her side, limp, shielding her from another volley of bullets. Andrea fought the sudden dizziness that dragged her toward oblivion: she had to reach Steve. Andrea pushed the fresh corpse aside and tried to shift her weight to her knees, but her left arm failed. A ripping pain in her shoulder stunned her. She glanced at the wound and saw the jagged piece of her collarbone protruding through the bleeding hole in her shoulder. The sky turned pink and she collapsed—nauseous. She lay helpless, watching Steve.

Steve had heard Andrea's warning and saw the men. He gathered his daughter in his arms and started to run but two armed men cut his retreat. The men surrounded him and a half-dozen other hapless civilians on the dock, then rained bullets in their direction.

Andrea winced with each report of gunfire. She saw Steve crumple and fall to the bricks, sheltering her child. Andrea tried to force herself into the fray to help them, but with her useless left arm, she barely struggled to her knees.

The men in gray continued firing as they converged on the wounded clustered at the pier. The random firing ceased as each gunman worked a sector. They moved to the groaning bleeding men, searching each. *For what?* Andrea held her breath as a gray man walked over to Steve. He turned Steve over with the toe of his boot and Steve lifted his left arm as if to fend off a blow. Then with excited gesticulation, the gunman summoned his accomplices. They surrounded Steve. On the leader's orders, they emptied their pistols into Steve's torso. Andrea watched in stunned disbelief and horror as the percussion of the bullets and the backsplash from the bricks levitated Steve's mangled body. Then the leader calmly spoke into a small black transmitter as the pack ran down the dock to a waiting speedboat.

Andrea closed her eyes and tried to will the image

away. She opened her eyes and there Steve lay, in an ocean of blood. *This can't be real!* She finally struggled to her knees and crawled down the steps to the pier. *This is a bad dream. This isn't real!*

She crawled through slicks of blood, past the dead juggler. Andrea felt her heart bursting as she fought reality, as she struggled through her own pain to stand. Then she ran through the gore, finally slipping and falling to her knees beside her husband's riddled body. "Steve! Oh, my baby. . . ."

Steve heard his name and rolled onto his side, exposing their lifeless daughter. His lips moved but the sound was a faint, unintelligible gurgle, and Steve went slack.

I must get help! Weak from her own loss of blood, she managed a hoarse, "Help them!" She looked around. The dead and wounded lay still. The living cowered behind buildings, peering around corners at the carnage; their bewildered stares offered little sympathy—only a worse than useless sentiment: *that might have been me.* Her eyes settled on the one figure standing, a senior Jod Fleet officer. He wore a dark gray uniform, appropriate to oversee death. His large hands grabbed the railing. Younger officers tried to coax the older Jod away, but he stood like flint, his dark, pained eyes staring back at Andrea, communicating his unspoken condolence and the terrible truth: *your husband and child are dead.*

And the truth burned more than the hole in her shoulder. Andrea wailed. She clutched her daughter to her breast with her good arm, rocking as if consoling a frantic infant. But the child was tattered, lifeless flesh; her husband stared up at her in death. Andrea fell over them, soaking their blood into her clothes, sobbing: "Please don't go. Don't go . . ."

chapter 2

The sounds of gunfire and screams gave way to the oscillating pitch of sirens. Less shrill was the soft din of concern around the harbor, and from the middle of the carnage, one heard the pained howling of a wounded animal—a wounded woman cradling a dead man and child. The Jod, Hal K'Rin, stood respectfully at a distance as if watching a solemn rite. The five rings from yellow to violet beneath his eyes made his face look more somber—nature's way of advertising a Jod's age, roughly ten years per ring. He had a powerful jaw.

Behind him, his small entourage watched with morbid fascination. The harbor square just moments ago effervesced with laughter and life, now awash in blood and littered with the dead. But it was the sound of one woman's howling that tore at his heart. He shook his head and whispered, "Butchers!"

"Sir?" The aide, Kip, attended every word.

K'Rin took a large, deep breath of what was for him thin air. "Dismiss my guard. There is no further danger here."

"But, sir. I must insist . . ."

The flash of anger was genuine. "Do it, Kip."

"Yes, Hal K'Rin." With a subtle wave, the aide signaled the small squad of Jod warriors, and they dissolved into the background—not dismissed as K'Rin had ordered, but out of the way and alert. Kip considered Earth's political system of competing states a hopeless morass; consequently he had nothing but contempt for Earth's internal security.

K'Rin ran his hand over his hairless scalp. "Kip, you just witnessed your first Cor Ordinate Hunter operation."

"How shall we explain to the Council of Elders the fact that they slipped through our surveillance?"

K'Rin glowered. "None of your concern, you two-ringer."

"Yes, sir." Kip's neck flushed slightly, not because of the rebuke. He was used to K'Rin's temper, his bark. Kip rebuked himself for failing to read his master's mood. He had one failing as K'Rin's aide-de-camp: he wanted too much to know the inner workings of K'Rin's mind. So he asked questions better left unasked. He probed where he shouldn't.

K'Rin pointed to the corpses littering the panorama. "Did you observe the Hunter's technique?" K'Rin hesitated to call such brutality a technique, but if not technique, what? A style? "Maximum shock to create chaos, isolate and kill the target; no scruples about collateral damage. Fear—always fear."

Kip nodded, "Very thorough . . ."

K'Rin looked at his aide, partly admiring the young Jod's simple, dispassionate critique—excellent training, devotion to duty—but did his young aide completely lack a sense of tragedy? *Soldiering is more than technique.* K'Rin pointed with gloved hand. "Watch. These

Earth security forces are about to make a regrettable error." K'Rin had spent two years studying human behavior—an obsession according to the ruling council on his home planet. "Humans react in different ways when one tries to remove the corpse of a family member. Sometimes they act with simple resignation, but this female won't."

"How do you know?"

"Watch and learn." K'Rin gave his aide a sideways glance that bid quiet. Kip bowed slightly to acknowledge his bit of impertinence, then moved up to the railing and watched the drama below. A policeman in blue tried to distract the woman while white-coated technicians moved in to take the bodies of the man and child. The woman quickly figured the gambit and lunged at an inoffensive man who had laid hands on her mangled child. She shrieked and tore at his face with her good arm, and she might have gouged his eye with her thumb had not two paramedics grappled her into submission, injecting her with a powerful sedative.

"There, Kip, witness the aftershocks of violence wrought upon civilians." K'Rin's neck flushed a pale brown. "Mark this well, Kip. If we allow the Cor Ordinate to extend their reach, someday these scenes will again be common on Jod. If they murder their genetic cousins, what will they do to us?"

Kip kept silent although he knew history well. The worst violence is always internecine. No third-rate Terran massacre could impress a student of the Jod Clan Wars.

K'Rin continued and the raw edge of anger sounded in his voice. "The council should be here and see what you're seeing today. Maybe then they would drop their official opinion that the Ordinate is benign. They ought to ask that woman what she thinks of the Cor Ordinate."

He pointed toward the Earth woman fighting the effects of the drugs given her. Dazed, she pulled the intravenous tubes from her arms and stripped the bandages from her shoulder. K'Rin cocked his head slightly and commented, "She wants to die."

Kip had no other comment but, "Yes, sir—would appear so."

Then the anger returned to K'Rin's voice. "Take a squad of Tenebrea. Find the Ordinate Hunters. Kill them."

"They're as good as dead, Hal K'Rin."

"On your word, Kip. If they get out of this system alive, I'll hold you responsible. I want those Hunters' disrupted bodies commingled in one bag and sent back to Cor."

"Sir, the council expressed displeasure with you the last time you violated protocols for treatment of the Ordinate dead. Are you sure you want me to send their remains back in a waste bladder?"

K'Rin clipped his speech, "They are garbage: treat them as such."

"Yes, sir."

"Don't leave a trace. Sweep the area when you're done."

"Yes, sir." Whatever his orders—even rash—they must be accomplished. As a Hal, a prince, of an ancient house of Jod, K'Rin had power that often exceeded the authority of his military rank. Until recently, his family occupied a seat on the Council of Elders, and K'Rin would occupy that seat had not his father been expelled. Even so, the Rin Clan maintained considerable political influence. Despite failing political fortunes, the Rin Clan remained tied to the Jod military and thereby remained useful to the ruling council. The Rin Family had for five hundred years commanded the Jod forces responsible for offworld intelligence. K'Rin was born into a life of service to his clan and the Jod.

Kip risked another rebuke. "Sir, if you belay your order about sending the Hunters back in a waste bladder, I can make the Hunters disappear. The Terrans—even the Jod outside the Tenebrea—need not know."

"Your point?"

"Sir, Hal Pl'Don has convinced the majority of the council that you have taken on your father's xenophobia and that you have concocted the Cor Ordinate threat to exonerate your father and for personal aggrandizement. The council may interpret your decision to violate the Ordinate dead as an attempt to sabotage any diplomatic chances that may exist. Sir, with six more votes on the council your friends can reinstall you to your family seat. But the more you agitate—"

"Enough." K'Rin managed a sardonic smile. "Diplomatic chances? I'm not going to wait for the Ordinate to attack our homeworld. As for my seat on the council, I can do more good out here than I can cooped up in Heptar. Follow my orders to the letter, Kip."

"Yes, sir." Kip turned to leave.

"One more thing . . ."

"Yes, sir."

"I can't stand watching the Terran authorities mishandle that poor woman. Send my doctor to the Earth woman. Take her into our care. Billet her in my guest quarters aboard the *Tyker*. See that she has the best shock and trauma treatment. At the most basic levels, these humans are psychologically not so different from the Jod. Get her composed. Also, I want a level-one interrogation to find out what she knows about the incident. She may know something of use to us."

"Yes, sir."

"And inform the Earth protocol officer that I hereby invoke Alliance jurisdiction in this matter. The Cor Ordinate government will naturally claim provocation—that Earth gave asylum to a renegade clone. Earth need not respond. We are going to send the appropriate response."

The Jod light cruiser, *Tyker*, sat parked in one of the Earth's five libration points. K'Rin stood in the small briefing gallery and waited for his staff officers to assemble. He stood before a glazed wall that separated him from the eternal black of space. From his perch he looked at the planet Earth below: the blue planet with the turbulent swirls of clouds, ice caps, and broken continents, not like his placid Jod.

He looked at Earth, yet he thought of Cor, home planet of the Ordinate. He'd never seen Cor: no Jod had. However, intelligence reports—mostly secondhand from Chelle sources—painted a picture of Cor as similar to Earth, except that Cor is a planet of greater contrasts: two massive ice caps at either end of a massive ocean; one continent with stark red deserts penned in by towering mountain ranges and verdant forests. Like Earth, Cor had a thin shell of atmosphere, most of it cloudless and benevolent. Yet always somewhere a system of violent weather rushed in from the ocean to rake the land.

The Jod had no experience with the Cor Ordinate's closed society, yet a soldier's intuition told K'Rin that their cultures would soon clash. When he was just a boy, he studied the "mysterious" Ordinate, a species of humans who suddenly appeared in a system once claimed by the Chelle. The Ordinate fascinated him, because his father, known for his guarded opinions, said the Ordinate were evil. *Evil? Why?* The young K'Rin asked his aging father. And his father's face turned to flint as he said, *Because they manufacture clones—beings like themselves—that they use as slave labor.*

Now that his father had passed, K'Rin wanted to ask, *What part is evil, the manufacture, the use, or both?* What K'Rin feared was an army of clones raised against the Jod.

For thirty years, the great debate in the Council of Elders was what to do about the Cor Ordinate. The tough-minded Rin insisted: *We must use the Alliance to contain the Cor. In any case, Cor membership in the Alliance must be conditional on the Ordinate repudiating cloning as a technology.* The opposition argued as fervently that the better course was to absorb the Cor into the Alliance where they might manage the problem or even exploit the situation. Considered the first among equals, the old Rin prevailed.

For thirty years, Rin played on the fear of upsetting the balance in the Alliance. Jod would find itself between two aggressive human cultures. But the cost of Rin's policy was expensive vigilance, an expensive fleet, constant uncertainty, and foregone commercial possibilities—markets abandoned to their rivals, the Chelle. Rin had an enemy on the council, a younger prince from the Don Clan, ambitious to become the first among equals—Hal Pl'Don.

Pl'Don joined, then later led Rin's opposition,

patiently, relentlessly chipping away at the old Rin's arguments, using this issue as a wedge to splinter away the old Rin's allies. By all measurable variables Hal Pl'Don was right. The Jod Fleet was expensive and only recently used in the Chelle Drug Wars. *Like using a cannon to kill a gnat*, K'Rin reflected. The Chelle ignored Alliance policy and maintained an unofficial relationship with the Cor and got wealthier, using their wealth to exert more influence over the Terrans and buy their forbearance. Jod conventional wisdom assumed that the Chelle would successfully sponsor the Ordinate into the Alliance, whereupon the Chelle-Cor-Earth alignment would replace the centuries-old Jod hegemony. Rin's argument became increasingly abstract. Pl'Don accused: *Rin has whipped the empire into an anti-Cor frenzy, and he can't show one benefit to the Jod.*

Hal Pl'Don eventually persuaded a slim majority of the council that K'Rin's policy of isolating Cor was a diplomatic debacle. They abrogated the Rin policy without committing to a new one. And Pl'Don rose in the council to first among equals. Not satisfied with Rin's political defeat—the old Rin had rallied after other setbacks—Pl'Don destroyed the venerable Jod. He accused the elderly Rin of fostering the dangerous "old xenophobia," a powerful catch phrase remembered from the crippling Clan Wars of the previous millennia. He engineered the council's majority vote to strip the Rin Clan of its counselor rights for a generation, the standard punishment meted out to families who recklessly disregarded the "common good."

The council, however, did not consent to Pl'Don's desire to cashier Rin Clan members from other posts of authority. The Rin Clan had been valuable servants to Jod for many centuries. Even Pl'Don recognized the difference between removing a titular family head and disenfranchising thousands of capable—indeed militarily gifted—Jod. Disgracing one old man creates certain manageable problems: attacking the whole clan was too reminiscent of the old ways. Pl'Don took a different tact: he made outwardly sympathetic gestures to the son, Hal K'Rin.

The hot-blooded K'Rin would have used the opportunity to get within arm's reach of Pl'Don to send the usurper straight to Hell, but his father begged him: *Endure my rebuke quietly. Do not provoke Pl'Don. Outlast him. Watch the Ordinate from afar. If you never get to sit on the council, don't worry. You haven't missed much.*

K'Rin remembered his own intemperate words. *Father, how could you let this happen?* The old Rin said bitterly, *I am old, tired, and dying soon. I have lost my honor. Have I lost your respect as well?* K'Rin never forgave himself for remaining silent. When his father died soon thereafter, he swore upon his family crest that he would restore the old Rin's honor or lose his own in the effort. At that moment, K'Rin's professional interest in the Cor Ordinate became an obsession. But information about the Cor Ordinate was scarce and nearly impossible to substantiate.

That situation changed abruptly three months ago. One of his Tenebrea brought in a bedraggled human, half-starved, unshaven, smelling of urine, lice infested—a stowaway on a Jod freighter. The human claimed to be a renegade clone from Ordinate's home world, Cor. K'Rin remembered the short encounter as if it were yesterday: Two Tenebrea, wearing gray duty uniforms, brought the manacled clone to an interrogation cell and set the disheveled man onto a cold chair.

The first few questions established the clone as the experimental ERC model, number 1411, with fewer than three years in service—and much more intelligent than expected. "And what was the experiment?" K'Rin asked.

"The geneticists engineered the ERC model to augment the Ordinate Security Force. They hatched two hundred prototypes, of which I am one. We were coded to maintain order within the clone precincts."

"Interesting—so the Ordinate has a problem controlling their clones."

The prisoner nodded. "The old-order clone is harder to program, not as predictable; we develop a sense of . . . belonging yet not belonging. We don't have a word for it. We are curious and need considerable supervision." Then the ERC clone described in exhaustive detail a technology involving a two-stage incubation lasting five years, during which the hatcheries introduced artificial stimuli to give the larvae a virtual life experience plus rudimentary training. He called the life experience an imprint that faded over time.

"Fade? Do you mean *forget?*" K'Rin wanted to understand the nuances.

"No. The imprint fades as we remember." The clone pointed to his head. "We learn according to our curiosities. We can disobey. We can learn to love, and we can learn to hate. That's the fatal flaw: we outgrow our virtual memories. And that is why the Ordinate has developed NewGen technology—a more perfect clone, from their point of view."

"More perfect in what way?" K'Rin folded his heavy arms.

"Control. The Ordinate correctly views the old-order clone as a time bomb—they created millions of us that might in time turn against our creators. So now they clone the NewGens directly from tissue, and they manipulate the DNA to make the NewGen asexual."

The ERC continued. "I've seen the NewGen prototype with my own eyes. I've been in the Ordinate's genetics laboratory at the Clone Welfare Institute on Cor. They've already started several hundred thousand NewGen larvae. I've seen how they converted the hatcheries. In less than four years, the Ordinate will produce millions of these NewGen models. Then, the Ordinate will cancel the old-order clones in favor of the NewGen model."

"Living machines." K'Rin rubbed his hairless pate as he pondered the significance. "Reliable, expendable."

"The Ordinate can grow a new generation of NewGen every five years. Heretofore, the Ordinate has been reluctant to manufacture too many old-order clones for fear they'd lose control. But with the NewGen model, they'll expand their hatcheries. They'll make and control billions of the NewGen clones. This NewGen technology spells the end of the old order. As soon as the Ordinate has a crop of NewGens in operation, they'll cancel all the old-order models."

"So you ran away." K'Rin loosed this verbal barb just to see the ERC's reaction.

"I came for help." The clone sat straighter in his hard chair.

"Help to do what? To find you a soft life on Anduras Four?" K'Rin feigned surprise.

"To defeat the Ordinate!" The ERC's voice rose.

Now K'Rin had to suppress his real surprise. Collecting his wits, he rejoined, "To usurp power from your creators, it seems to me." K'Rin paced the metallic floor, playing devil's advocate, trying to gauge the clone's convictions.

The ERC clone tugged at his manacles in frustration. "You don't believe me."

"Why should I believe you—a clone, a copy, one of a thousand copies? You come to me a stowaway, smelling like dead fish, pressing me, a Jod Prince, to urge my people to wage a bloody war against the Ordinate. You have no credentials, no family—you have no standing, especially in matters of Jod security interests." K'Rin stood over the clone, his words and posture designed to intimidate. If the clone were lying, he was an ambitious liar. If he told the truth, then his late father's worst fears might come true. K'Rin must press the clone to find out.

But the clone didn't flinch. "I have a name."

And K'Rin continued to badger him. "Favor us with your name, clone."

"I am called Eric."

"A derivative from your model number?"

"That is our custom. I'm sure K'Rin is derivative of something."

K'Rin thought: *These clones are not the hapless creatures I had envisioned.* He kept a stern note in his voice. "Finish your story, Eric."

"Soon after I learned about the NewGen prototype, I defected. I brought many ERC models with me. We worked with a handful of other old-order clones to form an Underground. The Ordinate immediately canceled all the ERC models that remained in service. They dumped a crop of ERC larvae, then hunted us relentlessly. Most of us died fighting, many given up to the Ordinate by *loyal* old-order clones—the fools. I escaped offworld—smuggled aboard a mining tug. As I said, I'm looking for help."

Perhaps the clone told the truth; perhaps not. K'Rin

prodded, "And why should the Jod help you and the old-order clones?"

The ERC clone straightened himself and spoke defiantly. "Purely for self interest, of course. As an ERC larvae I was programmed with this overriding truth: *A threat to clone technology is a threat to Ordinate society.* I haven't forgotten everything. The Ordinate will methodically and pro-actively eliminate any threats to them, and right now, the Alliance is the only power in the galaxy that might raise a finger against them. As soon as they can, the Ordinate will manufacture their clone armies. They'll eliminate the Chelle, then the Jod, then whoever is left."

"The Ordinate has a small fleet—light starcruisers and small interceptors: purely defensive in nature." K'Rin waved his hand in dismissal.

"The Ordinate fleet may not be as small as you think, Hal K'Rin. They are building hundreds of small attack ships: long-range interceptors with an array of quark and neutrino torpedoes."

"You have an answer for everything, don't you?" K'Rin paused, then began pacing again. His boots fell hollow on the metal floor. "What you describe is nonsense. A small craft armed with quarks couldn't withstand the backblast of its own weapons."

"You don't understand, do you?" The ERC clone shook his head. "They don't care about the backblast. They'll overwhelm your dreadnoughts with a swarm of small attack craft. Only one need get through your short-range defenses and launch its torpedoes. The Ordinate expects to lose their small ships and crews: they'll just make more. If you could expend pilots like ammunition, I imagine you'd use a similar strategy. The NewGen clones will execute their missions even if they know the certainty of backblast."

K'Rin pondered this sobering scenario. *A dreadnought takes six years to build and has a complement of four thousand crew plus tender craft. We haven't commissioned a new dreadnought in more than eight years. We have no capital ships under construction. I can't risk our aging fleet to an ill-advised adventure. And I can't risk the fleet by waiting to absorb a suicide raid. Two sides of the same coin.*

At last, K'Rin said, "Suppose I succeed in getting the Alliance involved in a war against the Ordinate—in the process we'd devastate your world. We cannot delicately discern what is Ordinate and what is clone—nor do we particularly care. We'd reduce your cities to ashes. Many more clones than Ordinate will perish."

"My kind is dead already if you don't deal with the Ordinate—they'll cancel the old-order clones as soon as they have NewGen models in production. Then they'll come after you. On the other hand, if you succeed, my kind can build a new future from the wreckage."

"How? You can't propagate."

Here, Eric floundered as he tried to extrapolate from his scant three-years' life experience. "I figure if the Ordinate can genetically engineer clones to be sterile, we might reverse the process and make a generation of clones that can reproduce. We'll teach them to work, pass on our culture; then destroy the clone technology for good."

Clone culture? K'Rin bit his tongue. K'Rin had no more questions for that first interview. He turned to the Tenebrea guards and ordered, "Clean him, delouse him, feed him. From this moment on, his existence is a state secret." Turning to the clone he said, "This interview will continue tomorrow. You are—as it were—under house arrest."

K'Rin didn't send the council all the details of his early interviews with Eric. He did, however, send his assessment that the Ordinate appeared to be developing a clone suitable for military purposes. He requested permission to send sensor drones into the Cor system. And the council responded with an official yawn: *Technological progress is the Ordinate's right as a sovereign species. You will take no action nor conduct surveillance that might jeopardize ongoing diplomatic efforts.* K'Rin sent more requests.

Now, three months and many interviews later, K'Rin looked down at Earth and thought of Cor. He contemplated billions of NewGen clones that lacked any sense of self. He recalled Eric's warning: *The NewGens don't bond. They are incapable of any society except the utilitarian process programmed by the Ordinate. The NewGen has a genetically engineered brain that favors linear thinking. It can manage some creativity in problem solving but is incapable of changing a goal. It has no sense of self beyond the initial memory imprint. Perhaps the consummate warrior, bred in five years, not trained over a lifetime.*

True, the NewGen was a cheap investment by military standards. With such an army, a military governor might subjugate worlds and commit soul-numbing atrocities without any of the unpleasantness rubbing off on his soldiers. He need never worry that the horror might wend its way back to sour his own pleasant society. Warfare without the commensurate horror might be the most horrible of all.

As K'Rin contemplated the future, four staff officers filed in quietly and took seats around a semicircular table. Each wore the simple duty uniform, gray tunic and pants. As K'Rin settled into his chair in the center, he opened with the comment, "This is an informal briefing. There will be no transcript." Then he asked his first question. "What is the status of the shore party?"

The tactical officer reported. "As ordered, a squad of Tenebrea neutralized the Cor Ordinate Hunter team as they waited for transport out. A clean mission. No friendly casualties. No witnesses. The Tenebrea squad is in their quarters giving a debriefing."

"And the mortal remains of the Hunter team?"

"In a hermetically sealed waste bladder." After a pause, the tac added, "Sir, you don't need to send the Hunters' remains back to Cor in a waste bladder."

K'Rin snapped back, "Clear communication develops trust among species. I learned that at the academy, didn't you?"

The ship's engineer suppressed a smile. "You can't be faulted for ambiguity, sir."

The tactical officer quickly closed the subject. "I'll see to it that the package gets delivered to the Ordinate outpost on Clemnos as ordered."

"Their equipment?" K'Rin prompted.

"We have their weapons, communications gear, and their recorders."

"Keep the hardware but erase the recorders."

"Sir, we haven't exploited them yet. They may have useful data."

"I said *erase the recorders*. I don't want some council auditors sniffing around. I quite specifically do not want a record: theirs, ours, yours. Do you understand perfectly?"

"Yes, Hal K'Rin. I understand."

"Now," K'Rin nodded to set the officer at ease, "the Ordinate ship? Have you found it yet?"

The tac spoke plainly. "We believe an Ordinate Class E intelligence ship is hiding within the asteroid belt or behind Triton."

"You don't know?" K'Rin chaffed at guesswork. He tapped his knuckles on the table.

"Sir, Ordinate Class E ships are lightly armed but carry a full sensor countermeasure suite that can throw their image and electronic signature a considerable distance, and they are very agile." Anticipating K'Rin's thought, the tac continued, "They can outrun us to deep space; then lose us."

K'Rin grunted some annoyance, then changed the subject. He turned to his senior intelligence analyst. "Any news from the council?"

The analyst began his report as if cued. "Not much, just that some members criticize your efforts to catch Ordinate Hunter teams as expensive and unnecessary."

K'Rin sat up straight. A slight flush colored his neck, everyone at the table could see that he was becoming increasingly annoyed. "I asked the council to authorize me to intercept and inspect Ordinate mercantile shipping to their Clemnos outpost—technically within Alliance jurisdiction. Any reply?"

The analyst answered K'Rin. "No, sir. They have not even acknowledged your request."

K'Rin grumbled, "Then, they don't want proof. They want the status quo. But, gentlemen, whether they want it or not, we're going to give them proof. When we're done, every child on Jod will be able to see the truth, even if the council refuses to see it."

He pointed to his analyst and tac officer. "Here are my two intelligence requirements. First, I must know the Cor Ordinate's capability. We have heard from our resident clone—a potentially unreliable but presumably knowledgeable source—that the Ordinate has developed a NewGen clone. I must know if this technology is real and if the NewGen can indeed be used in warfare. Second, I must know the Ordinate's intention. Will they manufacture clone armies? Does the Cor Ordinate intend expansion? Do they intend to remain in rigid isolation? Do they intend a preemptive strike to neutralize the Alliance?"

The senior analyst misjudged the rising ire in his superior. "Yes, sir, but the council sent a directive—"

K'Rin stood and slammed both fists onto the table. His neck flared crimson as he let his passions show their full strength. "The next officer that quotes the council's official position to me without my asking for it . . ." He pounded the table again, "I will personally throw that officer off the *Tyker*. Is everybody clear on that point?"

All four answered, "Yes, sir."

K'Rin turned to the analyst again. "Have you learned anything new from the clone, the one called Eric?"

"He described the Ordinate capital, Sarhn, and the surrounding clone precincts in great detail. He also described the clone Underground: a small cadre of clones led by a female he knows personally—I think intimately. Sketchy on details, sir. He won't talk to me about her, but he'll talk to you. Also, he wants to know why we've restricted him to deck five."

K'Rin waved a hand, "Tell him the truth. We have the human female aboard. For security reasons, he stays on deck five until she leaves. Meanwhile, continue interrogating Eric about topography and Ordinate capabilities. I'll pursue the details about his underground organization. He's the best source of intelligence we have at the moment."

Risking a flare-up, the tac officer reminded K'Rin, "No matter what the clone tells us, the council will reject the information as tainted. We've got to get some corroborating evidence. We need nothing less than a pair of Jod eyes on Cor."

The analyst picked up the discussion. "How can we accomplish that with zero access to Cor? We have no embassy, no diplomatic or cultural exchange with the Ordinate. We do not trade with them. Our closest contact is an occasional glimpse of their activities on Clemnos, from which we can tell almost nothing, except that they're buying technology from the Chelle. A Jod can't get within twenty parsecs of their system. We can't intercept communications; we can't get imagery. We are forbidden to send a probe or inspect their shipping. We can't get near them."

K'Rin paused in his own thoughts. "We can't get near them if we rely on doctrine. I'm sure there is an answer to this puzzle, and I'm equally sure that the answer is unorthodox." He gazed around the table looking each officer in the eye. "Gentlemen, start being creative."

With that, K'Rin dismissed his staff—all except the ship's surgeon. "Yes, Hal K'Rin. You want to see me alone?" the surgeon asked with a frayed edge to his voice. He looked tired.

"I do." K'Rin leaned back in his chair and asked, "How is the human, Andrea?" K'Rin had asked this question each day since the massacre. The woman had refused food and drink for days, despised all counseling, all offers of help. She didn't sleep, except under heavy medication, and even sedated, she preferred to prowl the decks. She spent long hours bathing and staring at the walls.

"Medically speaking, she's in no danger. We rehydrated her, and she is beginning to take food. We had to fabricate Earth eating utensils and devise recipes bland enough for the human gut."

"Make her feel at home." K'Rin looked away. "I'm indebted to you."

The surgeon bowed slightly to acknowledge this bit of praise. He continued, "Her wounds are almost healed. She needs to wear the bone knitter for another twenty-eight hours. After that, we can send her home."

K'Rin pressed for details. "Does she have a home? Any family?"

The surgeon shook his head. "No. Her mother died from natural causes when she was young; her father died in the line of duty in one of Earth's internecine conflicts, the Patagonian Revolt. She has no one."

"No clan?" K'Rin shook his head. He could not comprehend a social system where family ties were so shallow.

"Her clan by marriage consists of two aged, timid parents, Dewinter by name. I took the liberty of contacting them. They seem to have no affection or sense of duty toward their daughter-in-law. I'm afraid Andrea is alone."

K'Rin asked, "Do you think she can make it on her own? Has she given any indication of what she *wants* to do with her life?"

"She's been asking a lot of questions about the Harbor Massacre, what we know, and the status of the investigation. She asks very dispassionate, detailed questions: numbers of assailants, types of weapons, and such. Of course I'm the wrong person for her to ask." The surgeon folded his delicate hands on the table.

"She sounds resilient—emotionally tough."

"Or emotionally dead." The surgeon added.

K'Rin did not like what he'd just heard. He fixed his eyes on the surgeon and asked, "Anything else? There's got to be some reason for her to get up tomorrow morning." K'Rin looked for any indication that a spark of life had survived in this husk of humanity.

"She did mention something about going to Earth's Space Academy." The surgeon brightened momentarily, but the fatigue returned to his face. "Unfortunately, sir, she's too old for admission."

Nevertheless, K'Rin smiled at the news, saying, "We'll see if we can get her a waiver. I doubt they'll refuse my personal request."

K'Rin rose to leave, but the surgeon intercepted him with another question, "Sir, I'm puzzled by something. Perhaps you can shed some light on it for me."

"Yes. What's the problem?" K'Rin responded briskly. K'Rin's mind was already working the problem of getting the waiver for Andrea.

"As part of my inquiries about the human female, I discovered something odd about the dead and wounded at the harbor."

K'Rin raised an eyebrow. "What?"

"Sir, they were all accounted for."

"So?"

"All the victims had families: records . . . birth certificates. Sir, none of them was a clone."

"Oh, really?" K'Rin folded his arms across his chest with smug satisfaction. "Rather an ironic bit of justice—we put the disrupted bodies of six Cor Hunters in a waste bladder, and this time, the clone got away."

chapter 3

Utterly friendless. After eighteen months in the academy, Andrea Flores found herself accused of numerous honor violations. She stood at rigid attention before a panel of three officers and two cadets. They sat in high-back chairs behind a green felt-draped table on a platform flanked by flags. The room was cold yet awash in white light. The internal room had no windows, just opaque mirrors mounted within thick molding, made to look like windows—fakery. The whole business had an air of fakery, and she saw no way out.

Andrea fought a rising tide of pessimism, recalling her father's advice, advice she believed as a child but failed to understand. *Don't run from your troubles.*

Her mind rehearsed so many arguments, none of them sufficient to turn back the decision that already appeared in the faces of her accusers working hand in glove with her judges. More dismal still, she had no idea what they knew or the case they planned to make against her—not that it mattered. *Don't run . . .* A rap of a gavel brought her mind back from its internal exploration.

A cherubic Captain O'Donnell in white uniform carefully enunciated his prepared remarks. "This formal inquiry shall determine if cadet Andrea Flores is fit to continue in the Space Academy. This administration doubts the psychological fitness of Cadet Andrea Flores to serve in an armed force. Therefore, we intend to prove Cadet Flores is obsessed with personal problems that make her a security risk, that she violated numerous security regulations. Specifically, she used academy computers to access databanks illegally at the Fort George Meade National Archive. Furthermore, she employed subterfuge to hide her motives and illegal activities from her counselors and superior officers. Consequently, the administration recommends that Cadet Flores be terminated from the academy without prejudice."

Captain O'Donnell directed his next comment directly to Andrea. "At this point, you can still elect to resign from the academy and thereby close this inquiry. If you continue with the inquiry, and if the administration prevails in its case, then you may receive a dishonorable discharge that shall be part of your permanent record. The choice to proceed is yours alone. Do you still wish to exercise your right to a formal board inquiry?"

Don't run . . . She knew fighting the inquiry was pointless. Behind her sat a couple of rows of unsympathetic spectators. Beside her stood a lieutenant senior grade, a legal lackey appointed by the board—not to help Andrea win—but to ensure that she lost fairly, without hope of appeal. They kept the witnesses in the anteroom next to the witness box. She could only speculate whom they'd recruit to disparage her. Three cardboard boxes on the exhibit table held files, books, maps, and her privately owned Marquis 7mm pistol.

An easel held an oversized and particularly cruel photograph, a picture of her out of uniform, sitting on the dock in the same spot she'd held her slain husband and child. *What bastard would stalk her for that photo, then use that sentiment against her?* Her nostrils flared and she gritted her teeth.

"Well? We're waiting for your reply."

The hell with the lot of them. They've been trying to run me out of the academy for almost two years. They still blamed her for getting into the academy under false pretenses: at twenty-three, she was too old. But her new patron from Jod, K'Rin, discovered a loophole: The long-lived and slow-maturing Jod could enter the academy exchange program up to age twenty-seven. So K'Rin sponsored Andrea with a Jod appointment.

Pressured by K'Rin's sponsorship, the academy was forced to adhere to the narrow language of its own admissions policy and admit her, but the administration never forgave her for pulling a fast one. The hidebound administration quickly patched that hole in the regs; then set out to rectify their oversight. They badgered her often, telling her that taking Jod sponsorship was sneaky, disloyal to her species, and unpatriotic. *When push comes to shove, are you going to side with us or with the Jod?* Andrea quickly learned the unofficial lesson that as far as the Terran Fleet was concerned, when push came to shove, the Alliance was just a piece of paper.

The administration planned a three-prong attack. Wash her out for any egregious violation or an accumulation of picayune transgressions. Drive her out with discretionary demerits: she could either spend her weekends pounding the quad in a hard suit or she could resign. Or flunk her in the academics.

Andrea walked off the demerits with stone-faced stoicism, and stayed on the academic honor roll. Now this.

"Cadet Flores. I must insist that you answer."

She collected her thoughts. *I won't quit. You boys would like that. No, if you're going to tar and feather me, you're going to have to get your hands dirty.* Then aloud, she answered, "I won't resign. I choose the board." She clipped her words short, reluctant to add to their show.

The captain intoned in a voice affected to sound like doom itself, "Let the record show that Cadet Flores submits to the formal board of inquiry. Fleet regulations regarding evidence apply."

At that moment the double-doors in the back clattered open. A pair of befuddled marines back-pedaled their way into the room unsure how best to resist K'Rin and his personal guard. Andrea turned and witnessed his entrance. K'Rin did not wear the pale duty uniform of a Jod captain; instead he and his small cohort wore a foreboding gray with black piping, without rank or insignia. The tunics were open collar: these were the work uniforms of the elite Tenebrea. Each wore a black utility belt and from each belt hung an assortment of pouches, a utility knife, and a handgun of sorts.

The board captain stood and addressed the uninvited Jod. "Hal K'Rin, this is a surprise."

K'Rin's neck flared a hot red. He growled, "Imagine my surprise to learn through unofficial channels that you are trying to cashier a cadet whom I sponsored."

"This is not a matter that directly concerns you."

K'Rin ignored the captain and led his band to the front bench, and with sheer intimidation of presence, his armed men persuaded the spectators to vacate. The Tenebrea took their warm seats. As K'Rin settled into an aisle seat, he said, "You may proceed."

Andrea wanted to leave her post and go kiss the old Jod, so glad was she to see any friendly face. She remembered his kind, solemn eyes from his brief visits abroad the *Tyker.* She remained grateful for his favors. For these eighteen months she treasured his weekly correspondence and his interest in her studies, his encouragement. She had not dreamed of involving him in this unsavory affair, afraid that she might embarrass the great Jod or worse, dishonor the Rin Clan. Nevertheless, she was glad to see him.

In the first phase of the inquiry, the administration built their case that Andrea was obsessed with the death of her husband and child. They called the academy surgeon to testify.

"I remember looking at the scans and telling Cadet Flores that she was in excellent health. Then I discussed the matter of her scar."

"A scar? How unusual."

"That was my opinion as well. She received the scar from a bullet wound that punctured the platysma and pectoralis major, shattered the clavicle, broke through the scapula, and exited through the infraspinatus fascia. Her medical records indicate that she received emergency medical treatment on the scene and was transported to a Jod ship for surgery. I know for a fact that Jod doctors can effect tissue reconstruction to eliminate scars. When I asked her why the Jod doctors left her with a scar,"—the fleet surgeon consulted her log—Cadet Flores replied, *"I didn't authorize that procedure."*

"Is that true?" The captain, still the spokesman for the board, asked Andrea.

"Yes."

"Please continue, doctor."

"I told Cadet Flores that I could remove the scar—no need for anesthesia, a perfectly safe procedure. She became almost abusive, telling me to mind my own damned business."

"Is that true?"

Andrea felt the scar beneath her tunic, a warm pain. Several doctors said the healing was complete; therefore, her *feelings* were just imaginary. Imagined or not, she felt the warm pain and cherished it. *This scar is all I have left*, she thought. Then she answered the captain's question. "Yes."

"Do you think this behavior indicates any obsession with the Harbor Massacre?"

K'Rin stood to address the board. "Sir, you are asking the doctor to speculate. I thought your inquiries had some basic rules of evidence."

The captain gaveled the murmuring room to silence. "Hal K'Rin, Cadet Flores has counsel."

"Him?" K'Rin pointed his gloved hand at the reticent JAG Lieutenant seated next to Andrea. "He's incompetent."

The JAG Lieutenant didn't respond but looked to the board for help. Again the gavel commanded silence and the captain spoke, "The doctor can give us her professional opinion."

The fleet doctor brushed a wisp of hair from her face. "No rational person elects to keep a scar, especially one as disfiguring as Cadet Flores's. Obviously, she feels guilty about surviving the Harbor Massacre. We call it *survivor anxiety syndrome*. She keeps the scar as some sort of physical penance. I'd call that obsessive behavior."

Seated next to the captain was a highly decorated veteran—a commander by rank. He asked, "Why do you keep the scar, Cadet?"

Andrea answered coldly, "A souvenir."

The veteran looked at the rest of the board. "That doesn't sound obsessive to me. I know a lot of guys who've kept scars as mementos of combat." Annoyed at the seeming indifference of the board captain, he added, "Combat. You know, Captain O'Donnell, where people shoot at each other. Some people get hurt, others die—something you rear echelon personnel types don't have a lot of experience with. I could show you a couple scars."

"That'll do, commander. You made your point. Nevertheless, we have expert testimony that Cadet Flores's interest in her scar indicates obsession."

The matter of Andrea's scar didn't hurt her case; rather, it won her the sympathy of the veteran. Yet the scar lingered as a metaphor for her time in the academy. The discipline of academy life may have helped anesthetize the immediate pain, but healing? O'Donnell introduced more evidence to show that she didn't want healing—not the forgive-and-forget kind.

"Next we submit a copy of Cadet Flores's term paper from the course in Galactic Culture, titled *The Coming Ordinate Wars.*" O'Donnell flipped through a couple pages. "There's some irrelevant stuff about the Ordinate economic system and clone labor . . . ah, here's her conclusion. I quote: *A war with the Cor Ordinate is inevitable. They have little if no regard for the Alliance or natural law, and they have proven their aggressive intentions by their brutal attacks against runaway clones into Alliance space."* O'Donnell looked up from the paper and continued, "And finally we come to Cadet Flores's recommendation. She writes, *Earth needs to invoke the Alliance Treaty, section 2—An attack on any member is an attack on all members—whereupon the Alliance must mobilize its combined resources and mount a preemptive expedition to neutralize the Cor Ordinate threat.*

"I think it's safe to say that Cadet Flores means what she writes with every fiber of her being. You see, she has a theory that Ordinate Hunters are responsible for killing her husband and child. I also think it's safe to say that she'd use her position as a fleet officer to exact revenge if possible." Captain O'Donnell ended this segment of the inquiry saying, "I think it interesting to note that Earth and other Alliance members, even the Jod Council of Elders, entertain hopes that the Ordinate will end their isolation and join the Alliance. I think Cadet Flores, by her own words, demonstrates that she would be unfit to serve in a military allied with the Ordinate. Does the defendant wish to contradict me by declaring herself indifferent toward the Ordinate?"

Andrea glared. Now, she despised O'Donnell. Yet she kept her wits and replied, "So, the fleet wants indifferent—perhaps ambivalent—officers? Then, God help the Terran Fleet: it won't know how to help itself."

She saw O'Donnell's face turn red. In the back, she heard the Jod laugh. Andrea enjoyed this brief success, but she knew damage was done to her—O'Donnell questioned her loyalty in fairly blunt terms and she responded with a clever dodge, but a dodge nonetheless.

O'Donnell retaliated on a personal note, "We cannot help but notice that you took your maiden name, Flores, instead of your married name, Dewinter. May we ask why?"

"Sir, that is none of your business."

"I think the matter is relevant as to your state of mind. I believe you are estranged from your husband's parents. Please tell the board why."

Andrea looked at the JAG Lieutenant seated next to her, expecting him to object on some grounds, but the lump sat there in preprogrammed silence. Andrea then answered reluctantly, "They were never very fond of me either, to tell the truth. They didn't approve much of Steve leaving the nest to marry me. I can deal with that. But they didn't come to Steve and Glendon's funeral. They were afraid that whoever killed Steve might strike again. Cowardly behavior. I told them that I didn't care to see them again if they missed the funeral. I tried to give them some of Steve's personal effects, but they refused. I didn't want their family name if I couldn't have Steve. Steve was adopted anyway—who knows what his real last name was."

O'Donnell merely added, "That's very odd."

Next, the board heard testimony regarding Andrea's private investigation into the Harbor Massacre. She sold everything, even Steve's boat; then she exhausted a small personal fortune on research. Baltimore City showed her nothing but an empty file with a one-line explanation: *presumed terrorist activity.* Six people dead, fifteen wounded, three of them permanently crippled, and no records? The board produced copies of angry correspondence in which Cadet Flores accused Baltimore of a cover-up. The city replied that the case was taken out of their jurisdiction for investigation. *By whom?* Andrea asked. *Where did the case go?*

On nights, weekends, and during snatches of duty days, she pursued the matter to state offices in Annapolis, and after a month of haranguing the bureaucrats with information requests, she left convinced only that the state had no knowledge except for the death certificates of the harbor victims. She contacted the families of the other victims, and they knew less than she did. *The matter remains under investigation.* By whom, they didn't know.

She searched for similar crimes occurring around the same time, and she did uncover a peculiar blotter report, a deposition made to a Maryland state trooper by a soybean farmer on Kent Island. Andrea hunted down the man and she interrogated him, adding his bizarre story to her burgeoning files—a copy of which found its way into evidence at the board of inquiry. It read:

> At 5:45 in the evening on the day after the Harbor Massacre, Mr. Joseph Broomtree, a truck farmer from Tunis Mills on the eastern shore, sat in a neighbor's duck blind drinking malt liquor. He saw six men dressed in civilian clothes in a boat shed. They acted as if they were waiting for someone or something because one of them would periodically step outside with a pair of fancy binoculars and look into the night sky. Then the farmer saw about sixteen big men, soldiers likely—"they had shoulder pads or something"—wearing black uniforms and helmets with face shields. The soldiers crept up, surrounding the boat shed. One of the soldiers threw a small bomb into the shed, which gave off a blinding white light—beams shot through the window,

through holes in the tin roof, even through the cracks between the wall boards—but "made no more noise than popping a paper bag." The six civilians staggered out of the shed with hands covering their eyes, they fired handguns blindly. One of the bullets hit the duck blind just above my head. Then the soldiers in the black uniforms shot the civilians with something like a "flash-light" that made sounds like a bug light zapping insects. The weapon killed the civilians outright. Then the soldiers stuffed the six dead ones in big shiny plastic black bags and left.

The board captain handed a copy of Andrea's summary of the Broomtree interview to the other members of the panel. He asked, "Do you think this report has any connection to the Harbor Massacre?"

Andrea answered, "I think that's self-evident."

"Really? Let me read a little from the state trooper's report. He says and I quote, *Joseph Broomtree is a habitual drunk who's been thrown out of every bar on the eastern shore for failing to pay tabs and lying about it.*" Looking up from the paper, O'Donnell said, "Cadet Flores, you're just clutching at straws."

Andrea looked across the room at the captain, genuine malice in her eyes. "The trooper says more in his report that you left out." Quoting from memory, Andrea said, "State Trooper Edmond Cooke also wrote: *However, I did find a fresh large-caliber bullet hole in the duck blind.*"

"So what?"

"Aside from the solitary bullet hole, there was not a scintilla of physical evidence; no bodies, no blood, no weapons—not even a missing person's report."

"Precisely, there was no crime . . ."

"Begging your pardon, but I talked with Joseph Broomtree, and he was not making up a story. Six unidentified men slaughter civilians less than thirty miles from the site of the massacre on the same day as the massacre. Broomtree saw them vanish. Nobody on Earth just vanishes without a trace. Everybody here has a past—unless their past is of another world."

"Very metaphysical! So, Broomtree's apparitions were in fact the same gunmen behind the Harbor Massacre. Then, who shot them with the so-called flashlights?" the captain asked, his eyes narrowed with disdain.

"Lasers or disrupters . . ." Andrea shook her head. "Broomtree was no technologist: he would not know the difference."

"Whatever. Who shot them with lasers, assuming the six apparitions even existed."

"I don't know who killed them. Federal antiterrorist units use antipersonnel lasers. All I know is that the federal government won't say, and that alone makes me suspicious. I know you gentlemen have rifled all my files, so it's no surprise to you that I tried to access federal crime records without result. But I did learn one thing: There is in fact a record of that day. But the Harbor Massacre files remain under a thirty-year seal for national security reasons." Just saying it raised her blood pressure. *Thirty years! Damned bureaucrats—*

Captain O'Donnell mused, "So because you can't find the six gunmen, you assume they came from the Cor System. And you've ruled out the possibility that the Harbor Massacre gunmen were Earth First terrorists. How did you manage that?"

Andrea smiled to herself. She knew where this

inquiry was going now. She had not been careful enough. They could link her with Earth First extremists. Should she answer? Why not? They could hang her for her silence as well as her testimony. Clever jackals. She tried to put them off by saying, "If the murderers had been Earth First terrorists, and if federal troops had slain them, the government would have been crowing. The government is very public with cases that it solves. That's why I suspect that the Harbor Massacre remains unsolved: the six civilians were not Earth Firsters."

"Then what do you think?"

Andrea felt she had nothing to lose. "One theory that I have is that someone within the federal government is covering up the Ordinate attack. I know many people in government are sympathetic to our galactic siblings, as it were."

Captain O'Donnell's face immediately flowered with a grin and wide alert eyes. "Do tell us more about your antigovernment sentiments."

"Don't put words in my mouth, sir."

O'Donnell's smile did not fade in the least at her rebuke. "I'm sorry for jumping to conclusions. Rather, how do you know that people in government are sympathetic to the Ordinate?"

"Open sources, mainly: the Commonweal Net. I entered the Net with near-anonymity . . ."

O'Donnell interrupted her. "Oh, please. Everyone knows that the Net is just an electronic sanctuary for the social fringe: oddballs and conspiracy theorists."

"People characterize the Net that way. I think it's a research tool."

"I'm sure you do." The captain handed out another ration of paper and continued, "In fact, Cadet Flores, you fed the Net a ration of your own conspiracy theories. I have here a sample of the questions you posed to the riffraff on the Net. *Is Earth security so lax that Ordinate Hunters can smuggle themselves onto Earth undetected? Or, is it possible that Earth Security aids and abets Ordinate Hunters?*" Captain O'Donnell addressed his next comment to the board, "These are the questions of a delusional paranoid—a typical antigovernment technoid in search of conspiracy."

K'Rin rose and spoke out. "I think those questions are prudent. I applaud the cadet's inquisitiveness."

"As you wish, sir." Captain O'Donnell dispensed with Hal K'Rin quickly to get back to the scent. "But Cadet Flores didn't limit her research to open sources on the Net. She contacted Earth First militiamen directly." He faced Andrea and accused her. "You consorted with enemies of the state. You masqueraded as a civilian and met secretly with outlaws, terrorists. What did you talk about?"

Andrea's face flushed as she suppressed her rising ire. "I met with knowledgeable people who satisfied me that the Earth Firsters had nothing to do with the Harbor Massacre. I had no reason to believe these people were criminals."

O'Donnell asked with dramatic sarcasm, "Help me out here. You're so astute when it comes to deducing the criminal activities of a species on the other side of the galaxy, yet you are too naive to know when you are face-to-face with known enemies of the state. You can't have it both ways, Cadet."

Andrea swallowed, stiffened, and said, "I'm entitled to my opinions."

"Of course you are. These knowledgeable people who know all about but are not a part of the Earth

Firsters—they showed you how you could use Academy computers to hack your way into the federal files. You accessed the National Archive at Fort Meade under the codename Methuselah."

Andrea sat silent.

"You successfully broke into the archive, but you couldn't get past the thirty-year seal. Do you know why?"

Andrea just glared at the Captain. "I don't know what you're talking about."

O'Donnell brushed her protest aside, saying, "The Meade internal system told you why: material under the thirty-year seal is not on-line. On the contrary, the information you sought resides on a stand-alone computer. However, while you were in the archive, you looked into personnel records. Why? Did you think you might blackmail someone into providing you this sensitive data? You looked into crime reports, especially ongoing investigations. Do you have any idea how many regulations you violated? And finally, you inspected special agent reports about Earth First activities. Were you providing payback for their help?"

Andrea's mind raced. Her pulse quickened. She felt a powerful urge to step onto the platform and slap the pusillanimous smile from the captain's face. They had enough circumstantial evidence to bounce her from the academy. But perhaps they weren't content with that. They wanted an admission of guilt—certainly would make their job easier, a nice tidy report tied with the ribbon of the cadet's own admission.

Well, they could go straight to hell. They had no hard proof: if they had she'd already be in prison. And she wouldn't be cowed into giving them anything. Her personal records were purposefully silent about her illegal hacking efforts. While there may be a record of access into the National Archive, they could not pin it back to her, except with circumstantial evidence. The academy provided wireless access for all cadets. Anyone who could break into the academy's wireless system might circumvent the security protocols and use the academy link to federal systems to hack into the National Archive. She recalled a recent report that the National Archive endured twenty thousand hacking attempts per month—about one percent of them successful. So what if they matched a successful break-in with her personal interests? They had no physical evidence, no accomplice. They wanted a confession to close an embarrassing physical security breach—a confession that would likely get her a jail sentence to go with her dishonorable discharge. After a long pause, she answered, "I know nothing about breaking into unauthorized files."

"You want us to believe that you got hacker instructions from Earth First Militia, and although you desperately wanted to see the sealed records of the Harbor Massacre, you didn't hack your way in?"

"Yes, sir." Andrea pursed her lips, trying to fight the color rising on her cheeks.

"I remind you, Cadet. You are under oath and bound by the honor code."

Although her face held rock steady, she almost burst into a nervous laugh. *Honor code?* They'd harangued her for two years, still angry that she'd finessed her way into the academy. They'd followed her, trying to entrap her for seeking the truth, for daring to hope for some modicum of justice. They mustered every confidential source who might promptly roll over to testify against her. They took her personal records, read her electronic mail, and tapped her phone. *Honor!* She owed them nothing.

Andrea looked up at the dais. Captain O'Donnell licked his lips. The veteran seemed rather sad about the whole business and the third officer, a hopeless dullard, had yet to utter a peep. The two cadets on the board had all the giddy anticipation of two boys at a burning building waiting for the smoldering bodies to be hauled out. At her side, the JAG Lieutenant simply occupied space like some wilted potted plant.

She glanced over her shoulder and saw K'Rin among the titillated spectators. He alone was on her side in this trial. His eyes displayed an attitude of stiff-necked resistance despite the certainty of failure. She measured her words, replying with a deliberate cadence, "On my honor."

chapter 4

She paused a moment from her rushed packing to look out the window. A breeze rustled the pastel leaves in the poplars—eight knots of wind from the west, perfect for a broad reach to St. Michaels. Just enough clouds to keep the glare down. In the distance, a small fleet of J-class boats huddled by a starting buoy at the mouth of the harbor. *Spinnakers!* Her memories shoved her troubles to the back of her mind. She closed her eyes and transported herself to the forepeak of *The Deeper Well,* Steve's other woman. *We'll start with the spinnaker.* Then from the back of her mind, another voice intoned words that echoed: dishonorably *discharged!*

She opened her eyes and stuffed another handful of her toiletries into a small suitcase. She carefully wrapped a brittle old cigar box of memories in a satin bathrobe and cushioned it among the mufti and old work fatigues. The dress uniforms hanging in her closet would stay there, ashes of her short career in the fleet.

Andrea heard a soft knock on her door. "Go away,"

she snapped. She no longer had to feign politeness to the academy officers who tossed her into civilian life.

But the voice on the other side of the door was not some gloating officer trying to rush her out the gate or just one more insincere cadet offering condolences just to get a good look at her distressed face. The familiar voice belonged to K'Rin. "May I speak with you, Andrea Flores?"

She unfastened the deadbolt and opened the door. K'Rin motioned to his entourage to stand outside and ensure the privacy of his conversation. He stepped into the room, looking around at the orderly display of books, nodding approval. "Much like a cadet's quarters on Jod." He fixed his gaze on Andrea.

She expected a rebuke for her failures and braced herself for his next words. But his eyes were thoughtful. He furrowed his brow, his loose scalp making shallow ridges to the top of his head. "I had hoped that you would get your commission from the Fleet Academy, then serve as a liaison officer on Jod."

"I'm sorry—" *Here it comes,* she thought.

"But your situation has changed." K'Rin rubbed his big hands together in contemplation. "What are you going to do now?"

She hung her head. "I don't know." Then looking K'Rin in the eye, she added, "And right now, I don't really care what I do. I just want to get out of here."

His neck raised a tinge of scarlet, but his eyes remained soft, and he controlled his voice. "I, however, do care. My family sponsored you: You are, like it or not, tied to the Rin Family now."

Andrea broke eye contact. "I said I'm sorry, all right? I can only say I'm sorry. I can't undo the damage."

K'Rin raised his voice. "You miss the point: I don't

want your apology. I want you to become worthy. No one in my family just throws up her hands and announces, *I'm beaten, and I don't care!* The Rin Clan does not broadcast failures or faint hearts. We know our share of failure, but in two thousand years, we have refused to admit defeat." He raised a fist.

Years of bitterness swamped Andrea. "Well, you might not want to face facts, but I admit it." Her eyes welled up with tears of frustration as she said, "I failed my husband and daughter: they're dead, as I should be. I have humiliated my father's memory—and dishonored you. I admit defeat. I am," she struggled with the word, ". . . *hopeless*."

K'Rin raised his hand to bat away this nonsense. "You aren't hopeless unless you choose to be hopeless."

Andrea looked up, annoyed that anyone would trivialize her pain. "Bad luck, then?"

K'Rin paced the floor. "Don't confuse luck with hope. Hopelessness is an act of will—a weak will, but nevertheless, an act of will. The natural consequence of hopelessness is despair, the easy way out for the weak will." He stood in front of Andrea and lifted her chin with his forefinger. "I never thought of you as having a weak will. In many ways, I see great strength in you."

Andrea gazed out the window to aviod eye contact with K'Rin. K'Rin took a deep breath and said, "A weak-willed person does not mount her own manhunt for her husband's killers. A weak-willed person does not hack her way into the Meade archives and lie about it so brazenly. A weak-willed person does not, for her final statement before sentencing, tell her judges that they are *gutless functionaries*. No, Andrea Flores, if you admit defeat, at least have the gumption to admit that you defeated yourself. Don't blame luck."

Andrea turned and looked up at the Jod. She thought those dark-ringed eyes had seen their share of pain as well. "I figured you came here today to dismiss me—"

K'Rin cocked his head and smiled. "As amply demonstrated today, institutions shoot their wounded—families do not. It's the same on Jod—probably an archetypal flaw of all sentient species. But I must say, Andrea, your academy officers lacked the loyalty of a goat. That charade they called a trial disgusted me. And by the way, Andrea Flores, for a Terran, you are an unusually incompetent liar. You have no talent for it. Resourceful, yes, but you have no gift for language. Leave the dissembling to older men of more august rank—like Captain O'Donnell."

Andrea returned an angry smile and shrugged. "I felt they had been worse than dishonest with me. I wanted them to have a taste of their own medicine."

"Perhaps." K'Rin's voice grew soft. "Truth is delicate, yet powerful. In my line of work, Offworld Intelligence, secrecy and misinformation—what laymen call lies—are tools of the trade. We lay false trails. We use camouflage and subterfuge. Sometimes we must protect the truth with a bodyguard of lies. But O'Donnell's performance today was inexcusable. He's a clerk, not a warrior. Your performance was understandable."

Andrea gave her patron a thin smile—not because she'd received a modicum of sympathy, but because she approved K'Rin's biting words, insults from an alien directed against humankind in general and the academy in particular. She let her disaffection show.

K'Rin continued, "So you are at loose ends again. What do you want to do now?"

Andrea stepped to her bunk and closed the lid to

her suitcase. "Before I lost Steve and Glennie, I thought the world was lovely. I thought the sun smiled on me. I was happy. I really was happy. Now I wake up in a world I hate, in a world—I am now convinced—hates me. There's only one thing I want from life now."

"Tell me, Andrea."

"I want to kill the bastards who killed Steve and Glennie. I want to kill the bastards who took my happiness away."

K'Rin leveled his proposition, "I leave on the cruiser *Tyker* for Jod at seven hundred hours tomorrow. If you want, you can come with me. Our little corner of the galaxy is far from this world and your troubles. I can guarantee useful work in my command."

"Doing what?" she asked impulsively.

He spoke slowly, almost seductively. "Very . . . special work, directly under my command. I want to bring a human into my household guard, an elite unit known as the Tenebrea. One of our missions is to track Ordinate Hunters operating out of their space. I may be able to create a situation whereby you can inflict considerable damage to the Cor Ordinate."

Andrea braced at the words. Her eyes narrowed. K'Rin had her complete attention now. "I'll do it. I'm ready."

"You are not ready yet. The training is difficult. And the commitment is absolute. I'll leave you now so you can make up your mind. Give the matter serious thought. If you join my unit, you'll never come back to Earth except in a Jod uniform under my orders."

"I said I'm ready. There's nothing left for me here." She buckled her suitcase. "I'll go with you now."

K'Rin stood on the bridge of the *Tyker*, alone with his thoughts. The bridge of a Jod cruiser presented a lonely dark theater of tactical displays and navigational equipment. On this routine trip, the weapons stations lay vacant, powered down. The communications officer worked offbridge in the cozier alternate tactical center. Only the first officer stood watch, seemingly unaware of the third soul on the bridge, the omnipresent helmsman who lay supine in mechanical concentration.

The helmsman wore a neural harness and lay on an ergonomic masterpiece, his arms resting at his side, twitching ever so slightly. From his coach, the helmsman works in the wireless grip of the ship's systems, allowing him to assess instantly the computer's suggestions and make instant decisions—very useful in tactical engagements. But more often than not, the helmsman verbalized any recommended course changes to the bridge officer. "Sir. Recommend four minutes of degree positive *Z*; duration twenty-nine cycles on your mark."

The clipped speech broke K'Rin's concentration and he looked down at the helmsman who, in spite of his crisp enunciation, looked as if he was lost in a deep narcosis. The deck officer didn't question minor course corrections. Everything in the galaxy remains in motion. With star systems in flux and rogue comets dashing about, the navigational system did a better job of making adjustments than forecasting a precise course. Until the Alliance finished surveying the galaxy—a millennium of pick-and-shovel work—they would make these minor compensations. The deck officer didn't bother to lift his eyes from his systems checklist. Instead, he grunted, "Mark."

The course shift was imperceptible, although the suggestion was enough for K'Rin to feel a phantom tug. He'd honed his stick and rudder skills with many thousands of hours flying in atmospheres. As a youth, he flew sixty-four aerial combat missions in the brief Chelle Conflict, an unfortunate but brief rift in the Alliance's solidarity—a tragic misunderstanding compounded by Jod overreaction according to the Chelle. His body never forgot the flood of sensations that comprise winged flight—sensations stripped away by the artificial gravity and inertial dampening in spacecraft. His trained reflexes braced only to meet no physical resistance.

A fourth figure walked onto the bridge: Kip. The young aide presented himself with stiff obsequiousness, a young Jod's clumsy attempt at challenging authority without getting into serious trouble. The sight brought a wry smile to the veteran K'Rin as the aide said, "Sir, may I have a word with you?"

"What's the problem, now?" K'Rin folded his thick arms.

Kip replied curtly, "Our guest." Kip referred to Andrea euphemistically as *the guest*. This bit of semantics was his passive resistance to K'Rin's plan to embrace this Terran female into family and service.

"I don't want to hear it, Kip." K'Rin put out his arm, a gesture intended to spike Kip's obviously prepared speech.

Kip bristled. "May I speak to you as a cousin and not as your subordinate?"

"Invoking family privilege?" K'Rin cleared his throat. "You are a very distant cousin, Kip. Don't overplay your advantage."

"I am only interested in your welfare, cousin." Kip pressed.

K'Rin concentrated to suppress the tinge of purplish annoyance rising on his neck. "You may find our blood a little thin, but very well. When you next see your father, you can tell him I listened to you with all respect. Speak freely."

"I believe your involvement with the Terran woman is a grave error."

"I've heard this lecture before. Can't you come up with something . . . fresher?"

"Sir, I fear for your reputation."

K'Rin furrowed his brow. He closed the short gap between them so he might communicate in a whisper. "Are you questioning my judgment or my integrity? Because if you are questioning my integrity . . ."

Kip recoiled. "On my word, *no!* But I fear your enemies on the council. They want to keep your seat vacant, and they'll attack you with innuendo. Already, they fill the council halls with whispers about K'Rin's pet human. Most on the council dismiss the gossip—allowing for your sentimental proclivities about our human allies. Yet Pl'Don keeps the rumors stirring."

K'Rin folded his arms, in part annoyed, in part bored. As chief of the Jod Intelligence Service, very little missed his attention, especially matters that affected him personally. "I watch the clans closely. I know who my enemies are and how they attempt to undermine me and my work. Pl'Don may yet undermine himself by promoting gossip."

"But sir, you're helping your enemies. You give them leverage by bringing the woman back to Jod into your private service. Your enemies will cast the worst motives on your decision."

"And what do you think, Kip? That this old Jod has tried to revive his waning appetite with forbidden fruits?" K'Rin laughed loudly, startling the sedate bridge officer.

Kip bit his lip. "The woman is not psychologically stable."

"I see. Now, I'm toying with my *crazy* pet human."

"Don't discount that possibility: she might be crazy. One minute she seethes with anger and won't attend to her studies. Then she makes a mistake and falls into self-loathing. After a good sulk, she becomes lethargic."

K'Rin's face turned for a brief moment to sadness, then recovered to hard purpose. "Except for the lethargy, these passions of hers can be made useful. You must do more to combat the lethargy . . ."

Kip did not give up. "Sir, she has no honor. I can't imagine her serving any Jod interests."

"We'll link her own interests to ours." K'Rin tried to deflect Kip's criticism.

But Kip continued, "She squandered her chances at the Earth Space Academy by chasing ghosts. You defended her against our allies, and you know full well that she lied under oath. You know the saying: *A fool tracks mud through his own house.* Sir, she's not worth the risk to your good name. She will embarrass you on Jod just as she embarrassed you on Earth."

"Cousin, I don't think you are in a position to judge whether or not I am embarrassed." K'Rin gritted his teeth; he'd heard enough. "Are you through addressing me as a cousin?"

"Not quite . . ."

"Oh, yes you are." K'Rin reached forward and grabbed a fistful of Kip's jacket, easing the young man closer. "Now, I'm going to address you—not as your cousin, but as a Prince of the Council, Hal and Headman of the Rin Clan, Admiral and Chief of Offworld Intelligence, as well as your immediate commanding officer. You haven't told me anything that I don't know except perhaps that you doubt my ability."

"Sir!" Kip protested.

As he spoke, K'Rin's voice rose. "After the Harbor Massacre, I brought that woman under my protection and that is a personal matter. As for bringing her back to Jod, I chose Andrea Flores for a special mission, a mission that a Jod cannot do. To accept this mission, she has to be half crazy; to succeed, she must be . . ." K'Rin shook his head searching for the right word, settling on a cliché, "unconventional. You will help me plan her training, and if I think you're competent enough, you may help me plan her mission. In the meantime, my enemies on the council will mount a whispering campaign, if not about the Flores woman, then about something else: my drinking, my temper, or perhaps an ill-disciplined cousin that I keep in a sinecure on my staff." K'Rin winked at his aide. "Anyway, Kip, you'd best understand, Flores is not the issue. The council's enmity is. They are . . ."

"Sir—" Kip raised his finger to his lips.

K'Rin checked himself and smiled, "Ah, Kip. Even out here." He pointed to the void of space, "I forget from time to time that I might be watched. Suffice it to say, cousin, that I can manage Flores."

"Take care that she doesn't manage you."

K'Rin's neck flared briefly as he muttered. "Your father was just as insolent."

"Sir, you mistook me. I find the woman impossible to manage. I can teach her nothing. Her indifference: I can't penetrate it. Her hostility: I can't fathom it. Half the time, I can't goad a response from her; half the time I feel like I'm defusing an Abileen bomb."

All the passion drained from K'Rin. His neck

returned to a calm pale. He asked, "What lessons are you trying to impart?"

"I started at the beginning with the standard inductee course: organization of the Jod military services, history of the Jodic Clan Wars of Unification, the Oath to the Council of Elders, the basic dictates of—"

"Oh, Kip." K'Rin groaned. "You ought to know better."

"What now?" Kip's face said the rest: this woman is more trouble than she could possibly be worth.

"Don't feed her that standard pap!"

"But she's just a cadet." Kip objected. "She has less than eighty-hours flight time."

"I don't need another pilot, so waive the requirement. And promote her. From now on she has the rank of First Order Mat—that would be her equivalent rank had she graduated from her academy. Draw up the orders to make it so."

"And what shall I teach this instant officer?" Kip straddled the line of humor and insubordination. He sighed.

"First, channel her anger. Her anger makes her valuable, but in its present mode, self defeating." K'Rin clenched his large fist. "Teach her to fight. Build her strength. Put her through the low-to-high gravity drills. Work her till she drops from physical exhaustion—that is, if you can keep up with her. Show her how to use a blade. Teach her the principles of weapon selection. Start her on a bland diet of Jod staples. Keep a schedule of twenty hours work with a four-hour sleep cycle. Take her off any medicines: those medicines just add to her lethargy. If she gets space sickness, then so be it. We've got a seven-hundred-hour flight ahead of us and I want her ready to train with the current class of candidates for the Tenebrea."

Kip's eyes widened. "But that unit has worked together for six seasons."

"Then, you've got seven hundred hours to close a six-season gap. You get her physically ready; her state of mind will follow naturally. Her personal motivation will make her an excellent member of my Tenebrea."

Every muscle ached: Andrea practically wobbled from lack of sleep. Yet she felt a strange relief. For a brief time she forgot the past and ignored the future. Her mind focused on simple, repetitive tasks—consumed by the *now.* She'd slept without dreams. She'd even heard Kip's reluctant praise: balm for her aches. But now the marathon of physical training ended. Andrea used her last hours of quiet time aboard the *Tyker* to sip a strong tea, enjoying the boost from the stimulant, while she inspected her new world, Jod, fifth planet from an auburn star.

The *Tyker* settled into a holding orbit around this planet of ochre continents bordered in green, surrounded by blue. Verdant archipelagoes stretched into the seas. On the dark side, Andrea saw glowing cities, thousands of bright specs fused to one lacy web, strands radiating from brighter centers. On the bright side, she saw sun glint from seamless rails crossing a flat and barren continent. Deep in the seemingly lifeless interior stood a tight jumble of block and mortar stacked on a reddish mesa: massive buildings, the fortress city of Heptar, capital city of Jod and seat of the ruling council.

Closer to the coast, ambitious irrigation widened the green band, but the enormity of the wastelands seemed to scoff at agriculture. Between clouds she saw white chevrons, the wake of large ocean barges—commerce, life. Clouds obscured coastlines and textured the oceans, but rarely did a puff manage to shade the interior.

Ironically, this least-lively planet in the Jod system was the source of Jodic life. Their outlying colonies, now centuries old, built on bioformed worlds, sustained populations way beyond the capacity of the planet Jod. But Jod was home to the Great Families, the cradle of Jod culture and learning, plus the principal port for the Jod Fleet.

After a quick shuttle ride to the surface, Kip delivered Andrea to a small garrison situated on a crescent of land hanging onto the sea. Archetypal stone barracks stood in formation around a large quadrangle of bright green neatly cropped grass. Kip led Andrea to the middle of the quadrangle, then stopped for a sentimental look around. Andrea dropped her bag. He said, "This is the Tenebrea's home. Over there," Kip pointed to an austere building with windows of black glass, "is the operations center. Most of the working space is below ground."

Kip turned about face. Andrea turned with him. "Those long buildings are the barracks where we billet the Tenebrea who do not have ship duty or work off-world at one of our outstations. The squat tower to the right is the school where you take classes. Behind the tower you can see the side of the gym and weapons lab."

Looming over the stone barracks, modern utilitarian piles of steel and glass stood. Kip panned the horizon with his hand and said, "Adjacent to our compound is one for the regular Jod infantry assigned to the fleet. I believe you Terrans call them marines."

Andrea nodded.

"It's a necessary distraction. They provide us service support, and we in turn provide the fleet intelligence. We conduct special operations. As a point of information, you ought to know that the regulars resent the Tenebrea in general, and Tenebrea students in particular. My guess is that they will find even less to like about a female Terran student. You'd be wise to confine yourself to our compound until you graduate. Even then the regulars may dislike you, but they'll stay out of your way."

Andrea knew Kip's was friendly advice. He started walking to the barracks and Andrea grabbed her bag and followed. At the entrance of the barracks, Kip paused in front of a weathered bronze statue that depicted a larger-than-life ancient Jod infantryman, burdened with pike and shield, a battle-ax tucked in a belt sling. He wore a battered burnie and ragged chainmail. The artist skillfully showed many wounds still open, and the jagged bronze flesh seemed to bleed green. Yet the warrior's face was serene: a peace that transcended the pain of so many wounds.

Andrea shifted her tote back to her left shoulder and asked, "Who's the statue?"

"Nobody." Kip replied. "Everybody. A myth called Mani. We're all supposed to end up like that."

Andrea snipped, "Near dead?"

"And glad of it." Kip added cynically.

"I'm not so sure I'm going to fit into your military gestalt."

"Oh, you'll fit in just fine." Kip could not have been more patronizing.

Using a set of Andrea's old cadet fatigues, a tailor quickly prepared a set of duty uniforms, serviceable but a bit baggy. The tailor interpolated the more sumptuous Jod female physique onto the proportions suggested by Andrea's fatigues—better too loose than too tight. The quartermaster assigned her a separate room, not out of any consideration for the Terran female, but for her classmates. As a matter of traditional bias, the Jod considered Terrans and other aliens roughly equivalent to domesticated animals, depending on the animal.

At her first supper in the open mess, she sat ostracized at one end of the hall, alone with her small bowl and improvised fork and spoon.

The rest of her class sat at table and ate from the communal platter. They viewed this skinny, hairy, offworld interloper as obviously some ill-conceived interoperability stunt concocted by some rear echelon subaltern with crap for brains. *An alien in the Tenebrea? Inconceivable.* A stocky Jod named Gem-Bar nodded in her direction. "Look at her. She eats with garden utensils."

A tall, refined Jod, H'Roo Parh, took Andrea's part and answered, "It is her custom to eat with tools. They consider the custom more refined than eating with fingers."

"I hear that Terrans will eat anything—*anything!*" another chimed in.

"I heard that too. They are particularly fond of eating flesh."

H'Roo butted in. "We'll eat flesh if need be. Don't be a hypocrite."

"And sometimes they leave the bones in and use them as handles!"

The group gave a collective grunt of disgust. Again, H'Roo took Andrea's side. "We should invite her to our table."

"What! So she can stick her hairy hand in our dish?"

Tamor-Kyl, the unofficial leader of the group, raised his voice. "I care nothing about the Terran's dietary habits. However, I do want to know what idiot sent this human debris to train with us? H'Roo, you always know the gossip."

Tall and thin by Jod standards, the trainee H'Roo Parh glanced in Andrea's direction as he answered the group. "She is here by Hal K'Rin's orders."

The group gaped in stunned silence. Admiral K'Rin, head of Jod Offworld Intelligence, was no one to trifle with. The Tenebrea was the Rin household guard and K'Rin its commander. Nobody joined the Tenebrea without K'Rin's blessing—no one. Each of the Great Families retained a small household force of two hundred eighty soldiers—a tradition held over from the ancient days when the clans raised their own armies. For three thousand years, the Jod honored that tradition. Other families kept ceremonial troops, a sinecure for the family incompetents. Their household troops were overfed and richly adorned in livery and plumed helmets, jeweled breastplates, and sparkling weapons. The Tenebrea had nothing but contempt for those parade warriors: they marched well, they'd make gorgeous corpses.

The Rin Clan had always taken a different path—perhaps because they'd always been associated with the Jod Fleet. Their guard, the Tenebrea, wore the simple black on gray—always trained for battle. K'Rin used the Tenebrea for special operations as Chief of Offworld.

No one, especially a trainee, questioned the commander of the Tenebrea. Tamor-Kyl quickly retracted. "Hal K'Rin always has a surprise for each class. This

Terran must be the surprise—perhaps one of his psychological tests. My guess is that she's supposed to break up our unity. We ought to keep her at arm's length."

H'Roo cut him off. "She's not here for your benefit, Tamor. She's a part of our unit. She wears the rank of First Order Mat."

Tamor-Kyl's neck turned indigo.

"Jealous?" H'Roo looked at Tamor-Kyl's neck.

"No." Tamor-Kyl lowered his chin to mask his blush. "H'Roo, why don't you persuade the female to join us at our table." Tamor looked at the faces around the large dish and added, "She's just a Terran. She'll learn her place soon enough."

H'Roo Parh approached the woman and quickly learned that she'd overheard much of the conversation among the Jod. At first she refused to give up her solitude for bad company, but H'Roo insisted and won with the argument that she might as well be done with the introductions. Andrea brought her small bowl, fork, and spoon.

At the Jod table, each trainee rose, bowed, and introduced himself. Andrea sat in the uncomfortable silence between Tamor-Kyl and the burly Gem-Bar. There she attended to her meal. Looking at her meager supper, Gem-Bar asked, "Are you ill?"

"No." Andrea replied. "Do I look ill?"

With genuine curiosity, Gem-Bar observed, "Your diet—weak cheese and mashed legumes—that is what we feed our sick, the very old, and infants."

The rest of the table chortled. Andrea didn't try to defend her small plate of mash and cheese cubes. "This diet was prescribed to me. And frankly, gentlemen, it's tasteless—two standard deviations beneath bland. This green juice isn't so bad, though—might go well with steamed crabs." Andrea looked at the leftovers in the communal dish and added, "Your meal doesn't look much better. No offense, but your Jod cuisine leaves much to be desired."

"Does your food need spice?" Gem-Bar reached to the center of the table for a glass tray of condiments. "We can fix that." He prepared to sprinkle an assortment of dried berries onto Andrea's meal.

H'Roo reached forward and stayed Gem-Bar's hand. "No!" He explained to Andrea. "We Jod have a two-chamber gut. The first chamber is alkali. We spice our foods with acidic flannerberries for the taste and to soothe our stomach. These berries, and for that matter, much of our foods would be for you unbearable—especially flannerberries. We'll find other foods more suitable to your palate if the legumes fail to satisfy."

Andrea thanked Gem-Bar for the thought and H'Roo for the warning. Then the conversation shifted to questions about Earth, and Andrea struggled to explain her world in terms the curious Jod could understand. Tamor-Kyl hovered at her side, feigning interest while palming a fistful of the multihued berries into her drink. At an appropriate lull in the conversation, Tamor-Kyl rose to propose a traditional welcoming toast: "To our new comrade, Mat Flores. To the Rin. To the Light. To the Tenebrea!"

All the Jod rapped their knuckles one loud knock on the table, then downed their drinks. Andrea imitated them. Instantly, the tender tissues in her mouth burned, as she felt the flannerberries wash down her throat with the liquid. Her neck began to constrict and her sinuses, in intense pain, began to flush themselves with mucus. Perhaps fifty times as potent as the hottest peppers on Earth, the flannerberries sent searing pain down her esophagus and into her stomach. All around her she heard boisterous laughter. Hardly able to see through eyes squinted shut in pain and watering, Andrea grabbed a fistful of the bland legumes and stuffed it in her mouth to absorb the burning chemical in her mouth. Then with no concern but for her pain, she spit the mash out—and into Tamor-Kyl's face.

The laughter stopped suddenly. Tamor-Kyl wiped the splatterings from his face and scarlet neck, then raised a hand to answer this insult, sputtering, "Human trash—" Andrea slumped over the table groping for water, ignoring Tamor's threat. Gem-Bar stepped between Andrea and Tamor-Kyl: "That was a dirty trick, Tamor."

Tamor shoved Gem-Bar aside only to face H'Roo, who pressed Tamor back away from the table. He calmly warned, "She's K'Rin's pet. Don't throw away your future."

"Welcome to the Pit." Feld Jo'Orom, the gnarled non-com, stood at the bottom of the concave arena, hands on hips. Twenty trainees stood along the rim. Andrea stood among them, her lips swollen, her eyes raw from rubbing and circled from a miserable night of no sleep. She looked across the Pit and saw Tamor-Kyl grinning back at her. She didn't hear the lecture in the Pit.

"We're through with classroom training for a while. Today we begin your training in hand fighting." Jo'Orom then droned on about defense being paramount, that a thwarted attack was . . .

Andrea's mind sought refuge from the unfocused noise, none of it news. She looked about the rim and sized up her opponents, especially Tamor-Kyl. She recalled the practical anatomy lessons she'd learned from Kip. Jod have a low center of gravity, short thick legs, and powerful arms. Instead of a rib cage, they have two plates of curved bone joined by a soft vertical seam of cartilage, like a subcutaneous shell to protect their big hearts and small lungs.

These powerful but bulky Jod lacked quickness and endurance. Their martial arts reflected these physical qualities: certainly, the defender held the advantage because the Jod can take physical punishment, but they lack the bursts of energy required for attacks. She judged her odds to be reasonable. Although twice her weight and capable of bone-crushing strength, these Jod could be beaten. She would have to evade the strong grip and pummel the face, neck, and head. The Jod had little advantage in bone mass around the eyes, nose, and ears. Indeed, they had no cartilage in their noses, just brittle bone. *If I can rattle their brains . . .*

"Mat Flores!" Jo'Orom barked. "I asked you a question!" The other trainees smirked.

"Sorry, Feld Jo'Orom. I didn't hear."

"Didn't hear?" He bellowed. "Get down here where you can hear better." Jo'Orom pointed to the center of the Pit.

Andrea skipped down the incline to face the instructor. He barked loudly, projecting past Andrea to the spectators above. "Flores is going to help me demonstrate the effective defense." Turning to her he purred, "Now, I want you to come at me with everything you have."

She studied the thick Jod standing before her. He raised his arms like a pair of thick swords and crouched slightly, shifting his weight low and to the center. She heard murmurs from above: "He's going to kill her," then a chuckle and more hushed comments.

Andrea threw a blizzard of quick punches. Jo'Orom's reflexes were keen for a big Jod. He batted away her blows, though his face registered genuine surprise at her speed. She backed off, then returned with another flurry of straight punches. He stepped past a blow, snatching her wrist, turning her thumb down, palm out: her arm locked against wrist and elbow. She dove through the hold, wresting her hand free, rolling on the spongy floor up the curved side of the Pit.

Jo'Orom smiled. "You're quick . . . but you haven't laid a hand on me yet." He congratulated and taunted in the same breath. "Try again."

Andrea crouched on the rubbery concave floor measuring her opponent. *He's good.* Then she rose and took a stance slightly higher than his, launching yet another barrage of fists. He adapted to her technique quickly, parried her blows with greater ease. Although he breathed heavily now, Jo'Orom's movements seemed unaffected by fatigue. She thought of a leg sweep—*no! He'd trap me.*

A voice from above cajoled, "Hit her!"

Perhaps she could beat her way through his defense, land one blow, then live with the consequences. She closed in with another series of punches, all blocked. But this time she kept up the attack, forcing Jo'Orom back, blocking punches with open palms, his arms like swords brushing aside her deeper thrusts. Then, she saw an opening, a shot to the nose and she put her full reach into this punch, leaning forward at the waist, putting her shoulder into the blow, losing her balance for a split second.

And he had her. He caught her fist in his right hand, pulling her through and tossing her like a rag doll onto the curved floor with a resonating *thud!* She slammed her free arm into the floor to brace her fall, but she lay there, her arm extended and twisted against itself. "Yield," Jo'Orom said in a paternal tone. Rumblings from above approved of her predicament.

Andrea didn't answer. Fighting her pain, she struggled to her knees, her cheek pressed against the floor. Jo'Orom added pressure to the leverage of his large upper body against her smaller arm. She breathed haltingly as she suppressed the sharp pains. Her sweat-soaked hair hung in her face. "Yield." Jo'Orom bid her with an air of authority. "In the Pit, we fight until one party yields. You're beaten." His voice shifted to mocking her, "Are humans too stupid to know when it's over? Yield and I will release you."

One voice from above, H'Roo Parh's, echoed, "It's no disgrace. Yield!"

But H'Roo's advice was soon lost among taunts from the rim. The laughter worked like a crude anesthesia to her pain. Andrea inched her way up the wall, slipping and struggling. Jo'Orom suddenly dropped her arm in disgust, saying, "Fool. I'd get in too much trouble if I broke your arm." And he turned to acknowledge the applause from the spectators on the rim.

Andrea didn't think twice. She jumped from her slight elevation and kicked, landing the side of her foot against the back of Jo'Orom's head. She pulled her kick, flexing her knee upon impact; nevertheless, the blow knocked the noncom to his knees, where he groped on all fours trying to refocus his eyes.

Andrea stood over her instructor, grinning, soaking in the howls of protest from above. With a lilt in her voice she said, "I yield."

Andrea received orders to stay in her quarters and not attend class the next day. Late that afternoon, she answered a perfunctory knock on her door and found H'Roo standing in the threshold. She watched his eyes dart about the room taking the measure of things and she saw criticism in his eyes, as if her room was not tidy enough for Jod standards. H'Roo said, "Jo'Orom asked me to speak with you."

"Why send a cadet?" Andrea moved to the doorway blocking H'Roo from entering. "Is Jo'Orom afraid to speak with me on his own?"

H'Roo bristled. "I assure you, Feld Jo'Orom is not afraid of you."

"Are you going to give me my demerit?"

H'Roo bent slightly to look Andrea more squarely in the eyes. His two rings of amber and indigo underscored his crisp hazel eyes, intelligent eyes. His neck tinged slightly, which Andrea presumed was annoyance. Although his voice was deliberately flat, his eyes showed concern or maybe just curiosity. He said, "They don't know what to do with you. Hal K'Rin has some special interest in you, therefore, the administration is afraid to expel you. They would have expelled any one of us for such a flagrant violation of Pit etiquette."

Andrea smirked. "Pit etiquette. How refined—"

"It's not a humorous matter, Mat Flores. Whatever chance you had to make friends among your classmates, you ruined yesterday."

"I didn't come to Jod to make friends. Why don't you just deliver your message and leave."

H'Roo gave a short sigh of resignation. "Fine. Commandant Bol-Don orders that you be isolated from the class until he can consult K'Rin about your fate. You are, therefore, restricted to your room in the barracks. You must take your meals in your room. However, Feld Jo'Orom wants your training to continue. You have access to the physical training lab and the technology lab, where you have assigned tutors. Feld Jo'Orom will personally supervise your combat and flight training. Bol-Don questions your loyalty, so you are denied access to sensitive data."

"Just like home, back at Space Academy . . ."

H'Roo braced himself to deliver the rest of his news. "One more thing. I must spend an hour or so each evening with you to help you learn Jod culture and keep you current with the class."

"Don't bother." Andrea put her hand on H'Roo's chest to press him back through the door.

H'Roo didn't budge. "I have my orders, Mat Flores. I return tomorrow whether I or you like it or not. If you don't want to learn about Jod, perhaps you can tell me more about your homeworld. Then the time won't be wasted for us both." H'Roo stepped back into the corridor, smiled sardonically, shook his head, and asked, "You really do think you're better off alone, don't you?"

Andrea shut the door in his face. Then, she stood for a moment looking at the faint shadow she cast upon her door.

Within a week, Andrea was glad that her petulance was overruled by H'Roo's orders. She didn't completely trust H'Roo yet but discerned that he lacked the pack instinct of the other candidates. H'Roo provided decent company partly because he remained aloof without any air of condescension. This young, self-assured Jod proved to be curious about Earth, but more importantly for Andrea, H'Roo was free with his considerable knowledge about the Jod. She hoped to get information about the Cor Ordinate from this curious, well-read Jod.

chapter 5

Jo'Orom and his staff tutored Andrea in tactics, weapons, and basic flight. She spent what might have been idle time in the physical training lab increasing the artificial gravity by fine degrees with every workout. She tested her reflexes in a computerized game much like tagball. In a large room, a person wears body armor and carries a small shield in each hand. Then the walls hurl balls—a faint hiss of forced air is the only warning, especially for balls launched from behind. Despite wearing body armor, Andrea rarely finished a drill without a dark round bruise. With Jo'Orom's instruction she became adept at defense. Her strength and agility made her uncommonly expert at attack. And when she sparred with Jo'Orom, he showed her no quarter, and she learned how to yield—so did he.

Andrea lay sideways on her cot with a cold pack pressed against her bare thigh. Her room was long and narrow with a plain workstation built onto one wall, one uncomfortable chair, and a closet. Her Spartan cot was a three-inch bladder of air on top of a large locker.

At room's end, a small, bare window offered a view of the training fields. She rarely bothered to take in the view.

At present she nursed a deep bruise, having lost a bout with the computer in the reflex drill. H'Roo sat in the chair eating fruit, watching with more than clinical interest. He caught himself staring at her muscular leg and said, "It's getting late. I'd better leave."

"Stay awhile, H'Roo." Andrea wanted to get back to her question. "You still haven't answered my question about the Ordinate. Are you forbidden to tell me any more?"

"No. There's really not much to know about a closed system. Lots of speculation, but little verified data."

Andrea sat up, dangling her legs from the cot. "Somebody knows something about the Ordinate and where they came from. No society is that closed."

H'Roo cut a piece of the fleshy fruit and handed it to Andrea. "Eat this: Hlulva juice helps the body heal bruises."

Andrea took a big bite. She wiped a dribble of white juice from her chin and beckoned him to continue, "Just tell me what you know."

H'Roo nodded. "Most of our information is suspect, but we know a few things for certain. More than a hundred years ago, the Jod intercepted a derelict spaceship drifting, tumbling into the Jod system—an Ordinate ship. The crew lay in an eternal sleep, desiccated by hundreds of years' travel in frozen space, encased in archaic, cumbersome suits. Their DNA matched human specimens. Geneticists say they've linked the Cor women among them to the prototype the Terrans call Eve. Therefore, we know that Human and Ordinate species share the same genetic origins."

Andrea leaned forward. "What else?"

"We know that the Ordinate are adamant about their isolation. However, we know for a fact that the Ordinate have some kind of commercial relationship with the Chelle. Recently, the Ordinate started building a port facility in the Chelle system on the planet Clemnos. We also know that the Ordinate augments their relatively small population with clones. A few clones have fled the Cor system to provide bits of information: shreds of evidence about basic technologies—hardly anything useful. The clones know next to nothing about Cor Ordinate history, politics, military, or society. Everything else we know is mostly myth and speculation." H'Roo peeled the husk from a milk white fruit, handing another piece to Andrea.

"On Earth, most myths are founded on truth." Andrea took the Hlulva slice.

H'Roo looked at the chronometer, then at Andrea. "We pick up gossip from Clemnos by way of the Chelle. Apparently, during the Earth's second millennium, the Chelle clandestinely took several thousand humans for research. With so much war and violence on Earth, I guess the Chelle assumed the humans would not be missed. For two hundred years, the Chelle took men and women to their laboratory planet in the Cor system. They wanted to observe human development on a small scale so they might anticipate how best to handle the billions of Terrans, who seemed poised to move into deep space by the middle of the third millennium. The Chelle are even more paranoid about Terrans than we Jod are." H'Roo smiled apologetically.

Andrea set her cold pack aside and sat up. "So they set up a lab experiment?"

"Why not?" H'Roo continued. "The Chelle placated their abductees by giving them an easy life. They referred to their abductees as *The Elect*, and quickly, this privileged class began to view their Earth cousins as a subspecies. Incredible, isn't it?"

Andrea raised an eyebrow. "Quite human, actually."

"The Chelle carefully selected humans who had limited technological knowledge," H'Roo continued.

"People might notice if the faculty of MIT suddenly disappeared." Then again, Andrea thought, she would not have missed most of her professors.

"Actually, I think the point was that the Chelle wanted to selectively introduce technologies into the experiment to see how the Terrans assimilated the knowledge. In four hundred or more years the humans increased their numbers into the tens of millions."

"Busy."

H'Roo nodded. "Not many people for a large planet the size of Cor. One of the technologies the humans acquired and perfected is clone manufacturing. The humans augmented their numbers with clone laborers so The Elect might invest themselves in the more profitable pursuits of science and technology. Although cloning was banned even then, the Chelle didn't intervene to stop the Ordinate. They considered The Elect/Clone paradigm just the technical equivalent of social evolution on Earth, so from their point of view, cloning helped their experiment."

Andrea chaffed. "It's not the same."

"I'm sure." H'Roo shifted the subject from cloning. "As part of the experiment, the Chelle tried to introduce their traditions into this artificial human society. They had mixed results. The Chelle have no concept of family as we Jod do; rather, they have a sense of the link in some giant biological tree and their loyalties tend toward their institutions—the Chelle Guilds that all take direction from the Supreme Guild. All of this is somehow fused into Chelle religion. The Chelle managed to organize The Elect into a Guild called the Ordinate—the centralized authority on Cor, and the Ordinate is still the political setup on Cor. The Ordinate Guild was supposed to take direction from the Chelle Supreme Guild. Unfortunately, the Chelle could not begin to understand the dynamics of human competition: inter- and intrafamily. The Chelle gave their human wards technologies way beyond human evolutionary development and then suffered the consequences."

"What consequences?" Andrea asked, although she already had a rough idea. She adjusted her cold pack.

"In a word, the Chelle's lab experiment failed. The transplanted humans divorced themselves from the Supreme Guild, violating the terms of their social contract with the Chelle. They turned against the Chelle scientists and project managers, then ran them off the planet. Fortunately for the fledgling Ordinate, the Chelle scientists refused to admit their failure. If they had any foresight, they might have eradicated the Ordinate then. Instead, they recorded the revolt as the natural progression in their experiment—just another key finding. Then they contented themselves to observe their experiment from a safe distance. They sent probes that the Ordinate methodically discovered and destroyed."

Andrea commented, "The Ordinate is fully human all right."

"The Chelle wanted their planet back, so they naively offered to ferry the whole Ordinate population to Earth where they might assimilate back into their eight billion kin. To the everlasting surprise of the Chelle, the Ordinate wanted nothing to do with Earth; instead, the Ordinate built defenses to protect their new home on Cor. This is all speculation, Andrea. The official history is silent on the whole experiment."

"Official history?"

"Chelle's Supreme Guild commissions the official history." H'Roo smiled. "It's huge, I've read just bits and pieces of the file: *The Official History of the Chelle: 43rd Revision*. I put more faith in their oral tradition."

Andrea motioned with her hand for H'Roo to give more information. "So what did the Chelle do—unofficially?"

"They are better technologists and merchants than they are warriors. They officially abandoned their claim to Cor and signed a secret accord with the Ordinate. Although the Ordinate proved a frustration to Chelle science, the rapidly growing Ordinate became an excellent market for Chelle manufacturers, and the clone farms and mines provided exports of food and raw materials—that is, until the Ordinate mastered faster-than-light drive and closed their frontiers. Again, the Ordinate broke their agreement with the Chelle, but the Chelle could do nothing without risking a costly and embarrassing war. After all, the Chelle created this whole mess. The Ordinate embarked on a utopian plan for their world. As The Elect, they determined to make themselves a single-class society. They expanded clone labor to perform all the menial functions."

Andrea wiped the Hlulva juice from her hands on a towel. "So now Jod finds itself flanked by two human systems, Earth and Cor."

"Yes—a troubling reality for us. We have no clear

policy for containing Earth and Cor." H'Roo added, "Many on Jod are afraid that the Ordinate and Terrans will eventually converge into a galactic power to challenge the Jod hegemony. The council believes we must join both branches of your species within the Alliance so the Jod can manage Cor-Earth development and undo the rift caused by Chelle meddling. Others believe we must keep Cor and Earth forever separated to keep the humans from cooperating."

Cooperating? Thinking of Earth's long fractious history and innate human belligerence, Andrea looked at H'Roo and thought, *nobody on Jod has a clue.* She asked out loud, "What do you believe, H'Roo Parh?"

H'Roo's neck blushed slightly. "No offense, but I think Earth is too disorganized to threaten Jod in the next thousand years, if ever. The Ordinate, however, had singular purpose. Their technology is advanced beyond their judgment. And I agree with K'Rin: the Ordinate has corrupted itself by using clone labor. If war comes in my lifetime, it comes from Cor. K'Rin is the only clan headsman who understands the Ordinate. Even within the Tenebrea only a handful agree with K'Rin, but everybody obeys."

The officers rose in unison as K'Rin swept in. He wore his battle sash embroidered with the Rin Family crest, plus his personal honors. His eyes flashed around the room, settling on the school commandant. "Bol-Don, what's going on?" As he spoke, his personal guard filed into the room and stood in a phalanx—all choreographed to intimidate.

Bol-Don stood behind the safety of his granite desk and straightened his tunic. He was meticulous. Every crease on his uniform was as straight as a cartographer's rule. His high collar framed a square jaw and a smile of perfect white teeth. "We've got a problem with the Terran woman you put into the class. She's disruptive and—"

K'Rin stepped up to the desk, interrupting. "My aide tells me that you've put my kinswoman, Mat Flores-Rin, in isolation."

"Kinswoman?" Bol-Don looked about the room for answers, only to find confusion.

"Very soon, yes. I've made the arrangements. I submitted my petition to the Clan Seat, of which I am head, so I believe my petition is going to be approved."

K'Rin read the shock on everyone's face. With an indifferent gaze, he dared them to speak. Then he broke the silence. "No law says I can't adopt a human, with her consent of course. She can't join the Tenebrea without a family connection." Turning to Bol-Don, he inquired, "Now tell me: why is she not in training with the rest of her class?"

Bol-Don retreated a half-step behind the clean desk, bumping his chair. Everybody in the room, including Bol-Don, knew that school commandant was an administrative post and therefore not esteemed in the Tenebrea. He enforced policy, submitted budgets, and coordinated with the Jod Fleet regulars. Jo'Orom led the faculty and candidates. Bol-Don had the good grace not to resent Jo'Orom; he did, however, chafe at this public and surprising rebuke from K'Rin. "She's training in isolation pending a decision—"

K'Rin flashed. "Whose decision?"

The commandant swallowed hard, then asserted himself. "Sir, this school is my command. You gave me the authority to dismiss a candidate for cause." Bol-Don recited the policy, expecting no relief, and getting none.

"And I retain the authority to cashier an officer in my chain of command. Shall we get busy?"

Bol-Don fired an angry look at his adjutant, then turned to K'Rin and with soothing tones said, "Sir, I had no idea that you were so personally involved in the future of Mat Flores."

K'Rin stepped forward till he was nose to nose with the school commandant. "Don't waste any more of my time than you already have. What's your complaint against Flores?"

"Sir. Your protégé, Mat Flores, resists instruction. She ignores matters of discipline. In brief, she's insubordinate." Bol-Don picked up a small data screen from the desk and pointed to a cluster of numbers in the lower quadrant of a scattergram.

K'Rin took the screen and set it back down on the desk without even a glance at the scores, then asked, "Have you any examples?"

Bol-Don nodded his head morosely. "I'm afraid so, sir. We gave her the battery of psychological tests. She purposefully engineered her responses to contradict each other. According to the test results, she is at the same time sentimental and ruthless; calculating and ruled by passion; given to fancy and goal driven. Yet her neural markers show no signs of schizophrenia—no signs of multiple personality."

"Maybe she's just complex." K'Rin spoke slowly with strained patience as if repeating a lesson to an inattentive child. He encroached further onto Bol-Don's spotless desk, leaning forward, closing the gap, daring Bol-Don to back away.

Bol-Don stiffened. "Or maybe she purposefully lied on the tests—I just wish we knew why. The contradictions make us question her integrity." Bol-Don took refuge in the cold hard facts while trying to act concerned.

"She beat your tests—don't accuse Mat Flores of lying unless you're prepared to back yourself in the Dyad. Mat Flores will soon be my cousin with all the rights of my family. She may, if she chooses, defend her name against slander, and call you to the Dyad. Frankly, Bol-Don, the smart wagers would fall on her side. Right Jo'Orom?"

The threat of the Dyad was two parts theater, one part real. The Tenebrea allowed the ancient satisfaction of personal combat to settle matters of honor. The Dyad was rarely invoked because the combatants fought hand-to-hand with razor-sharp claw gloves, rarely fatal but often disfiguring to both parties. The Dyad stressed the ugliness of animal passion as opposed to rational restraint.

Bol-Don glanced sideways toward Jo'Orom, who didn't even acknowledge the question. Jo'Orom enjoyed some notoriety for maiming a Jod regular in the Dyad. Bol-Don chose less incendiary language. "What is the point of beating a psychological profile test?"

"Perhaps to mock your feeble attempts to probe her mind. Perhaps she's just instinctively competitive." K'Rin mused, "Anyway, she beat your test. I like that. She's bright."

"And dangerous." Bol-Don added.

"I'm counting on that." K'Rin trumped Bol-Don's criticism. "What are the other problems?"

"She refuses to cooperate with the students and she distrusts the counselors and instructors. How are we going to train her? I give you another example: she ambushed Jo'Orom in the Pit; gave him a slight concussion by kicking him in the head."

K'Rin laughed aloud. "Shame on you, Feld Jo'Orom. How'd this happen? Are you getting slow? I could never lay a hand on you."

"I let down my guard, sir." Feld Jo'Orom answered stoically.

"And did you make this complaint against her?"

"No, of course not, sir. Mat Flores and I have been in the Pit since."

K'Rin asked, "What do you think of her abilities?"

"Sir. She's an excellent fighter, but unreliable. She will always choose the most expedient course of action to serve her interests. Sir, I would not want my life depending on her. I think she's using us."

"Did she tell you this fact?"

"I sense it." Jo'Orom wrinkled his brow. He was uncomfortable offering opinions instead of facts.

Bol-Don interjected, "And therein lies our problem. We can't trust her. She'll turn on us when it suits her."

K'Rin fingered his battle sash, as he paused to control his temper. "Do you just sense this treachery, or do you know something?"

"She's human." Bol-Don did nothing to soften the contempt in his voice.

"You are right. She's human. Ah, we finally get to your real objection: you don't like humans."

"I'm not prejudiced, sir." Bol-Don smiled around the room. "Humans cannot keep their intellects separate from their passions—especially this female. And I'm afraid her passions make her too inconsistent, too unstable to be a Tenebrea."

K'Rin thought a moment and answered. "Quite the contrary—this drive of hers to find and kill Cor Hunters. Pure passion. Senseless passion. She's constructed a complete—albeit personal—system of ethics to justify herself. She's given all her physical and intellectual energy to her goal. I'd place her powers of concentration up against any of our Britigan Monks. In her own mind, she's perfectly consistent. Don't discount her intellect: She is formidable."

Bol-Don amplified his misgivings. "If what you say is correct, then Mat Flores is, by Jod standards, pathological."

K'Rin paced the floor. "I suppose that depends on whether she's living in a fantasy world or the real one. Frankly, I think she's got an excellent grasp on reality as to how we ought to deal with the Cor Ordinate."

Bol-Don said with resignation, "Very well, you are determined to have the Terran woman in your household guard; I will do my best to train her."

K'Rin caught the half-heartedness in Bol-Don's voice, and he shot back, "Do you think, Bol-Don, that Mat Flores is just a passing curiosity for me? A hobby, perhaps? If you think so, you insult me. You have no idea how valuable she is."

Bol-Don braced himself and said, "Sir, I need an explanation of her *value* to the Tenebrea, because I don't understand. I might be able to train her better if I did."

Put off by Bol-Don's tone of voice, K'Rin nevertheless softened his stern expression. "Fair enough. I can trust you to keep this secret. I need better intelligence to persuade certain council members of the Cor Ordinate threat. We know too little about Ordinate capabilities and intentions. A recent intelligence source suggests the Ordinate is aggressive, that their resources are formidable. But my source may have reasons for drawing us into a conflict entirely against our best interests. Offworld Intelligence can confirm nothing.

So I'm going to rely on my Tenebrea. I need an eye witness account. I can't send a Jod in their midst, but I can send a human, Mat Flores."

The room fell silent as they absorbed the consequences of K'Rin's plan. Bol-Don bowed before the brilliance of the stratagem, speaking reverentially. "Now I understand, Hal K'Rin. We will do our best." With his index finger, Bol-Don reached down and turned off the data screen lying on his desk.

K'Rin noticed with some annoyance how Bol-Don's spirits rose. No longer were the commandant's Jod sensitivities stung by the prospect of a Terran female using the Tenebrea. Quite the reverse. K'Rin thought, *In the greater scheme, Bol-Don's myopia is useful. Andrea must prove her value to doubters like Bol-Don. I can't.*

Andrea's training returned to some semblance of normality. She excelled in weapons: blades, short-range hand lance, long-range rifles. But she remained a mediocre pilot, by Jod standards, having little sympathy for machines. She frustrated Jo'Orom in the cockpit just as she'd frustrated Steve whenever she took the helm of *The Deeper Well.* She heard Steve in Jo'Orom's admonitions: "Don't oversteer! Steady, woman. Don't oversteer!" Despite her heavy touch on the controls Andrea passed the fundamentals of piloting small starcraft.

Her classmates noticed that she now enjoyed encouragement instead of the heretofore steady ration of criticism. The rumor circulated that she was a privileged character, an adopted member of the K'Rin household. Tamor considered the rumor an effrontery, impossible, unthinkable for a Jod like K'Rin to become traitor to his species. He considered Andrea's success in the training undeserved, and he continued to despise her, constantly reminding his small following of the obvious: "The Terran female is not one of us. Soon she'll be out of our way: I'll see to it."

Andrea did not respond to Tamor's carping, but kept a weather eye. She thought of Tamor as a training aid, a combination of adversary to keep her edge and nuisance to test her patience.

At the end of a long season of training, Feld Jo'Orom divided the class into four groups of eight and delivered each group to separate atolls in the Odwa Sea for the survival test. Deposited with an opaque poncho, knife, and bottle of water, each student was free to work within a group or alone. He left them with these words: "This six-day field problem is a test of your self-discipline and endurance. There are no rules, except that you are here when we come back for you in six days. You have just enough water to last the exercise, if you avoid the heat and practice self-denial."

The shore was a lime crust with pulverized shell and coral masquerading as sand. At the water's edge cacti rose like barbed fence posts with three- to six-inch thorns as strong as Spanish steel and as sharp as fangs. Small leathery fruit clustered at the top of the cacti. Black birds with bright yellow eyes flew in to peck and tug at the cactus berries. Small blue lizards lay on the sun side of the cacti, nestled within a thicket of thorns, inching higher to stay out of the birds' reach. Larger sea birds bobbed offshore—adults and juveniles—preening themselves, squawking, complaining—*how dare these eight large unfeathered bipeds usurp their dry perch.*

One dead tree stood near the water's edge, a gnarled

species, long devoid of leaves and bark, just sun-bleached nubs for branches. Obviously, this seed washed ashore had managed to root in a hostile environment, grow to maturity, then die among the cacti. What a strange delight this tree must have been. Andrea claimed the bandy shade from the unknown tree as her own.

"This isn't so bad," Andrea opined. She looked at a nest built of driftwood and the dried fragments of eggshell. *Omelettes are off the menu.*

H'Roo found a patch of shade from a cactus next to Andrea. He shifted from one foot to the next as he swept jagged debris and exfoliated cactus spines to make himself a small place in the shade. "Six days."

Another pair of survivalists wandered off to find shade on the leeward side of the atoll. Tamor-Kyl gathered three of his comrades into a cluster of cacti, each sitting ramrod straight in the shrinking shade, meticulously self-administering tiny capfuls of water. One draped his poncho between two cacti to put up more shade. Andrea watched in disbelief, then called over, "Are you just going to sit there for six days?"

Tamor-Kyl scowled as he screwed the cap back onto his water bottle—already saving his breath from moisture-sapping conversation. H'Roo pulled Andrea aside. "You heard Jo'Orom—we need to get into shade. We have just enough water to stay alive for six days—*if* we have the discipline to do *nothing.*"

"You're kidding." She thought, *you're by the ocean, you fools.* With a chicken neck and string, she'd lured hundreds of blue-fin crabs to supper. As a young girl, she waded waste deep in Assawoman Bay, wriggling toes in the sandy bottom, feeling out cherrystone clams. Six days! Why, this was just a contest to see how much fish she could catch in only six days.

H'Roo seemed surprised. "Standard procedure. Every class goes through the survival test."

"Misery enjoys company." Andrea sat on her haunches and looked out at the ocean.

H'Roo unfastened his shirt. "Well, that's the fleet for you. We are supposed to sit tight and be miserable—in natural shade if possible." H'Roo crouched in the shade. "Worst part of the day. The sun climbs directly overhead. The breeze dies completely, and we bake. Tonight, after the sun goes down, we get just as cold. In your case, your sweaty clothes will add to your discomfort."

"What a bunch of city boys!" She smiled. "H'Roo, stick with me and we'll put on a couple pounds. I grew up by salt water."

Then Andrea shocked H'Roo by drinking half her bottle of water and giving the other half to him, which he refused to drink. "I insist." Andrea said. "I can't hold another drop, and I need an empty bottle."

Andrea took a large clamshell and began digging a hole three feet down. She beckoned H'Roo to help her. "Haven't you ever built a solar still?"

"A what?"

"A solar still—a way to extract potable water from the ground."

"No. We have excellent water reclamation equipment. This situation—stuck on an atoll in sight of the mainland with nothing—is totally artificial. We're here to test our self-discipline through self-denial." He dug earnestly to keep up with Andrea.

"You'd have been better off if they'd dropped you here with no water; then you'd have been forced to improvise."

"That's crazy: no water at all?"

"Look at Tamor. He'll subsist on a couple ounces of water each day because he can. All his energy is devoted to measuring water, counting time between drinks, and steadying his hand lest he spill a drop. He'll sit there thinking how miserable he is; then he'll try to figure out how to cheat the others out of their pitiful rations."

"He's tough, he'll pass the test." H'Roo defended Tamor-Kyl's discipline.

"What if they don't come back in six days?" Andrea grinned. "You said yourself, this situation is artificial. Do you think real life has a six-day limit on deprivation?" H'Roo swallowed hard, considering the possibility.

They cleared away the jagged pea-sized coral gravel to a finer strain of grit and shell fragments, then cool white sand. *Cool because it's moist.* Using the serrated blade on her knife, she cut a wider opening to her water bottle and set it at the epicenter of her pit. Finally, she laid her poncho loosely across the pit, anchoring the edges with coral.

"Your hole looks like a trap. Going to trap some water?" H'Roo observed warily as he wiped his dry lips.

"In a manner of speaking, yes." She explained, "The sun shines through the plastic and heats the wet sand below. Moisture evaporates from the sand and is trapped on the underside of the plastic before it can escape to the air." She placed a small round chunk of worn coral in the center of the poncho, forming a funnel shape in the acrylic cloth. "The moisture condenses on the underside of the poncho, then runs downhill, falling into the water bottle." Andrea raised an edge of the poncho to inspect the aim of the drip above her water bottle, adjusting it slightly to catch the first drip.

"We'll each take a quart or more each day from this still. See!"

"So simple." H'Roo bent down and to look under the flap. Already moisture rose and began to condense on the underside of the poncho. Gravity pulled the tiny droplets down the funnel, where they collided into fatter beads of water; then collected finally at the vortex, swelling to a full drip, and letting go into the altered water bottle. *Plink!*

Andrea walked to the water's edge and looked into the clear brine. Urchins brandishing purple and black spines milled about the floor. Live coral, a mottled red and yellow, clung to the chalk walls built from the tiny skeletons of past generations. Small iridescent fish swam among the urchins. A striped crustacean, a water scorpion, casually selected a small urchin and mounted the unsuspecting ball of spines. Then, with the jab of a green and orange striped tail, the water scorpion put the urchin spines into a rigid reflex as the poison did its work. A faint rivulet of inky fluid rose like smoke from the urchin—now the scorpion's meal. Small rainbow-colored fish hung about a respectful distance—a scavenger's deference to the predator—waiting for scraps.

Farther in the deep she saw a long shadow pass. She guessed the aquatic beast was most likely some bottom feeder, a ray or catfish—something gosh-awful ugly, but edible; size hard to judge given the refraction of light in the water. She looked up at the sun-dappled water. Steve would've loved this patch of desert raised in a tropical sea. How often he promised to show her the Pacific and spend a night on an uninhabited atoll. He promised to show her the Southern Cross; promised Easter Island—so many unfulfilled promises.

H'Roo called over. "Now what?"

"Why don't you put up a biminy," Andrea directed. Before he asked, she translated, "Put up some shade."

They sat back to back in their small patch of shade, napping and waiting for the noon heat to subside. Andrea asked lazily, "What do you want for dinner?"

"Don't tease. I'm just beginning to get hungry."

"Do you like fish?" She carved a pair of notches in a cactus spine. There, she fit a pair of barbs also whittled from the tough spines.

"Normally we don't eat flesh, but tonight I'll make an exception."

She pulled a heavy thread from her pants inseam and wrapped nylon thread about the barbs, fashioning a large fishhook. "We need some line and some live bait. When evening comes and the temperature falls, we work. I'll procure the line; you catch a lizard."

Dusk brought relief in the form of a fresh breeze. H'Roo and Andrea shared the precious extract from the solar still as they planned to use the waning light. Andrea cut the drawstrings from their ponchos to make twenty-four-feet of heavy fishing line. H'Roo took his knife and began stalking a small set of fresh lizard tracks.

While she waited for H'Roo to return with the bait, Andrea set out to build a fire. Waterbirds protested loudly as she savaged their nests, gathering driftwood. She pocketed small pinches of down, shavings from bark and fibers of sun-dried seaweed for kindling. From her collection of driftwood, she selected an eighteen-inch crescent to which she fastened a length of cord sacrificed from her new fishing line. She picked through her collection of sticks, selecting the hardest, straightest piece, which she trimmed with her knife. She put one wrap of cord around the straight stick, set it on a large piece of wood, then held her stick erect with a thick piece of shell smooth as glass. She lay the kindling at the base of the stick, then vigorously pushed and pulled the bow like a saw. Smoke! She bent down and blew gently on the hot spot till it burst into yellow flame. In moments, she had a respectable fire.

The novelty of fire on the atoll attracted attention. The other Jod left their shadows—all but Tamor-Kyl—and wandered up the shore to inspect Andrea's flurry of domestic arts. Reef crabs, likewise mesmerized by the light, climbed onto the shoreline, and squatted.

H'Roo returned triumphant with a fat blue lizard. It hissed and spread a pink neck cowl until Andrea impaled it on the double barbs of her field expedient hook. The lizard's mouth remained open in death; its legs hung limp. She tied a chunk of coral near the baited hook, then tossed the assembly into the soft waves, aiming for the deep trough between the coral heads. Andrea tied her end of the line to her wrist, pulled in the slack, and sat.

Nothing. The last sliver of sun fell beneath the horizon; the night came, and when she reeled in her hook, she had little more than lizard bones and skin left. The underwater midges had fleeced her hook. The dreary spectators slouched back to their patchs of dirt and went to sleep muttering about Andrea's failure. They might have at least eaten the lizard, now wasted. "We'll try again tomorrow." She coiled the line carefully.

H'Roo gamely answered, "I'll catch another lizard." Then they took turns tending the fire and snatching bits of cold sleep.

On her watch, Andrea lay on her back by the low

fire gazing at the canopy of stars. None of the patterns looked familiar: no Orion's Belt, no Pleiades. The same stars were there but rearranged. She did see the familiar band of white dust that she knew as the Milky Way. The Jod called it the Coandal Belt. She used to love to lie on the deck of *The Deeper Well* and look up at the stars. Stargazing was peaceful then.

Somewhere in that haze was her home and she could not help but feel an urge to orient herself toward her source of existence—her sun, her light, and also the source of her pain. But which speck in that luminescent dust was hers? Unable to discern even the general direction of her Earth, she felt strangely alone, and looking at the stars gave her a pang of loneliness much worse than the chill in the night breeze. She sighed, then played with her thick fishing line. She diverted her attention from the stars to the black water and the phosphorescence stirred to life by the gentle waves.

Morning came. The night sky vanished except a pale silver husk of a moon and a brilliant dot of light near the darker horizon—the docking station for the Jod dreadnoughts. At first light, H'Roo captured another hapless lizard and Andrea consigned him to the deep. She felt the line sink away, and she prepared to sit and wait. But then she felt a slight tug: she stood, carefully feeling the slack in the line. Then a strike that jerked her off balance and she fell, sliding in the rough gravel toward the water.

Quickly, she spun around and dug her heels deep into the ground. The noose about her wrist cinched, tightly cutting off circulation. "I got a big one!" She called H'Roo to help. The line pulled always toward the deep with sharp tugs left, then right. No finesse—just brute force. The loose gravel gave way, and the line dragged her inch by inch toward the water. She had no desire to swim with whatever wrestled the end of her line, so she grabbed her knife, contemplating cutting herself loose. "H'Roo! Slip your hips down here and help me haul this beast in!"

H'Roo caught a handful of line and halted Andrea's retrograde. He apologized. "I was looking for another lizard."

Together, they pulled the line in. The water surface broiled as their quarry fought the line. "What is it?" Andrea asked.

"An eel? I don't know the names of fish." H'Roo grunted as they gave one mighty heave and landed the frantic creature onto dry land.

"Ugly damn thing. Look at those teeth!" Andrea untied the noose from her sore wrist. The elongated fish did look like an eel. It had a rough eel skin. This vicious fish also had a flat oversized head, an underbite, and a mouth of wicked, serrated teeth—teeth that could take a hand off. It thrashed about the land coiling itself onto the line, biting and chewing—twenty pounds of wet fury.

Again, the commotion brought spectators and they formed a wide semicircle. Again, Tamor-Kyl observed standard procedure, content to watch from his shade cactus.

"Now what?" H'Roo asked.

Andrea kept a straight face. "You just go in there and kill it with a stick."

H'Roo's raised brow advertised his reluctance. "No disrespect intended, Mat Flores." He used her formal rank and name. "But why don't *you* kill it with a stick?"

The eel paused as if listening to their deliberations, daring one of them to come closer. *Yeah, why don't you kill me with a stick?* It continued to chew on the line. Soon the beast would break the line and wriggle itself back to the water, and their meal would disappear, their labors wasted.

Andrea took her knife and walked four paces to the gnarled tree. With one stroke she cut away a short branch, leaving a sharp stake protruding from the tree trunk, angled up like a meat hook. She tossed the remnant branch aside and returned to the eel. She stood between the eel and the shore, keeping a respectful distance from the snapping jaws. She sheathed her knife and walked around the eel, and the eel turned to face her.

Then as quick as a mongoose, she jumped over the eel, grabbed its tail, and began swinging it. Centripetal force straightened the thick eel—one swing, two; she stepped toward the tree trunk and slammed the eel against the meat hook she'd just prepared.

The eel writhed against the stake stuck through its head. Andrea took her knife and deftly sliced a ring around the eel's fat neck. She stuck her knife in the tree for the moment as she grabbed the eel's skin at the bloody cut, and with one violent wrench, pulled the skin away, throwing it casually in the direction of the gaping spectators. The wet rag of fish skin landed in Gem-Bar's lap. The eel bled a pale red from a thousand tiny pores as it continued to turn and twist. Andrea plucked her knife from the tree and cut two large fillets—five pounds of flesh each. She handed one of the filets to H'Roo, the other to the spectators, saying, "You can use some of our embers to make your own fire."

The eel managed a last twitch, then died. Nevertheless, Andrea would wait till morning to retrieve her hook from the jaws of needle-sharp teeth.

In no time at all, the atoll had no fewer than five

solar stills, three cooking fires, and a constant effort to catch fish. Even Tamor-Kyl left his shade and standard procedures to participate.

Andrea set her screen board on the desk and looked up at the proctor. "What kind of stupid test is this?" She noticed his front teeth were crooked.

"It's a peer rating sheet. You rate each of your classmates—everyone but yourself."

"On what grounds? I don't see any categories here . . ." She paged through the screen by stroking a small gray touch pad.

"Just your general impression. You rank everyone from first to last, and you offer comments. If you don't have enough information to form an opinion about somebody, you rate them U for unknown."

"What does the school do with our peer rating sheets?"

The soldier grinned at her. "Helps the cadre identify misfits." *Like you*—he didn't say the words, but Andrea knew what he was thinking.

Andrea looked at the form, the list of twenty-one. *This stinks.* She would not play their game. She wrote *U* by all the names but three: H'Roo Parh, whom she rated 1 without comment; Gem-Bar, whom she rated 2 with the comment *reliable*, and Tamor-Kyl, to whom she gave last place without comment. She actively disliked Tamor—she might as well make their mutual animus a matter of record. She could only imagine how her name would appear on the compiled list.

chapter 6

Andrea contemplated the rumors. The midcourse interview was a simple performance review, nothing more. Sitting in the anteroom waiting her turn, she knew better. The last time she wore a duty uniform and waited in solitude outside a heavy door, her life changed. She was expelled from the academy. For her these formal settings always seemed to portend some failure. Why should Jod be any different? She heard a rumor that they always pare down the class to eight finalists; some or all of those elite would graduate into the Tenebrea. The great majority of candidates return to the fleet for mundane billets.

Andrea mulled over her experience in the course so far. Suddenly she didn't think kicking Jo'Orom in the head was so clever. She recalled all the taunts she'd aimed at Tamor-Kyl—especially offering him root during the tension climb. She chewed the powerful stimulant and swung from her rope, hanging upside down as she handed him the black plug of root and coaxed him, "Don't be a baby: chew this, Tamor, and join the fun. It calms the nerves and takes away any fear of heights." The anxious Tamor chewed the root: the black treacle stained his lips. And there she left him dangling from a reverse slope in stirrups, two hundred feet in the air, nauseous, helpless, humiliated—she, all the while, cackling with satisfaction for this payback for her flannerberry cocktail.

She pondered other negatives she might encounter in her performance review. Andrea certainly had little use for show, but now as she waited for her performance review she wished she hadn't been so cavalier about Jod tradition and Jo'Orom's passion for clean lines and bright shine. The hard reality sunk in: she had nowhere to go if K'Rin turned her out. *Go back to Earth and start over? How many times can a person erase her past? Or am I to become a study in failure?*

Also, the specter of her peer rating haunted her. She slumped in her chair. Heretofore she'd not cared one whit what the Jod thought of her—except H'Roo. As far as she was concerned the rest were just so many training aids—things put in her path to test her growing skills, maybe competitors, but not team members whose opinions counted.

The door handle rattled and the heavy door opened. Out stepped Gem-Bar, looking pleased, but a bit concerned. Andrea asked, "What's happening?"

Gem-Bar rubbed his forearm. "Can't tell you: I'm under orders." He finished his sentence as he rounded a corner and disappeared.

Then she heard K'Rin's familiar command voice, "Next candidate, enter."

She stood, fought back a wrinkle in her trousers, checked her gig line, and marched through the door into a dimly lit room.

"Close the door, please."

She complied, pushing the heavy door till the lock

made a fateful click; then she stood waiting further instructions. K'Rin sat at a desk made of polished petrified wood. He jostled a handheld screen. Feld Jo'Orom stood by a draped window, his hands clasped behind his back. On the desk lay a parchment document, an ink pen, and a charged hypo-injector. A lone chair sat humbly in front of the desk.

"Sit down, Mat Flores." K'Rin paged through a set of screens, looking up just briefly to acknowledge Andrea's presence. Despite his abrupt greeting, his manner was relaxed. "I've looked forward to this day."

He's in a good mood. Andrea took her seat with renewed confidence. Whether by nepotism, merit, or luck, she didn't care: Again, K'Rin had come to this interview on her side, and in this forum, he was judge and jury.

K'Rin didn't waste time with preliminaries. "We decided you are suitable to continue the training. However, to continue, you must make a lifetime commitment, and take the oath—what you humans might call a blood oath. Do you understand, Andrea Flores?"

"Yes, sir."

"Feld Jo'Orom tells me that you are the most unusual candidate who's come through this course." K'Rin paged through the screen.

Jo'Orom stiffened. "That is my unprejudiced observation, ma'am. I neither meant it as a criticism nor as a compliment."

Andrea knew this was not the time or place to exchange barbs with the senior noncom. But she could not resist one small jab. "I'm glad I could add something new to your routine."

K'Rin suppressed a smile, then said frankly, "The cadre all think you're a pain, but they're resigned to take you back into the second phase of your training."

Andrea said nothing, but looked past K'Rin to Jo'Orom. K'Rin looked at the handheld screen as he spoke. "Let me give you an example. *The candidate Flores fails to work within the rules. She shows no inclination to repair this deficiency, using the excuse that the mission supersedes all other considerations.*"

Andrea asked, "Is that bad?"

Feld Jo'Orom answered. "Ms. Flores, our rules are designed for your safety and the safety of the other candidates."

Although she tried to sound sincere, one could not mistake the sarcasm in her voice. "Will you also design our missions for our safety?"

"As much as possible." Jo'Orom defended the policy.

"With the cooperation of the Cor Ordinate, I presume."

K'Rin snapped, "Don't be impertinent. We spend a lot of effort, time, and resources training you. If we want to get you killed, then that's our business. However, we won't tolerate you getting yourself killed. You no longer have that luxury. I hope you see the distinction?"

Andrea recoiled slightly at the sharp rebuke, shrinking further after this cold douse of reality. They were fashioning her as a tool. Like any soldier, she was property—valuable perhaps, but expendable. She looked at K'Rin and wondered, *Are you expendable, too?* She needed the Tenebrea to get at the Ordinate, and if that shackled her or made her expendable, so be it. Her voice turned matter of fact as if she were engaged in a commercial transaction. "Yes, sir. I see the distinction."

"Good." K'Rin switched off his wrath as he returned to his notes. "Now, this is interesting—your peer review. You come in the lowest quartile."

She'd expected worse and said so. "I expected to be dead last."

K'Rin paged through a few more screens, "Actually, yes. You got a couple of high ratings, but for the most part the men don't like you. Jod, like humans, typically despise what they fear. I suspect that they fear you."

Andrea nodded with a modicum of self-approval. "If I'm last and you keep me, then what's the point of the peer review?"

"I could not care less what the others say about you." He looked over at Jo'Orom and arched a hairless eyebrow. "They all believe that I actually care what the collective body thinks. Youth is terminally vain, eh, Feld Jo'Orom?"

"Yes, sir."

The Admiral set the screen filled with notes aside. "I don't care what they say about you—I'll form my own opinions. Rather, I'm more interested in what you say about the others, and not because I put any weight on what you have to say."

"I didn't write any comments; I only ranked three."

"Exactly. You withheld judgment where you lacked knowledge. In that you demonstrate that you are more discreet than the others."

"Thank you, sir."

"Don't let it go to your head, Andrea. Most of your record shows that you have a colossal dearth of prudence. My cadre cannot discipline this recklessness from you. In my experience, a reckless warrior is immediately unreliable and soon dead. Your passions override any natural sense of self-preservation. And this worries me. I can't teach self-preservation. Either you have the instinct or you do not."

"I do not expect to die before I can settle with the Ordinate."

"Therefore, I do believe we can teach you the simple common sense that you must survive to complete your mission. I'm inviting you into the Tenebrea, and I shall personally oversee your training, and your missions."

"So when do I get to kill Ordinate?"

K'Rin narrowed his eyes, displeased with Andrea's question. "Not until I give you orders. You will have a chance to kill Ordinate, but on my terms."

"Then, I accept your invitation." She knew better than to press for concessions now.

K'Rin walked around the granite desk to be nearer Andrea. He lowered his voice. "This rather extraordinary decision of mine reeks of nepotism. If you continue to make a mockery of our discipline, then you give my enemies on the council ammunition to discredit me. You hurt the unit integrity of the Tenebrea, and I must at some point wonder if you're worth the trouble. I am taking an awful risk with you, Mat Flores, and you have not made it easy for me. You can do me a great deal of harm, or you can make me immeasurably proud."

"Yes, sir." She understood the risk K'Rin took, probably better than he did.

K'Rin took the parchment from the desk and handed it to Andrea. "Now I want you to read the oath. It's simple enough."

Andrea looked at the short paragraph. *I, Andrea Flores-Rin, solemnly pledge to obey the orders of my superior officers within the Tenebrea. I promise to submit to the Tenebrea for the rest of my natural life.* She looked up from the parchment and took a breath. *I promise to keep all the secrets entrusted to me. If I ever violate this trust, I forfeit my life.* She finished by looking K'Rin in the eye, saying, "A strong oath."

"Yes, it is. And not in the least bit allegorical—when we say you are part of the Tenebrea for life, we speak of a biological certainty. To leave is death. If you join the Tenebrea, you can never unjoin. If you live long enough to retire, you live as a pensioner in relative luxury restricted to the Jod system. If ever you betray the Tenebrea, you have in effect already signed your death warrant."

Without comment, Andrea took the pen and as she did, Jo'Orom picked up the hypo-injector, rolled up Andrea's sleeve, and placed the injector on her forearm. She hesitated. "What is that?" she asked, referring to the hypo.

K'Rin answered. "When you sign the oath, we bind you to the Tenebrea with this injection. I'll explain everything when you are with us."

The hypo pressed lightly against her bare skin gave her pause. Something about this injection gave them control over her—more control than an oath, but was it any more control than they already had? Her curiosity burned. *What in the world?* She'd heard of the Chelle infusing parasites into their condemned criminals, which left them in a constant state of narcosis.

She fingered the pen. "You've had this injection?"

"We all have," K'Rin answered.

Now, she would belong to the Tenebrea, in every sense of the word. But they offered much in return, for how else could she find and slay Ordinate Hunters? Who else would feed her, equip her, and transport her throughout the galaxy to find and execute the Ordinate who killed Steve and Glendon? And what else could she do with her life? Was the Tenebrea asking anything more than the academy? Yes, they were—a death-do-us-part commitment, but she could handle that, for in her own mind, she had nothing else to live for anyway. They wanted a lifetime of secrecy—not a big problem. They might as well enforce a lifetime away from Earth. Nothing but bitterness waited for her there. The Ordinate had already robbed her of the only companionship she ever wanted; the prospect of forced solitude caused no anxiety. But, the Tenebrea also wanted a lifetime of obedience, and obedience came hard to Andrea.

She tapped the pen on the paper to start the wet ink and she scrawled her name; as she finished, she felt the pinprick of the hypo-injector breaking her skin. She rubbed her arm, remembering Gem-Bar soothing his injection. "So what did you pump into my arm?"

Jo'Orom replied, "Quazel Protein."

"I've heard of Quazel; it's illegal." Andrea searched her memory. "A drug, right?"

"Not exactly." K'Rin answered. "It's a prion—a self-replicating protein."

"I remember. The Artrix developed the drug for horticulture and livestock. Some unscrupulous Chelle merchants smuggled it to Earth and sold it as a great performance enhancer. No, a kind of fountain of youth. So you guys are trafficking illegal youth drugs."

Andrea searched her memory. The Chelle found a huge market on Earth. People who took Quazel felt like world-class athletes. Their ailments vanished, everything from acne to cancer; even viral infections such as hepatitis—all gone. People lucky enough to get the Quazel enjoyed almost instant rejuvenation and the promise of perfect health and a long life. The Earth doctors who recommended trials suffered derision.

Quazel was about to put most of the medical profession out of business! In less than three months, operating from a series of twenty-five clinics in Europe, the Chelle administered two million doses of Quazel. Andrea remembered the pictures, the assembly-line aspect of the clinics with the diminutive Chelle, with autoinjectors in each hand, trooping a long line of affluent humans. They charged ten thousand ecus per dose. And that was the bargain of the century. Suddenly the Chelle merchants left. And within a few months the inexorable and fatal side effects of Quazel put two million people in hospitals. The only palliative was morphine.

Andrea backed up, knocking over the chair. "Quazel kills humans."

Jo'Orom arched his eyebrows. "Quazel kills Jod, too."

She tried to read the bemused smile on K'Rin's face. She wrestled for a course of action, but her mind clouded as it jumped from K'Rin's motives to the deadly effects of Quazel. *Is this some kind of sick joke? Jo'Orom looks too self-satisfied.* She looked to K'Rin, whose calm visage helped her keep her nerve. One word escaped her lips. "Why?"

K'Rin picked up the chair and sat Andrea down. "Relax. Just let me explain Quazel. Our bodies age and deteriorate because the proteins in our cells break down, in part due to the damaging effect of free radicals. As the protein breaks down, the cell membranes break down; so our cells require frequent replacement. What is worse, our cells do not replace themselves with perfect copies, also a function of protein breakdown. As proteins fail, intercellular mass becomes dehydrated, slowing down enzyme functions needed for gene expression. So, with each cell copy, minute imperfections creep into the DNA—a kind of cellular entropy."

"So?" Much of the biology of aging escaped Andrea as she dealt with the reality that she had been poisoned.

K'Rin continued to lecture his distracted pupil. "Quazel is an extremely resilient protein. It replicates itself throughout the body—what you Terrans call a prion. Quazel replaces the body's weaker proteins. Much tougher than natural proteins, Quazel practically eliminates the effects of free radicals. Because Quazel Protein lasts many times longer than normal proteins, the cells do not slough away and therefore do not require replacements."

Jo'Orom added, "Consequently, your cells with Quazel Protein resist disease and aging. You enjoy greater strength and quickness. Also, a body built of Quazel heals at amazing speed. You become an enhanced physical being."

Valuable—enhanced even, but expendable. Andrea's eyes widened. "But within six months to a year, everyone who ever used Quazel died."

K'Rin read her mind. He pointed at himself and said, "I have the Quazel Protein in me. So does Feld Jo'Orom. You'll live much longer than a year, I assure you. The heretofore unmanaged side effect of Quazel was the inevitable hardening process. Most hardwood plants and simple organisms like insects or crustaceans get great benefit from the Quazel Protein. Why? Either they resist the hardening process or, in the case of livestock, they don't live long enough to suffer from the effects. However, complex beings like humans typically enjoy terrific health and vitality for a short time before the ossification destroys their tissues."

Andrea looked at her forearm. She knew that once administered, the Quazel could not be reversed. The self-replicating protein was already coursing through her bloodstream. If K'Rin were not telling the truth, then she was doomed. "Ossified?"

"In layman's terms, Quazel eventually turns people to stone. When the Quazel protein has completely replaced the organism's innate protein, the Quazel bonds with itself to become a crystal. Without intervention, your muscles, then your vital organs turn to stone—an excruciating death. After debilitating stiffening of the joints, the circulatory system typically fails. Blood cells crystallize. Every capillary in the body is cut with a million tiny razors. The subcutaneous bleeding literally inflames the nerve endings under the skin and the slightest touch is agony. The body goes into hemorrhagic shock. If one is unfortunate enough to survive, the intestines ossify. Very unpleasant. Some species like your salmon experience a sudden gerontologic collapse like Quazel demise."

"I think you'd better tell me about the intervention part." Andrea looked at the hypo-injector lying lazily on the desk next to her signed oath.

"Normally, the body has enzymes on constant patrol eliminating any foreign proteins. However, your body does not have an enzyme to attack the Quazel Protein. Unlike viruses or bacteria, you can't kill prions with a slight rise in temperature or by disinfectants. Any attempt to kill the prion kills the host. Except enzymes. Until recently, no body was able to create an enzyme to manage Quazel."

"But you and Jo'Orom—you both have the enzyme." Her mind was spinning with questions. She felt swamped in a deluge of information and emotion. But she cleared her mind of her fear to concentrate on the enzyme—the antidote to the fatal protein.

"Yes. During the Drug Wars I captured an Artrix wanted for Quazel trafficking. He knew the secret of making the enzyme. Instead of handing him over to the Artrix authorities for execution, I gave him a job. I built him a laboratory and assigned my best technical staff to help him. He's happily working for me now making the Quazel enzyme that keeps us all alive. The enzyme breaks the Quazel Protein into an artificial but digestible sugar. Tomorrow, we implant a supply of enzyme under your skin. The enzyme dissolves into your body over a period of months, providing you just enough enzyme to keep the Quazel Protein from crystallizing. In effect, you get all the benefits of Quazel while eliminating the deleterious side effects."

Andrea's eyes widened. "You mean you could double the life span of everybody? Why don't you take this to market? You could name your price."

"Again, you are correct. You may live to be one hundred fifty years old. However, so would everyone else. The population of the universe would double in one generation just due to increased life expectancy. Our economic systems cannot survive such a shock to the demographics." K'Rin's countenance grew stern. "That is just one reason why we guard this secret carefully. Nobody outside the Tenebrea knows about this enzyme; not even the council." He muttered, "They're living too long as it is."

Feld Jo'Orom frowned.

K'Rin paced the floor. "If anyone ever leaked the information about the enzyme, we would withhold the enzyme implants and let him die; and his horrible death would contradict his story."

"You sound as if you've already had to withhold the enzyme."

K'Rin smiled at Andrea's astuteness. "Yes, as a matter of fact, we had an awkward moment with one of the first assistants I assigned to Dr. Carai, the Artrix biochemist I mentioned. Like you, he instantly recognized the short-term commercial possibilities of the Quazel-management enzyme. He insisted that we let him present his findings to his fellow scientists. So we obliged him. We shipped him to a very public sanitarium on the Boltar colony, under the care of some of the finest doctors in the galaxy. His claims were dismissed as dementia of a Quazel addict, and they committed him to a secure cell. Away from his lab, without his notes, he couldn't duplicate his enzyme; soon he suffered from the initial symptoms of cartilage hardening and blood cell ossification. Within a month, the Boltar staff had to restrain him in isolation. One day after lights out, the poor wretch managed to break free of his restraints, whereupon he hanged himself in his cell."

Andrea's eyes narrowed. "Likewise you can withhold the enzyme and let the Quazel Protein kill us."

K'Rin chortled. "Andrea, if we wanted to kill you, you would be long dead. But you understand our purpose." K'Rin left no doubt as he continued, "You see, Andrea, the Quazel and the enzyme are not just a reward for performing dangerous work for us. The Quazel is my leash on the Tenebrea."

"I thought so." Andrea felt the filial bond between her and K'Rin fade as the Quazel Protein began to replicate in her body.

"What fool would train you to be what you are, then simply turn you loose? As part of the Tenebrea, you operate outside the laws of the Alliance. You perform missions that would cause great scandal to Jod if you talked. You could do us irreparable harm if you turned against us. You could do great damage to the Alliance if you turned freelance. However, the damage would be limited because, in any case, you would not last six months without a refill of the enzyme."

"So you don't rely on the integrity of the person taking your oath." A dull sense of loss replaced the initial joy of belonging.

K'Rin ignored Andrea's comment but held out his hand, not the typical Jod gesture, "Welcome to the Tenebrea, Andrea."

She took his hand and accepted his congratulations. She had hoped that entering the Tenebrea meant earning K'Rin's trust. *Perhaps the trust comes later*, she thought.

Andrea turned to leave when she heard K'Rin's voice at her back. "Cousin." Andrea paused at the word. K'Rin had never addressed her as cousin before. The voice shed all the edges of command, and took instead a haunting, warm lilt.

Andrea turned, wondering *now what?*

"I have good news." K'Rin stepped in front of Andrea and put his thick hands on her shoulders. "Today, if you consent, I may adopt you into the Rin Clan. My petition is recorded and all that is necessary now is your consent."

My consent? Andrea stood speechless. She looked into K'Rin's eyes and could not read the thoughts residing there. For a moment K'Rin resembled her father, whose inscrutable eyes mirrored the confusion of dipolar vocations: father and warrior. In K'Rin she saw the same disconnect in the soul, and she suddenly realized with a shudder of self-knowledge that in K'Rin she preferred the warrior to the father. This familial side of K'Rin seemed at once alien and unnatural. Or had she so hardened herself against affection that she recoiled at the tenderness in K'Rin's voice. *Consent?* Andrea felt as though her consent had been the cheapest commodity in these past three years. What did her consent have to do with anything? She was neither asking for nor giving consent. She was going to punish the Ordinate for . . . *for everything.* She closed her eyes.

K'Rin smiled and tried to draw Andrea into conversation. "All is in order. Jo'Orom is kin and can, therefore, act as witness." Andrea opened her eyes as K'Rin held out the document, a simple form that also served to procure the Jod equivalence of a marriage license. He handed her a pen. Andrea hesitated.

K'Rin whispered, "Andrea, protocol demands that you be part of the Rin Clan by blood, marriage, or adoption if you are going to serve in the Tenebrea."

Andrea took the pen. She took comfort knowing that the adoption was a means to an end. She signed her name where K'Rin pointed. All practical—as practical as the bonds of Quazel Protein. K'Rin said, "You must not tell anybody yet. I'll make the announcements at the appropriate time."

Jo'Orom then poured a stiff claret into a chalice carved of ivory and gilt in the bowl. He said, "The paperwork is for the registrar. In the old days, we just shared this ancient cup." He drank and handed the ivory cup to K'Rin, who took a deep drink of the potent wine, then handed it to Andrea. Jo'Orom admonished her, "Don't drink unless you mean to share our fate. The paper is nothing: The cup is everything."

Andrea took the cup and drained it.

* * *

Andrea returned to her room. Was it her imagination, or was her arm still tingling from the Quazel injection? As was her habit, she unfastened her collar as her door closed behind her, and she spoke to her private system: "Messages?"

The wall panel lit, and a disembodied voice replied: "You have two messages."

Andrea sat in the straightback chair bending over to unfasten her boots. "Play messages."

The wall screen glowed, displaying 1, the date, time, and the from lines. The first message was the daily training schedule. Andrea interrupted the audio recitation, saying "Save first message to calendar."

"Done."

The second message was from H'Roo Parh, delivered in H'Roo's smooth voice, but staccato format. "I heard the news, Andrea. Congratulations. Take a look at your wardrobe. I'll meet you at the open mess, as usual. Out."

The mechanical voice followed: "Save, Reply, Forward?"

Andrea ignored the machine, leaving it to the default. She peeled off her boots. *One hundred fifty years.* How casually they hand out seventy years of life, how casually she accepted it; yet, she didn't feel the least bit enriched by the prospects of such longevity.

In fact, she suspected that she hadn't even begun to consider the consequences of Quazel. For instance, a woman built of Quazel Protein would almost certainly outlive her spouse and children. This abstraction bit deep into her heart for she had already suffered that unacceptable loss. In a strange projection of ethics she mused, *a wife and mother must secure the Quazel for her family. How would H'Roo handle this dilemma?*

No wonder Gem-Bar wore such a giddy look as he emerged from his interview. He'd just added another century to a Jod's already long life. The happy fool. What happens when a member of the Tenebrea exceeds his or her life span and still has a middle-aged face and body? The slowest mind in the galaxy would see the pattern: the Tenebrea live too long. Perhaps few survived a career of special operations, but what of those who did? At some point, members of the Tenebrea must disappear because at some point their very existence betrayed their secret.

Andrea looked at her hands. They were nicked, scraped, and callused. Ironic, she thought her hands had become prematurely old. Another bit of irony: the thought of another seventy years tacked on to her life suddenly made her feel tired.

"Lights forty percent." The ceiling dimmed. The window ionized gray to block most of the sunlight. Andrea removed her heavy tunic and draped it over the chair, and she moved to her bed.

Her short-term memory echoed: *Look at your wardrobe.* She paused and opened the panel. Her duty and field uniforms hung in neat rows: they had been altered. Someone had sewn the Tenebrea flash over the left shoulder: an arch comprised of a dark metallic gray field within a black border; the word *TENEBREA* in black silk—mysterious in its simplicity. Something else caught her eye.

"Light one-hundred percent." The charcoal gray beret with the shield, bisected diagonally with the upper half gray, the lower a glossy black. And a dress mess uniform, the peculiar black-on-gray jacket tapered to her waist, and the high stiff collar, tailored to the proportions of her smaller human neck. Two columns of brushed titanium buttons added a dull splash of light to the uniform. The epaulets broadcast a thin streak of emerald on a platinum stripe: the rank of Mat. The stovepipe pants were pleated at the waist and hips. And from a thin leather belt hung the ornamental dagger, an eight-inch double-edged blade in a black leather sheath edged in platinum. The dagger's handle bore the triskelion crest of the Family Rin.

At the stroke of the sixth bell, Andrea stepped into the formal dining room of the officers' mess wearing her new uniform—complete with dagger slung low on her hip—not quite military fashion, but nobody was about to tell a Tenebrea what to do with a dagger. She wore her hair pulled severely back into a tight knot. She walked up to the bar. Her presence stirred the small crowd of swaggering young Jod officers and even the grizzled old commodores, who parted as this figure in gray cut through their ranks on her way to order a drink.

The other uniforms, a nut brown, looked pale against hers. They were supply officers, transport pilots, staff, and protocol specialists. But being Jod, they were thicker and heavier. She might have reminded them of a wisplike prepubescent Jod girl, except that her black hair and olive complexion gave her the aspect of the mythological L'Ee (*The Stalker*—Jod demon of Death). She looked immeasurably intense compared to the pasty rear echelon types.

No one spoke to her, except as required by formal convention. As a matter of mutual consent, the

Tenebrea didn't mix with the regular service. Prying questions were often rebuffed with threatening looks: The Tenebrea oath of secrecy was vaguely understood if not exaggerated by outsiders. As a household guard of a great house, the Tenebrea didn't answer to the regular chain of command, and cooperation was sustained by the thinnest formal courtesy. Jod Fleet Officers at once disdained and admired the unconventional Tenebrea, who did the offworld dirty work, but by Mani's Ax, they did it well.

Andrea held up one finger. "One Baldinale, if you please."

Promptly, the barkeep handed her a rose quartz tumbler, snow-white froth atop an effervescent red liquid. She took it and left the way she'd come. She found herself a seat in the arboretum, where she drank her ale and waited for H'Roo Parh.

H'Roo arrived soon with his tumbler of Baldinale. "Andrea! How glad I am that you suggested we put on our finery tonight." He paused to look at Andrea and added, "The tailors did an excellent job fitting your uniform. Do you like it?"

"Yes, I do. I just wish he were here so I could thank him in person."

Her remark caught H'Roo off guard. He lowered his tumbler of ale and asked, "Whom?"

"Why, K'Rin of course."

"Oh, you think K'Rin bought you the mess dress?"

Andrea held up the dagger, pointing to the Rin Family heraldry, a triskelion of three raised fists. But looking at H'Roo's face, she knew better. "Don't tell me you bought the uniforms."

"Yes." H'Roo shrugged.

"I'm floored." Andrea was embarrassed, partly

because of her gaffe, and she was inexplicably peeved at her patron, K'Rin, for not making the gift. Plus, she felt a bit compromised wearing clothes purchased for her by this young male Jod—her partner.

"What's *floored?*"

She rephrased. "I'm overwhelmed by your generosity. You should not have spent so much money on me."

H'Roo beamed. "The uniform was but a small token . . ."

"I must give it back."

"Earth etiquette?"

"Yes." Andrea snatched at any bit of common ground.

"And what am I supposed to do with a set of Tenebrea uniforms cut to fit an Earth female?"

"I'm sorry H'Roo, but this isn't right."

Now H'Roo looked puzzled. "But you would have accepted the uniforms if K'Rin had given them to you."

"Yes, but he's family." Andrea nervously polished off the rest of her ale. A fat head might feel good about now. The last thing she needed or wanted was some Jod two-ringer taking a shine to her—for any number of reasons, most of them deeply personal, some of them anatomical.

But Andrea's refusal didn't seem to dent H'Roo's spirits. He downed his Baldinale, grabbed her quartz tumbler from her hand and left saying, "Stay right here. I'll bring us—or as you might say, fetch—another pair of drinks." For a lumbering Jod, he practically bounced out the arboretum.

Damned awkward, Andrea thought as she sat looking at the exotic flora. Small signs propped on thin rods bore the botanical name and place of origin. She saw an especially exotic flower: a three-foot stalk bearing a white airfoil shaped like a hang glider, and beneath this bleached roof, a cluster of black purple cubes—like some delicate origami. Three of the fine cubes opened to reveal a small white flower with six tiny petals around a tiny yellow stigma. Just below the black cubes, the giant flower had a tumescent chin, and from the chin a dozen long iridescent purple strands hung like a magi's beard just brushing the ground below. *Where in the galaxy could such an oddity come from?* She got up to see the sign: an unintelligible jumble of Latin for a name: *Tacca integrifolva nivium,* with a subtext common name, *Bat Flower*—origin India, Earth.

"I'm back."

Andrea turned around to find her second Baldinale staring her in the face. "Thank you."

H'Roo took a seat, obviously pleased with himself, and he drank heartily. He effervesced as much as the ale, and his exuberance bothered Andrea, who after an awkward silence, said, "You seem awfully pleased with yourself."

"You don't know the first thing about me, do you?" H'Roo saluted with his glass, enjoying his advantage. "But I know a lot about you. I know where you're from, and why you're here. Meanwhile, you know practically nothing about me."

Andrea cradled her glass in both hands. She was embarrassed to admit that he was right. "I know that you're a friend." She winced at her own superficiality. The cold truth was that H'Roo had been a useful source of information about everything she'd inquired, but she'd never asked a single question about H'Roo. She didn't need to know H'Roo's story. Now, the one-sidedness of the relationship embarrassed her. "So, tell me about yourself."

"Very well. Let me fill in a couple of details. K'Rin asked me to look after you. He asked me to make you welcome on Jod and treat you with respect. I was supposed to help you manage your way through the thicket of Jod manners and prejudices, and when necessary run interference for you with your classmates. I must admit, at first I didn't like the assignment, but K'Rin trusts me and I wouldn't disappoint him." H'Roo laughed out loud. "Ironic, but in the process I developed a fondness for you."

"Oh, no . . ." Andrea drowned a groan with a long swallow of Baldinale. *He's drunk. A drunk Jod is hitting on me.*

"K'Rin said that when the time was right, I could tell you that I'm his cousin."

"What did you say?" This bit of news brought Andrea forward in her seat.

"Yes. I'm K'Rin's cousin—one of many. He treats me like a nephew, though, because I am competent. His mother is my mother's eldest sister. So we can settle one dilemma outright: if you can accept the uniform as a gift from K'Rin because he's family, then you can accept the uniform from me—cousin."

Andrea's brown eyes widened and she took another drink. She managed, "Then, I accept. Thank you."

"You are most welcome." H'Roo grinned.

"Do the others know about you and K'Rin?"

"Of course. The marriage ties between the Parh and the Rin families is common knowledge. Someday I'll take you to my family seat, the city of Gyre, and you can get to know some of the eccentrics in the Parh Clan."

"Tell me about K'Rin."

H'Roo's countenance turned sober. "He is both the

pride and disappointment of the Rin family. He had the claim to the Rin Seat on the Council of Elders taken away from his father. Our families have suffered without representation on the council. Most of us believe he could force his way back onto the council—the Rin Family has many allies, such as the Parh Family, and Hal K'Rin has powerful friends in the fleet. Instead, he chooses to serve the council as Chief of Offworld Intelligence."

"Perhaps he wants to earn his place on the council."

"If that's his plan, he's doing it badly. He constantly criticizes the council, especially Hal Pl'Don, the council's first among equals. I think his plan is to become indispensable for Jod security; then the council will have to take him back on his terms. Force won't do. He wants an invitation. An invitation erases the insult done to his father. An invitation is an admission that the council erred."

Andrea set her drink down. "So he needs to prove the Ordinate threat for political reasons. I didn't think he was politically motivated."

"Who can say?" H'Roo struggled for words. "K'Rin's a contradiction. One day he acts like a mystic, but he demands practical solutions to every problem. K'Rin can be exceedingly kind and exceedingly ruthless. He exudes honor—very scrupulous about piety and honor, yet he is positively cynical about backing every promise with raw power. He is ambitious, but denies it. Do you think it's possible to be ambitious and selfless?"

"I don't know. I suppose . . ." Andrea had never thought of K'Rin in any terms but grand. She recalled the first time she saw him, braced against a balcony railing looking down at her as she cradled her dead family. His eyes! His eyes reflected her pain completely. In retrospect, she realized that from that moment on, her destiny was tied to his. "What did K'Rin do before I met him? Go way back."

"As heir to the Rin Seat, he should have stayed at Heptar as the understudy to his father, but K'Rin thought Heptar was too confining. He wanted to be a pilot. To make matters worse, he refused to marry the woman chosen by his parents, a carefully arranged match. His stubbornness caused a bit of a scandal, and his father never quite got over the flagrant disobedience."

"You still have arranged marriages?"

"Not for everybody—just persons of high rank. Me for example, I'm available." H'Roo grinned at Andrea. "Back to K'Rin: He would marry for love or not at all, and his childhood sweetheart was given to marry into another powerful family. So he left Heptar and became a pilot. He flew special operations in the Chelle War. He earned a reputation as a formidable warrior. Since then, he worked in Offworld Intelligence for three rings. When the old Rin died, K'Rin took over the Tenebrea. Now he has the rank of Admiral in the Fleet, and as Clan headsman he commands his Tenebrea.

"What's her name?" Andrea asked automatically. "The sweetheart he left behind."

H'Roo killed Andrea's inquiry. "We're not going to gossip about K'Rin in that way. I'll give you specifics about his professional life, but nothing else."

Andrea shrugged, "Fair enough . . ."

As the evening wore on the entire officers' mess became their private sanctuary. One by one, the staff cleared rooms and doused lights. The mood music died and cleaning equipment hummed in the background.

Management timidly informed the two inebriated Tenebrea that the facility had closed, but none had the balls—one of Andrea's metaphors that the Jod did not comprehend—to evict two Tenebrea. Rather, the genteel manager bid them "Help yourselves," and he retired to his office to catch up on paperwork and otherwise wait them out. H'Roo and Andrea moved to the bar to be closer to the Baldinale spigot.

H'Roo snuffled as he poured another pair of ales, "I've got to ask you just one more thing before we end this lovely evening."

"Ask me what?" Andrea did not want the conversation to turn serious again.

"I've watched you for six months do the craziest things."

"Really?" Andrea licked the white froth from her upper lip.

"It's unnatural . . ." H'Roo gesticulated as words failed him.

"For a woman—" Andrea tried to bring H'Roo's thought to closure.

"No, no, no. Unnatural for anybody. You take risks no one needs to take—this place is a school. It's make-believe here."

"I like to push the envelope."

"Like the orbital jump? You were supposed to fire retros at thirty thousand feet. Even in combat, you're supposed to allow forty seconds' slack in case of malfunction. You waited to fire at ten thousand feet. That's insane!"

"I wanted to get to the ground first. I was seventh out the door. I had to make up the time somehow." Andrea raised an eyebrow, annoyed at H'Roo's choice of words: *risk is not insanity.* "I got to ground first—"

"But you could get yourself killed. Don't you know fear?"

Andrea didn't answer. She pushed her drink aside. *I know fear. I know death.* She hated death, but she didn't fear death.

"Fear is natural." H'Roo pressed her. "Aren't you the least bit afraid of anything?"

Andrea's face hardened. "No. I am already dead—I died with my husband and child three years ago." She unfastened her collar button.

H'Roo lowered his eyes sadly. The Baldinale's bubble of elation had been pricked by the mention of death. He said, "I don't completely understand. We Jod live in the present for the future." H'Roo whispered, "Today, you and I were given a second lifetime. Why would you want to spend so much time acting like one who is already dead?"

"Because, cousin, being dead to the world uncomplicates my life."

chapter 7

Another hundred days of technical training followed: doctrine, sensors, phenomenology, intelligence processing—the part of the course known as *Scopes*. Andrea endured the classes, learning foremost that she wanted no part of Tenebrea technical support, and she worked off her mounting frustration in the physical training lab. Finally, word came down that they would go back to the field, for the final test.

Andrea looked about the room. Three of her old classmates, H'Roo Parh, Gem-Bar, and Tamor-Kyl wore the gray and black uniform. Another four candidates joined them. The Jod looked bulky and dangerous in their dark uniforms; their faces bright and confident. Next to them, Andrea looked small, wiry, withdrawn. The eight stood silently yet formally at rest around the briefing platform.

Each knew the agenda for the meeting: *the final test* to determine each candidate's standing in the Tenebrea for years to come. Only the best in the field would earn billets in special ops, the dirty and deadly cat-and-mouse game of finding and dispatching the increasing number of Cor Ordinate Hunters violating Alliance space.

Andrea had not come this far to lose her right to kill Ordinate Hunters. She looked across the briefing platform at Tamor-Kyl, and she smiled. How he'd made the final cut, she'd never know, but if at all possible, she'd make sure that blowhard would fail at her hands. In turn, Tamor-Kyl smirked: obviously he cherished the same thoughts, that he might finally eliminate this human female, whose very presence besmirched his chosen profession.

The door hissed open and a squad of instructors marched into the auditorium. Feld Jo'Orom walked to the platform and the seven Jod Tenebrea trainees snapped to chin-tucked, feet-locked attention. Andrea stood comfortably erect, her head cocked slightly to observe her rigid companions.

"At ease." Jo'Orom grunted. He looked around the platform before he spoke. "You and you alone determine your success or failure in the final field test. Hal K'Rin directed us to build an exercise in which you hunt each other."

The young Tenebrea looked at each other, and Jo'Orom remarked, "You like that, don't you, Mat Flores?"

With the slightest tinge of a smile, Andrea replied, "I certainly do."

"I thought you would. So, eventually, the test comes down to two persons, and the winner of that duel takes highest honors. The last candidate standing wins. The winner gets first choice of assignments, second place gets second choice, and so on." Jo'Orom pressed a button that simultaneously dimmed the auditorium lights and presented a holographic map on the platform. The hologram depicted an island: a ridge of steep, dormant volcanoes; the windward side a mass of vegetation bisected by a river flowing to the sea by way of a saltwater marsh. The leeward side offered a mass of black barren crags, ancient lava flows stretching to black sand beaches. "This is Dlagor Island."

Andrea watched the others check each other's reaction. She had no reaction because she didn't know the island.

Feld Jo'Orom circumnavigated the island with the light pointer. "The island is surrounded by a reef of blue flame coral."

A bright yellow grid marked the boundaries of the exercise area. "You must stay on the west side of Dlagor River and south of the mountain ridge. Above the cataract, the Dlagor River flows at a rate of two meters per second with dangerous undercurrents. Above the cataract, the water is potable. Brine lizards, some up to twenty-feet long, own the alkaline tidal portion of the river. The water there is not potable, and we will not give you purification tablets. The marsh is infested with biting insects and poisonous reptiles."

Feld Jo'Orom pointed with his light pen to an area above the marsh. "The liquid sandpits are well marked, but they shift. Each of you will get a written briefing and virtual charts of the terrain that you may study before time of departure at nautical twilight, 0520 hours."

The holograph switched off and the room lights brightened. Feld Jo'Orom placed a handful of items on the platform. "We issue each of you a basic set of equipment for the exercise. You wear your standard field uniform with harness. In addition, you get three pieces of hardware. First," Jo'Orom picked up a small handheld weapon, "each combatant gets a handlance with twenty shots."

Andrea noticed that the Jod candidates' necks turned pale. "However," Feld Jo'Orom smiled wryly at his students' discomfort, "we throttled each handlance to stun. Of course, it still packs quite a stun: knock you flat on your ass and unconscious for about five hours. You wake up with a headache that makes a hangover seem tame. Safety tip: don't shoot someone more than once; even throttled to stun, your lance might put the target into convulsions."

Andrea raised her hand and the Feld acknowledged with a grunt. She asked, "And three shots? Would that be lethal?" She could not suppress the smile creeping onto her face.

"As ever droll—and crass—Mat Flores. Three shots would cripple if not kill. I promise you, if you, even by accident, inflict three shots on one of your comrades, I'll personally see to it that you spend the rest of your days in a small, windowless box; Earth citizen or no; K'Rin protégé or no."

H'Roo Parh rolled his eyes and the other candidates scowled. Feld Jo'Orom continued. "You each take a utility knife." He held the blade to the light—rugged, polished titanium forged in a hard vacuum with a razor-sharp edge.

"Your third piece of equipment is this simple transmitter, no bigger than a button, that we rivet to your uniform below the collar. If for any reason you need to be extracted from the problem—for example, if you get injured—you simply rip this button from your uniform. Pulling the rivet loose activates the transmitter, and we hover in to extract you. Of course, if you call for extraction, you lose. By the way, when you stun one of your classmates, be a good soldier and tear off the transmitter button so we can get the poor wretch before the small carnivores do. Are there any questions?"

Tamor-Kyl asked, "How long is the exercise?"

"As long as it takes."

Gem-Bar stammered, "But what are . . . I mean, what are the rules?"

Feld Jo'Orom answered with a booming laugh and walked out of the auditorium shaking his head.

H'Roo Parh stood in Andrea's open door and knocked. The room was dimly lit by fading daylight filtered through tinted windows. "Mind if I come in?"

Andrea slowly turned in her chair, her face illuminated from the screen depicting the virtual chart of Dlagor Island. She rubbed her eyes. "Sure, H'Roo. Come in." She wore a thin cotton shirt, cut to fit a Jod. Instinctively, she pulled the loose collar to cover her bare shoulder and crossed her bare legs. "What's up?"

H'Roo shut the door. He approached her desk, taking a seat on the unmade cot. "You know that there are only three billets in special ops."

"That's a rumor. Most rumors are crap."

H'Roo smiled quizzically. "Another Earth acronym? Well, I think it prudent to operate on the assumption that the rumor is true. I don't want to be stuck in the rear echelon watching a scope. Or worse—liaison to the fleet. I propose we work together to make sure we are among the last three, maybe the last two. You are the best in the field. Everybody knows it and—"

Andrea sat up straight. The baggy shirt slipped off her shoulder again. "H'Roo! That's so sweet. You want me to cheat."

H'Roo grinned and added, "I prefer to think of our

cooperation as a special operation within a special operation."

"I'd feel rather peculiar helping you, and at the same time planning how to take you out." She kneaded the air with her hands and winced. "It's messy."

"I don't mind. I'm not picky. I just need to be in the top three."

Andrea stood up and walked to the open window. Her face turned to flint. "Sorry. If you want to be sure to make the final three, you just make sure you're not the first, second, third, fourth, or fifth Jod I come across."

"We could work opposite ends of the exercise area. I'll take the marsh and . . ."

"Forget it, H'Roo: My plan is simple enough. I'm going to win. I'm not going to worry about who I stun first. K'Rin designed this test; I think he designed it for me. I've always wanted a test like this one. I'm not going to waste this opportunity. I'm going to find out if I'm the best. I'm going to win this contest on my own. The rest of you can make excuses—not me." She stood up.

"I thought we were partners." H'Roo got up to go to the door.

"Not on Dlagor Island." Andrea shook her head. "But good luck, anyway."

"You don't mean it." His neck tinged dark with anger or disappointment, Andrea couldn't tell which.

"No, H'Roo. I *do* wish you good luck. On Earth, we wish each other good luck, then we work like the devil to beat each other—like I'm going to whup you."

"You are a mendacious species." H'Roo tried to step away to avoid further argument. "I've got to go. Bol-Don's office called. I have a secure message—probably my mother wishing me good luck," he added sarcastically.

Andrea stopped him, saying, "H'Roo. At the end of the trial, we'll remain friends, okay? Let's agree: if I win, I'll honor you with a banquet. Hal K'Rin cannot refuse me this favor, if I bring this honor to his house. If you win, you honor me with a banquet." Andrea held out her hand.

"All right. I'll never understand why humans always grab each other." H'Roo clasped her hand with a firm shake. Disappointment still showed in his face as he said, "What you propose is now a promise."

They ate as much breakfast as their stomachs could hold—everyone except Andrea. She nursed a cup of coffee and watched the little fraternity of Jod candidates. H'Roo sat alone with a sullen countenance, eyes fixed on a large glass of fruit juice.

They reported to the ready room, where the staff issued each a tray with a clean field uniform, and harness. As promised, the transmitters were riveted to the uniform collars. Each took a belt with holstered handlance and sheathed utility knife. Andrea inspected her weapons, shaving a bit of lint from her harness with the titanium blade.

Feld Jo'Orom led them to the air transport, an empty windowless cargo bird. Each buckled into a web seat and sat—no talking but profuse toe tapping, knee bouncing, arm stretching, and equipment checking. This flurry of silent activity amused Andrea. Each Jod candidate stubbornly refused to be the first to break the nervous silence. Unbidden speech at such times was an admission of nerves. Andrea cackled derisively once, breaking the awkward silence, then resealing it.

They flew through turbulent air for two hours, whereupon Feld Jo'Orom announced, "Okay, Tenebrea.

Get ready to go in. Now to make things as interesting as possible, I want you to put on these blindfolds." He handed each an elastic black band that wrapped tightly over the eyes.

Andrea felt the Feld's large hands and stubby fingers adjust the band securely over her eyes and she stiffened, indignant, but unable to protest because everyone had to wear a blindfold. *But did they?* she wondered. How could she know unless she stripped away her blindfold? The temptation to do so gnawed at her.

The transport zigged and zagged around the island, periodically stopping. Andrea heard the Feld's voice bark, "You next." She heard the bay door open, letting in a rush of fresh air and the whine of the engines, followed by a slam and renewed silence. Then the transport accelerated up and away. Seven times the door opened and shut.

"You next." She felt a pair of hands unbuckle her seat straps and haul her to her feet. Quickly she patted her web gear to assure herself she still had her handlance and utility knife. Then she felt the hot breath of the Feld Jo'Orom at her ear. "Mat Flores, knowing your highly developed sense of humor, I arranged a special insertion for you." She heard the bay door open.

"What—" Andrea started to ask but she felt strong hands grab her and toss her through the door. Instinctively she tucked her knees, expecting to hit ground—but she didn't! She felt nothing but air and her heart stopped as she accelerated. She ripped off her blindfold and saw the ocean coming at her. Andrea braced herself, straightened her legs, and pressed her hands at her side, using her abdominal muscles to keep herself as perpendicular as possible.

Andrea slammed into the water with bone-rattling force; it was difficult to be sure she hadn't hit pavement. But she was intact—unsure how far under water—encumbered by wet clothes, not much air in her lungs, and mad as a snake. She struggled to the surface, her legs useless with the heavy boots acting like anchors. Her lungs burned. When her head broke the surface she sucked in an atmosphere of fresh air and exhaled a loud, "You bastard!"

The air transport swooped past her low and fast, wagged its stubby wings: the Feld had waited nearly a year for this bit of payback.

Andrea bobbed in the thick brine; her eyes scanned the beach. A current pulled her south to a spit of gravel: coral sands mixed with shells, bones, and teeth. There she touched bottom and rested while she took stock of her situation. The turquoise sky was empty save for a pair of seabirds. The beach was the narrowest band of taupe fouled by bits of rot lapped up from the lagoon by insipid waves. Trees skirted the beach, dropping roots to prop up the thick overhanging branches.

Having studied her immediate refuge, Andrea let her eyes peruse the grand panorama of the island. One hundred meters from the shore, looking over the wall of dense vegetation, Andrea calculated her bearings based on her recollection of the virtual charts. The ridge of volcanoes began far to her left, practically dipping into the sea. They arched before her—a formidable wall hemming in this tropical garden—then disappeared in the interior. A lone peak rose as an afterthought like some ancient white-capped giant, but in fact, this youngest of the volcanoes was not yet extinct. She was on the west side. *They must have dropped us from east to west. Good, I have no one at my back.*

She waded ashore, holding her handlance above water at the ready. Once ashore, she disappeared into the brush, jogging up a dry creekbed to higher ground. As thirsty as she was, she refused to stop to search for water. Speed is in itself security. And she didn't need water to comfort her thirst, only enough to fill her pores and cool her against the tropical heat. The Jod, on the other hand, needed frequent drinks of water.

As explained in the briefing, the island offered almost no potable water except the upper river and its estuaries. She knew the Jod must congregate there, lumbering up from the shallows. She'd come down on them from the rock slopes.

She trotted along for an hour, always to higher ground. From time to time, at a break in the fleshy vegetation, she saw above the canopy of leaves, and thus kept her bearings. The source of the river was less than fourteen hours east, and there she could slake her burning thirst that had of late begun to occupy her mind as much as the hunt.

The sun skimmed the southern horizon. The sky turned red, then gray as a stiff breeze shoved black clouds ashore. Rain, blessed rain followed, stripping fifteen degrees of heat from the air. Lightning shafts crashed all around the mountaintop above her, but Andrea thought of nothing but the rain: cool and wet. She stood beneath one of the fleshy broadleaf trees, turning one top leaf onto a lower, catching the heavy rain in these verdant gutters, running them at last into her mouth and down her parched throat. And when she had filled her stomach till she could drink not another drop, she turned the water onto her hair to wash the ocean salt mixed with the salt of her sweat off her itchy scalp and from her sweat-stained clothes.

The evening deluge passed as suddenly as it came. The breezes dwindled, and the calm enticed the night insects, and the creatures that hunted them into the muggy air. The cacophony of love-struck amphibians grated on her ears but also covered the sounds of her movement. The pair of moons shone through the lingering mist, providing just enough light to guide her way. This was a night she could use.

Andrea quick-stepped eastward, searching for the source of the river. The relatively pleasant temperature became uncomfortably cool as her wet clothes dried. And the slight chill made her hungry, but not miserable. *H'Roo: he'll be miserable.* The Jod had no sweat glands to cool themselves. They had no hair to trap heat. The thought of their discomfiture brought a smile to her face. They'd be exhausted; with luck, disoriented if hypothermia sets in. One could hope. Anyway, she'd heat them up soon enough with her handlance.

All seemed right, even peaceful, for her night trek. Andrea congratulated herself on her own stamina: second, third, and fourth wind. Even her fatigue seemed like a narcotic, dulling some of the minor aches from her endless uphill climb. Her life, synchronized with this mission, became surreal. She floated above her pain as she plodded along. Then she slipped on a patch of wet fungus: Her feet flew from beneath her. As she slid down a gully into fast water, her conscious mind rebuked her: *You fool! You can't react—you're in a stupor.*

Dlagor River! Sucked under the wild current, tossed head over heel, she lost her sense of up. Down the sluice she tumbled, torn between the instinct to fight and the odd premonition to tuck and ride.

She fought the water, unwisely, and the water fought back with the indifference of omnipotence. The current thumped her against a stone; she gasped and inhaled a mouthful of the broiling water. Jolted alert, she thought of broken bones, and worse: failure. With some difficulty, she turned her feet downstream to fend off other boulders, and each time she felt the jar of rock or bottom, she steered to the right and flailed the air for any hold. She sputtered and floundered till her hands groped a tangle of exposed roots. With all her strength she held. She put a wrap of roots around her wrist and the roots bit deep, but she needed a moment to take a breath in between her coughing fits.

The stream pummeled her. *The water wants to pry me loose. It knows it can crush me on the rocks below.* She knew she could never outlast the torrent. The relentless current sapped her strength, and seemed to mock her as it did—a helpless, hopeless, empty feeling that pricked her subconscious and raised a fountain of anger.

An unnatural strength, beyond her training, buoyed Andrea. She hauled herself up the roots and onto the slippery bank. And there she lay, bruised and coughing. She patted her harness: the handlance was in its holster, the knife in its sheath, *thank God*. Then she tried her arms and legs and all her joints. She'd been lucky.

She lay exhausted on the silt, wet grasses, and ferns flattened by the gushing eastern tributary of Dlagor River overflow. She closed her eyes and slept. Her last thought was that a carnivore might find her there on the ground. "So be it," she croaked.

* * *

Judging by the sun, she'd slept four hours. Her side ached with a deep muscle bruise, but she made quick time sluicing down the estuary to the main river. There, as she expected, she saw tracks—deep clumsy tracks. Fresh tracks. Moreover, she discerned at least two pair of tracks. Perhaps one of her colleagues had already made the first *kill.*

Andrea crept through the bush, staying parallel to the tracks. *Patience,* she warned herself. The danger in tracking is that to catch up, one must move faster than the quarry, and fast usually makes more noise than slow.

Voices. Who in the world is having a conversation out here? Andrea could hardly believe her ears, but the voices were real; very matter-of-fact, and less than fifty feet away. She dropped to her stomach and slithered over the rotting leaves and animal spore. She found the voices: all seven of them—including H'Roo Parh.

Those sorry bastards. She inched closer to hear their conversation. They were arguing about rules—*rules!* The apparent leader, Tamor-Kyl, argued emphatically, "After we get rid of this human interloper, we break up into our buddy pairs: standard procedure. We'll have a four-hour truce to disperse, then we resume the exercise, but we work as teams—the way we were trained."

The group murmured assent, "Teams, yes . . . teams."

H'Roo asked, "Whose team do I join?"

Tamor-Kyl quipped, "You know the deal, H'Roo. You set her up; we agree that you shall be one of the three last standing. After we get Flores, you can just sit under a shade tree on the beach—you've already secured your slot."

Andrea waited for H'Roo to say something—anything—to deny this treachery, but H'Roo only pulled out a small black baton, and pressed a small toggle on the handle. He reminded them, "The direction finder gives no indication of distance."

H'Roo's bad faith stung. She sat on the wet ground, confused for a moment, not about the information she'd just learned, but about this ache in her chest. Was it anger? Hurt feelings? If it were hurt feelings, she'd turn it to anger. She hunkered down to watch. H'Roo turned in a broad circle watching a small red light at the base of the baton. Andrea watched him stop and point the accusatory stick directly at her, saying, "She's downriver."

Tamor-Kyl boomed, "I've got her, this time."

"Don't be so sure," H'Roo countered. "You might have the misfortune of being the first to run into her."

Tamor ignored H'Roo. "Okay, let's go. Let's get this over with." They all stepped in Andrea's direction in a leisurely gait, spreading out in some semblance of a tactical march.

Andrea slipped back under the cover of thick vegetation, and when she was safely out of sight and beyond hearing, she broke into a run, constantly turning her shoulders to slip her slender body past the crowded saplings that choked the forest. The thicker Jod would have to fight the vegetation, much of it bristling with three-inch thorns. Andrea took some comfort in knowing that she'd build a couple hours' lead. As she ran, she began to devise a plan.

She'd seen and heard correctly: the black baton pointed right at her like some magic wand—she'd settle the score with H'Roo later. What did the black baton see? How was it tracking her? Andrea took off her uniform and inspected it for wires. Crouched over her uniform, boots, and equipment, she carefully ran her fingers over the seams. The lining of her boots, the inside of the holster, even the metal in her handlance and knife were suspect. She knelt in the underbrush, naked, pondering her situation. For certain H'Roo had marked her equipment, but how? Perhaps the transmitter button she wore issued a beacon—some safety precaution turned against her. But wouldn't all their buttons create a signature? In any case, she could not tear away the transmitter button without disqualifying herself from the exercise. Probably not the button. H'Roo had marked her.

And H'Roo didn't need to use a transmitter—nothing so mechanical. Always the elegant solution for H'Roo: physics or chemistry. *Perhaps chemical.* Andrea smiled at the cleverness of a chemical tag. Perhaps H'Roo tagged her with pheromones, which was in itself ironic: seven males tracking the one female like so many luna moths. *Or physics.* Perhaps H'Roo treated her gear with a tailored molecule to create a nuclear magnetic resonance. With each movement she made, the molecules would create a paramagnetic signature against the planet's natural magnetic field. *Now that's elegant—much more H'Roo's style.* And if he'd had access to any piece of her gear, then he'd had access to all her gear. He may have marked one piece or all of it, and she hadn't time or the opportunity to sort out which piece. *The clever son of a gun. But not clever enough.*

Andrea gathered her clothes. She wrapped her handlance, knife, and boots in her tunic and trousers. Then she used her equipment harness to bind them to a chunk of deadwood. She carried her small raft to the river's edge. The river flowed broader and slower. She hesitated to launch her clothes and weapons, but her anger outweighed any nascent modesty, and she shoved her bundle into the current, and watched it glide away, pausing only to spin in eddies churned up by the irregular bottom.

The small raft disappeared behind a curtain of vegetation. Andrea stood knee-deep in the river shallows, and spied her wavering reflection. All her senses flooded her memory. She smelled wet vegetation. She felt cool water on her legs, coarse sand between her toes, and warm air on her back. Her wet hair clung to her forehead and dripped the slight salt taste of a day's perspiration. Andrea was suddenly standing in the cool water in the quiet sand-bottom coves along the Chesapeake Bay, Steve's sloop swinging about an anchor. There, wearing nothing but moonlight, she bathed with Steve. He would wrap his hands around the small of her back, his forearms resting on her hips. He would pull her toward him. Steve was warm in contrast to the cool water. He'd whisper, "I'll always remember you like this . . ."

She blinked away the memory to see herself again, changed in the short three years. She'd become thin—no, not thin: lean. The months of physical training showed about her shoulders and arms, even her stomach—a definition of muscle unbecoming on a Jod female. The scar over her left breast turned purplish in the chilly water.

From the debris along the riverbank, she selected a dense length of stick to serve as a club. Then she waded upstream, watching for any sign of the seven Jod. Periodically, she traded in her club for a smoother, denser copy. She vacillated between a stave and a short bludgeon, settling on the latter. *What could be taking those slugs so long?*

* * *

H'Roo and company sat in a clearing, taking a short respite. They pulled thorns from their clothes and took turns visiting the river for a drink of water.

Tamor-Kyl addressed the couple who would listen to him. "K'Rin was unwise to bring this human female into our inner circle."

"The Tenebrea is *his* inner circle." H'Roo spoke just to irritate Tamor.

"You are always sticking up for the female. Is she your pet? Have you had such bad luck with Jod women?" Tamor asked with mock sympathy.

The rest of the party knew better than to join this sport. The tall H'Roo stood up to challenge Tamor-Kyl. The other Jod prepared to intervene, but H'Roo calmly said, "You're just jealous because *you* are not my pet."

Tamor growled, "Are you mocking me, H'Roo?"

"Of course not." H'Roo's sarcasm was palpable. "I'm your accomplice, which is in your case lower than a pet."

"Don't act so superior. You wouldn't be here if you weren't in the Parh Clan. Admit it: your people bought their way into the Rin household. Your relationship is more money than blood. You're no better than the rest of us." Tamor raised his voice so the rest might hear.

H'Roo's lips were tight with acrimony. "I'm afraid you're right. At present, I am no better than the rest of you." Under other circumstances, no Parh would stoop to collusion with a Kyl. The Kyl Clan had always been minor players. Having little influence, the Kyl had few allegiances of consequence. Nobody feared the Clan Kyl, and so the innocuous Kyl intermarried with all the big families at the low level of third and fourth cousin. Therefore, the Clan Kyl remained the perennial poor relations.

Tamor accepted H'Roo's admission and offered

some gratuitous, paternalistic advice. "You need to set a goal for yourself, H'Roo. If you distinguish yourself in the Tenebrea, then someday you can say the Parh's reputation is based on merit, not money."

H'Roo had had enough. He tossed another sarcastic barb. "Well, one thing about this test is certain: it's all based on merit, not family connections, right, Tamor? Oh, except for one thing. We haven't enough merit between us to handle this human female. What a fine little team we've become." H'Roo pointed a finger at all of them and said, "The only way to beat her is collusion. None of us could take her one-on-one."

The others bristled at the accusation, but only Tamor spoke. "Teamwork is what you called it yesterday, H'Roo."

"Treachery, I should have called it. She's better than all of us."

"Really? Then why is she running as fast as she can downriver?"

"Perhaps she knows we've banded against her. Even so, I would have expected her to be more aggressive, unlike you, Gem-Bar." H'Roo showed him the palm of his hand, meant as an insult.

"Don't berate me, H'Roo. This whole plan was your idea. You marked her, I didn't. Beside, you were right when you said a little humility will be good for her—make her more a team player."

H'Roo muttered, "Regrettably so." He sat down on a rotting log and turned his back to the group.

Gem-Bar tried to put matters in a better light. "Besides, you can't back out now. And don't be so hard on yourself, H'Roo. You know Andrea. I bet she's already cheated: gone out of bounds to the forbidden side of the river."

"Oh, I'm counting on it."

Tamor jumped back into the argument. "Don't sulk. In or out of bounds, she's headed for the marshes soon and she'll have to double back. Nobody can struggle through the marshes. And with all the brine lizards, staying in the river is suicide. She'll come to us."

"I wish she would," interjected another.

H'Roo spun around and cautioned, "Be careful what you ask for."

Gem-Bar offered his final opinion for the evening. "I say we rest here a few hours. We've only a couple hours of daylight left. We might even build a small fire and eat a hot meal."

Tamor gave his blessing. "Good plan. Set a guard and sleep in shifts."

From her hiding place, Andrea heard their voices as distinctive in the wild as a pistol shot. And the voices were downstream. She had them.

chapter 8

With nightfall, the daily torrent of rain blew through. Andrea used nature's tantrum to conceal her movement: she crept within sight of the Jod's sodden camp and watched them scramble to save their doomed fire. The last flicker of flame brought a chorus of curses. Then each Jod grabbed a handful of roasted tubers from the coals and sought the shelter of a tree branch—all but H'Roo Parh. He straddled the dead fire and watched.

Hidden in a stand of reeds, Andrea sat on her haunches, waited, and watched. Her teeth chattered from the chill and her stomach growled from hunger. She watched them eat, then turn their collars up against the driving rain—it seemed like luxury to eat roots and wear wet clothes. She caressed her wooden club and consoled herself thinking that she would have the last laugh at their expense. Her feet sank in the fresh mud and her hamstrings ached.

The rains left, and the insects appeared. Andrea endured the bug bites on her naked back. In the small clearing before her, the Jods drowsily swatted flying insects, till one by one, their heads nodded; arms fell limp at their sides and they lay exhausted, asleep.

At last. Andrea selected the smallest Jod at the periphery. Taking her club, she crawled toward him, stopping at the least snort or sniffle. It seemed hours as she inched her way closer, finding herself at last kneeling beside the sleeping Jod, club raised.

She struck him—too hard judging by the dull crunch. The Jod jerked his head back, arched his back for an instant; a rush of air came from his lungs and he collapsed, limp. Blood poured from a ragged gash over the forehead. She'd always thought Jod skulls were thick as the rest of their heavy bones. Afraid that she'd killed the Jod, Andrea felt an artery on his pale neck to check his pulse: it was strong.

She dragged the unconscious body into the underbrush, and there she stripped him of his clothes. Andrea bound his hands and feet with his boot laces, cinching them tight, offering him to the insects, already attracted to the sticky blood oozing from his cut. She fashioned a gag from a stick tied tightly into his mouth with a strap from his harness.

She paused a moment, having never seen a naked Jod before. Instead of the complex, opposed, almost stringy muscles that comprised human strength, these Jod seemed to have sheets of rugged tissue layered over large bones. If the Jod were strong like blocks of stone, then humans were strong like coils of steel. She noticed the gut was a bit distended. Being hairless, pale, rain-soaked, and unconscious, this hapless Jod looked like a sea creature tossed ashore.

Then she crawled back into the brush, and donned the uniform, still warm from the Jod's body. Jod boots did not fit her smaller human feet. She buckled the equipment harness, then inspected the handlance and knife. She felt whole again. She tore off the transmitter button and threw it to the ground. *One down.*

Andrea crept barefoot along the camp perimeter. She measured each step for sound. She skulked by tree trunks, staying in the dark shadows away from the dappled moonlight filtered through the trees. *There!* A second Jod, Gem-Bar, lay asleep on his back. A small pile of roasted tubers lay by his side: probably breakfast. With one hand she unfastened the holster strap and ever so gently extracted the handlance. And at a range of one meter she fired at Gem-Bar's midsection—the handlance emitting a barely audible, high-pitched wheeze.

"Ugh!" The muffled cry rose and fell. Gem-Bar shuddered from the jolt, then tucked into a fetal position, cramped about constricted stomach muscles. He lay like a stone: he would not open his eyes for a couple hours at least. Andrea quickly looked about to see if the others had heard the handlance discharge or Gem-Bar's guttural lapse into unconsciousness.

No one heard. She looked down at Gem-Bar and whispered, "I want you to know that I'm the one who knocked you out." Then with perverse pleasure she pulled out the titanium blade, peeled back Gem-Bar's arms, exposing his chest. Then with a clean swipe, she severed his nametag and tied the ragged trophy to her harness. With the other hand she plucked the transmitter button from his collar. Then she sat next to Gem-Bar's body and ate his breakfast: roasted tubers and rhizomes. She peeled the charred skin and picked away the burrowed—now toasted grubs—with her fingernail. As she ate the tasteless but filling roots, she listened to Gem-Bar's shallow and fitful breathing intermixed with the light snoring from the other Jod around her.

At morning twilight, H'Roo Parh stirred to muffled groans. From the corner of his eye he saw a shadow slip into the brush and thought it wise not to follow; rather, he went to investigate the wretched sound at the other end of the camp. He saw one, two, three of his colleagues in various states of unconsciousness—stunned by a handlance. "Andrea," he muttered, as he unholstered his weapon.

Searching the perimeter for the rest, he stumbled upon a naked Jod writhing in his bonds, his head caked in dried blood. H'Roo Parh's first instinct was to pity the poor fellow. He loosed his stick gag, and the young Jod sputtered, "I'll kill her! I'll kill her with my bare hands, if it's the last thing I do!"

H'Roo gazed wide-eyed at the petulant figure: hairless, naked, dirty, beaten; wrists and ankles swollen in their bonds. H'Roo shook his head at the helpless Jod booming potent oaths into the forest. "When I get my hands on her . . ."

"Oh, really?" These grand threats coming from the hog-tied Jod soured H'Roo Parh's sense of pity, replacing that nobler sentiment with bitter mirth. He imagined the recovery team's unsympathetic smiles and rolling eyes. Jo'Orom would laugh out loud, further debasing Andrea's victim. All richly deserved. H'Roo tossed the black baton into the brush and ran in the opposite direction, leaving the hog-tied Jod cursing him as well.

Tamor-Kyl woke upon hearing the commotion. Quickly he roused his companion. Both drew weapons, crouching and shuffling around the perimeter surveying the damage. At first they suspected H'Roo of treachery, but soon they learned from their hog-tied companion that Andrea Flores was responsible.

"Untie me!" The naked Jod demanded.

"Oh, shut up," Tamor snapped. "You fell asleep at your post. Untie yourself." Tamor and his companion walked away from a string of oaths.

"What shall we do?" The Jod holstered his handlance.

Tamor rubbed the back of his neck. "Well, there are four down. We need just one more loser to secure a place in the top three."

"I see. Shall we go after Mat Flores or H'Roo Parh?"

"First things first—" Tamor-Kyl casually leveled his handlance and squeezed the trigger, shooting his hapless companion. The stunned Jod flushed crimson, lungs collapsed at the shock. Breathless, he was unable to utter a word of protest. He crumpled facefirst into the dirt, adding a bruised face to the unforgettable headache he'd have upon regaining consciousness. Tamor-Kyl stepped over the palpitating body, pulled the transmitter button loose. Then he ran into the brush toward high ground.

A transport hovered above the tree canopy. Andrea knew one thing: the transmitters were accurate enough. Rappelling ropes and body harnesses dropped from side doors. She saw pilots' faces looking down from the cockpit trying to spot bodies through the thick tree canopy. A pair of uniformed Jod snapped themselves to the dangling rope. They came to retrieve the losers.

Andrea crouched in the thick brush and watched them

reel in unconscious Jod, still as death, dangling from thin lines, slowly twisting in the hovercraft propwash. The naked Jod rose last, now limp from humiliation.

Tamor-Kyl scrambled up the scree toward the jagged rocks where the vegetation grew less dense. He knew from experience now that the heavy underbrush gave Andrea the advantage. In the barren rocks he might have the advantage of height and a several hundred yards field-of-view. There he might become the predator. In the dense vegetation, he was certainly the prey. The Flores woman must not be allowed to sneak up on him.

Smack! Tamor turned to see a single rock bound from the obsidian face and rattle down the hill. *She's ahead of me!* He lunged for the shelter of a protruding ledge, banging his knees and skinning his hands on the ragged, brittle rock. He waited till his heart stopped pounding against his chest plates. Then he drew his handlance and waited, periodically wiping the blood from the small cuts on the palms of his hands.

I'm overreacting, he thought. *Chunks of rock fall all the time. She's behind me, and I'm wasting time.* Tamor-Kyl stood and gingerly worked his way up a narrow crevasse. With little more than finger- and toeholds, Tamor inched his way higher.

Crack! A stone as big as Bebwa melon smashed the stone wall above his hand and showered him with chips of pumice. He slipped and broke his fall with his feet and hands pressed against the jagged stone walls, tearing his boots, further mangling his hands. He stifled a cry of pain.

Tamor rebuked himself for scaring so easily, and he doggedly climbed the crevasse. A small stone bounced from the wall with a thud, then hit him in the leg. Tamor grit his teeth against the pain and studied the trajectory of the stone. It had lobbed from a high overhead arc. *She's ahead of me, all right. To the left. She knows roughly where I am, but she can't see me. Otherwise, she'd use her handlance.*

Tamor surveyed his route to the top and calculated that he could continue his climb unseen, even if harassed by the stone-throwing harridan. He decided to take a less direct route to the top, sidestepping to another crevasse, a winding lava tube. At the top, he'd have the cover; she'd be exposed, and he could get off the first shot. *The first shot must count. The first shot means everything.*

He watched for more missiles and in time another sailed overhead without effect. As the stone clattered harmlessly below, Tamor congratulated himself: *She thinks I'm in the other crevasse.*

At the top he waited and watched. Providence provided him a watchdog of sorts. A blue and green lizard sat in the open, back sail raised to catch the sun. Any sudden movement would spook the lizard and warn Tamor. Another rock sailed overhead and disappeared into the rocks below. *Where is she?*

The sun baked Tamor for three hours. His arms and legs ached as he clung to his perch. Thirst began to take its toll. And the rocks stopped. The stalwart lizard finally meandered away. Tamor peeked over the ledge and saw nothing. *Is she gone?*

Ten minutes later, with handlance ready, he crawled onto the ledge, and lay there prone. The view stretched for a hundred yards. Except for scrawny cacti and a few tufts of grass he saw no vegetation. A few isolated weatherworn boulders, coughed up from some volcanic spasm, sat about the plain like giant marbles: all of them out of handlance range.

Tamor stood up, ready for the worst: *She is out there—hiding in the comfortable shade behind one of those boulders. Very clever,* he thought. *If I move into the boulders, I'm no better off than I was in the forest. And I'm too tired to go back down the rock; if I tried, she'd hurl more rocks at me. Out here I'm exposed. In the shade she can outlast me.*

Then Tamor-Kyl spoke out in a loud voice. "Andrea Flores! I know you're here watching me from your hiding place. Is that all you can do, hide? Come out and show yourself, if you're not too frightened to face me."

He waited for a reply and got silence from the stones. "Are you waiting for night so you can sneak up on me like the serpent you are? I won't fall asleep like the others. You won't club me half to death, or stun me in my sleep as you did Gem-Bar. That was cowardly, wasn't it?"

No sound but the rasping caw of a distant scavenger bird. "Flores! I will holster my handlance and we can have a fair fight." He put his handlance away and lifted his arms. "If you're as fine a marksman as you say, then surely you won't refuse an offer to fight a duel, warrior to warrior."

He felt foolish making a speech to the boulders. Andrea mocked him with silence, and he began to lose his self-control. Tamor-Kyl raised his voice a halftone and swore, "If you will not show yourself and fight me face to face, I swear I'll denounce you as the coward you are!"

Not a sound but the hot breeze. "Coward!" The word echoed against the volcanic cliffs in the background. "You disgust me, you human garbage! You are all cowards! If you won't face me here and now, you'll have to shoot me in the back . . ."

"Then you'd better turn around, asshole."

She'd been behind him all along. Tamor-Kyl spun around as he fumbled his holster strap. He saw her standing a scant two meters away, grinning, her hand-lance raised. She fired, and Tamor felt the jolt—like someone had hit him in the chest with a five-pound sledgehammer. His chest cramped. Still fighting to remain conscious, he felt his knees buckle. He fell, although his senses could not distinguish falling from floating. His sight dimmed, and just as well because he despised the grinning woman standing in front of him. He felt his bladder empty as he landed with a dull thud on the ragged gravel. His last sight was her bleeding bare feet. And the last thing he heard was, "Tamor-Kyl, you talk too much."

As with the others, Andrea pulled his transmitter button and took his nametag as a trophy. Her thoughts turned to H'Roo Parh. *Clever H'Roo—treacherous H'Roo.* She limped down a goat path to the forest and the softer ground. The occasional thorn from the Kaltrop tree added to the misery of her lacerated feet.

She backtracked to the small campground to pick up H'Roo's tracks. The campground was now vacant except for the black ash from their fire. She accounted for each set of tracks except for one that headed down-stream: *H'Roo's footprints.* His tracks for certain: H'Roo had narrow feet for a Jod. The length of the stride showed haste: a loping gait, not quite a run.

The tracks followed the river, periodically stopping at the edge. Andrea drank where he drank. She wondered if the water refreshed him as much as it refreshed her. In addition to drinking, she paused to rinse the dirt and twigs stuck to her swollen feet. She feared infection now more than any other possibility. The cuts stayed open, the calluses shorn away, replaced by blood blisters. Did her feet feel warm from infection? She'd get medical attention later. For now she thought, *H'Roo's tracks are fresh. His steps are short and measured. Another mile and I'll have him pinned against the marsh.*

As she willed herself back onto her feet, she heard her name. "Andrea."

She knew. H'Roo was behind her on the path: he had her, but his voice betrayed a sense of guilt and with it hesitation. "Yes, H'Roo?" She surreptitiously unfastened her holster strap and slipped her hand on the handlance.

"I'm sorry."

"I forgive you," she lied. She spun around trying to put H'Roo in her sights, but too late. H'Roo knew her too well. He fired his handlance. The jolt to her ribs sent a wave of pain through her body. Her mind began to blank, but not before she managed a bit of tactical calculus. If she could hit H'Roo, neither could pop the other's transmitter button: The winner would be the first to wake. The winner would be the one with the strongest constitution. She took aim as she fell, squeezing the trigger as she blacked out. She saw panic cross H'Roo's face, a wishful thought, because she knew she'd missed her mark.

As the world around her went black, she had the odd sensation that she had no pulse—as if some white noise had suddenly been damped, leaving her in perfect silence—that she was dying.

chapter 9

Andrea regained consciousness and quickly regretted it. She lay on a stiff recuperative bunk with a skull-crushing headache and a wicked case of dry heaves. She blinked away the light that stabbed at her eyes. She felt the intravenous tube tied to her left arm, through which a small pump rammed fluids into her dehydrated body. A loose bandage covered the handlance burn on her sternum: the dead skin peeled and itched. And someone was wetting her cracked lips with ice chips.

"You've been unconscious for two days."

Andrea focused her aching eyes and H'Roo came into focus. She croaked, "You! So I did miss."

"Yes. And it is a good thing you did."

Her throat hurt, but she spoke anyway. "Says who? I might have won. I might have recovered sooner than you."

"You would have died."

Feeling as she did, Andrea didn't find that bit of news hard to believe. "How so?"

"They set the handlance to stun a Jod. We are physically denser. Apparently, our nervous system can handle more volts than a human system. After I stunned you, you turned blue. Your tongue slipped back into your throat. I resuscitated you." H'Roo beamed great satisfaction at giving her this news.

If Andrea were grateful, she didn't show it. H'Roo pestered her further. "So, Andrea, if you had managed to hit me with your handlance, I would have been unconscious and you would have died. Your grab at vengeance would have been the death of you."

Andrea whispered, "My mistake was tracking you last." And she closed her eyes to suppress the pain lodged behind them, remembering her father's advice: *Always finish the hardest task first.*

"I saved your life." H'Roo put the ice to Andrea's lips and she let him minister to her.

"Am I supposed to thank you?" Her voice was flat, tired, but not weak.

H'Roo tried a different tack. "I spoke with K'Rin during our exit briefing."

Andrea just lay there fighting the nausea, leaving the conversation to H'Roo Parh. "I told him how you ambushed us; how you clubbed and trussed that one fellow like a goat, then left him naked in the bushes."

"Did you tell him about your treachery?"

"He knows." H'Roo's neck rushed to scarlet. Andrea raised herself on her elbows to look H'Roo Parh in the eye. "You're blushing."

H'Roo put his hand to his warm neck, "I feel like I betrayed you."

"You did betray me, H'Roo." Andrea spoke with disembodied, indifferent candor—the kind of candor reserved for strangers.

H'Roo paused to measure his words. "Please don't

use that tone of voice with me, Andrea. I couldn't . . . I didn't have a choice."

"Why, is treachery second nature to you?" She winced as a twinge of nausea triggered a spasm around her wound.

"Please, Andrea. I was hoping that you can—as they say on Earth—forgive and forget."

Andrea pushed away H'Roo's hand and the ice. "Forgive? It costs me nothing to forgive you, so I'll do it. But forget?" She shook her head. "Only fools forget."

"I see." H'Roo sat back in his chair somewhat defeated. He had squandered her trust, so easily given a first time, so difficult to earn a second time. K'Rin was right about these humans: all imps of the perverse, bundles of contradictions, randomly pliable; then rigid. No wonder K'Rin found them so fascinating. H'Roo had no idea where to take this conversation so he came straight to the point of his hospital visit. "We agreed that the winner of this exercise would host a banquet for—" H'Roo caught himself.

But Andrea filled in the missing word: ". . . the loser. I can stand to hear the word applied to me, H'Roo. So far, I've heard it seldom enough on Jod."

H'Roo paused. Only a human could launch humility and sink it in one breath. "We have three weeks leave and I want you to come to my city, Gyre, where my family is preparing a feast to honor you. I invited kith and kin. Also, because you are the guest of honor, K'Rin accepted an invitation to visit our household."

"You are some piece of work, H'Roo—shameless." She slumped into her bed. "I will not go to your house. I planned to take my leave visiting Heptar."

"The capital? Nobody spends free time there. Heptar is landlocked, nothing but a flat plain to look at. The city is not much more than a garrison and a dormitory for bureaucrats. The only buildings worth seeing are in the Council Fortress on the obsidian rock—they're sumptuous, but you can't go in."

"Why not?"

"As a Tenebrea, you are attached to K'Rin's household. He and his family are exiled from the Council Fortress indefinitely. Even K'Rin cannot enter Heptar without an invitation from the council. You might visit the outskirts, a collection of support services for the council. Even then, the local constables follow you—a human, an outsider, and that would just make trouble for K'Rin. No, Andrea. You'd better come to Gyre with me if for no other reason than to stay out of trouble."

"I'd rather stay here and rest."

H'Roo bit his lip and made his last argument. "You made a promise. Plus I spoke with the doctor; he wants you out of here by tomorrow. We will keep our promise, and I shall hold a banquet in your honor. If you wish to embarrass me in my own house, you may speak as the honored guest and expose me . . . well, I deserve it, and you'll have no better venue from which to exact vengeance."

Andrea knew from her scant understanding of Jod manners that she was supposed to cave at this point, deny herself any vengeance—kiss and make up, as it were. But the glint in her eye returned, and through her pain she managed a thin smile, "Now, that offer is too good to refuse."

The city of Gyre grew over the millennia as a set of concentric rings, each marking the next burst of cultural and technological progress. The Gyrt—as the people refer to themselves—were natural antiquarians.

Ever since the War of Unification, they preserved everything old, not so much out of reverence but from curiosity. The very concept of modern was simply a relative notion: modern compared to what? And their answer: compared to the next inner ring.

Within the innermost ring stood the Walled City, built around a deep harbor at the base of sandstone cliffs. Masonry walls narrowed the mouth of the harbor to the sea gate, where ten thousand years ago the ancients sealed the harbor entrance with log rafts. Nonfunctioning catapults—once capable of hurling fireballs a thousand yards—sat on the harbor walls, an odd adornment for a city that had not heard a shot fired in anger for a hundred generations.

The Walled City's architecture consisted of granite walls and slate roofs. It had become a living museum of Gyrt history and culture. Artisans practiced old arts and lived above their shops. Exclusive boutiques and restaurants filled many of the narrow lanes. The old halls, completely renovated with every modern convenience, served as the municipal offices. And the Gyre's architectural jewel, the Residence, housed the city's most prominent clan, the Parh.

Andrea had had no idea. She'd thought H'Roo Parh was some poor relation to the venerable K'Rin. True and not true. The family Rin held power at the council, but getting and maintaining such power nearly exhausted the Rin fortune. The family Parh left all political ambition to their cousins and continued to amass wealth. The families became far more entangled than mere bloodlines. The Rin needed access to Parh money: the Parh needed political protection—the Jod Council was forever sniffing around Gyre for any loose change. H'Roo explained the politics and economics to Andrea with uncharacteristic candor, and he was greatly impressed that this female from Earth understood this symbiosis completely.

Andrea stood on the balcony, leaning over the balustrade. She looked down upon the slate roofs, clumped in irregular polygons bisected by streets. She saw open windows in the upstairs apartments built over the shops—apparently the Gyrt eschewed curtains—and shadowy figures of family members crossing rooms, stepping in and out of artificial light, sometimes as couples or threesomes.

H'Roo tapped Andrea on the shoulder. "I have something for you, a gift. Come." H'Roo led Andrea back into the house to a drawing room. Laid out on a set of embroidered pillows lay a robe of iridescent blue.

"What is it?" She asked.

"A formal Drimdel Gown—traditional dress for Gyrt women. You'll need such a gown for the banquet tomorrow. Please, try it on."

Andrea took the gown behind a wooden screen, and there she shed her military tunic and trousers. Then she pulled the seamless robe over her head. The quilted fabric looked heavy, but in fact was light as silk. As the cloth slid down her torso she caught the sleeves with her arms. Her head popped through the wide collar and it lay gently on her shoulders. The ankle-length robe reacted to her body heat, changing colors, the cooler, looser cloth ranging from the iridescent blue to green. The tighter fitting, hence warmer cloth flashed yellow, orange, even red.

Andrea saw this marvel in the mirror—her body heat crassly advertised by the garment. She didn't want to see the back. She stepped into the open room and said, "H'Roo Parh, is this your idea of a joke?"

"Why, no." He looked genuinely perlexed, even hurt. "The Jod women are very proud of the Drimdel Gown."

"It's like a full-length mood ring, only worse." Andrea scratched the healing handlance burn, causing the fabric there to turn claret red. "I won't wear it."

"But why? True, you look a little warm in places, but . . ."

"I look like a slut."

H'Roo's command of Earth slang remained limited, but her tone of voice was clear. "Is that bad?"

"Never mind." Andrea tried to explain. "Earth women simply do not advertise their body's hot spots. We certainly don't compete as apparently your women do: you're only orange, but I'm *red* hot . . ."

"I beg to differ with you, Andrea. I've seen pictures of Earth costume. Your women use shape and color—combined often with remarkable tattoos. Our women only use color, and with practice they control the flashes on their Drimdel Gown like artists."

"If you don't mind, I prefer something that stays solid blue."

"That takes years of practice . . ."

"No, H'Roo, that's not what I meant. Either you modify this neon come-hither Drimdel Gown into some basic Earth fabric or I'll wear my uniform."

"A Drimdel Gown without Drimdel cloth? I've never heard of such a thing, but I'll ask my mother. If *she* allows the change, no one in Gyre will have the nerve to argue. Supposing she agrees, do you want blue cloth?"

"Something with a cool shade of aquamarine, thank you."

* * *

K'Rin arrived at the Parh residence without his usual entourage: this was a sign of respect. He summoned both H'Roo and Andrea to meet him in the Parh Trophy Room—a smallish chamber embellished with enameled copperplate, littered with jewel-encrusted commemorative goblets, gold plates, and platinum bowls. On the inside wall, shelves of polished burl housed ancient hidebound books—books written by generations of Parh. These books were the trophies. Three ivory chairs sat in a circle in the middle of the brightly polished wood-inlay floor.

H'Roo and Andrea found K'Rin leafing through one of the old Parh genealogical accounts. H'Roo stepped ahead of Andrea and announced their presence. "Hal K'Rin, you honor our house."

K'Rin carefully put the book back onto the shelf and replied, "Thank you, cousin. The Parh Residence is a treasure that I could never afford, yet by your family's gracious hospitality, I enjoy it without the burden of ownership."

An awkward compliment by Jod standards, but H'Roo Parh beamed, "You flatter us, sir."

K'Rin crossed the inlaid floors to the young pair and gave each a thorough head-to-toe look. H'Roo wore civilian attire, a garish Gyrt tunic embroidered with the Parh Family crest. H'Roo's pantaloons, baggy at the waist, tapered to a skintight fit around his ankles. On the wide Jod feet, Gyrt shoes looked like flounders with side fringe and a pair of semiprecious stones at the toe. K'Rin snorted his disapproval of the foppish Gyrt costume, saying, "You chose wisely to join the fleet if for no other reason than to get a decent set of clothes."

K'Rin stood before H'Roo, his silence inviting him

to speak, but H'Roo prudently kept his mouth shut. K'Rin then turned to Andrea, who wore her plain, comfortable work uniform. "Simple is better."

Then he motioned for everyone to take a seat in one of the ivory chairs. "I asked you to come to talk about business and to bring you some news to cheer you. Immediately, I am detailing you two for a special assignment under my direct command. So I'm especially glad to see you two getting along."

"Thank you, Hal K'Rin." H'Roo looked across at Andrea but she, showing little emotion, failed to echo his gratitude.

Andrea punctured the moment of elation saying, "I'm not so sure I want to work with H'Roo." She looked K'Rin squarely in the face and asked, "Did H'Roo tell you how he manipulated the Dlagor exercise or did he skip that part and just tell you about saving my life?"

"He didn't have to tell me anything." K'Rin rubbed his hairless chin. "You were programmed to fail in this exercise, Andrea." K'Rin shifted his gaze to H'Roo and said, "Tell her the truth."

H'Roo braced himself. "The plan to set everyone against you on Dlagor Island: it was not my idea. Hal K'Rin ordered me to set the seven Jod against you. The nuclear resonant tracking device was, however, my own innovation."

Andrea quickly fixed a hard look on K'Rin. Her nostrils flared as her anger welled up inside her. Her hand slipped down to rest on the hilt of the ceremonial dagger and squeezed the K'Rin crest till her hand hurt.

K'Rin quickly defended his actions. "I had to know if you could beat unbeatable odds. I've had special plans for you since your first day in training. So I designed the problem, and I ordered H'Roo—the only one I could trust—to set the other seven Jod against you."

H'Roo interjected, "Tamor-Kyl was only too eager to lead that bit of collusion."

K'Rin glanced at H'Roo, a glance that meant hold your tongue. "In fact, this entire test was for your benefit."

To Andrea's mind, some of the facts didn't fit. "H'Roo said that the stun would have killed me, had he not intervened."

"That was an honest mistake," K'Rin answered.

"Honest mistake? If H'Roo and you were in cahoots—"

"In where?" H'Roo asked.

Andrea rephrased her point. "If you two were running the Dlagor exercise just for my so-called benefit, if both of you knew, why did H'Roo stun me with the handlance?"

"I'll answer that." K'Rin stood with his hands behind his back. "First, H'Roo didn't need to know my reasons; he just needed to follow my orders, so don't blame him. Second, I can't have the other six candidates thinking I used them as props in an exercise for the human female. They are Tenebrea after all. It's bad enough for them that you beat them." K'Rin smiled. "—literally clubbed one of them, so I hear."

K'Rin waited for Andrea's response, and after an awkward silence, he asked, "Are you angry with me, Andrea?"

"Yes, I am."

K'Rin stepped closer. He looked Andrea in the eye and said, "Understandable. But I could not risk sending you on this mission unless you triumphed at Dlagor Island. Cousin, you are the best." He stood rigidly to see how she absorbed this praise.

Andrea coldly replied, "Perhaps you'd better tell me about this special mission."

K'Rin recoiled slightly. "You do come to the point, don't you." K'Rin motioned them to a trio of ornate chairs stationed around a short inlaid table. "Sit. Please." K'Rin sat in the ivory chair in the middle. "Very well. I need you to go to the Cor System, to their capital city."

Andrea's face brightened immediately.

"Being human, you can pass as a native. On Cor you will infiltrate the clone population and contact a female clone there. This female clone has information we require. She will most likely come with you willingly. Also, I need your firsthand assessment of Ordinate strengths and weaknesses. I need to know, in particular, if they are manufacturing a new generation of clones that have military potential. After you collect the female clone and your information, you will hijack an Ordinate shuttle to escape the Cor System, and we shall have a battle cruiser just outside their sector to pick you up."

Andrea looked askance across the ornate table at H'Roo, then at K'Rin. She'd just heard their glib explanation of how they lied to her for her own benefit. And now they dangled the prize before her—a chance to hurt the Ordinate. "Sir, I'm tired of the surprises. May I ask you a few questions?"

K'Rin's neck raised a pale shade, a tinge of outrage at her impudence that he quickly suppressed. He exhaled deeply and with the last breath of resignation said, "Of course. I'll answer any question you care to ask, Andrea."

Andrea pondered K'Rin's mission summary. "You've been planning this mission for almost a year—since the day I arrived—haven't you?"

"Even before you arrived."

Andrea glanced sideways at her partner. "How much of this did you know, H'Roo?"

"No more than you, at this point. On my honor."

Andrea faced K'Rin and asked, "What do you want me to do on Cor?"

"I need independent verification. We have reports from a Cor source. If the source is correct, the Cor may be in the early stages of preparing for war against the Alliance."

She cut him off. "What source?"

K'Rin leaned back in the ivory chair. "I hadn't planned to go into this much detail with you tonight, but you have a need to know. A clone from Cor claims that the Cor Ordinate have developed a NewGen clone." K'Rin described the threat of NewGen armies.

He finished with his political assessment. "The Council of Elders regards speculation of the Ordinate's NewGen technology with mixed emotions. They think the NewGen might be a solution to the uncomfortable problem of renegade clones. The placid NewGen are in every sense a manufactured species with no will of their own: they'd stay put and out of trouble, and the Cor might evade the opprobrium attached to cloning fully sentient beings. But I see in the NewGens the raw material of soldiers. Although they'll stay put, the NewGen will also go wherever the Ordinate orders them. They'll kill whomever the Ordinate tells them to kill, without compassion, without regard to self-preservation."

"The perfect soldiers."

"I disagree. They might be the perfect ammunition, but not the perfect soldiers. However, here's why I need your independent verification: The old-order clones, of which my source is a copy, have everything to gain from a war between the Ordinate and the Jod. If we slaughter the Ordinate, we in effect liberate the clones. In their own obtuse thinking, they'd prefer serving their new Jod masters than their old Cor masters. I'm not so sure I share the clones' optimism on that point." K'Rin looked at H'Roo for verification.

H'Roo just shrugged his shoulders, "Ancient history. Long forgotten."

"Hmmm." K'Rin shook his head and under his breath said, "Even ancient history repeats itself." Turning back to Andrea he continued. "Be that as it may, I think our clone friend is telling the truth about the NewGen threat. If unchecked, the Cor Ordinate will expand. Already they claim territorial rights that conflict with our colony on Corondor Six. At present, nobody is worried: the Ordinate is no match for the Jod, but if our clone source is right, the Ordinate will manufacture armies of NewGen clones. They can grow armies to rival Jod power in less than twenty years, perhaps less."

Andrea quipped, "You ought to annihilate the Ordinate now."

"You'd like that, wouldn't you?" K'Rin returned to the serious part of his conversation. "The council is not so glib about warfare, especially genocide. So far I haven't even been able to convince them that we have a threat. But suppose I do convince them and suppose I'm wrong. Suppose this clone is using me to instigate a conflict. I've got to know the truth. The cost of mobilization alone staggers the imagination. But compared to the cost of an Ordinate invasion? If we prevail, the cost is too high. If we lose . . ." K'Rin's voice trailed off.

Andrea's eyebrows furled, "I intend to draw blood."

K'Rin pointed his fist at her. "You must not jeopardize your mission for a vendetta. You would become an unreliable source yourself. The council would discount you as if you were just another renegade clone. I need results. I promise you, if you do your job, and if the Cor Ordinate are guilty, you'll have vengeance on a scale beyond your wildest imagination. But you must act like a Tenebrea, not like an impertinent child."

"Yes, sir." She stiffened at his rebuke.

"Besides, the Ordinate is part of your own species. I'd rather trust your discipline for this mission than your passions. Passions are too often disordered, and passions can change like the wind."

"Mine won't." Andrea braced herself. She felt her face flush.

K'Rin took a deep breath. His jaw muscles relaxed. "Curious species, you humans. Reckless, yet in many ways, Andrea Flores, I admire you chaotic humans. Even the few contemplative sorts I've met seem bent on proselytizing. Half of you have a pathological drive to take what is not yours—the other half have an equally pathological drive to share things others don't want. No offense, cousin, but you humans are a species of exuberant busybodies."

"No offense taken." Andrea felt no particular pride in being human. In terms of misery and happiness, humanity was at best a wash.

"And this is what frightens me. The Ordinate is restless just like Earth folk, but there the similarity ends. With the Ordinate there is no irritating sharing to offset the avarice. Everything on Cor is on a grand scale because the Ordinate is the opposite of chaos. Even their name boasts of their linear purpose—*the Ordinate*. You may not see it now, but your involvement benefits Earth as well. As part of the Alliance, Earth would be drawn into a war with the Ordinate."

"Ha!" A cynical laugh erupted from Andrea's soul, but she quickly composed herself. "Hal K'Rin, I beg your pardon, but you have failed to learn one of the most basic qualities of human nature—procrastination. Add dumb hope. It might take the Ordinate a thousand years to slaughter the Jod. I assure you, no one on Earth will give a hoot in hell for the first nine hundred ninety-nine of those thousand years. And I daresay, the Chelle and the Artrix will wait with Earth to see how you fare."

Silence crawled a long minute as K'Rin and H'Roo Parh considered the human female's casual dismissal of the Great Alliance. She had articulated with a caustic laugh what most level-headed Jod were afraid to admit in public—that when push came to shove, the Chelle would sell their loyalties to the highest bidder; the Artrix would send nothing but bouquets of sympathy; and the Terrans would do little more than place bets and watch the spectacle.

A sobering reality. K'Rin asked, "So will you accept this mission? Do you give a—how did you say—hoot in hell?"

Andrea found herself without a ready answer. Did she care? She certainly didn't care about the Alliance. But did she care about her training, about the Jod, K'Rin's patronage, or H'Roo's stumbling friendship? She most certainly cared about punishing the Cor Ordinate. She answered, "With pleasure, I'll take this mission."

Andrea stood first, which was poor etiquette. The Admiral had not dismissed them. "From the day you brought me to Jod, you planned to send me to Cor as your assassin and spy. You should have told me, K'Rin. You squandered an opportunity to motivate me even more. Instead of a few Cor Hunters, you've given me the entire Ordinate world. I won't let you down." Then Andrea gave H'Roo a sideways glance and added, "We just might have a little fun."

H'Roo looked at the wicked glint in Andrea's eyes. K'Rin stood from his ivory chair and raised a hand, "Reckless talk often presages reckless deeds, Andrea. We are not sending you to Cor merely to kill a few Ordinate. Foremost, you will gather information that will prove the Ordinate threat to Jod so I can convince this tepid council to mobilize. Second, you will retrieve a certain old-order clone named Tara 2862. Our source claims she is the key to organizing a clone insurrection. If the old-order clones rise against the Ordinate, the Ordinate civilization will be wiped from existence. There's your revenge, if that is what you seek."

"Oh, I do."

"Then, have your revenge on a grand scale, Andrea. Your passion, which serves you so well in the field, limits your vision. With you everything is tactics."

Andrea gave him the slightest affirmative nod.

"On the other hand, my strength is strategy. If you will just follow my orders and conduct the mission according to plan, you will get your revenge. But if you manage to get yourself killed in some pusillanimous bit of blood lust, I cannot replace you. I will never get my proof; the council will not mobilize until it's too late; the old-order clones will be slaughtered like sheep, and the Ordinate will flourish behind their NewGen armies. If you do not keep a cool head, you in effect assure the Ordinate's success. Do you understand the importance of maintaining discipline in this mission?"

"Yes, sir." Andrea cringed inside. She had not thought that she might unwittingly help the Ordinate and that reality unnerved her slightly.

"One more thing; I need to cut your leave short. Attend your banquet tonight and return with me tomorrow to the operations center. We have urgent work."

Andrea returned to her room, her mind flooded with thoughts about her upcoming mission.

She found a new gown lying on her bed, a shiny, blazing red dress—sleeveless, tight around the bodice with yards of shimmering cloth flaring out from narrow hips. Andrea had to smile as she put the dress on. Her respect for H'Roo's mother rose a notch.

At the banquet, H'Roo sat Andrea at the head table between his widowed mother, matriarch of the Parh Clan, and Hal K'Rin. The widow wore a flowing Drimdel Gown that she maintained in mottled greens and yellows. Her face sagged with old age, but nothing about this old woman was grotesque. Her jowls and her wrinkles simply offset her sparkling eyes. She wore no jewelry except the necklace given her in marriage and a thick brooch with the Parh family emblem: a wave-riding porpoise.

All rose to their feet as Andrea took her seat, but all eyes were fixed on the matriarch who smiled graciously and held Andrea's hand.

Missing from the table was Andrea's customary bowl, knife, and fork. Instead, her place setting was like the others: an embroidered linen place mat and finger bowl. The communal dish lay before her with an assortment of fleshy steamed vegetables, candied fruits, thick pastes, stacks of paper-thin pancakes, and many more delicacies. Everybody sat quietly and watched, because Andrea as the guest of honor must begin the meal by putting her hand into the dish. The old matron quietly assured Andrea, "You may safely eat anything on this table, my child."

Andrea thanked her hostess by reaching for a sautéed plum. Eating it, she smiled and whispered softly aside, "I love my new dress."

"I knew aquamarine was not your color."

chapter 10

After disembarking the shuttle, Kip escorted Andrea through the grassy quadrangle. But this time, instead of marching her toward the cadet barracks, Kip steered her toward the large ops center. Across the quad, she saw another clutch of cadets standing rigidly as some instructor she could no longer recognize railed and boomed intermittently about their worthlessness and an ennobling profession. *Military life is an archetype.*

Shortly after they arrived at the base, Andrea bid H'Roo Parh farewell. Dressed as a rich Parh merchant, swathed in fine fabric, he boarded a cargo ship bound for Clemnos, a Chelle trading settlement that served as a free-trade zone between the Chelle and the Ordinate. His assignment: find a way to smuggle Andrea to Cor, then get her back.

Andrea immediately introduced herself to the small Tenebrea operations center. She passed through a series of physical security checks: a neural scan that mapped the subject's unique electromagnetic signature. "Mat Flores, you are cleared Alpha through Gamma for access to the files."

"Is that everything?"

The duty officer shook his head, "Nobody is cleared for everything." Then he offered her a courtesy tour, to which she responded, "Just put me in front of a data screen."

This time, when she asked for information about the Ordinate, the computer didn't brush her off. Rather, it displayed a search engine to take her through thousands of files. She skimmed through the raw transcripts of interrogations of the eighteen clones in Jod custody. The poor wretches, hatched in adult form, were preprogrammed to work at menial tasks: farming, construction, manufacturing. Sketches depicted the clone precincts outside the urban centers. They lived in monotonous beehive dormitories.

Andrea performed a Boolean search under the subject headings Cloning and Cor Ordinate. Most of the information came from an unofficial Chelle source that criticized the Ordinate's technical approach to cloning. Apparently, the Ordinate combined their own highly developed work in animal husbandry and biosciences with new Chelle technologies and after a few grisly missteps, they developed clones. At first a novelty, clones became the basic commodity of their managed economy. Already built as a society of specialization, the Ordinate gracefully evolved into a system with The Elect at the top and all the lower rungs of the ladder occupied by clones.

The Ordinate carefully reserved management and security functions for themselves. They manned their fleet with an adept officer corps and an elite cadre of technologists. They too had a special operations unit: Cor Ordinate Hunters. Even with near-perfect controls, the sheer millions of clones ensured that some would inevitably get out of line. The Hunters dealt ruthlessly with clone malefactors—the messier the better in order to intimidate. Andrea read in most of the eighteen clone dossiers accounts how they'd find a mutilated renegade hanging from a tree or on a wall in their housing complex as a warning. The Ordinate treated any threat to their internal order as a threat to their very survival.

After twenty years or more service, the clones *retired.* Andrea presumed *retirement* was a euphemism, because the literature spoke of nothing after retirement: no housing, leisure, or medical attention. Apparently, clones disappeared after retirement. Clones that failed to work satisfactorily or otherwise threatened the natural order on Cor risked cancellation, another euphemism, although less obscure. One anonymous Tenebrea intelligence analyst opined that for every renegade clone that successfully found sanctuary outside the Cor system, thousands of renegades must have been caught and killed.

For a clone sanctuary was hard to find. The Chelle and the Artrix considered the clone renegades and their pursuers, the Cor Hunters, an offworld matter, none of their business. Earth ignored the problem. The Jod were of two minds. Some saw the wisdom of letting the problem burn itself out; others like K'Rin, considered the Hunter intrusions into Alliance space acts of terrorism and dealt with them accordingly, hence, the counter-Hunter mission of the Tenebrea.

Andrea browsed through a catalogue of two hundred thirty-seven known Cor Hunter incursions in Alliance space. Many, including the folder for the Baltimore Harbor Massacre, offered scanty details, a few painful images, and the caveat—investigation continues. *At least they're still looking.* She read with interest some of the files about successful anti-Cor Hunter operations. She approved of the Tenebrea policy of dealing ruthlessly with the Cor Hunters. *Terrorists understand terror better than compassion.*

Reports from Jod merchants visiting Clemnos painted a picture of cautious, deliberate expansion, lately accelerated. These files included pictures of Cor ships, graceful craft that functioned well in atmospheres as well as deep space. Analysts annotated the pictures, extrapolating from their displacement. Some merchants had gotten close enough to measure the ambient energy indicating the ship's power plant and weapons capabilities. Andrea skipped the slough of equations to the speculative conclusion: Cor ships had excellent speed, but they had weak shielding and they lacked heavy long-range weapons.

She read screen after screen till her eyes ached. Andrea studied the thousands of bits of information—mere specks of data. She was trying to build a puzzle with too many missing pieces. She cross-referenced and sorted her findings, trying to build patterns and memorize details, frustrated at the inundation of unsubstantiated, random details. The problem was that the specks of data easily conformed to biases. At best they might provide a sketchy picture of the Cor's capabilities but no indication of Cor intentions—nothing about their state of mind. Now, she understood why K'Rin needed to send a pair of eyes to get firsthand information from Cor.

Andrea took advantage of her freedom of movement throughout the operations center. Organized functionally like the *Tyker*, this land base had the sole advantage of mass: bigger on-line files, more staff, better food. Even K'Rin's office replicated his ready room aboard the *Tyker,* a quiet refuge, a place where he might read and think and hold private conversations.

Andrea looked about the small room, waiting for K'Rin to finish reading a short stack of dispatches. In the background, a civilian orderly poured two cups of tea and set out a plate of dried apricots. The walls were bare except for a black lacquered frame holding a tattered battle flag—red silk embroidered with the Rin triskelion in black and gold. On an end table sat a model of an outdated Jod air support fighter, the kind K'Rin flew in the brief Chelle War.

The furniture was austere. The room was not a place to relax the body. Andrea sat silently on a backless chair with her hands folded on the simple wooden table. The smell of the spiced tea caught her attention, and she noticed that the orderly had left.

K'Rin dropped his dispatches on his desk, picked up another folder and approached Andrea. He didn't greet her, and Andrea was for an instant annoyed at his brusqueness. She was not, after all, just another member of the household guard.

K'Rin slid the picture across the table where Andrea sat. "Take a good look at this computer composite sketch."

"Who is it?" She mimicked K'Rin's mood.

"This is Tara 2862, the clone you're going to bring back from Cor. She is the head of an elaborate cell system. She is a major part of a plan to organize an old-order clone insurrection."

Andrea took the stiff piece of paper. The picture, as good as any film process, showed a sweet face. Despite close-cropped auburn hair and lack of makeup, the face expressed warmth without heat. The gold-specked hazel eyes, set below arched eyebrows, beckoned one to converse. This Tara had an oval face, bowed lips—in a word *classic* good looks. She wore a plain white smock with half sleeves, and on the smock her identification: TRA 2862. "Where did you get this information?"

"My source."

Andrea set the picture on the table. "Who is your source? What's the name?"

K'Rin paused, squinted slightly, then answered, "A clone. He calls himself Eric. He's an ERC 1411 model—"

"I haven't read any mention of Eric or an ERC model in the literature."

K'Rin raised an eyebrow and smiled. "Aren't you the thorough one? Eric's interrogation is still in progress. Supposedly, he's an experimental model, and he's my private source—he is either a very knowledgeable and valuable asset or a talented and dangerous liar. I will not broadcast his information until I can verify his story."

"But you will tell me now, won't you." The tone in Andrea's voice was slightly accusatory.

The smile evaporated from K'Rin's face. "I'll tell you what you need to know, and no more. And don't you dare question my motives." Then, K'Rin took a sip of tea, setting his cup down hard to punctuate his pique. He continued his briefing. "Tara 2862 works as a records clerk in the factory where they manufacture, repair, and retire clones."

Chastened, Andrea added, "The Clone Welfare Institute."

"Very good. Tara is alleged to be quite the computer hacker—so you two will have something in common.

And according to our source, Eric, she has access to the Ordinate's most sensitive files. She has studied their weaknesses. Eric claims that he and Tara can lead a clone insurrection, but they need offworld help—help that Eric was supposed to find. Meanwhile, this Tara builds their organization. This story might be true; it might be an elaborate ruse. I want you to bring her back, and I want you to bring back as much of her technical knowledge as possible. And I want you to see with your own eyes and record evidence of the NewGen technology."

"Finding her among a million clones—thousands of whom look just like her; I don't know if it's possible . . ."

"The task is not as hard as it sounds. Fewer than a dozen of her model work at the institute. She lives in Precinct 15, and she's the only model number 2862. Plus, she has a distinctive mark."

"A birthmark?" Andrea held the picture to the light.

"No. Apparently, a lot of the old-order clones took up the fashion of distinguishing themselves from other copies. Eric says that some clones cut notches in their ears, some raise ornamental welts on their flesh, and some wear tattoos." K'Rin slid another graphic across the table: the upper torso of a full-figured, soft young woman. "The Tara you seek has a very distinctive tattoo: gull wings just below her collarbones."

"I see." Andrea matched the two photographs. Noting the precise lines and color of the gull wings over the breasts, she commented, "Your source Eric seems to know this Tara in what I'd call intimate detail."

"Eric and Tara were mates."

"Mates?" The term sounded cold to her ears, even if applied to clones.

"That's their term. Although the old-order clones are genetically engineered to be sterile, they are still sexed. The Ordinate tolerates serial relationships, but they forbid pair bonding. Nevertheless, the clones are gregarious. They tend to develop personal affections and enforcement is difficult. From the Ordinate's point of view, it doesn't matter much, because the record of their engineered sterility is almost perfect."

Andrea cocked her head. "*Almost perfect* sounds like flawed engineering to me." These bits of news were revelations to her, not part of the files she'd studied.

"As a matter of fact, Eric mentioned that there have been rare cases of clone females conceiving. The Ordinate watches for such mishaps and treats fertility as a malfunction in their process—they catch the pregnant clones and cancel them quickly. Eric related a secondhand story whereby a clone female successfully hid her pregnancy and did in fact have a male child. The renegades hid this solitary clone progeny. This would have happened before Eric hatched, so I discount his story."

"I believe his story."

K'Rin allowed a thin smile to cross his lips. "That, dear cousin, is what I believe you call your constitutional right."

"No, sir." She looked K'Rin in the eye. "The Ordinate system demands perfection. Nature won't allow it. And that's a weakness we can exploit. The Ordinate can't control the clones' instincts or psyches. Nor can they control Nature."

"I think you exaggerate the weakness. Yet, despite Ordinate strictures, many male and female clones secretly bond in a ceremony we'd recognize as marriage: Eric and Tara are an example of monogamist clones."

"I'm not surprised." Andrea smirked. "She looks like the marrying kind." Then her smile withered as she remembered that her father mocked her with those same words.

K'Rin shrugged his shoulders. "It's hard to say how deep these emotions run. Take Eric for example: he doesn't seem to miss Tara the way human literature suggests."

"Literature exaggerates. Humans don't necessarily pine away."

"Well, I have my own theory. I think their behavior is purely an attempt to imitate Ordinate culture—slaves adopting the affectations of their masters. Rather pathetic, don't you think?" K'Rin didn't give her time to answer. "Eric admits that in a perverse sense, most clones look up to the Ordinate as we might look up to parents and grandparents. But the point is: these rudimentary clone families, although bereft of progeny, serve as the basic elements of the clone cell organization—*if* Eric is telling the truth."

"Then, unless they eliminate the old-order clones, the Ordinate is doomed." Andrea looked at K'Rin with sudden recognition. "No government, no institution however brutal has outlasted the institution of the family."

"Clones? I don't think you can call a pair of sterile clones a family. Yet I agree with your conclusion. The Ordinate planners fear this nascent solidarity that starts with the sexes. They see the old-order clones' gregariousness as a major genetic flaw, especially as it tends toward pair bonding—a consequence of the old-order clones' two sexes. Biology is destiny."

Andrea considered the paradox: differences cause solidarity. She dropped the notion as one of K'Rin's superficial side trips into human psychology. Too often his accurate observations of human culture led him to inaccurate conclusions about human nature.

K'Rin continued. "Consequently, the Ordinate engineered the NewGen clones to be sexless or unisex. Frankly, I fail to see the semantic distinction."

Andrea set the photos aside and said, "Perhaps this Eric clone is just trying to get his mate out. Do anything; say anything. That's how I'd act."

"Perhaps. But I told you: he doesn't seem very emotionally attached to the female clone. All Eric talks about is organizing the resistance, then going back to Cor. He needs Tara to bring him enough proof to get the Jod involved. And he knows one thing for sure: I'm going to send him back to Cor one day to fend for himself, for good or ill."

"Okay. If he's lying, then he's pronounced his own sentence. I've got some questions for this Eric of yours. When do I get to see him?"

"You don't. Not yet. However, I'll take your questions to him and see that you get complete answers. You will not lack for information."

"I don't understand why I can't interview him," Andrea protested.

K'Rin shook his head and answered her protest without the usual ire he meted out to those who questioned his reasons. "I have no way to verify Eric's story, and until I do, I won't trust him. He might even be an Ordinate spy who's infiltrated my operation. So, I'm not going to let him see my agents, especially the one I plan to insert into Cor to verify his story. He doesn't know much about you either, and I want to keep it that way for now."

"Okay." Andrea nodded. "Then let's talk about the hard parts: getting me on and off Cor."

* * *

The Tenebrea planners taught Andrea everything they knew about Ordinate security. The Ordinate had excellent redundant security evolved from their technical genius in genetic engineering and centuries of angst. Their greatest fear as a society was that their clones might infiltrate their species. They developed a DNA scan. Each Ordinate at birth got a DNA tag—a record of his or her DNA for identification. The scan sampled the body's DNA, head to toe, and matched the DNA with the identification tag. As a matter of irony, these scans became the way an Ordinate woman learned that she was pregnant: the hypersensitive scan would report two sets of DNA: the woman's and her baby's long before the woman felt other symptoms. Technicians who ran the DNA scanners would sometimes joke with an Ordinate matron, *'Scuse me ma'am, but we're showing four—no five!—sets of DNA here.*

K'Rin's staff had studied the Ordinate security. They decided the weakest point in the system was its lopsided application. Ordinate security was like a one-way valve. Whereas the Ordinate were obsessed with keeping non-Ordinate out of their cities, they were not nearly as concerned about securing the clone precincts. Their system was geared to make sure clones could not leave Cor, not to keep clones from getting onto Cor. As a clone Andrea would simply slip through the cracks in their security system.

Andrea resisted the idea of blending in with the clones on Clemnos. She didn't offer a reason, she just felt that as a clone, she'd lack resources, freedom to move. Slipping through the cracks sounded like relying on dumb luck. However, she kept her silence, deciding that arguing with the Tenebrea planners only gave them reason to forbid her options. Her father always said: *When dealing with any bureaucracy, it's easier to get forgiveness than permission.* She'd wait and see what transpired at Clemnos. Besides, whether she masqueraded as a clone or an Ordinate civilian was academic until H'Roo found a way to get her to Cor.

Three weeks later, K'Rin reported, "I have a communication from H'Roo: he sounds optimistic. The Ordinate are building a permanent garrison on Clemnos. In his travels, H'Roo saw Ordinate surveying teams marking off a huge facility with landing pads just the right size for Ordinate cargo shuttles. He even saw what he thought was some labor under guard, which he's convinced must be clone labor. He says the main Clemnos spaceport is crowded with Ordinate traffic coming and going. The area is thick with Security Troops, even a handful of Hunters."

"That's bad."

"In the short run, it's good. With almost weekly, sometimes daily flights between Cor and Clemnos, security must be a bit lax. If they're bringing clone labor, that's perfect. All you have to do is move in, assume the person of a clone or Ordinate female, then take her place on the trip back to Cor. With the influx of humans on Chelle, you can blend in. But we need to move before they build a permanent garrison. Then you can bet security will tighten up."

The next communication from H'Roo pleaded: *Send Andrea to Clemnos as soon as possible.* K'Rin quickly acquired the *Kam-Gi*, an old scow from the Jod Maritime Fleet that hadn't seen a paintbrush in more than two thousand parsecs. He staffed it with a taciturn crew and fabricated a reasonable commercial excuse for the trip.

The time had come for Andrea to leave Jod. She mothballed her uniform, packed her weapons and other personals, then donned her old civilian attire. Now tight in the shoulders and loose everywhere else, her misproportioned clothes just helped her blend with the rest of the crew and the ambience of the *Kam-Gi.* She cut her black hair in the severe Ordinate style.

The dingy old *Kam-Gi* seemed embarrassed, sitting on the civilian landing pad next to the other gleaming commercial craft. With a small duffel slung over her shoulder, Andrea climbed the corrugated ramp into the belly of the ship. A sign riveted to the bulkhead, also worn with age, advertised: Safety Inspection—Unsatisfactory.

Oh that's just great, she thought. She stopped to read the fine print. "This vehicle lacks the structural integrity for in-atmosphere takeoffs and landings"—*That's just great.* A crewmember followed her through the hatch, pausing only to pat the red sign, commenting to Andrea, "It's our lucky sign."

"Are you sure this thing can fly?"

This Jod had an attitude as raw as any waterman she'd known from the bay. "We didn't carry it here—"

"You have a point," Andrea conceded.

And like a waterman, he didn't take kindly to criticism of his ship. "She can cruise at thirty-four parsecs per standard hour; seventy-three if someone's chasing us. She may lack some of the amenities you Earth females are accustomed to."

"You don't say." She probed a hairline crack in the internal wall patched with liquid weld. "For example?"

"The artificial gravity comes and goes. It's not so

bad when it goes out. Mostly the trouble happens when it comes back on."

"Why don't you just leave it off?"

He smirked, "Why don't we just leave it off." *Gads! What a stupid question.* The Jod crewman wiped his hands on a rag and chuckled, as if trying to explain this highly technical stuff to an Earth dame was like teaching a pig to sing. In his most condescending voice he said, "Because, Earth lady, most of the time, it works just fine. You just learn to hold onto stuff and cross your legs when it shuts down, and you sleep under straps."

"Oh." *This is pointless.*

The crewmember took Andrea below, and showed her the crew compartment. She stowed her modest gear in a drawer built into her bunk, took a double dose of space-sickness medicine, drank two fingers of a distilled beverage loosely resembling rum, and settled back for a long nap, cinching one cautionary strap across her stomach. As consciousness ebbed away she heard the engines fire and felt the craft vibrate. Dust rose in the cabin and flakes of graphite composite fluttered down from the bulkhead. If they were going to disintegrate on the jump past light speed, she'd just as soon be asleep.

Andrea slept through most of the trip, which took twenty-eight hours thirty-seven minutes. In astronomical terms she was farther from Earth than she'd ever been before, a fact she noted without caring.

Chelle ground control kept the *Kam-Gi* in orbit for four hours, partly to extort a greater landing fee and partly to demonstrate Chelle's unofficial neutrality to their Ordinate onlookers. The planet Clemnos turned slowly on a fourteen-degree axis. Clemnos was a giant ball of dirt, wrinkled with wadis leading to dry lakebeds—an ugly planet rich in minerals and poor in water. At present the continent lay in daylight. The city below was a patchwork of low-rise buildings of cheap construction. The place exuded a lack of permanence. In stark contrast, the construction outside the city was meticulously surveyed. Deep excavations and pilings presaged large institutions. Someone was building a new city outside the old one.

The landing was teeth-clattering rough. On the way down Andrea thought the ship's "lucky sign" might shake loose from its rivets. But they reached the tarmac in one piece. The Jod crew powered down the systems and lowered the corrugated gangway. Immediately, a Chelle duty inspector boarded the craft with an electronic clipboard, arguing with whoever would listen.

Andrea grabbed her bag and slipped down the gangway. Chelle ground crew had gathered around the decrepit *Kam-Gi* to insult her obsolete technology. They paused to take notice of Andrea—she wanted to look like a female Ordinate disembarking a Jod ship. Andrea glanced backwards with practiced indifference. Smaller than humans, the Chelle were sleek creatures with pale gray skin, silvery hair, and round doleful eyes with large black pupils seemingly always wide with amazement. Their ears were mere indentations on either side of the head. Their oblong heads were disproportionately large like children's heads, their mouths small, their delicate four-fingered hands disproportionately long.

She tried to mask her face as they pointed at her and chattered in their own tongue: *a female human coming out of Jod ship. These little gray blatherskites will have that bit of news broadcast about town soon enough.*

Andrea avoided further attention, hustling herself into a crowd on a public tram that took her directly to the aliens' ghetto—somewhat of a resort catering to the non-Chelle. The rank-and-file Chelle avoided contact with aliens, and their fear was understandable. A big Chelle might reach five feet and weigh eighty pounds. Fine boned, near-sighted, and tone deaf: the Chelle relied on technology for their strength and most of their pleasure.

Consequently aliens, especially in large numbers, intimidated them. Despite their technological superiority, they felt puny compared to the burly Artrix, or the sturdy Jod. But most of all, the Chelle feared the human species, both Earth and Ordinate. They'd watched Earth for millennia: long wars interspersed with brief timeouts. Earth contact was a dismal failure. Of the few explorers they sent, half ended up on slabs in refrigerators in a place called Goddard; the rest got away in a panic, recommending that Chelle have nothing to do with aboriginal Earth. They resorted to sleuth, gathering specimens for their ill-fated experiment on Cor.

The alien ghetto was filled mostly with Artrix and Ordinate. Earth travelers had only begun to reach this far into the galaxy, and few Jod traveled out of their system. Also, each species tended to further segregate themselves within the ghetto—sort of subghettos. Most establishments catered to their own kind. Andrea noticed the small brass plaques with the same curt message written in various dialects: Artrix Only or Jod Only or Ordinate Only. Occasionally she saw a hard-up establishment with a sign that read, All Species Welcome.

Andrea found H'Roo Parh just where he said he'd be: standing by a giant sculpture of a Möbius loop in the central park. H'Roo Parh muttered, "Let's get off the street and find someplace where we can talk."

She answered with a nod, but whispered, "H'Roo, you look too nervous. Relax. Blend in."

"I'll relax when I'm off this main street." H'Roo walked ahead.

With her conspicuous lack of style, Andrea looked like a pickpocket following a rich Jod, but the few Chelle security troops looked the other way. Their only job was to keep these foreigners from harming Chelle citizens or Chelle property; they had little or no interest in other intramural activities that stirred within the ghetto.

Andrea and H'Roo passed a dark tavern, and the smell of roasted meat and fried potatoes drew Andrea to the door. Six empty cafe tables adorned with menus and cut flowers sat on the sidewalk waiting for patrons, and Andrea suddenly felt like eating a hot meal with a cold drink. She inspected the menus, didn't recognize the names, but the pictures spoke of rack of lamb—or rack of something good. She muttered just loud enough for H'Roo to hear, "I'm starving. Let's spend some of those credits."

H'Roo grabbed a fistful of her blouse and pulled her from the tables. "Not here, of all places." As he led her to a safe distance away, he chided her. "That particular restaurant is a favorite of the local Ordinate Security Troops."

"Hunters?" Andrea stopped. She felt her heart beat faster.

"A few of them, yes. Check the epaulets. The regular security troops wear epaulets made of black cloth; the Hunters wear shiny black epaulets made of plastic or polished animal skin."

H'Roo tapped Andrea on the shoulder to motion her to hurry up. He said, "I know a place about five blocks from here where nobody but civilians eat. I rented two rooms in a tenement near the ghetto wall." H'Roo led her off the tree-lined avenue onto a small side street strewn with litter.

"Let me guess," Andrea switched shoulders with her small duffel bag, "all species welcome."

"You catch on fast. We can't be seen together without raising suspicions. The Ordinate types won't talk to a Jod for any reason. If they see you, a human, with me, they will quickly deduce that you are not Ordinate."

"They'll think I'm a clone." Andrea's eyes narrowed as she conjured a plan. There is something poetic about using your opponent's prejudice to cause his downfall—cosmic justice.

"Precisely." H'Roo amplified Andrea's thought. "They'll think you're a clone who escaped their labor camp. Furthermore, they'll think you're talking to a Jod trying to buy passage off Clemnos."

As he finished speaking, H'Roo rounded a corner into a deeper level of deprivation, an alley that dead-ended at an unhinged door. The smell of urine and effluvia swamped her appetite, and Andrea turned her back on the poverty and asked, "We've got to live here?"

H'Roo just pointed to the corroded tin sign, All Species Welcome, and said, "We have the two adjoining rooms on the top floor where the smell isn't too bad. Why don't you go up and settle in? I'll bring back something to eat."

Andrea put her hand on his chest to stop him. "I want you to get me something else as well."

"Anything—just name it."

"Find me some used Ordinate clothes—something a clone might scrounge up in an attempt to get off-world."

During the day, H'Roo worked at the launchpad terminal gathering information about Cor-bound flights. The Chelle ground workers chatted amicably about manifests, missions, and crews. In the meantime Andrea worked from the shadows in the ghetto, spying from out-of-way niches as she carefully selected her prey.

Andrea lay on a roof with a binocular recorder watching the comings and goings at the forbidden tavern. During the heat of the afternoon, the off-duty Ordinate Security Troopers stayed indoors. During the cool evening breezes at sunset, they favored the sidewalk tables. She counted no fewer than eighteen Security Troops, a mix of males and females, but so far no Hunters. Their pattern of visits indicated that they worked in shifts. She had difficulty identifying individual troopers because they tended to wear their face shields in public.

Andrea watched as an Artrix civilian took a seat at one of the empty cafe tables. He was an older Artrix judging by the white in his fur and his slight paunch, probably a merchant. After prolonged inattention, the Artrix rose, filled the doorframe, and summoned the proprietor. Instead of the proprietor, a lone female Security Trooper walked to the door and exchanged words with the Artrix.

The gentle but stubborn Artrix was a head taller and eighty pounds heavier than the Ordinate female, but she didn't flinch. She stood ramrod straight in her black uniform, average height but muscular. Andrea squinted, trying to get a better look at her epaulets—*they shine. I've got a Hunter!* Her tight black pants tucked into black boots. The left boot had a sheath and a blade with an onyx handle. Her double-breasted tunic boasted rows of military honors. It tapered to fit snugly at the waist, held in place by a wide metal belt; attached to the belt, a small hand weapon. Andrea knew from intelligence reports that the Ordinate still preferred the old kinetic kill devices: good old-fashioned pistols to tissue-disrupting beams. The uniform's shoulder padding exaggerated the woman's military physique.

The Ordinate woman raised her face shield for no other reason than to let the Artrix see the gleam in her eye. The Hunter had a serious face. Her lips seemed to hardly move as she spoke. She had smooth skin and she wore her raven hair short cropped, tapered, and slicked back.

The Artrix got more animated as words exchanged, yet the smaller Ordinate woman felt no need to brandish a weapon. She stood with her feet comfortably apart and her arms slightly flexed at the elbows—a very understated martial stance, but this woman was ready for the Artrix to do something foolish.

He obliged. The Artrix blurted some curt burst of language and stepped toward the tavern door. The Ordinate woman sidestepped to block his path; then the poor Artrix made the fateful mistake. He reached with his long right arm to grab the Ordinate by her jacket. *Bad move,* thought Andrea. The rest happened in the blink of an eye. In one fluid motion, the woman widened her stance, turned one-quarter to her left, and reached across with her right hand to seize the Artrix's beefy hand. She turned his thumb down, turning his wrist against itself. The Artrix howled as she put all her strength against the joint, driving her much larger adversary to the pavement, now helpless, howling for mercy. His cries drew a crowd from inside the tavern and out. Her Security Troop colleagues cheered her on. A pair of Chelle policemen watched from across the street.

The Artrix lay there, face pressed into the pavement while the Hunter toyed with this hand, wringing cries of pain by selectively applying pressure and giving some relief. She spoke a few more words to the Artrix, who nodded and groveled. It looked as if the altercation was done. Then the Ordinate woman smiled to her comrades, raised her boot, and kicked down with brutal force while turning the Artrix's hand till it cracked: she dislocated the beast's arm, and the screams of pain echoed throughout the ghetto. She dropped the Artrix's limp arm as if it were diseased.

With laughter and much backslapping, the Security Troops retired into the tavern. A Chelle medical unit arrived to extract the whimpering Artrix.

Andrea had found her target, the Ordinate Hunter—a good fit for clothes and easy to take. For certain the Ordinate woman was her physical match, perhaps physically stronger. Yet Andrea had the advantage because the Ordinate woman had a fatal flaw, a flaw that Andrea could exploit better than any physical weakness. The Ordinate woman was cruel. She was no common security hack: she was a Hunter. She was accustomed to beating craven clones and other weaklings. She could have brandished a weapon and easily run off the Artrix, but no. She wanted the fight. She'd quickly sized up the Artrix as some lumbering civilian, unskilled in hand fighting. This Ordinate woman suckered the poor Artrix, fed him a slab of sidewalk, then crippled him—must've felt like a god as she accepted free drinks and accolades from her comrades.

This will be too easy, thought Andrea as she climbed down from the roof.

Back at the room, Andrea showed H'Roo the video of the Ordinate woman trashing the Artrix. H'Roo winced as he witnessed the lopsided affair. "You can't be serious, Andrea. I'd rather wrestle a Fraxile than tangle with that."

"She's not so hot. Besides, can you think of a better way to walk onto a Cor-bound ship than as a Hunter?"

"What makes you think she's a Hunter?"

"She has the epaulets and she likes her work too much. I'll just put on her uniform, and put on her attitude; then the rest of the Ordinate will just get out of my way. Who's going to stop me?"

"This is a radical change in plans, Andrea." H'Roo Parh grimaced as he saw the finale: the woman stomping the Artrix's arm. "K'Rin will not approve."

"We won't ask his permission, will we, partner?"

H'Roo argued, "You're supposed to infiltrate as a clone laborer."

"I don't know much about being a clone, but I know a lot about being a Hunter. It's a lot like being a Tenebrea, don't you think?"

H'Roo grumbled, "This is not what we agreed."

"I didn't agree to anything." Andrea turned and smiled flirtatiously, but her smile hardened as H'Roo looked back disapprovingly. Then she dropped any pretense of their partnership, telling him curtly, "You can just watch and learn. In the meantime, we've got to find out who this Hunter is, and when she's due to ship out."

H'Roo closed the door behind him and sat in one of the rickety chairs next to Andrea. "You're in luck."

Andrea sat in a dim light running her titanium blade over a whetstone. She paused to feel the edge. "Good. What's the news?"

"You were right: She is a Hunter. She has the rank of Senior Lieutenant. Her last name is Tapp. Nobody calls her by her first name. She's got orders to return with the contract labor ship back to Cor to rotate a load of construction clones. They rotate the clones between Cor and Clemnos to prevent them from organizing themselves. They're traveling on a merchant ship."

"You're amazing. How do you do it?" Andrea grinned with admiration.

"I can flatter the Chelle out of anything." H'Roo basked in Andrea's praise.

Andrea asked, "Is she traveling alone or with her comrades?"

"Alone. Only four other military personnel are on the manifest, no others from her unit."

"When does she leave?"

"The day after tomorrow."

"Perfect." Andrea held the blade to the light. "Let's give Lieutenant Tapp a little going-away present." She jammed her blade into a crate, set upside down as an end table. Then she walked across the room to a dingy porcelain bathtub. She turned the hot water spigot on and began to disrobe, talking to herself.

H'Roo averted his eyes.

* * *

The Clemnos sun dipped low in the red sky and the evening breezes rose. H'Roo went ahead to set up a watch across the tavern.

Back at the room, Andrea carefully modified the clothes H'Roo had pilfered from the labor camp. She hid her blade in her belt at the small of her back in the loose folds of her shirt. She practiced a slump-shouldered, whipped-dog look in the mirror. Andrea became the embodiment of weakness and fear.

She jogged through the tenement section of the ghetto working up a heavy sweat to stain her clothes and to mat her short hair. Appearing harried, weak, and fearful, she was now ready to meet Lieutenant Tapp. Andrea jogged up the side street toward the tavern and there she slowed to a halting gait. She came up the sidewalk pausing to take a seat at one of the cafe tables with her back to the door. There she waited and she did not try to control her rising pulse, the natural anticipation of combat. Any sign of anxiety would draw Lieutenant Tapp to her like a moth to flame.

"Hey, you." Andrea heard the insulting tone, but didn't move; rather, she tried to hide her face in a menu, farcical but effective. She noticed a long shadow to her left, then the black boots. "I'm talking to you."

Andrea looked up and forced a look of shock having come face to face with a Hunter grinning back at her. Tapp had arrived on cue. "Me?"

"Oh, yes." Tapp pulled her black gloves out of her belt and began putting them on, snugging each hand into the tight leather. "Where are you from, dear?"

"I . . . I'm from Earth." Andrea stammered, hoping Tapp would not detect the affectation.

"Oh, my!" Tapp clapped her hands once and addressed the handful of black uniforms standing around with drinks in their hands. "She's from Earth! They're always from Earth."

"Your clothes . . . now I've seen this cut of clothes before. Want to guess where?"

"I bought these clothes: I didn't steal them."

The Ordinate Security Troops laughed aloud, and Lieutenant Tapp purred, "I wouldn't admit to buying these clothes, no matter what. Mind if I sit down?"

"Take the table. I was just leaving." Andrea pushed her chair back, but the lieutenant reached across the table and took her hand. She had a strong grip. Andrea looked at the Hunter's gloved hand, the first human touch she'd felt since she left Earth.

"You can't leave just yet. I need to ask you a couple questions—clone."

Andrea sat down and pleaded, "I'm from Earth. You must believe me."

Tapp reached across the table and playfully ran her finger down Andrea's cheek. "You are quite the looker. What model are you?"

Andrea leaned away shaking—with anger, not fear—but the Hunter didn't know the difference. *These arrogant Ordinates, they can't tell a human from one of their own clones.* She thought of Steve, and hate swelled in her breast like a hot cyst, and for the first time in this charade, Andrea had to fight to calm herself.

"Oh, don't be difficult. We've been alerted to you—an attractive clone trying to get to Jod. You were seen with a Jod. What model are you?" Lieutenant Tapp turned to her audience and opined, "Looks like a Gwen."

A male voice from behind answered, "Naw; I did a Gwen once. She's not a Gwen. I'd love to do this one . . ." A chorus of crude laughter followed. "How about it, Tapp? Let us have her a half hour."

Andrea felt her plans suddenly begin to unravel and her heart began to race. She needed Tapp's identity, none other. She had to engage Tapp; exclude the others. She looked at Tapp directly with pleading eyes. "You mustn't let him hurt me. You have no idea who I am."

"Well." Lieutenant Tapp looked annoyed. "I'll find out who you are. Let's see if you've got a mark . . ." She reached for Andrea's blouse and Andrea slapped the black glove away. "Don't touch me!"

Instantly, the black glove struck back, slapping Andrea across the face, a hard blow that left a small cut on the inside of her swelling lip. Andrea needed every ounce of her will to cringe at that blow as months of training prompted her to strike back. Cowering, she raised a quivering hand to shield herself from a second blow while maintaining eye contact with the predator. *I've got her,* Andrea thought. *It's personal now.*

Lieutenant Tapp addressed the other uniformed Ordinate. "And to think that I thought this assignment was a waste. Three months here and I haven't bagged a single clone—and now providence smiles on me."

Andrea took that as her cue. She bolted, purposefully tripping over her chair, scrambling toward the side streets. She heard Tapp laugh, "Greon, be a good man, tell the porter to take my bags to the ship. I've got just enough time to take care of this scum and catch my flight home. The rest of you stay here and enjoy your drinks. See you on the next rotation . . ."

Around the corner into the shadows Andrea ran, slowing to an easy jog waiting for the Hunter to close the gap. *Ah, here she comes.* Andrea ducked down an alley littered with squalor. Some idle refugees and bankrupt travelers poked their curious heads from windows to watch the bit of drama run through their otherwise dull lives. A block apart, Andrea turned to see the Hunter gaining.

"You can't get away. Give up and I'll kill you quickly." Tapp spoke with cold authority.

How reasonable and reassuring you sound. Kill me quickly, will you? You delight in the prospect of a clone cooperating with the executioner. Well, Lieutenant Tapp, let us reason together . . . Andrea patiently lured the Hunter. She flung some debris behind her—a purely dramatic gesture of contrived desperation to whet the Hunter's appetite. The chase continued as Andrea led Tapp deeper into the belly of the ghetto. And finally, the dead end. Tapp slowed to a walk, adjusting her uniform, pressing some of her black hair into place. "Trapped?" Her voice was smooth. The Hunter recovered quickly from the chase.

Andrea didn't answer.

"Now, maybe we can finish our conversation. No offense, but you don't seem bright enough to figure out how to manage an escape by yourself. Who helped you?"

Andrea cowered against the wall.

"Now, if you won't talk to me," the Hunter scolded her in mock tones, "I'll get very cross and start breaking your bones." The Hunter loosened her hands. "I know you scum are trying to start an Underground to help runaway clones. I just want a name—something to take back with me to Cor. Just a name, and I'll see to it you feel little pain."

Andrea looked terror stricken as the Hunter approached. Finally she found her voice and uttered a purely rhetorical question, "What are you going to do?"

Lieutenant Tapp didn't answer, but began to close in, slightly adjusting her stance to center her balance. Andrea knew this dangerous dance, thanks to the countless hours with Jo'Orom in the Pit. But she must not react yet. She must concentrate on the mental game: *feed Tapp's confidence.* Andrea cringed.

This latest show of fear piqued the Hunter's cruelty. Andrea watched the Hunter's hands and feet. *Come to me, Tapp. Come to me. Just one more step . . .*

Lieutenant Tapp moved in with her fist clenched and she struck at Andrea's face. Andrea sidestepped and Tapp's fist struck the wall. Instantly, Andrea stood in the open alley. She crouched; her arms poised; all outward fear vanished.

"Well, I'll be damned." The lieutenant shook the sting from her hand to assume a more defensive posture. "I've never had a clone fight back before. What a rare treat."

Tapp stepped in with a roundhouse kick. Andrea ducked the blow and parried with a low kick behind the Hunter's knee, followed by smashing her right palm into the Hunter's face. *Smack!* A bruise swelled about the Hunter's left eye.

The lieutenant jumped to her feet hobbled by bruised knee ligaments and returned with a desperate set of blows, each blocked or parried. Andrea caught Tapp's arm, put it in a lock, and carried her forward momentum, smashing her body into the wall. Disoriented from the blow, the Hunter tried to pry her pistol from her holster, but not nearly fast enough. Andrea grabbed the Hunter's hand, made a half-turn, and jammed her elbow into the tender flesh just below Tapp's ribs.

The pistol clattered to the pavement as the Hunter

sagged, her chest heaving for air, her knee ligaments torn, her left eye swollen shut: a pitiful sight, if Andrea were disposed toward pity. Andrea just saw a Hunter. And had she been able just four years ago, she'd have saved Steve and Glendon. Somehow, she'd have killed the six hunters as they pressed through the crowd. She'd have taken her knife—her razor-sharp titanium blade and—

"No! Don't!" Andrea heard H'Roo's voice coming up the alley. "K'Rin will want her for interrogation."

Andrea blinked. She had her knife against the Hunter's neck, not knowing when she'd pulled it from her belt. The Hunter looked back at Andrea with her good eye staring.

"Don't do it." H'Roo stood a few paces away.

Then Andrea said to the Hunter, "By the way, I really am from Earth." And she slit her throat to the bone.

chapter 11

The collar of the black Hunter uniform was still wet, sticking to the back of her neck. She'd had to soak and scrub the blood-soaked garment, oddly similar to her own Tenebrea uniform, except that hers was gray with black trim; the Hunter uniform was a silky monochrome midnight black.

H'Roo and Andrea worked through the night to prepare Andrea for her trip to Cor. Cleaning the garment proved to be the least of their problems. H'Roo had to dispose of Tapp's body, and he had less than two hours of night left. Under cover of darkness, he'd have to haul Tapp's stiff body into the desert and dig a shallow grave. H'Roo fumed. He considered Andrea's treatment of the Hunter rash and excessive, but she snapped, "I know what I'm doing: butt out."

H'Roo's silence proved more unpleasant than his arguments. H'Roo had always wanted the best for her, even on Dlagor—strange as that seemed to Andrea. And now she saw in his kind eyes something she'd never seen before: disapproval.

So be it. Andrea wasn't in much of a talkative mood.

H'Roo wrestled with his lifeless load, beginning to stiffen with rigor mortis. He trussed the body into a ball with strips of linen. Tied so, the Hunter looked small and helpless; not dead, but no longer able to struggle. Then H'Roo struggled to stuff the corpse into a laundry bag, occasionally glancing at Andrea. His neck was scarlet with undisguised anger. He pulled the drawstring with tight-jawed disgust, then he wiped his stained hands on a rag,

Meanwhile, Andrea took what she needed from the late Lieutenant Tapp. Andrea inspected the military hardware that came with the Hunter uniform. The pistol was a kinetic device that fired twenty lethal rounds in bursts or single shots depending on the flick of the switch above the trigger guard. A small transceiver built into the uniform sleeve had a blank crystal display and sixteen buttons arrayed as a square. She left the transceiver inert. In a breast pocket, she found Tapp's identification card: computer analysis determined that the card held little more than identification, DNA markers, and a set of access codes. Tapp had a first name, date and place of birth, and home address, all of which she memorized.

She ran her finger around the collar to momentarily separate the clammy wet from her skin. She wore the reflective face shield, marveling at the subtle tactical displays it offered: a three hundred and sixty-degree moving-target indicator, plus scan detection. If she focused her eyes up and to the right, she saw her weapons status: she still had twenty rounds in her pistol. She had no concussion grenades, and no authorized indirect fire support—*must be a link to other platforms during coordinated field operations*—very much like the Jod tactical system.

Andrea heard the door close. H'Roo had left with Tapp's body. Andrea muttered to the empty room, "Not even a good-bye."

Hours later, Andrea stood at the plate glass window watching civilians board the Cor-bound starcruiser. The Ordinate ship was long and narrow, tapering like a rapier. The ship had thin retractable wings—now fully extended and sagging under their own weight. The wings looked incapable of supporting the weight of the ship, let alone the brutal forces of takeoff and reentry. She'd read about the Cor systems' genius for structures—materials that sensed heat and stress, responding with waxing or waning rigidity, shape-memory metals.

Looking about the terminal, Andrea noticed a trio of black uniforms, regular Cor Security congregated in the lounge, enjoying the privilege of a leisurely drink while the clone laborers and civilians processed themselves aboard. Clone labor shuffled past the gangplank to a yawning hatch at the rear of the ship. There, they waited like cattle. A technician issued each a lozenge—a strong, long-lasting sedative. With supreme indifference, the clones took the drug and laid themselves in metal coffinlike boxes that the ground crew then sealed, stacked into modules, and rolled into the cargo hatch.

Ordinate civilians walked up the gangplank, each carrying an identical traveling case for their personal effects. Black uniformed security agents checked documentation, placed their identification keys in the scanner; the passengers walked through the DNA scanner, whereupon the Security Troop handed them back their identification—very routine.

A young Ordinate male, apprentice pilot, walked over to Andrea, inspected her name tag and said, "Lieutenant Tapp, we're ready to board you. Your cabin is ready. A porter brought your luggage last night."

"Thank you." Andrea acknowledged without eye contact. She was too busy surreptitiously studying her fellow passengers.

The apprentice wandered off to invite other privileged passengers to board—some of them wearing the black uniform. Security Troops certainly were a privileged class within the Ordinate, the Hunters more so. She was the only Hunter in the boarding area, and Andrea would use this class system to her advantage.

She followed the other troopers from a distance. She projected a surly mood—one that discouraged conversation, and when she reached the security checkpoint, she handed the technician Tapp's identification card. He slipped it into a slot, then invited her to pass through the DNA Scanner. Andrea swaggered through and held out her hand for her card, but the technician hesitated.

"Lieutenant Tapp?"

"Yes." Andrea paused.

"A porter brought your gear last night."

"As I ordered." Andrea tried to look bored to the point of being annoyed. "I hope you haven't lost my luggage."

"No, ma'am." With a wry smile, the technician winked and said, "Lieutenant, your scan shows two sets of DNA. Are congratulations in order?"

Andrea didn't reply immediately; rather, she reached into her pocket and pulled out a fresh but withering ear, and held it right under the technician's nose. "Why? Are you congratulating me?"

The technician recoiled at the sight of the blood-encrusted ear. He blanched and exhaled, "What the . . . ?"

"A trophy. From a renegade clone I retired last night. Hadn't you heard? I've got the other. Do you want to see it?"

The onlooking Security Troops chuckled at the technician's discomfort. He swallowed, held his breath, looking away from the grisly souvenir. "You may pass."

Andrea walked triumphantly to her small cabin thinking: *Sometimes the best cover is to stand in the open.*

She shut her cabin door behind her and pondered her temporary lodging. Tapp's cabin was little more than a four-by-seven compartment—a bunk to lie on, a storage locker, a shelf, a mirror, a communications suite; no running water, no window. Down the companionway at a hub, showers and toilets provided common service. Barely eight paces away, a meal dispenser operated in another cramped cubicle. Not a lot of frills. But it beat the hell out of living for ten days in sedated stasis stored in a chilled box belowdecks. Andrea congratulated herself for wending her way aboard as a Hunter instead of a clone.

The ship's intercom advised passengers to take a seat or find a handhold during the flight through low atmosphere. Then the engines fired, and the ship accelerated smoothly. Andrea leaned against her cabin. The Clemnos winds buffeted the winged ship—minor jolts, just a nuisance to anyone stubborn enough to insist on a cup of coffee during takeoff.

In a few moments she felt the ship break through the atmosphere into smooth space, and she heard the hum of the antimatter drives powering up. Then the lights momentarily dimmed as a great surge of power energized the ship's artificial gravity and synthetic space shield for the jump to FTL speed. She felt the slightest shudder as the synthetic shield bulged and reset during the acceleration past light speed. *What a fine ship!* If anything, the Jod had underestimated Ordinate technology, a vain and often fatal error.

Andrea lay her face shield aside and sat on the firm bed, careful not to bump her head on the steel cabinet above. She pulled off the tight boots and wiggled her sore toes, then methodically shed the utilitarian uniform, folding the tunic and trousers carefully and laying them at the end of her bunk.

She opened the locker to rummage through the late Lieutenant Tapp's clothes—something cotton, light, open collar, loose. She found a muslin two-piece ensemble that cinched at the waist with a tie and hung generously from her shoulders. And slippers! Fur lined and subtle, as soothing as running water.

She found an antique brush and comb made of ivory and other toiletries and cosmetics, which she set aside for her own advantage. A set of baggy athletic togs and various uniforms filled the bulk of the locker. Cradled in a set of soft towels, she found gifts: two bags of candy and a bottle of Vocloch Brandy—a famous patented delicacy from the Chelle system.

Beneath the gifts, Andrea found a thin leather-bound binder, worn by much handling, tucked at the bottom of the trunk. Andrea opened it and found an old fashioned family photograph: a somber man with shoulder-length hair forcing a smile for the camera. Beside him stood Lieutenant Tapp, who broadcast a look-at-me self-confidence. Two stair-stepped children stood like diffident foothills beneath the looming parents. For some bizarre reason, the image reminded Andrea of a magazine advertisement for real estate, and Andrea momentarily was embarrassed by her own callousness.

She gazed deeper into the photograph. The eldest child, a seven-year-old boy, favored Lieutenant Tapp in looks, the dark eyes, straight mouth, long graceful neck—except that he appeared sad. Or perhaps Andrea projected too much into the boy's image. His mother was dead: he should look sad. The younger sister seemed oblivious, smiling blandly. A tiny bit of pink tongue showed behind a pair of missing teeth. The girl had her father's delicate nose, thick black hair, and square jaw.

How curious it is that children tend to favor the parent of the opposite sex. Glennie favored Steve. Even then Andrea felt a twinge of jealously mixed with pride knowing that her daughter would be more beautiful than she. *Beautiful child.* Had she lived, Glendon would be the same age as the boy in the photograph.

Andrea didn't breathe for a long moment. Her mind, reacting to an undisclosed angst, told her to toss the picture away, yet she found herself staring at it. Was the ache her old wound or remorse, or both?

In the photograph, the proud Lieutenant Tapp wore a simple gown, resting a hand on either child's shoulder. This woman she'd killed was a mother—a mother like herself, with a husband like Steve and children like Glennie. And this woman, whose throat she slashed, would have butchered the anonymous clone that Andrea pretended to be—Tapp would have played with her the way a cat torments a downed sparrow, squeezing every last dram of fear from the doomed creature before sending it into oblivion.

This woman, Tapp, was cruel, yet her children certainly wouldn't think so. *Would Glennie think her mother cruel?* Children only judge cruelty directed at them. If the Tapp children knew their mother's vicious profession, they would deny the truth or justify it. The husband—Andrea looked at his stiff countenance and his indifferent eyes: he knew his wife was cruel, and he was beyond caring. *Steve would care.*

H'Roo cared. Andrea reflected on H'Roo's quiet revulsion when she sliced the ears from Tapp's pale dead face. *H'Roo thinks I'm cruel, perhaps depraved. So what? I had a purpose . . . a plan. And it worked. In any case, the deed is done, and I haven't time to worry about what H'Roo thinks. Tapp signed her own death warrant.*

Andrea took one last look at the children standing in their mother's restraining hands, one last look at the husband. They would miss wife and mother terribly. This pain Andrea knew. This pain was not speculation.

She closed the binder and let if fall from her hand into the locker. She resolved to put the picture and any remorse associated with it out of her mind. Pain is a fact of life. Remorse is a bitter luxury for survivors.

During the 240-hour trip, Andrea stayed in her cabin, feigning space sickness, emerging only to take a quick meal, visit the head, or stand briefly in the shower. She carefully avoided the crew, especially her fellow Security Troops who preferred to waste the hours away in the forward lounge. In consideration of the distemper that accompanies space sickness, and remembering her ghoulish collection of severed ears, the passengers and crew were content to leave Andrea alone.

She used every minute of her forced solitude. With Tapp's identification key, Andrea accessed the ship's computers. She studied the Ordinate fleet of spacecraft. Later she turned to maps of Sarhn, the capital city on Cor. She memorized as many details as possible.

Although the largest concentration of Ordinate, Sarhn houses fewer than two hundred thousand citizens. The city is the jewel of the Cor System: center of art and learning. Sarhn is situated below the first cataract of a deep river, just east of the confluence of three fast, fat mountain streams pouring freshwater from the snow-capped mountains situated in the north and west. Between Sarhn and the ocean, twenty miles of masonry banks manhandle the navigable river.

Andrea detected in the simple exposition an overriding civic pride in the capital city. Despite the authors' understatement, every building is a joy to contemplate, every edifice, whether commercial, private, or civic—even the grandest halls—all have human dimensions, a comfortable face, a genteel attitude. All technology remains unobtrusive. The citizen sees handwrought iron and polished stone, etched crystal, and fanciful terra-cotta. They see no wires, no smokestacks. Most mechanical transport operates underground or in the air. Ordinate planners save the surface for pedestrians, who wander along decorative walks among the building facades or through elaborate flowered gardens.

Andrea noticed a morose shift in the texts as the authors moved to the topic of clones. Suddenly, the adjectives were gone, the details sparse. She analyzed this first insight into the Ordinate mind regarding clones. She guessed that the authors subconsciously took pains to separate the triumph of Ordinate culture from the economy of clone labor. *What is their state of mind?* She wondered. *For the typical Ordinate, the clones represent the serpent in paradise, a serpent of their own making, a serpent ironically responsible for their paradise.*

More than three million clones live outside Sarhn in hivelike barracks of cement. The clone city has no name; rather, the Ordinate divided it into precincts. The clone precincts surround Sarhn on three sides: east, south, and west. The northern quadrant is a great greenway following one of the streams through open spaces toward the foothills. There the Ordinate citizens play. Beyond their playground stretches wilderness and mountains.

Ordinate city planners take great pains to hide the ugliness of the clone habitat from their idyllic existence. Sarhn is surrounded by a great wall, quarried from deep veins of granite. Once an indomitable barrier to shot and shell, the wall is now a tourist attraction, one of the few ancient relics that predates Cor's independence from the Chelle.

Outside the stone wall, one finds the real barrier, a ring of fifty-foot towers emitting sound waves powerful enough to emulsify blood and lymph without breaking the skin. The sound-wave barrier cleverly warns would-be infiltrators. As they approach within one hundred feet of the barrier, they hear a painful low-range noise and feel some stirring in the gut. The intensity of the barrier increases as an inverse square of the distance to the towers. If an intruder is foolish enough to proceed, the pain to the ear grows. The eyes feel the throbbing. A few feet closer, eardrums burst. The cornea tears: the intruder goes blind. Another ten feet and the now deaf and blind intruder suffers massive internal disruption.

They are afraid that the clones might rush the c[illegible]y. They don't have enough bullets to stop all the clones. Do the clones know that?

Beyond the sound barrier, two thousand meters of ancient coniferous trees stand in a thick forest, a massive screen to hide the industrial noise, eyesores, and smells. On occasion, usually in the hotter months, an easterly wind wafts up a pungent odor—a potpourri of waste management, slaughter yards, and chemical manufacturing—called the Clone Winds.

Aside from the occasional olfactory reminder, the typical Ordinate can live a full life unaware of clone heavy labor. They never see the precincts. The typical Ordinate only knows clones as carefully screened day laborers, artisans, clerks, or domestics—stolid, semi-skilled workers. The rough-hewn clone laborers, bred for strength and limited problem solving, never see the refined citizens of Sarhn—except of course the Security Troopers and the Clone Welfare Institute staff.

Nestled in a secure area, one finds an appendage to the otherwise symmetrical City of Sarhn. Two secure facilities reside there: the spaceport and next to that the Clone Welfare Institute. A heavily armed garrison guards both.

On a decapitated hill, within the granite wall and sound barrier, the Clone Welfare Institute stands as the largest single structure ever built on Cor. A magnificent structure. Although not the highest volume clone-manufacturing facility in the Cor System, the institute provides the best that biotechnology has to offer, including the laboratories where the geneticists design hybrid models and the neuro-ontologists map new neural imprints.

The massive building covers eighty acres, and stands

as a seven-layer ziggurat over eight hundred feet tall. Built of ceramic and glass, it sparkles in the sunlight and glows from within at night. Temple to Ordinate technology, the great Clone Welfare Institute produces more than two thousand clones per day. Plus it maintains the sick and injured, and retires the old and ineffective. Managing the rapid growth of so many organisms, the institute becomes in effect a city within a city, having all the energy, supply, and hygiene challenges of a typical city of fifty thousand souls. *Does K'Rin have any idea how technically advanced these people are?*

Andrea devoted one afternoon studying the Security Troop, particularly the select group designated as Hunters. She found that the Security Troop operates along military lines: squads, platoons, companies, and battalions. Doctrine emphasizes shock and firepower. All soldiers volunteer. Theoretically, every citizen between the ages of eighteen and fifty can be called into military service at a moment's notice, but none of the civilians receive training. The officers rise through the ranks in a strict meritocracy.

She noted with interest an essay from one of the Ordinate's shining examples of military thought: *The decisive virtue of the Security Force officer is "decisiveness."* Andrea mused that military thinkers have a universal penchant for conundrums, tautologies, and mediocre poetry. But the rest of the essay delved into dark practicalities. The greatest inhibition of the Ordinate officer candidate is to apply deadly force. Their remedy for this natural inhibition is to elevate cruelty to a virtue and rename it *decisiveness.*

She queried the computer for information about NewGen clones. The machine curtly responded with a screen filled edge to edge with the word, *DENIED.* With that rebuff, Andrea scoured the ship's library for information about the old-order clones. The library provided a sort of catalogue that described current offerings: forty-nine root models and the roughly two thousand hybridized branch-models—all categorized by suitable jobs and given serial numbers comprised of three letters and four digits. Each had a synopsis of genetic attributes scored for utilization.

She wanted to learn more about this Tara 2862 that she needed to extract from Cor. Andrea asked for the synopsis of the T-model, subset Romeo-Alpha hybrid. The computer replied, "Clone Female Model TRA remains in production. However, we have a three-month backlog. The Clone Welfare Institute reports 268,462 units produced, of which 12,615 remain in service throughout the Cor System. One of the more successful hybrids of T-species, the TRA enjoys high reliability, experiencing only eighteen cancellations for cause and four-hundred thirty-six early retirements for illness or injury."

The screen proffered a picture of the TRA clone—a pleasant female with fair, freckled skin and auburn hair; beneath the picture, a table of scored attributes:

problem solving	84
short-term memory	97
long-term memory	88
minor motor skills	94
major motor skills	72
health	84
height	54
strength	43
compliance	82

The computer summarized the TRA model saying, "The TRA model remains one of the more popular models for clerical duties. Attractive with an excellent short-term memory and docile, the TRA model has one significant drawback—a tendency to be overly solicitous of Ordinate supervisors. However, on a positive note, the TRA model tends to develop loyalties to the organization for which it works. Records show that one ought to keep TRA model clones in one job from initiation to retirement as they suffer some dysfunction when reassigned."

Andrea tried to access the ERC model and got a terse screen message without a picture: "Prototype Clone Male Model ERC removed from production. Formerly used as clone constables. All units recalled and retired. No orders accepted."

She tried again, searching for records about clone constables, ERC prototypes, prototypes in general. She found nothing but generalities about clone manufacturing. Andrea paged through volumes of clone data. She marveled not so much at their superhuman qualities: they had none. She marveled at their ordinary human foibles. The clones had a crude class system of their own, built around their assigned work: low-level supervisors, technicians, skilled labor, and strong backs.

Some lucky clones got to work inside the city of Sarhn as day laborers and domestics, but the vast majority toiled in factories and farms outside the city barrier. Every evening, the relatively few city clones made the mandatory exodus back to their drab dormitories—often in a rush to avoid severe penalties for curfew violations. Andrea made a mental note—a person might lose herself in that daily swarm of bodies.

The library confirmed what she'd learned from briefings on Jod: the clones were biologically human in every way like their Ordinate "parents" except that they'd been genetically engineered to be sterile. They had all the appetites, innate curiosity, and fears that their parents had—all of which led to some periodic messy situations requiring mass retirements and attendant work stoppages. The literature lamented that there was only so much that social conditioning might accomplish for clones: the answer lay in further genetic research.

Andrea felt a sudden chill. Further genetic research—not to make greater humans, but lesser humans—lesser humans, more expendable.

chapter 12

The two weeks of hiding in her cell-like cabin and skulking around the ship for necessities came to an end. The ship's intercom instructed the crew to begin the resuscitation of the "cargo" in the hold and advised the remaining passengers to brace for deceleration to sublight speed.

A few hours later, the Ordinate starcruiser began a controlled vertical descent twenty miles above the light-speckled city of Sarhn, just waking up in the predawn shadows. Rose-colored clouds lay as a dappled screen between the ship and the dark ground.

Andrea stood in the forward observation deck to watch. This descent provided a high-altitude personal reconnaissance of the city, and she watched with keen interest the shadowy terrain, the pattern of lights in the city. She listened intently to the pilot's chatter with ground control. Her acute focus augmented her reputation as being unapproachable. She wore Tapp's black uniform, slightly altered. She removed Tapp's nametag from the breast pocket—anyone who knew Tapp could compare the face and the nametag and discover her fraud.

The boots pinched her feet, and she accepted the discomfort as a benefit: it kept her in a pose of physical tension, which others interpreted as agitation. They gave her wide berth as she turned her back to the room and occupied her porthole.

The trip straight down lasted barely eight minutes. Andrea's porthole gave her a western panorama. She saw the ink-black scrawl of the creeks pour into one straight line spilling into what looked like an eternity of black—the ocean hid deeper within Cor's shadow. Meanwhile, Sarhn dazzled. Effulgent splashes of white and blue light marked the larger thoroughfares. The older buildings shone with a million luminescent eyes. Newer crystal architecture rose like glowing spears of quartz. The Clone Welfare Institute shined like a bright eye. The ship's library had so understated the beauty of Sarhn as to be guilty of libel.

From high altitude, Sarhn's great wall—brilliantly lit to the outside—looked like a fine diamond bracelet. Andrea squinted to see the sound-barrier towers and the few passages. Heavy land transport crept along light rail through the barrier and beneath the wall. She made a note: They use clone labor to haul in their victuals and cart away their garbage before dawn.

With her own eyes, she confirmed that a dense forest rose as a monstrous privacy hedge between the much larger, industrialized clone city and Sarhn. And beyond the forest was the smoke-stained gray of cement and cinderblock with red clay roofs. The clone city was a patchwork of squares called precincts, one of which was Precinct 15: dormitory 6, room 227—Tara's room. The clone city disappeared behind a curtain of trees as Andrea lost her vantage of height. The starcruiser, just barely above the city roofs, stalled to a slower landing, the rumbling dampened by harmonics. Even so, the great buildings seemed to leap from the ground—just a moment before delicate, diminutive; now massive, intimidating. The spaceport pad seemed surprisingly small in this man-made canyon. She felt the slightest jolt as the ship touched down, and heard the final word from the pilot: "Weight on gear—prepare forward hatch to disembark."

The view of Sarhn was hard to quit: the spaceport a modest ten-acre field of steel blue ceramic surrounded by shimmering buildings, the tips of which now reflected the hard white light of the Cor sun. Spreading trees of a high-gloss green skirted the buildings. Andrea grabbed Tapp's small satchel of civilian clothes. She took the rear of the procession as the column of glad passengers shuffled down the metal ramp. She kept her face shield up, mimicking the other Security Troops who disembarked.

Outside the confines of the ship, the impact of the scene took a ratchet up. In a moment of self-awareness, Andrea saw herself standing back as the others walked away. She caught herself staring at the skyline like some rube colonist on a first trip to the home world—not a self-assured Hunter on her homecoming. Rather, she saw herself as a round-eyed child on her first trip into Baltimore, lost in the majesty of the grand buildings, absorbed in the curiosities of marine commerce, titillated by the clamor of the crowd, separated from her irritated father who finally backtracked to find her, filling her ears with his oft-repeated rebuke: *Pay Attention!*

Now Jo'Orom's voice echoed the warning, *Pay attention or you'll get yourself killed.* Andrea blinked. She willed herself to concentrate on her tactical situation, the people, and her options for egress. Eventually, she'd need to remember the details of this spaceport, her only way off this hostile world. Andrea surveyed the buildings, the hangars with yawning doors, spacecraft lined up on the tarmac, and technicians in khaki suits ministering to the sleek machines.

Closer, at the back of her transport ship, flatbed carts rolled up to the cargo bay to accept a load of clone crates. In front, a crowd of welcomers stood anxiously and obediently behind a short barrier. Mostly civilian, they wore gay pastels. Older children stood on tiptoes, toddlers sat upon shoulders; the few infants sat in crooked arms, peering wrongway over shoulders—missing the event. Already, the first passengers embraced family, and the din rose as more passengers poured into a pool of good cheer.

Andrea recognized Lieutenant Tapp's husband and two children straining the barrier. The children pointed at the lone female in black uniform—her. From a distance and carrying the familiar satchel, she would look like their mother. The little girl jumped up and down. The older child tugged at his father's shirt to broadcast the happy news—*Mother is home!* The husband smiled broadly, ignoring his children's commotion while concentrating his energy on the distant image of his wife.

Andrea stopped for an instant in the middle of the field, seized in a moment of panic. She couldn't go back or take another route without arousing suspicion. She grit her teeth and walked toward the crowd obliquely to a side exit. From the corner of her eye she saw the Tapp children waving frantically to steer her back toward them, but she feigned indifference and continued, careful not to accelerate her steps—although never before had she felt such an animal urge to flee.

The husband swept the girl child into his arms and muscled his way through the crowd, creating a wake for the boy child to follow. Andrea quickened her step as much as she thought observation could bear. She could no longer see the Tapps with her peripheral vision and dared not turn her head. But she heard the children yell above the din, their pitch rising to a shrill desperate note, "Mommy! Mommy!"

She passed through the gate and needed to cross less than fifty feet of walkway where she might disappear into the terminal building. Then, she felt a small pair of arms clasp around her leg and a voice squealed, "Mommy!" Andrea thought her heart would burst. A small hand enveloped her kneecap; the child's face burrowed between her legs. That tactile rush of joy was burned forever in her memory—now turned bitter beyond anything in this life. If she looked down, her heart might see Glennie grinning back. She could commit no violence to others that compared to the violence that her memories inflicted on her rational mind now. The child's caress set her soul on fire.

Andrea froze. She found herself face-to-face with the husband from the picture, a face suddenly crumpled by disappointment. He spoke first, "I'm sorry. The children . . . I thought you were . . ." (he forced a nervous laugh) "my wife."

The tight little grip on her leg went limp, and the girl groaned as if by child's intuition she knew the awful truth. Andrea refused to look down at the child but kept her gaze on the husband and said nothing.

"I'm Jorg Tapp. Did you see Karool Tapp aboard?" He brightened slightly.

"Lieutenant Tapp didn't leave Cor. I don't know the details," Andrea lied.

"But I saw her orders. I saw the ship's manifest . . ."

Andrea stepped away. "Like I said, I don't know the details." As she turned into the crowd, she shuddered.

Andrea ducked into a quiet lounge nestled into an old stone building. The door lintel sported an archway of bas-relief stylized faces progressing right to left from stern sobriety—the face on the keystone was the model of mellow conviviality—then sliding into the riotous and finally stultified drunkenness.

Her distinctive uniform kept the curious at bay. She sat at a corner table in relative quiet observing the bar patrons. Nobody exchanged coins here. The barkeep handed over effervescent drinks and the patrons handed over metal discs, which the barkeep passed through a device to debit some unit of money.

Andrea opened Tapp's small bag and retrieved the silver disk. *So this was Ordinate currency.* With it she took a seat at the bar, procured a meal and large tumbler of brew that tasted much like Earth coffee. Most importantly, she caught the bartender in the mood to chat. After a mouthful of a meat pie, she grunted: "It's good to be back. The food on Clemnos is awful."

The barkeep lowered his voice. "Been offworld, have you?"

"Rotating clones. Boring work. We're using a lot of clone labor there."

"So I heard. These clones are nothing but trouble if you ask me."

Andrea smiled, "Without them, I wouldn't have a job."

"We all make our little contribution . . ." The barkeep fished for more tidbits that he might share with his patrons. Being the bearer of news raises the stature of any profession. "So what's going on at Clemnos these days?"

She whispered, in a manner to engage his confidence, "We're building a garrison there—complete with port facilities. Give us another two years, we'll own Clemnos."

The bartender nodded, "It's about time."

"Clemnos could use a good bar." She raised her glass in a salute, a gesture that the barkeep misinterpreted as a request for a fill-up. He took the glass and put it under a tap. Then Andrea took her turn prying information from him. "I've been away for a year—don't get any local news." She accepted her drink and slid her silver disk across the bar.

"As you can see, I can't get any help. I think maybe they're sending all the fresh issue to the colonies or something. I used to keep three Dana models. The CWI recalled two and retired a third. I haven't got my replacements for four months. Used to be I could get a replacement or at least a loaner in just one day." The man snapped his fingers. "During the evening trade, my wife and I can't keep up; so a lot of my regular customers are staying home."

"What does the government say?"

The barkeep laughed skeptically. "No offense—you being in the government and all—but the government doesn't tell us much. All I can tell you is what I see."

"And?"

"Remember the huge rush at the East Gate just before curfew?"

She nodded to encourage him, and the barkeep continued. "I used to go for the laugh. You security guys would prod them through—seems that you could never get a clone to move but so fast. When we were kids, we'd sit on the wall to watch the flood of dullards disappear into the woods. I always wondered where they all lived, and I never got tired of hearing all those shuffling feet."

"I remember." Andrea nodded, affecting nostalgia. She tried to echo the delight in the man's face, encourage him to reminisce.

"Well, the crowds just aren't what they used to be. What I'm saying is, ma'am, the clones are disappearing."

"And you think the colonists are getting them."

"I sure do, must be millions of them. You said yourself; you've got a bunch of clones working on Clemnos. And those not going to the colonies are building our fleet—five hundred new light attack ships, so I've heard. Now, I'm not complaining or second-guessing policy. I'm all in favor of the expansion—official or unofficial."

Andrea quashed the conversation by simply raising an eyebrow. *Five hundred new attack craft?* Andrea nodded as if this revelation were old news. "Loyal citizen—of course."

"That's right." He disengaged to go dry some glasses.

She thanked the barkeep for the conversation, put her disc back into her pocket and left.

Andrea walked up a steep set of granite stairs to the top of the Wall. She found a leisurely perch, a roofed casemate with a dry stone bench by a large gun port. Pedestrians meandered, periodically stopping for a view—first the wild and gangly forest outside, then the ordered and ornate buildings inside. Pairs of self-absorbed adolescents weaved and bobbed along the Wall, arms draped around each other, oblivious of the scenery.

Her seat on the Wall gave her the advantage of watching the East Gate and preparing for the curfew exodus. Already a few clones beat the rush through the sound barrier and caught the light rail that disappeared into the forest. Two squads of Security Troops flanked the corridor with machine guns slung over their shoulders. They seemed supremely bored with the nightly routine. She'd wait another hour for the chaotic crush; then she'd join the crowd and drift with it into the clones' world.

Her perch also let her keep a wary eye on the lounge because she realized upon leaving that she'd made a serious blunder that if discovered, might unravel all her plans. First, she must assume that Tapp's husband files the Cor equivalent of a missing person's report. Second, the starcruiser's manifest shows one female Ordinate Hunter boarded, having passed the DNA screen. Third, a lone female Ordinate Hunter disembarked, but positively identified as *not* Lieutenant Tapp. They would find Lieutenant Tapp's bags unclaimed at the terminal. And fourth, someone just used Tapp's credit disc. How soon these four facts collided, Andrea merely speculated. But she knew one thing for certain: the four facts would collide and trigger the correct conclusion that the Ordinate Hunter organization had been compromised. She did not relish being the focus of such a manhunt, and for the first time she considered K'Rin's wisdom in insisting that she infiltrate Cor as a humble clone.

A new distraction competed for her attention. The light trickle of clones wending their way to the East Gate quickly swelled to a torrent of bodies. Andrea rose, dusted some lichen from her pants, and started down the steps. She turned to merge with a throng of outbound clones when she saw a boxy squad van roll up to the bar where she'd eaten dinner. The van's side doors swung open and out stormed eight heavily armed troops wearing body armor.

Andrea folded her face shield and secured it into the case by her holster on her utility belt. She did not want to advertise herself as a Hunter now.

She slipped into the crowd shuffling down the broad avenue to a line of fifty head-to-foot turnstiles—the East Gate. Above the gate stood a sign, an arch of glistening chrome letters: **WE LIVE TO SERVE!** Thousands of beings lumbered along: no conversation, no "How was your day?" She heard only the shuffle of feet and the grind-click of the fifty turnstiles. Each clone seemed intent on the back of the predecessor's neck, and they seemed to have perfected this mass maneuver without trodding on each other's heel.

The evening sun cast a dingy light onto the crowd; the wall and forest broke the light with shadows. Scant artificial illumination further muddled the image. Being of average height, Andrea felt reasonably concealed, as if floating down a slow river, only her head and shoulders visible to the sentries on the bank.

All around she heard, even felt, a rumbling hum. Fifty-foot black panels emitted subsonic waves that worked in perfect phase with the lethal sound barrier. The harmonics negated the disrupting sound waves, creating a safe bubble through which the East Gate passage carried the evening traffic. With the flick of a switch, the Security Troops could collapse the protective harmonic bubble and pulverize anybody unlucky enough to be in the killing zone. Clones instinctively clustered near the center of the road and thereby in the center of the bubble. Perhaps if it did collapse, this bit of caution might win them another split second of existence.

Within this swarm, her uniform proved particularly repulsive—the clones feared the black, didn't want to touch it, leaned away lest they annoy the wearer, but they had no room and had to endure the discomfort of walking beside a Hunter. Even so, Andrea felt a certain amount of slack between her and her fellow travelers. She wanted to pull the clones around her like shrubs for camouflage.

The sentries still had their machine guns shouldered and they seemed to look over the crowd rather than into it. *Good. The authorities aren't going to let Lieutenant Tapp's disappearance upset the entire workings of the city.*

The slow march to the turnstiles tightened her nerves. She half-expected the bars to freeze on her, trapping her in a steel cage. She found herself momentarily paralyzed, staring at the bars. She'd traveled the length of the galaxy on an enemy starcruiser with little angst; this simple steel gate scared her. She told her legs to move: they refused.

A burly day laborer sidled around her to take her place. Without comment, he brushed by her and passed through the gate. Standing, holding up the progression might draw attention to her. Andrea willed her fear away. She stepped forward and put her hands on the bar, then pushed her way into the pie-shaped cage. The gate clicked behind her—a sound amplified by her apprehension. She flinched as if she stood in the maws of a man-eating machine. But a second push loosed the catch and the bars opened—immediate relief. Andrea found herself breathing in infrequent shallow puffs. This intense fear was new to her.

She followed the herd onto the train. No seats, everybody stood, holding straps worn smooth by thousands of hands. The clones kept their distance from

Andrea, as much as the press of the crowd allowed. Those closest to Andrea nervously watched her. *Apparently, Hunters do not ride the trains.*

The train accelerated quickly, and the clones expertly shifted their weight to compensate. *Just like commuters back home,* she thought, *but something's very different; something's missing.* Then she saw. The clones carried nothing: no newspapers, books, shopping bags, purses—no flowers, no briefcases. Andrea looked at their clothes, plain overalls with flat, empty pockets. All but one woman, who stood less than an arm's length away: her right pocket bulged.

The clone woman perceived Andrea's stare and she nervously slipped her hand into her pocket, to retrieve or further conceal her possession—a weapon? Andrea didn't know. But under Andrea's continued glare, the clone woman began to shake. *From fear or rage?* Andrea didn't know; didn't care.

Andrea grabbed the woman by her wrist firmly. The woman emitted a hushed, pitiful, "Oh, no!" And she began to weep. Not another soul on the train made a move to help their fellow clone. Andrea firmly pulled the woman's hand from her pocket, and she found clutched in the thin fingers a porcelain teacup and a broken handle. "I don't steal it, I swear. I don't break it neither. They throwed it away. I picks it from the trash, I swear." The woman's eyes pleaded for her life.

Andrea saw that this crowd expected her to summarily execute the petty thief. Any other response might give away Andrea's disguise. Yet, Andrea slowly pushed the woman's hand and teacup back into the pocket. Then she commanded, "Go away."

chapter 13

The crowded train passed through forest, then a patchwork of truck gardens. From the carriage window, Andrea saw men laboring among rows of vegetable plants, harvesting delicacies for the Ordinate. Tanned men stripped to the waist, burnt by wind and sun, gathered fruit from an orchard: food they were forbidden to taste. The train passed under an archway that seemed to be under construction, then turned into a dull urban setting, the precincts.

At each stop, the train disgorged scores of clones, but nobody got on. Each platform was a copy of the last—nothing but a sign identifying the precinct: no cover for inclement weather; no benches, no old people waiting. Even the nearby buildings repeated in colorless monotony: rows of dormitories, even numbers on the right, odd numbers on the left, and a granite cobblestone street down the middle.

The street rose to shallow cement curbs that doubled for sidewalks. She watched a cleaning crew squeegee some antiseptic swill along the sidewalk and gutter into a wide-mouthed storm sewer. Two pair of light rail split the street, and in the distance, Andrea saw bright blue taillights of the railcar stop ahead. Also ahead, she saw a pair of white headlights announce another railcar coming to offload workers from the nearby factories.

At her stop, Andrea left by the train's side door and wandered into Precinct 15, instinctively keeping a keen eye out for Tara 2862. But the more she tried to look clones in the face, the more they averted their eyes to hide from the threat.

The clones, often in identical pairs, stepped aside or crossed the street to avoid her. She was like the shadow of death wandering through the neighborhood. Nobody spoke to her. They merely glanced at her epaulets to ascertain her branch of service and rank—officers could summarily execute judgment on a clone; Hunters had a reputation for doing so. They perused her belt, the holstered gun, short knife—as they picked up or slacked their pace to put more distance between themselves and her weapons. She heard murmurs behind her, curiosity tinged with fear, so she ignored them for the most part. Rather, Andrea focused on the possibility that she might stumble across another Hunter.

The large, complex economy of the clone precincts dwarfed the elegance of Sarhn. Ugly, but the precinct's teeming life required food, shelter, and maintenance. By far, most clones worked to maintain their own numbers. Surplus labor percolated up through many gradations to take the form of luxury goods, the finest bits of food, art, and leisure for the Ordinate. For every clone that made the daily commute to work inside Sarhn, one hundred and fifty clones labored in farms and factories outside the city walls.

Dormitories, six stories high, looked like a long row of beehives or kennels—exposed cement pillars and floors with cinder block and mortar skin, delimited with rows of small windows. No window shades. An occasional houseplant leaned into the glass or the sad face of some overfed house pet—cats mostly.

She found Dormitories 4 and 6, a pair of bleak buildings separated by a narrow strip of untrampled grass and a cement sidewalk. No shrubs. No trees. No sandboxes or playground equipment.

Andrea turned into Dormitory 6, an old building. The cement floor, although swept clean, bore a smooth, stained footpath. Naked ceiling lamps provided cones with intermittent light within the hallway shadows. Steel steps freshly painted with an industrial green led the way to the upper stories. She took the steps and found Room 227.

The door was open, a hand-scrawled sign hung askew above the lintel: Woton's Room. Andrea peered in. The small eight-by-eight cubicle had the barest essentials for furniture, a few items of clothing, and a towel hanging from a wooden peg on the wall. A small handmade clay bowl sat next to the thin mattress on the floor. A net bag of toiletries hung from the doorknob. Scraps of paper—pen drawings, notes, an old identification photograph—hung from the walls by straight pins. And a young man sat in a rickety chair, his chin resting in his hands as he stared out the bare window.

"Are you Woton?"

The clone turned with lethargic ease, rising abruptly upon seeing the black uniform. After an awkward silence, he found his voice. "I'm WTN 932."

"I see." Andrea stepped into the small room. "I'm

looking for a female, Tara 2862. I was supposed to find her here."

The clone's anxiety evaporated upon learning that he was not the subject of the Hunter's inquiry. "She moved. I got her apartment."

"Why did she move?"

"She's got seniority so she gets a newer place. I've only got three years' service, so I get the old building."

"Where did she go?"

"One of the newer buildings, next to the dining hall." With almost civic pride, Woton pointed up the street. "But I don't know which. I have seen her around, though, and you can't miss her."

Andrea was both amazed and saddened at the ease with which the new clone fingered Tara for her, ostensibly a Hunter. "You mean she doesn't look like all TRA models?"

"No, ma'am. The Tara you want wears her hair in a long copper-colored braid—not normal." He shook his head disapprovingly. "This time of day, you might find her or some of her friends at the new dining hall."

"You've been a big help." Andrea turned to go.

Woton sent her away with the slogan, "We live to serve."

Andrea quickly backtracked to the newer dormitories—in no way different from the old except that the building skin was a shade lighter, having endured less mildew and mold stains. She found the small dining hall nestled among the dormitories.

Andrea smelled hot food. She recognized the odor of yeasty bread, but the other smells lacked any hint of spice: a simple smell of simmering beans—maybe an onion thrown in. Many clones, walking in pairs and foursomes, followed the smell to a large hall.

She peeked through a window to see them queued. She looked for a TRA model with a long braid. A plump matron festooned with a long apron issued each a partitioned tray, a spoon, and a cup. Farther down the line each received an issue of bread, a ladle of yellow mash in one partition of the tray and a dollop of a white pudding substance in another. None had the temerity to question the size of a portion, but a few sniffed their meals. Most shuffled down the line with sublime indifference, a herd of gregarious cattle, chattering and grazing.

What clones talked about, Andrea could not guess. They had no families, no possessions to speak of. Their jobs were stultifying, unending repetitions of yesterday's task. They had no recollections of a past beyond a neural imprint, and they had nothing to decide about the future. Yet they sat on benches at long tables, where they spooned their dinner, sipped a weak tea, and pestered each other with animated conversation.

However, not all appeared docile. Andrea studied one of the surly clones. Who else would be the more likely to be in touch with a subversive cell organization? The thick-necked clone wore grease-stained overalls: *A mechanic, perhaps?*

He ate his meal in a hurry, one tray partition at a time, then drank the tea in long swallow. He abruptly finished and shoved his tray aside as he left amidst protests from the neighbors. They pointed to another queue where everyone else took the dirty tray to the conveyer belt. The malcontent brushed off his detractors with a flippant hand gesture and marched to the side door. Andrea left the window and caught him as he reached the sidewalk. "You! Stop!"

The man stopped and slowly turned, curious

enough to pause and note the female voice ordering him to do anything. Up close, Andrea saw the strength in his arms and chest, the white dust on his clothes. This man worked with brick and mortar. He wore his hair in a burr cut. Around his neck, he bore an intricate set of raised welts, like runes, set within a purplish band, a tattoo that circumnavigated his twenty-inch neck. His identification tag read CPP 6124.

His lips were parted as he'd prepared to spit some invective at the nuisance hailing him. Then his eyes betrayed his surprise at finding himself standing before a black uniform. His eyes instantly focused on her hands and weapons and his legs flexed. Andrea knew the clone was calculating his chances, trying to decide whether to attack or flee.

Andrea spoke again. "I just want to talk with you, just talk." She held her hands open.

He made no sound but watched her hands intently, but without the insensate panic of the other clones she encountered. This large fellow intended to do something about his fears. Andrea tried to reassure the brute, but how much can one say in just a few moments, and how much should she divulge about her situation? She said plainly, "I need to make contact with Tara 2862. I hear she has friends that come to this dining hall."

She had barely finished the words when the man leapt at her, smashing her chest with an open palm, knocking her backward to the pavement. Andrea knew enough to fold beneath the heavy blow. She tucked and somersaulted into the street, looking to see her assailant run back into the dining hall. *He's going to warn Tara. He knows where she is.*

Andrea sprinted after him. The large CPP had speed

as well as size. He raced through the long dining hall, straddle-jumping tables. The clone effortlessly shoved tables sideways to block Andrea's path. But each effort cost him distance as Andrea matched him stride for stride. He paused at one end, asking for help, then dashed away through the kitchen doors. His would-be helpers didn't lift a finger as Andrea raced past them, slamming through the swinging doors, slipping on the wet tile floor, falling, crashing into a large stainless steel bin. The CPP model ran between a row of ovens and large steam kettles. He pulled the handles, dumping the bubbling bean mash on the floor, then ran out an exit. *Damn! He's getting away!* Andrea leapt onto a long preparation table that bridged the steaming barrier and scrambled to the end, knocking steel mixing bowls and utensils to the floor.

The footrace continued down a grassy corridor between two dormitory buildings. He was slowing down. Good, if she couldn't beat him with naked speed, she'd wear him down. Obviously, he didn't know how to evade a pursuer. He never stopped to watch his back. He didn't double back. Andrea surmised that the Ordinate manufactured the CPP models for size-seven hats and twenty-inch necks: linear thinkers, and that assessment was charitable. But this fellow had pluck, he made quick decisions, and he knew how to find Tara.

He rounded a corner and scampered down a stairwell, through a metal door into the basement of a dormitory. Andrea followed, pausing a moment to ensure with a gentle nudge that the door was unlocked and unbarricaded. She slipped into the dimly lit room—more of a cavern built of right angles. Steam pipes, air ducts, and other plumbing littered the ceiling.

Oversized pumps and fans occupied cubicles spaced in regular rows and columns. The cement floor was well swept, hardly a particle of dust, not so much as a grease stain. *Maybe he does know how to lose a tail. Never underestimate your opponent.*

She listened for the sound of footfalls; but the whine of the machines masked the other sounds. Andrea stepped briskly from cubicle to cubicle, adding some caution to this hot pursuit. Either she would corner him here in this basement or he must find another exit.

She planned her progress like a chess move, she the rook, always keeping an eye on a column and a row, to box her opponent into a corner. Judging the distance to either wall, she would corner him soon. She passed the building's workshop where idle lathes, bandsaws, and planers stood within a mess of sawdust, wood shavings, and metal filings.

He must be close by. Her pulse quickened. Even if the CPP were thick as a plank, he must expect her to have her gun drawn. He would wait for her in a blind spot, surprise her, probably use some crude weapon, a bludgeon—certainly he had the strength. She quickly surveyed the workshop and saw an arsenal of potential handheld weapons displayed on the wall. A dust barrel displayed lengths of board and metal pipe.

She thought she might dash over and grab herself a sweet piece of pipe, but then what? Would she stand a chance in a quarter staff duel with this ox? Doubtfully. Given his physical strength, he might absorb a half-dozen hits, then land a lethal blow. Andrea took stock of her situation and considered backing out of the building to neutral ground.

But there was no neutral ground on Cor. If she were right about this CPP—and his helter-skelter flight confirmed her suspicions—he could lead the way to Tara. He was part of her cell organization. Consequently, if he escaped, he could alert Tara and send her into hiding, a complication she must avoid. And killing the brute might send just as dire a warning through Tara's cell. She must finish what she started. She must reason with this CPP clone. The very thought brought a wry smile to her face.

She'd finished the boxing maneuver. If he were in the building, he would have to be on the opposite side of this last cubicle. She thought about hailing him, but what would she say: *I need to make contact with Tara 2862?* Didn't work the last go 'round. Andrea left her pistol holstered, but just in case the big man wielded a blade, she put on her black gloves—a fairly standard composite of body armor. She looked right and left for any sign: a shadow, telltale breathing, a bump, a shuffle, anything. She half-hoped he'd found a way out, that she'd round the corner and find an open door.

She took a deep breath, rehearsing in her mind the likely scenarios. All required her to spring to where he wasn't; then maintain a safe distance, draw her weapon if necessary, and pray the ox could be moved to conversation. Andrea jumped around the corner and dove into the open floor, crouched low, rolling on her shoulder, recovering to her feet in a wide stance, her arms raised to parry a blow.

Andrea looked up to find an assembly of four: three men and one woman. She recognized them immediately—the last ones the CPP spoke to before he fled through the kitchen. She'd been drawn to this private setting for a quiet execution. The CPP model approached with a five-pound sledgehammer. The others held less formidable instruments: an eighteen-inch length of one-inch pipe, a claw hammer. The woman held a thick wooden dowel. All seemed eager for a piece of the Hunter.

Escape was impossible, the odds of surviving a melee worse. Should she use her pistol? Kill the ox, perhaps two, maybe. The result would be the same. No, they all seemed poised to rush her without hesitation. Andrea raised her hands. "I surrender."

The CPP clone erupted into belly laugh and began to close his side of the circle around Andrea. Andrea backed up. "Just listen for a minute, please."

They continued to close the circle. The urge to pull her gun grew even as the futility of such a move became more obvious. "I bring a message from Eric 1411 for Tara 2862."

The swarthy male clone spoke. "You lie. Everyone knows that you Hunters killed Eric."

However, the four paused. A tall woman with light brown hair and steel gray eyes restrained the ox with an outstretched arm. Andrea noticed the spark of curiosity—in no manner was it sympathy—from the tall woman. Andrea spoke to her. "I am not an Ordinate Hunter."

"Then explain the uniform."

"I killed the Ordinate woman who owned it. I come from the Earth system by way of Jod."

The CPP clone grunted, "A lie. Don't believe her."

"Coop, stand fast," the clone woman ordered.

Andrea observed the discipline at work here. The four clones seemed to be peers, but somewhat in competition for status within the group. The CPP model shifted his weight impatiently. He had a night's work invested and thus far, he'd been denied his reward of seeing a Hunter's brains splattered. He held his sledgehammer ready to collect his due.

"Listen to me. Let me deliver the message to Tara with the gull wings, and let her judge the truth of it. Imagine Eric's anger when he learns that you killed his messenger. What will Tara do when she hears how you cheated her out of a message from her mate—news that ensures their reunion—"

"Don't listen to the Hunter," the CPP insisted. "Tara warned us what might happen if ever the Ordinate Hunters found us. We can't take that chance." He raised his hammer.

The tall female clone snapped, "Use your brain, Coop. The very fact that she knows about Tara tells us a lot."

The thin male argued, "But Deedo, they probably tortured Eric. They can take information if they want it."

"Then wait four years to use that information? I don't think so. This woman knows Tara's number and hidden mark. She knows Tara's tie to Eric. Think, Coop. If the Hunters knew all this, would they send one woman to make inquiries? No! They'd snatch Tara from her workstation. This woman apparently doesn't know how to contact Tara 2862 directly—not a particularly difficult task for a bona fide Hunter. I don't know who this woman is, or why she's here, but she's no Ordinate Hunter."

Coop lowered his hammer, disappointment registered on his face. Andrea relaxed a bit.

The tall female called Deedo approached saying, "I'm going to take your weapons now. If you so much as flinch, I'll let Coop kill you."

Andrea raised her hands slightly higher. "Understood."

"Good." Deedo undid Andrea's holster flap and removed the heavy pistol. She cocked the hammer back halfway to the safety position. Then, she unsnapped the short sheath and removed Andrea's blade. Then without a sound, she searched Andrea for any hidden hardware, her legs, inside and out, her crotch and buttocks. Andrea stood like a wooden statue as the woman ran her hands up her sides to her armpits, examined the small of her back, even felt her breasts to ensure that the bulges and cleavage were flesh and nothing more.

Deedo stepped aside and continued to walk around Andrea. "You certainly have the physical conditioning of a soldier."

"I am a soldier."

"So what's your name?"

"Flores." Andrea purposefully volunteered nothing more. Their curiosity was her best ally. Let them wait for her audience with Tara to learn her secrets.

"Very well, Flores." Deedo stood behind Andrea bending down to put her mouth just behind Andrea's ear. In hushed tones she added. "We'll take you to see Tara."

From the corner of her eye, Andrea saw the clone woman raise the pistol high like a mallet, hand grasping the cold barrel. Andrea steeled herself for the blow, forcing her neck and shoulder muscles to relax, one of the hardest things she'd ever made herself do.

The pistol fell in one violent stroke. Andrea heard the crack of metal against bone from inside her head. The impact rattled her teeth and her eyes dimmed. She let her conscious mind fade. Her knees buckled as she crumpled to the floor: Her knees struck the hard floor and instinct jerked her arms forward to cushion the fall. Nevertheless, she felt a second whack as her forehead hit the cement. The room spun, as she fell into unconsciousness. She didn't fight it. She'd expected worse.

Thirst. Her first thought was water, water, and an analgesic. A pain that seemed more an itch migrated from a spot on the back of her skull above her left ear down to a throb at the nape of her neck. She tried to raise a hand to feel the wound, but straps retrained her to a metal cot.

Andrea pieced together her last moments of consciousness. How long had she been out? Had they drugged her as well? She lay still as death to observe her situation unmolested. She lay alone in a small anteroom. A trio of male guards—she recognized no one—sat at a table playing a game that involved much banter between moves. Her pistol lay in the middle of the gaming table.

Her room was stark: bare walls with exposed water pipes sweating, no observation cameras, and no windows. She lay on a stiff cot flanked by one wooden armless side chair and a side table. On the table, she saw a cobalt-blue jar of cream and a dwindling roll of bandage, a clean scalpel, scissors and sewing gear—all primitive by any standard. A porcelain bowl held a bloodstained washcloth. Apparently, she'd needed a stitch.

Her black uniform was gone. Instead she wore a clone's standard baggy one-piece suit made of a rugged fiber. The top three buttons were undone. She had no shoes. These people did not mean to kill her—at least not until they studied her. She licked her lips, then calmly addressed the guards. "I'm awake."

All three heads turned in unison. None replied. The oldest of the three grunted an inaudible command, which sent the younger spry clone bounding away with the news.

Andrea didn't have to wait long for results. She recognized the female clone Tara 2862, who stepped through the doorway past the armed guards. The woman carried a terra-cotta bowl filled with fruit. Tara was in every way soft, softer than the picture she'd seen on Jod. Tara's face was more heart shaped than oval. Her hazel eyes were sadder than the picture, but bright and beautiful, watching Andrea intently. Full lips waited, comfortable with silence. Her face was a bit drawn with care. Her skin was perfectly smooth but adorned with freckles about the nose and cheeks. She was full-figured; in no way athletic; indeed, she had small bones and delicate hands with long, precise fingers. Hers was a quiet strength, an inner strength. Tara wore her hair long—a sign of mourning among clone women. Her one thick long braid of auburn hair bisected her shoulder blades.

Unlike the other clones, Tara wore a knee-length smock tied at the waist by a thick copper cord. A sheer undergarment extended from the smock to cover her arms and legs. She wore sandals bound at the ankle with a thinner version of the copper cord. This female clone had stature beyond her average height and build.

Tara set the fruit on the side table, then unfastened the straps that bound Andrea's hands to the cot. She said, "Many of my people think you are just another Ordinate Hunter trying to infiltrate our cell organization."

Andrea sat up. "And what do you think?" She rubbed her sore wrists.

"You would be the first foolish enough to attempt it dressed in a Hunter's uniform. You're no Hunter." Tara handed Andrea a fig.

Andrea ate the fruit. What she really wanted was a cup of water. "I must be sure you really are Tara 2862. May I see your mark?"

Tara raised one of her fine eyebrows as a silent rebuke to Andrea's brazen request. "My adjutant, Coop, told me that you knew my mark." Tara pulled her smock down a bit. A pair of thin powder blue wings stretched above her pectoral muscles as a lazy *M* below her collarbones. The upper edge of the wings was drawn as a crisp navy blue; the under edge was ornately feathered. Andrea wanted to lean forward to inspect the artistry of the tattoo, but she resisted. Tara pulled her smock back up, saying, "I have already seen your mark."

"My mark?" Andrea asked. "I don't have a mark."

"Yes, the red pocks, above your heart, front and back." Tara reached forward and touched Andrea's scar.

Andrea felt Tara's soft fingers probe her old wound, which at that moment felt as fresh as the day she'd bled. The light went out of her eyes as she said, "Scars from a bullet wound."

Tara cocked her head. "A bullet? Straight through you . . . your medical arts must be good for you to survive such a wound." Again, she touched Andrea lightly and, through the cloth, felt the shallow divots dug from Andrea's flesh. "How did it happen?"

Andrea's jaw tightened. She did not want this stranger probing her old wounds; nor did she want to put the memories into words, for doing so brought them back to life. But she told her, "A team of Ordinate Hunters attacked a group of civilians on Earth, killing six, wounding many others. They killed my husband and daughter; they only wounded me."

"That is interesting. So you come to Cor to get revenge."

Andrea felt a grudging admiration for the clone's direct approach to interrogation. No impetuous questions. No rush to learn about Eric. No blasé curiosity, no sentimentality; the clone woman didn't blink at the concept of revenge. How should she answer? Would Tara consider revenge a potent or dangerous motivation? She crawfished her way out of the question. "I am here under orders."

"Whose?" Tara reached into the bowl and retrieved a fig for herself.

"I serve the Jod."

"I've heard of them. The Ordinate fears them. I heard of some clones that fled to Jod space."

"A few made it." Andrea wanted to entice this clone with tidbits of news. She saw the recognition in the woman's eyes. Tara had distilled the essence of Andrea's story from a few short questions.

Then Tara spoke directly. "What do you know about Eric 1411?"

"Eric is alive." Andrea rationed this vital fact with an indifference that meant she had more to share.

At those words, Tara took a deep breath and held it. She struggled to keep her stoic composure, but her eyes shut, pressing a pair of tears down either cheek. "I want to believe you." Tara dabbed her cheeks with her sleeve.

Andrea offered no sympathy but reiterated the fact. "Eric lives on Jod under the protection of Hal K'Rin, an admiral of the Jod Fleet."

"We heard Eric was hunted down and killed. The Ordinate touted his death as the end of his model."

"Obviously, the Ordinate made a mistake. Your Eric has enjoyed relative peace because of that error in fact."

"Is Eric a prisoner on Jod?"

Andrea looked about her cell. "He's enjoying better

care than I am. Eric stays of his own free will as he tries to convince K'Rin to recruit the Jod Council of Elders to your cause. But Eric has no freedom of movement, and K'Rin controls all his contacts."

"How is his health?"

"Fine, I'm sure."

"Well, how does he look?"

"I've never seen him." Andrea admitted. "He sends a message."

This last bit of news sent a shudder of fear through the clone Tara. "Then your report is third hand."

Andrea understood the loss of not knowing. Third-hand reports are less than shadows of the truth, often outright distortions, or sometimes raw magnification. Yet one cannot know the simple *yes* or *no* of it. "Eric is guarded for his own protection. The only danger to Eric is if the Jod decide he's been lying to them." Andrea decided cynically to raise the stakes for Tara and tie her fate to Eric's. She added, "I suppose if Eric's been lying to them, the Jod will hand him over to the Hunters."

Tara's eyes widened. "Eric has no reason to lie about anything."

"The Jod don't know that. K'Rin sent me here to verify Eric's story." Andrea kept a straight face, but inside she smiled. She had just turned this lopsided affair into a standoff. Without saying as much, she inferred that Eric was a hostage. In similar fashion, Andrea tried to suggest that Tara take a personal interest in her safety, saying, "K'Rin takes personal risks protecting your mate."

Both eyebrows raised at the indelicateness of Andrea's use of the word *mate*. Tara scowled and said, "Watch your tongue. It is very dangerous for clones to presume Ordinate prerogatives and bond in that way. Tell me Eric's message."

"Eric wants you to come with me to Jod. There, you two will work in exile to plan the liberation of the clones as the Jod Fleet plans the defeat of the Ordinate. Hal K'Rin sent me to Cor to bring you back to Jod."

Tara wrung her hands. "Eric told me to keep the underground cells alive until his return."

"Apparently he changed his mind. Eric believes he can make an ally of the Jod."

"Or the Jod changed his mind," Tara accused.

"Perhaps. I don't know. Nevertheless, he wants you to bring back proof of the Ordinate's development of the NewGen clone. K'Rin believes NewGen clone technology, if real, threatens Jod, but he must convince others who have the power to act, a Council of Elders, and they won't be moved without strong proof."

"I can show you abundant proof of NewGen clone manufacture."

"Good. Eric also asks for tactical data about Ordinate security forces, Sarhn, and the surrounding terrain."

Tara paused. "I can access that data."

"Also, Eric specifically wants you to bring plans, locations, and inventories by supply cache, and your cell organization. He intends that you both will plan a clone uprising with Jod support."

Tara sat silently staring back at Andrea. *Plans, locations, caches, cell organization:* with such information, the Hunters would eradicate a five-year effort in one bloody week. Andrea understood that such a treasure of information is not casually divulged to an outsider who arrives in a Hunter uniform, despite a good story.

Andrea sensed the reticence. "You don't trust me, do you?"

Tara stiffened. "Not completely; maybe not at all. And here's the little predicament you've forced on me: either I cooperate with you fully, or I kill you. Either way, if I make the wrong choice, all is ruined. You may think I'm grateful to hear this news. I'm not. Eric was supposed to return and make these decisions—not me. I need time to decide."

Andrea boldly interjected, "You don't have much time. None of us do. The Jod are waiting for better information that only you can provide. Eric's waiting. You are waiting for more perfect information about me. And while everybody waits, the Ordinate acts. If you wait much longer, Tara, you won't need to make a decision: the Ordinate will make it for you. And that rather sums up the present relationship between the Ordinate and their clones, doesn't it?"

Tara frowned at her prisoner, this interloper, goading her. She warned Andrea, "Most of my people want you dead. Maybe I should let them rush me into a decision. Or maybe I should take some time to convince them to change their minds . . ."

Andrea paused to reflect on Tara. *There is some steel hidden inside this woman. She just might be able to lead this rabble.* Andrea took a deep breath and withdrew her criticism, saying, "Take your time."

chapter 14

Andrea settled into captivity. The clone guards moved her deeper into a labyrinth of forsaken tunnels to another cheerless four walls of cement, graced with a similar cot, chair, and end table. However, this concrete jail boasted a spigot and a four-inch hole in the floor, and a hand towel. Lime leached from fissures in the damp wall: stalactites hung from the ceiling like small teeth.

She had not seen the sun since she arrived in the clone precinct, and she had only the intermittent arrival of food, and natural periods of fatigue to tell her approximate time of day. Tara made one visit to remove the sutures from Andrea's scalp. Otherwise Andrea had nothing to occupy her mind during the day but memories. At night she fought with cruel dreams: she began on *The Deeper Well* in calm seas, then a storm. Steve and Glendon fall overboard in an ink-black ocean, they cry for help, she stands frozen to the deck, afraid to leap into the water. Steve holds the child above the waves until his strength fails and they both slip under the water . . . she stands frozen on deck, watching. As they disappear into the black water, she screams, *Please don't go!*

"Be quiet in there!" The guards beat on her door, jarring her from the dream. Sweat soaked, she sat up in her pitch-dark cell, panting and confused. All she could think of was, *I'm not afraid of water. Why don't I jump in to save them?*

The guards worked shifts. Andrea watched them through a barred porthole in the door; they huddled in their own conversations: banal talk of food, games, and work. She tried to engage them in conversation, but they ignored her. As much as she chafed at her confinement, she suppressed the very thought of escape, because escape was tantamount to abandoning the mission. She'd already risked her life getting in. But she needed to fill her days and her mind to block her imagination, and exhaust her body so that she might enjoy dreamless sleep. So, Andrea filled the droughts of inactivity with every kind of physical exercise she could manage in her confinement, and she spent many hours crouched beneath the spigot, washing herself and her clothes.

One morning, Andrea woke to the rattle of the iron dead bolt on her door. In stepped Tara and a small cadre. The CPP clone called Coop was with her: he stood in the background and exuded suspicion. Tara wore the simple one-piece work uniform. On a belt she wore a heavy knife. She'd cropped her auburn braid, and her hair seemed a shade redder cut close to her scalp. "Quick! Get dressed. Come with me."

Andrea obeyed. She followed Tara into the corridor with confidence. She tried to hide her relief in stepping out of her cement cell: she'd long determined that if they were going to kill her it would be in her cell. A squad of ten lightly armed clones followed. They walked down many steps into cool damp air. Andrea saw her breath. The cement walls suddenly gave way to the raw chisel marks of cut stone, and the floor became slick from the perpetual dew in this underground world.

As they walked, Tara talked. "The Hunters are searching everywhere for you. They found the mutilated and bloated corpse of a Lieutenant Tapp in a shallow grave on the Chelle planet Clemnos. They know you stole aboard the starcruiser, impersonating Lieutenant Tapp."

Andrea could not suppress a slight smile that earned a rebuke.

"You think that's funny?"

"Just ironic. I had a better time bunked with the enemy than with you."

Tara stopped Andrea with a hand against her sternum. Her face hardened. "Here's another bit of irony. The Hunters have rounded up a thousand clones for questioning. They grabbed two members of my cell. My people are disciplined with reasonable fortitude, yet the Hunters may break one of them. If they learn about our lair in these tunnels, all is lost. You may have brought our destruction."

How could Andrea reply? *I'm sorry?* She didn't feel sorry. *If one waits around long enough to be discovered, one eventually gets discovered.* True enough, her arrival may precipitate a fight, but their destruction? That greatly depended on their fighting ability. Apparently, Tara had no confidence. Why? The clones had a huge advantage in Mass, that is, the overwhelming advantage of numbers. For certain they lacked Knowledge about warfare. But worse, they lacked the Spirit for warfare, the commitment to rise victorious or perish in the attempt.

Every cadet memorized this lethal formula: *No one*

element, be it Spirit, Knowledge, or Mass, is dominant; a combination of any two of these factors gives a strong presumption of success over an adversary relying on one alone, and the three combined are practically invincible against any combination of the other two. The Ordinate had long used their superior Knowledge and an indomitable *Spirit* to negate the clone's overwhelming advantage of *Mass.* Andrea considered the clone's *Mass* an advantage over the Ordinate's *Knowledge.* The warrior *Spirit* held the key.

Andrea knew she must assess the clones' potential for success for K'Rin. On one hand, the great majority of the clones were worse than useless. They cooperated with the enemy. But Andrea had hope for Tara's clones. She'd seen signs of discipline, solidarity, and sentimentality among Tara's cadre. These few clones had some spirit, however, cautious. A dormant spirit can be jolted, perhaps painfully, to alertness. An alert spirit can grow in courage and be disciplined by trial to become a warrior spirit. Had that not happened to her?

These clones needed a leader, but at present, Tara lacked the will to fight. Tara deferred to Eric's stale instructions. She relied on Eric's authority—Eric, who for the past four years had served as the absentee leader of the Underground. *A phantom can't lead flesh and bone.* Andrea saw clearly: Tara—not Eric—must lead these people.

Andrea asked, "Where are we going?" She ducked beneath a concrete rib that buttressed the rock-hewn tunnel.

"I'm going to give you the proof you need to take back to the Jod. Turn right." They came to an intersection in the tunnel and they walked out of the artificial light down a stygian hall. "Now take my hand."

Tara's grip was gentle, warm, neither tugging nor resisting. Tara led the way down a series of turns. In the subterranean black, their eyes were useless. The stale air became thick with the odor of mildew. Then Tara stopped and felt the wall, finding a wheel. With a counterclockwise jerk, she unsealed a hatch that opened, flooding the hall with soft blue light. A guard met them at the door with a pistol in hand. He recognized Tara, and backed away to let her enter.

Andrea stepped through the hatch into a cool dry room. She took a deep breath to clear her lungs. She stepped over a harness of power cables that snaked across the room to a metal crate. Suspended in a clear plastic material, a waffled black cube served as the brains for the room. Tara said, "This room is the nerve center for the movement."

Andrea looked around. The hodgepodge of equipment provided dozens of workstations, but there were no operators. The screens sat blank, saving power. A hand-drawn map of the area surrounding Sarhn hung on the wall beneath clear plastic, but the map lacked any annotations to indicate a plan or even intelligence gathering. A wall of blank screens seemed odd. Did anything happen here? Everything seemed carefully maintained, but scrupulously unused. "Nerve center?" Andrea asked. She bit her tongue to avoid adding, *your organization is in deep hibernation.* She asked, "Are you connected to other precincts?"

"We are connected to two precinct cells with fiber optics passed through tunnels."

"Only two?"

"You must understand, Andrea, all this equipment is refuse we salvage and rebuild. The Ordinate forbids clones from using any unauthorized communications device or computer. If the Hunters found this room, they'd hang us from the city walls. And yes, the machines work: old technology, slow, but the best we have. The other precincts have only the most meager systems. We use runners and infrared signals when needed."

Andrea ran her fingers over a keypad. Powered down, worn, and obsolete, the keypad begged to be brought back to life. "Eric says you're a pretty good hacker. Certainly you've hacked your way into the Ordinate data bases."

"He said that?" Tara smiled at the compliment. "Actually, we access their systems through passive means: side lobes from their low-grade microwave comm links—but they don't pass much data of interest on that system. Instead, we built our data banks by stealing data cubes. Our information technicians purloin a few gigabytes here and there: it adds up. We have about twenty percent of the city's total records."

"Are you processing anything now?"

Tara glanced at the lone technician sponging dust from a workstation. The technician in turn shook her head *no.* Andrea had been correct: not much happened here. She protested, "What are you waiting for?"

"We're just supposed to stay ready."

"Ready for what?" Andrea's voice grated with irritation.

"Eric will tell us when he returns."

"Oh." Andrea felt the urge to shake Tara. *Until I arrived, you thought he'd never return! All your preparations are phony! The initiative belongs to the aggressor. All this waiting serves the Ordinate. Wake up!* Instead she played on what she thought were Tara's chief motives. "Come back to Jod with me. You and Eric can develop a course of action with Jod help."

"I cannot leave my people." Tara's face tensed at these words, and her face revealed an emotion that had eluded Andrea.

This clone, sterile by design, had a maternal instinct for those simple persons left in her care by her mate, Eric. Her maternal instinct eclipsed the affection she had for Eric, and here lay both an opportunity and a hindrance. Her reluctance was not a sentimental attachment to Eric; rather, Tara could not bear the responsibility of making a decision that might cause harm to her wards. On the other hand, she could be motivated to action to protect them from the Ordinate, perhaps motivated to lead. Andrea thought, *I can use this strength of hers: a mother's self-sacrifice, without calculation, beyond fear.*

Andrea carefully probed Tara's maternal instinct. "It may not be enough to be here and die with your . . ." she chose the next word carefully "friends. To save them, you may need to come with me to get help. There is no shame in running for help when the odds are impossible."

Tara said flatly, "No. I can't leave. You can take what information you need back to Jod. You send Eric back to us. I know he'll come back with or without help."

A good mother. A bad decision.

Then Tara turned to her console. "I'll show you what you came for." Tara tapped a few keys and a four-foot screen brightened. The computer's disembodied voice led Tara through an authentication ritual, then waited for instructions. As her fingers danced over the console, Tara said, "Before you can understand NewGen clone technology, you've got to understand the first generation clones. Here's a simple digitized training session used for adolescents at Ordinate schools."

Andrea turned her attention to the screen. She saw the entrance to the Clone Welfare Institute heavy with pedestrian traffic and the dramatic title of the video: Manufacturing and Using Clones. An affable male in a white lab coat entered the screen: "Hello. My name is Doctor Sandrom and I work at the Clone Welfare Institute. I'm sure you've seen our large chrome-and-glass building above our eastern skyline. Today, you're going to learn the fundamentals of manufacturing a clone."

The doctor walked through a series of automatic doors that parted as he approached, never breaking stride. "Our first stop is the clone inception nursery."

The camera panned what appeared to be acres of eight-foot metal shelves holding large translucent bottles of opaque liquid. Lodged in each was a squirming mass—a shadowy and jumbled resemblance of a head, torso, arms, and legs. "We start with carefully selected DNA grafted into eggs harvested from unhatched female clones. Female clones are of course sterile; so the eggs were of no use to them in any case."

The camera shifted to a technician inserting an engineered egg into one of the bottles. "For a period of three months, they grow flesh and bone in a nutrient bath. As the clone gains bulk, you note that the surrounding liquid becomes cloudy. The kidneys have begun to operate and now hygiene becomes a key consideration."

Sandrom beckoned the camera into a second room. It had the aspects of a morgue. Large vertical crystal vats of amber liquid held suspended bodies ranging from small plump children to skinny adults. The adults' long hair drifted through the solution hiding the molded plastic mask that shielded their faces. Wires and catheters hung about the bodies. "After the brain, heart, liver, kidneys, and other vital organs demonstrate functionality, we transfer the human-shaped larva to a cocoon—these crystal tanks you see—in which the larva grows to maturity. The process takes another four years. We fit each larva with auditory pipes, an ocular mask, and neural cables."

A close-up showed a set of neural cables entering the back of a pale neck at the hairline. "The cables administer stimuli to stress the muscles and build strength. In the early stages of development, we use a combination of the ocular mask, auditory pipes, and neural stimuli to manage the other senses and thereby maintain a quiescent state, or state of bliss. You might think a clone is unhappy. But when you see the clone larva writhe in the solution, pressing against the crystal shell, contorting into a ball or stretching, you really see reflex actions designed to give the clone strong bones and muscles. Be assured that at the same time, within the larva's mind, the growing creature enjoys a sedate pleasure. All clones long to return to this state of sublime satiation. The cables, pipes, and mask fill the senses in a balance much like a pleasant dream. Gestation is a happy time for these creatures. In fact, you'll often see clones gaze upon the Institute with fond memories."

Tara stopped the digitized presentation. "What he said is true. Most clones remain docile on the premise that their good service shall be rewarded at retirement, when a grateful Ordinate returns them to this bliss."

"Back to the womb."

Tara did not understand the allusion. "No. The retirees are never seen again. I can't prove it, but I suspect retirees are dissolved into nutrients and fed to new larva. That's the practical answer for disposing depreciated clones, and I can't account for the mass otherwise." She pressed a console button to animate Dr. Sandrom.

"At approximately twenty months, the larva reaches the juvenile stage and shows signs of sentience. We start getting active feedback through the neural cable." The picture changed to a close-up of the pale face of an adolescent girl suspended in a large canister of liquid. The long hair captured tiny bubbles, causing it to rise upward and out of the child's face. The hair flowed slightly in eddies caused by the body's slight movements. The girl wore black goggles, the ocular device Dr. Sandrom spoke of. Tubes protruded from her ears and a thin insulated cable wrapped loosely around her throat, piercing the skin in the back of the neck just below the hairline.

Sandrom continued, "Now comes a very delicate procedure, called the neural imprint. We use a combination of the ocular mask, auditory pipes, and neural cable to give the maturing clone as much language as it needs. We teach the repetitious motor movements needed for the programmed job assignment. Plus we give the clone a background memory to help it assimilate into society."

Andrea glanced sideways at Tara and wondered what artificial memories still resided there. The soul is the treasury of our memories. She sensed that the damage done to these inoffensive clones was beyond her ability to grasp. Andrea grit her teeth and faced the screen.

The camera followed a neural cable from the back of the female's neck to a small harness at the base of the canister. Then accelerating, the camera followed the harness to an intersection of many lines, feeding to a trunk and into a large computer. Off camera, Sandrom commented, "The institute's computers serve as the nervous center for the developing clones. We interact with more than two hundred thousand clones at a time and customize neural imprints according to specific requisitions. Moreover, for the safety of our citizens, we imprint a strong reluctance toward violence."

Tara paused the program to comment, "That statement is part propaganda. Clones become less docile in time." She immediately resumed the presentation.

Sandrom's voice continued. "The neural imprint process is long and tedious—taking almost twenty-four months to complete. But the results are worth the effort."

The scene changed abruptly from the institute to a long greenhouse filled with red lettuce and a crop of gnarled squash. "The hatchling arrives with all the basic skills needed to be productive. For example, an RBT model used for hydroponics farming arrives programmed to know the precise sequence and quantities of minerals and nutrients required for the crops grown at the specific farm where we assign it to work. The hatchling can leave the institute after seventy-two hours' observation for quality control, then report to work." With a close-up of the industrious RBT clone, Sandrom's voice continued, "The clones live simple, happy lives serving the society that creates and sustains them. And so the harmony of nature is maintained."

Tara turned the screen off. "He goes on to explain that the clones need Ordinate supervision as much as the Ordinates need clone labor; that ours is a symbiotic relationship and that any threat to the system is a threat to both species."

"To both species? I can certainly see how you are a threat to the Ordinate. Do clones believe you threaten the clone species as well?"

"Most definitely. Our neural imprints provide us a virtual past—artificial memories, and those memories are of people like this Dr. Sandrom, smiling, holding our hand, speaking with us for hours, defending us from other abusive clones, healing our hurts, and protecting us from the forces of nature. Like most young clones I carried cut flowers to the institute barrier on the anniversary of my parting. Even today, you see mounds of withered flowers, small baskets of food, and handicrafts left as offerings. Most young clones hope the institute will remember them in a good light and take them back at the time of their retirement."

"But you changed." Andrea marveled at the complacency. "You lost your strong tie to the institute."

"The memory imprints fade. After a couple of years working, one cannot help but realize the indifference of the Ordinate in general and the cruelty of Hunters in particular. For most of us, fear of being canceled replaces the fatuous hope of returning to preparted bliss. Most of us get to work for twenty years, then . . ." she snapped her fingers, "we retire. Larva food."

"I see."

Tara folded her arms, leaned back in her chair and her voice filled with pride. "Here's a bit of clone psychology for you. The memory imprints fade, mostly because we are a species consumed with curiosity. For those of us working in Sarhn, we wonder what's the difference between an Ordinate and a clone? And we chew that question day in and day out, because we can find no satisfactory answer. A clone working as a swineherd, almost as dumb as the animals she watches, still watches the sow breed, bear a litter of small pigs, then suckle them. Of course she wonders, why are those teats, so essential to animal husbandry, a useless decoration on the clone female? In a short time, a clone comes to understand that our existence is unnatural. Consider the plumber or a mason: they get an idea how to better work their craft—an idea! Where do ideas come from? Not from any neural imprint, I tell you. None of us are manufactured for art, yet one dreams up a melody, another becomes adept at tattoos, another thinks of a joke. How can a drudge be inspired?"

Andrea looked around at the ingenious kludge of discarded computer equipment and murmured, "The flaw in the old-order clone is creeping self-awareness."

"Yes!" Tara exclaimed. "But we were never able to overcome our reluctance to do violence to the Ordinate, whom we consider our parents. We might run away and hide, but never raise a hand against the Ordinate. Anyone that would even talk violence was obviously sick in the mind, and we'd hand them over to the Ordinate to be canceled." She shook her head. "As a species, we don't understand."

Andrea pondered this strange contradiction: the Ordinate infusing a reverence for life into these clones. She reiterated Tara's point. "You became aware of what? Justice?"

"In part. Older clones began to resent the Ordinate and some began to make trouble—even steal and avoid work. The Ordinate was manufacturing clones in greater numbers, and they did not want to increase the size of their security force—that is, they didn't want to increase their force with Ordinate personnel. So seven years ago, they introduced an experimental hybrid: the

ERC model, a clone constable to augment the Ordinate Security Force. The ERCs were different from other developmental efforts."

"How so?"

"They didn't use the standard genetic library at the Clone Welfare Institute. They used the old methods—very slow, complex. They started with a Beta model using some genetic material from an Ordinate donor—truth be known, probably from the best Hunter they could recruit. They hatched the Betas young, at thirty pounds, then they manipulated the genes for desired qualities: strength, coordination, intelligence, and sterility. Basic lab experimentation. Some Betas died in the process. They saved the best Beta from which they harvested genetic material. They canceled the rest. Next they created a limited production model for operational tests before going to full production."

"Your Eric was a prototype?" Andrea watched Tara pace the room.

"Yes. He's the Batch 1 Nursery 4, Number 11. They manufactured two hundred prototypes here at the institute. The neural imprint was designed to make the ERCs intensely loyal to the Ordinate. Eric told me of visions from his artificial memory—memories of rapacious clones attacking his parents. According to his memory, he saves his parents and the Ordinate lionize him for his courage.

"Eric and his fellow prototypes worked in teams of four, patrolling the precincts, wearing a facsimile of a Hunter uniform. They were armed, skilled in fighting, and ruthless. We called them the Ordinate's Wrath. Soon, even the most complacent clones who still worshiped the Ordinate grew to fear and despise the ERCs. That was the Ordinate's first blunder: they created an object for our loathing. Before the ERC model, we had never loathed anyone but ourselves."

Andrea sat forward in her chair trying to absorb the volumes of information thrown at her, trying to analyze and test the assertions.

Tara's voice softened. "Then even for Eric, the imprint began to fade. Not only did Eric feel used, but used as a scourge against his own kind. He recruited other ERC models and they banded together to strike back at the Ordinate. They ambushed a patrol of Ordinate regulars and the conflict began. Eric had more than one hundred twenty-five men under his command. I met him then. I brought him bits of information from the institute." Tara raised her chin and looked Andrea in the eye. "I was his eyes and ears."

And so much more. Andrea took the measure of this voluptuous clone and might have smirked, but she saw steel in Tara's soft eyes—a look that answered a question she dared not ask. Tara did not defy the Ordinate because she loved Eric. The reverse was true. She loved Eric because he defied the Ordinate. Tara picked Eric because he might accomplish for her what she was afraid to attempt on her own. *Typical, yet ironic. He's gone; she's here.*

Instead, Andrea asked, "What happened then?"

"One of Eric's men betrayed them and led the ERCs into a trap. Eric escaped the slaughter, but the Hunters killed and captured one hundred seventeen others. They hanged them from the city walls, and there the bodies rotted until the citizens had them removed to quell the stench. They canceled all the rest of the ERC models as flawed—including the traitor. Only Eric survived, because I hid him in this room. We slept on the floor." Tara motioned with her hand to the bare concrete where Andrea stood. "Back then, this room held nothing but vermin and Eric. I spent all my off-duty hours here, helping him. The Ordinate mounted an intense hunt for Eric, who hid in my care for six months. He taught a few of us to use weapons. I designed a cell system to block infiltration."

"Why didn't you recruit another force?"

"Everyone was afraid. The smell of rotting corpses was too fresh in our minds. Plus, Eric has no patience for the old-order clones. The only ones willing to fight are the old ones due to retire. The Hunter's sweep came within two blocks of this safe house. Eric felt his presence was too great a danger for us. Finally, Eric fled to get help when we learned about the NewGen experiments. He said we might get help from Earth."

"Why Earth?"

"The Ordinate talks about Earth as if the Earth people were clones. But we knew that Earth was older than Cor with billions of people. If the Ordinate despised Earth, then Earth would most likely help us."

Andrea nodded, but she thought, *Non seqitur. Eric was lucky to end up in Jod.*

Tara continued, "Eric infiltrated the Sarhn spaceport and hijacked a freighter bound for the Chelle system, and that was the last we saw him. Clones have bribed their passage or slipped away in cargo holds before, but Eric's was the first hijacking—created a great stir." Tara smiled feebly. "He's been gone so long."

Tara returned to her console, sat in a swivel chair, and tapped the color-coded keys. The screen revived and she said, "Now watch. We copied the record of some of the NewGen prototype tests. You can take a copy back to Jod."

A monotone voice announced, "NewGen Prototype:

First Battery Tests." An Ordinate technician explained how they placed a barrel of burning white phosphorus in the middle of an industrial kiln that could handle extreme temperatures. Three identical NewGen clones stood at attention nearby. Each wore a military-style uniform and held a hose connected to a backpack of pressurized water. The NewGens were strong, well proportioned, and pleasant to look upon. They carried the heavy-water packs with ease. They listened intently to instructions. One could see intelligence in their eyes, but no hint of humor, no sense of irony, no mischief, no foibles. Andrea added, *no spark*. They nodded to signify comprehension, and the test began.

The voice narrated the action. "This test demonstrates the NewGens' suppressed survival instinct, their ability to perform complex tasks, their ability to learn, their incomparable obedience to unambiguous orders, and their extremely high tolerance of pain. Here, the first NewGen receives orders to extinguish the white phosphorus fire."

The first NewGen entered the kiln. He edged his way to the fire and unleashed the water. The barrel nearly exploded from enhanced combustion, splashing hot liquid back onto the NewGen. The clone flinched at the pain, but continued to pour water on the fire. The voice said, "The NewGen is unaware that water poured onto a white phosphorous fire creates phosphoric acid, one of the few materials that can dissolve bone in moments."

The camera zoomed in to see the NewGen's flesh bubbling and steaming from the splash of acid. Now blind, the NewGen sprayed water in the direction of the heat for a few moments until death spared him more agony.

The narrator continued, "The second NewGen has witnessed everything, yet upon receiving orders to extinguish the fire, he goes into the kiln, taking only the precaution of first dousing himself with water."

Andrea watched in awe as the scene repeated. The phosphoric acid melted away the flesh and bone, and the second NewGen collapsed with a perpetual grimace beside the first. She could not believe the sadistic third trial. The third NewGen tried to smother the flame by stuffing the two corpses of his fallen brethren into the white phosphorous barrel, a tactic that spawned billowing smoke, yet failed to subdue the fire. Then the NewGen rigged the three hoses to deluge the fire. Getting as close as one might stand the heat, the NewGen doused the fire, causing a brutal splash of acid that corroded the flesh from his bones. Hair burnt to the scalp and ears melted away, the NewGen finally groaned in protest as he watched the flesh peel from his arms. In a futile attempt, the third NewGen, now groping about, tried to smother the inferno by throwing himself onto the burning white phosphorus.

The screen flashed an antiseptic "End of Test," then faded to black. Tara said, "That is the NewGen clone. And in less than six months, the production models begin to hatch. The Sarhn Clone Welfare Institute has the capacity to generate about two thousand clones per day. We know that they've stopped manufacturing old-order clones. Yet the institute is running at full capacity."

"So you expect two thousand NewGens per day . . ." Andrea ran her hand through her short black hair. *Sixty thousand each month. Already disciplined, in a crude sense, for combat as they emerge from their crystal cocoons. All these NewGen clones need is transport and weapons. The Ordinate will have transferred the advantage of Mass to themselves.*

Tara continued. "As far as we know, Sarhn has the only clone factory that has begun NewGen production. After their disastrous experiment with the ERC model, they understandably proceed with caution."

"That might buy us a little time."

"A little." Tara raised her hands only to let them fall limp in her lap. "I see a future in which there are no old-order clones. As the NewGens hatch, we become obsolete. They've accelerated the retiring. When they have enough NewGens in service, I expect the Ordinate will kill us off with starvation—or worse. Even then, most of my people will do nothing. They think, *perhaps the Ordinate will overlook me until my time to retire. After all, my job is essential . . .*" Tara laughed bitterly with acute self-awareness. "An indispensable clone!"

"Why do you wait?"

Tara snipped, "I don't know what to do." She shifted in her seat. "But I suppose we've got to try something. I don't want to be the last of my kind."

Someone to come after me . . . my children. Andrea thought she could never hate the Ordinate race any more than she did, but now the NewGen threat seemed to climb over the dead bodies of her husband and child to jeer at her. The Ordinate view of life was clear: either you are at the top or the bottom; either an Ordinate or no better than a clone. And losing your place at the top dooms you to a life at the bottom. No such thing as peers. And who might upset their world order? Species who refuse to relegate themselves to the bottom: the Jod, and in a pinch, the equivocating Terrans, even the meddling Chelle, or the placid Artrix.

The Ordinate would be tough adversaries in the best of circumstances. The NewGen technology tipped the scales hard in the Ordinate's favor.

Andrea agreed with Tara's assessment of Ordinate intentions: grow a cadre of NewGens soldiers to protect NewGen propagation, then replace the old-order workers with the more efficient NewGen model. The barkeep's casual reference to five hundred new light attack ships echoed in her brain. K'Rin's worst fears were about to come true. The Ordinate would build ships and raise clone armies to eradicate the species of the other systems. Thereby, they reduce the equation to Ordinate and clone and ensure Ordinate dominance. Andrea asked, "How many clone factories do the Ordinate have?"

"They operate seven factories on Cor. Sarhn's is by no means the largest. They're building their largest factory south of here in the city of Qurush. Word in the city is that the Ordinate plan to subdue the Chelle outworld of Clemnos and build a series of NewGen factories there."

Andrea calculated NewGen production in her head. Sarhn would start with seven hundred and twenty thousand NewGens in the first year. If Tara was right and the Ordinate converted all their capacity to the NewGen model, they would within five years start hatching more than twenty million of these perfect soldiers each year, and they could increase the rate of production exponentially. These NewGens feared nothing, and the Ordinate would spend them like munitions.

Andrea placed her hand on Tara's shoulder. "I believe we can make a strong case that the fate of Earth, Jod, Chelle, and Artrix is indeed the same as the fate of the old-order clone."

"Then, the Jod will help us."

"Yes. But the Jod will need a year to mobilize a galactic campaign."

"We don't have a year!" Tara stood. "Eric should have come back. Now it may be too late."

"It's only too late if we do nothing. How many people do you have in your Underground organization?"

Tara thought the question offtopic, but she answered rather than argue. "Two hundred and thirty-seven. Some of them are too old."

"We can buy a year's time."

Tara looked deep into Andrea's eyes. "How?"

Andrea took her by the shoulders and said, "We must destroy the first NewGen crop while they are all still in the nest."

Tara threw up her hands. "Oh, right! Just like that! We operate in small cells of three and five. I've never even met the great majority of the Underground—secrecy is our only defense." She stepped backwards, stumbling on one of the thick cables, righting herself.

Andrea pursued. "It's time we go on offense."

Tara shook her head, objecting strongly. "I don't know who's trained to fight. Eric never taught me or any of us how to organize an attack. Without Eric here, who'd plan such an operation? Anyway, who'd be crazy enough to attack the institute? They keep a garrison of their best troops inside the perimeter. Who will lead?"

"You will."

Tara sat down on the stool, her shoulders slumped under the weight of this promotion. She muttered, "I can't. I'm a TRA model, designed for clerical work, programmed with some light problem-solving abilities. I have no physical strength. I have little mechanical ability. I can manage the cell organization like a data maintenance problem, but plan an assault on the institute? What you suggest is beyond the scope of my programmed capabilities."

"No!" Andrea slammed her hand on the table, jolting Tara into eye contact. "Nobody can keep you programmed." She spit out the word as if it were a piece of putrefied meat. "Unless you want to stay programmed. Listen to me, Tara. You must lead. I'll help you plan; I'll help you fight. But these people need you to lead them. They will become your physical strength, but you must have enough spirit for all of them."

Tara wiped her hands on her pants legs. "I suppose it's the only way. Maybe—"

Andrea interrupted. "No maybes. Either you lead your people to victory or we all die in the effort."

chapter 15

While Tara worked her normal shift at the Clone Welfare Institute, Andrea prowled the tunnels escorted by one of Tara's lieutenants, an older renegade male clone, Gerad: a GRD model—an agricultural laborer by design. He looked like he'd spent the better part of his twenty years' service baling hay and feeding cattle—becoming more like one of the taciturn brutes he tended.

The escort was no longer to protect Tara's cell organization from Andrea, but to protect Andrea from her cell members. Many Underground clones still distrusted the outsider, Andrea, and they openly debated the wisdom of letting this so-called Earth woman live.

Despite suspicions, Andrea was much safer hidden in the tunnels. The loyalists above thought Tara's Underground a dangerous aberration that caused enmity between the Ordinate and the clone, exacerbating an otherwise tolerable situation. They'd turn Andrea over to the security forces and feel patriotic about the deed. Hunter teams combed the precincts looking for Andrea, threatening reprisals to the whole precinct for harboring the fugitive. Indeed, many loyalist clones organized search parties during their time off as an act of good faith. So Tara limited Andrea's freedom to exploring the dimly lit, dank tunnels.

Tara assigned Gerad to act as Andrea's guide and protector. She outfitted Andrea with their standard clone work clothes to which she added a belt and knife. This eleven-inch blade of clone design had a spike point and a serrated edge. The handle was thick cast steel, the butt end splayed for a better grip and to act as a hammer or bludgeon.

Gerad had a sun-wrinkled face more recently pallid from too much time in the tunnels. This cowherd had many physical aspects of his wards: thick neck, big head, and sad brown eyes. His mark was a pair of notches cut in his left ear. He seemed wary of everyone, programmed to stay alert for predators.

Gerad quietly steered Andrea through the tunnels, answering her questions as best he could. Andrea looked through the labyrinth carved from solid rock and asked Gerad, "Who built these tunnels?"

He answered. "Clones carved these more than three hundred years ago. They cut blocks of rock from two hundred feet below the surface and hauled them to the city. Dangerous work, so the storytellers say. They built the big wall with the block."

"How far do the tunnels go?" Andrea pointed down an unlit corridor: it disappeared quickly to black.

Gerad shrugged his shoulders. "No one knows for sure, yet. We have maps of two hundred miles of tunnels. The tunnels link more than fourteen million square feet of open space—including some large caverns carved from the rock. We have some underground ponds—perfectly still: the water casts back light like a black mirror. Some tunnels go under other precincts. Be careful. Even we clones sometimes get lost in here—you can wander in circles till your light goes out."

Andrea looked down a dark lonely tunnel: *wander in circles until your light goes out—just like ordinary life.* Only two simple precautions needed: don't go alone; take light sticks. Andrea calculated the amount of living space in the tunnels and she surmised that the underground labyrinth could shelter half a million people. "Why do so few clones join the resistance to the Ordinate?"

The grizzled Gerad thought a moment and replied, "Some of us know what we know. The others, they don't know. Most never find out."

"Find out what?"

"I show you now." Gerad beckoned with his large hand. They walked to the end of a tunnel, then stepped through a fresh cut in the wall, buttressed with an arch of fresh masonry block laid by his own farmer hands, he proudly pointed out. The narrow passage led to a lime cave, dimly lit and populated with as many people as shadows. Andrea was taken by the strangeness of what she saw: old people with white hair, thin and pale, most of them engaged in some way to take care of the infirm.

"What is this place?" Andrea asked. She winced at the odors: pungent antiseptics, urine, putrefaction, and cooked cabbage.

"Hagion—the hiding place." The smell of sickness and death didn't disturb Gerad.

"And who are these people?"

"These people didn't retire. They ran away. They get old here." Gerad smiled impishly. "I ran away, too. I finished my twenty years' work. On the last day, they think

I go to the institute to retire. But am I a fool? I raised dairy cows for the Ordinate. I see the transport come take old cows away and give me young cows. Somebody eats old cows, I figure. So I work twenty years, knowing what I know, and they think they can treat me like an old cow? Not me. I know." Gerad winked.

Andrea stood in the man-made cavern and gaped. "I would think the Hunters would look for so many missing clones."

"They think we run away to the wilderness to die. Many do. The younger, healthy renegades flee to the wild to join Brigon's tribe. But Brigon won't take just anybody, just those he can use. If he doesn't take you into his tribe, you die alone in the wilderness. That's why most sensible renegades work in Tara's cells for food and bed till we are too slow. Then we spend the rest of our time in Hagion. Come."

Andrea gabbed Gerad's shirt and stopped him. "Brigon? Who's Brigon? Tell me about Brigon's tribe."

Gerad looked away. "Nomads. They hunt and steal."

"Steal from whom?"

"From us, who else?" Gerad reared back, surprised by Andrea's lack of understanding. His voice fell to an angry whisper. "Brigon's men steal our cattle, our materials—always want electronics and metals. A precinct clone is caught between the Ordinate and Brigon. Some help Brigon pilfer. They hope that when their time comes, Brigon takes them into his tribe."

Andrea lowered her voice to a whisper as well to keep Gerad's information flowing. "And who is Brigon?"

"The old one. He grew up in the wilderness."

"Grew up?" Andrea thought she'd misunderstood. "Don't the Hunters search for Brigon's tribe?"

Gerad tensed, seemingly annoyed at these basic questions. "The wilderness is a death trap to Ordinate. No surface water. The spur toad, the brown spider, the Cor adder, the fire lizard, the beaded hornet—all of them—bite or sting with a neurotoxin that kills you fast. Even what's not poisonous, can kill you. The pungee flies lay their eggs under the skin. When they hatch, you watch their little white worms eat your flesh—spreading sores that turn to rot. Hunters figure the wilderness kills renegades. What do they care how a clone dies? They never see Brigon's tribe, so they think they're all dead. Brigon knows how to hide."

She'd seen the tip of the wilderness during her descent into Sarhn, and she comprehended the vastness. A clone might reach the wilderness in a two-day march, then meander for years like a speck of dust tossed about a wasteland. Andrea pressed. "But if precinct clones report thefts by Brigon, won't the Ordinate investigate?"

"You don't know." Gerad folded his big arms and tried to dismiss her question. "Forget about Brigon's tribe."

"I want to know. Why doesn't the Ordinate investigate Brigon's theft?"

Gerad looked about nervously. "The Ordinate says that precinct clones lie about the Brigon thefts to hide their own pilfering or to cover their own losses. Precinct clones don't want trouble. We fake inventory: a diseased cow, wind-damaged crop, we don't get punished. But Ordinate punish us for theft. They can catch us. They never see Brigon's tribe. If you tell Ordinate that Brigon stole your cow, Ordinate thinks you stole the cow. They cancel you for stealing. Better to keep mouth shut or say cow fell in river."

"Did Brigon ever steal your cows?"

Gerad's eyes sparkled as he admitted, "Many cows."

"Where did Brigon come from?"

"He's the clone child—the old one." Gerad grit his teeth. "Now I've told you everything I know about Brigon."

I knew it! Eric's story is true! A clone had conceived—the old-order technology is flawed. Andrea resisted the temptation to ask another question: She'd raise the subject later when Gerad was more amenable. They walked forward, stepping gingerly around pallets on the ground, soiled heaps of clothes, and bowls filled with water or scraps of food.

As they pressed farther into the cavern, Andrea began to hear low groans. They stepped into a misshapen ward of natural origin, carved from the rock by a relentless trickle of water. The floors were leveled with coarse gravel. Cots lined a damp wall that glistened like so much melted wax, and in the cots men and women lay dying.

Andrea bent over a cot to view an ancient man taking shallow gulps of air, his eyes squinted shut in pain, his cheeks sunken, his jaw slack. She was simultaneously repulsed and drawn to this skeleton covered with skin, aware of nothing but the pain in his body. A wet cloth lay in a porcelain bowl by the cot, and Andrea took it to wet the dying clone's chapped lips. A drop of water trickled down the man's chin through wisps of a beard. A slight quiver in the jaw was all the thanks the old man could muster. The eyelids opened and opaque eyes acknowledged this simple kindness as something to remember in the last few hours of life. Gerad remarked reverently, "He knows. Life is pain."

Gerad led Andrea to a closed room staffed by a

gray-haired woman. The birdlike woman restrained a young male clone by placing her hand against his sternum; then the two of them, patient and doctor, tugged his wrist to set a fractured radial bone. The much younger male clone bleated as the woman jerked his arm. She praised the young male for his stifled howl, his stoic restraint. Andrea turned to Gerad. "Don't they have a bone knitter?"

Gerad observed the crude medical procedure without comment. The old woman overheard, and her voice betrayed years of frustration. As a PTR model nurse, she'd practiced the healing arts with the best technology in the institute. "No, we don't have a bone knitter. We have only the old ways medicine to offer these people: old ways and the peace of death. We have poppy crystal to numb the pain." She did not turn around but continued to tie a bundle of flexible rods around the broken arm. "You must be the Earth woman we've heard about."

"I am."

The old woman turned and offered Andrea one of her delicate hands in a gesture of friendship. "I'd pause to chat, but I've got patients waiting. Later perhaps. Stay well."

Gerad and Andrea left the clinic in the cave past her line of patients: one dabbing a septic wound, another shivering while wrapped in a blanket, yet another with a fist-size tumor growing from the base of the skull. "Some of these people are too young to retire. Why don't they get their medicine from the Ordinate?"

"Times are changed. Once the Ordinate used to repair clones—good medicine—but for many months now, a clone goes in for repairs and never comes back. They cancel the sick and wounded now."

"The young man with the broken arm, will he go back to work, then?"

"Impossible. He's a renegade now, like it or not. Taking a cure outside the institute is a crime. The Ordinate cancel him sure now. If he's lucky, that young one will join Brigon's tribe. Brigon will take him into the wild to live out his time."

Again, this Brigon fellow. Andrea seized this opening. "Why didn't you go to Brigon's tribe?"

Andrea saw that Gerad had become uncomfortable with these questions and more reticent: he had much more useful information that he refused to volunteer. Silence; then a petulant, "I'm too old."

"Why doesn't the precinct Underground work with Brigon?" Andrea tried to keep the discourse alive. "Brigon's tribe and Tara's clones are natural allies."

"Brigon doesn't work *with* anybody. Brigon doesn't like precinct clones. He thinks he's better than clones, but I think not. He is the child of a clone, after all."

Ironic, the clone child thinks he's better than his clone parents. How lonely. Who taught him that rubbish? The parents, likely. She looked at Gerad, who spoke with such an air of authority about the child and the mother, yet he had no clue. At best, Gerad applied the simple calculus of animal instinct to this extraordinary mother and child. She didn't have the time or the patience to try to fill the giant gap in Gerad's experience. Instead, she stayed with practical matters. "I think you mean Brigon doesn't respect you."

Gerad became defensive. "Brigon thinks the precinct clones are weak because we cling to our few comforts here. He thinks we are fools—giving twenty years' service in exchange for a painless retirement. He says we are sheep and need to be shorn, if not by the Ordinate, then by him. Also," Gerad added as if it were the ultimate rebuttal, "most precinct clones don't like Brigon either."

Andrea said, "You agree with Brigon, don't you?"

Gerad's face flushed. "He's not Ordinate, and he's not clone. Yet, he is still alive, so he must know something." Gerad turned his back to Andrea, a sure sign he did not want to talk about Brigon anymore.

Brigon knows what he's not. But does he know what he is? Andrea pressed. "Maybe I'll get to meet Brigon and he can tell me about himself."

A flustered Gerad replied, "Nobody sees Brigon just because they want to. Nobody. Brigon chooses to be seen."

"Of course." Andrea smiled to signal that she'd dropped the matter. She'd peel another layer of information off Gerad at another time.

Later that evening, Tara rushed into the subterranean dormitory where Andrea slept. Tara was rain-soaked, her suit stuck to her skin, her short hair matted into short red spikes. Her shoes squished as she left puddles in her footsteps. She shook Andrea and in a forced whisper, bid her "Wake up."

Andrea sat up straight, instantly alert. "What's up?"

Tara pointed to the ceiling. "We have perfect weather for reconnaissance: an electrical torrent. Don't you hear it?"

Andrea did. Even fifty feet of rock could not attenuate all the *crack-boom!* and rumbling.

Tara tossed Andrea's work clothes onto the cot, then talked while Andrea dressed. "The kkona wind blows up the coast dragging ten-mile-high clouds. When they strike the cold night air coming down from the mountains, they can dump up to eight inches of rain in a matter of hours. And the lightning! The electromagnetic flux scrambles the Ordinate's sensors. The lightning forces the Ordinate to shut down their communications."

Andrea pulled her boots on, sensing the urgency in Tara's voice.

Tara helped Andrea dress, handing her a belt with the sheathed knife. "I don't understand the physics, but they use a laser uplink to their satellites. The laser links set off a stream of ions that attract lightning. So the whole city of Sarhn practically goes off line during a kkona storm—two, three, sometimes four hours. The security teams go to shelter and wait for the storm to pass. So we're going topside for a bit of reconnaissance."

"It's about time. What are we going to look at?"

Tara glanced sideways to make sure others couldn't overhear. "We're going to a hill on our side of the barrier where we can see the institute, the security forces' barracks, and the spaceport. We're going alone. It's too early to involve Coop and the others."

"Involve them in what?"

Tara wiped some rain from her face. "I've been thinking about what you said—about destroying the New-Gen crop."

"And?" Andrea smiled, trying to wheedle some kind of commitment from Tara.

Tara stiffened. "I think we can do it. I've got some ideas."

They stopped by the armorer, where Tara took two pair of night goggles, weatherworn equipment reassembled with glue and wire and jerry-rigged with a clumsy alternative battery. She admonished Andrea to use the night goggles sparingly. She offered Andrea a poncho against the rain. Andrea refused. Too much loose clothing restricts movement. She'd rather be uncomfortable than constrained. Tara insisted they both take earplugs: "Trust me. You'll want these . . ."

Earplugs? Fifty feet below the surface, the ominous thunder sounded like timpani—dramatic music announcing Andrea's return to the surface—the louder the better. Andrea snapped the buckle on her utility belt and followed Tara through a long maze of tunnels.

Tara took Andrea to the "back door," a vertical shaft dug to the surface, lost within a cluster of nitrogen silos at a fertilizer plant on the outskirts of the precinct. Andrea climbed the ladder first: she had to use all her might to press the rusty hatch door open. Water spilled into the opening, drenching them both, nearly knocking Tara off her perch.

Outside. Breathing air untainted by the smell of mold spores, cement, and paint, Andrea climbed into the driving rain. Pellets of cold water smacked her back as she bent down to grab Tara's hand and haul her out. The sky flashed with a web of splendiferous blue and white sheet lightning. Farther west, more shafts of lightning split the sky. Despite the downpour, the flashes illuminated the heavy black clouds like giant paper lanterns—enough to cast shadows. Scores of cement silo covers stood above the waterline like lily pads floating in the ankle-deep water. Heavy wind gusts lifted sheets of spray from the ground.

What had been rumblings below the surface amplified to a head-splitting concussion. Both women quickly dug their earplugs from their pockets and jammed them into their ears. Then, they sealed the shaft cover.

The air smelled of electrically discharged ozone. Andrea had never seen such pyrotechnics even in the calamitous September squalls that used to crash up the Chesapeake Bay. How Steve would have thrilled to be here! He'd give her the helm as he'd set up the storm jib and reef in the main—but never, never would they strike all their canvas and hide belowdecks. Not Steve. He'd fight the storm in proportion to its strength, not out of pride, but seamanship. If one surrenders to nature, one invites calamity. A gale can shove you onto the rocks and break your back. Point into the storm and hold a course. She believed in Steve's ability, and this storm on Cor was little more than a thrill. Andrea stood on a silo cover like the deck of a boat. A gust blew a sheet of water in her face, stinging her cheeks and making her smile.

"Follow me!" Tara yelled above the storm. She wrapped herself in a black poncho and trotted toward the trees.

They stepped through a freshly dug ditch that ran several hundred yards; then they paused by a stack of cement block to scrape the heavy clods of sticky mud from their shoes. Andrea looked at the excavation and the piles of building materials and asked loudly, "What are they building here?"

Tara pointed in both directions. Squat towers rose at hundred-yard intervals. "A fence to keep us in." Then, Tara turned and marched away, calling out, "Head for the trees."

A flash of lightning illuminated the field. Andrea thought she saw something move. She crouched and turned a full circle to survey the silo field, dilapidated sheds, and old equipment. An overhead flash lit the area like a flare and she saw movement. She wiped the water from her face and strained her eyes. Was she seeing things? Two dark shadows disappeared behind an unfinished squat tower. Dressed in black? Everything looked black in this storm. Her stomach tensed.

The searing light faded as the thunder crack shook the ground. Andrea backed away. She pulled her night goggles from their pouch and fastened them by an elastic headband onto her face. The black night turned amber. The goggles' electronics muted the flashes. The heavy rain took the appearance of gauze, but in all she saw as if through a light morning mist. And she saw a pair of cloaked men watching back through some handheld device. One made an arm signal that could only be meant for others. Then, the pair seemed to fade away—disappear! Andrea tapped her goggles and looked again, but the men who had been watching her were completely gone.

She knew that Hunters work in teams of six. And by the men's gesticulations she knew: they'd seen her, and perhaps worse, they knew that she'd seen them.

She must use her own speed and the storm's chaos. A team of Hunters would envelop their prey. She ran after Tara and caught her in the tree line. The trees' thick canopy slowed the rain from a beating to the slosh of a million rivulets. The trees blocked much of the light. Andrea pulled Tara close and spoke into her ear. "We're being followed."

The carnival excitement on Tara's face withered. "That's impossible!"

Andrea didn't pause to debate the evidence; rather, she added, "I saw two men. They motioned to others—who knows how many. They saw me."

"Then they saw us come out of the shaft! They can

find the way to the Underground." Tara wrung her hands. "We have to go back! Warn the others."

"Wait." Andrea grabbed a handful of Tara's wet poncho to restrain her. "Let's think. Their comms are down. They can't call for backup, right?"

"Right." Tara nodded.

Andrea explained between thunderclaps. "They need to get us out of the way—" *Kaboom!* "—before they can deal with the shaft."

"You can't know that."

Andrea nodded. "They know that I saw them. They'll track us. I'd do the same. They can't leave us at their backs. They must get rid of the witnesses. Then they come back heavily armed to probe the shafts. If this is just a team of six Hunters, we might be able to stop them. We'll see if they're any good in the brush without their sensors." The thunder roared.

"You are insane."

"Without a doubt." Andrea pulled her knife from its sheath, held the heavy blade between them. "Are you with me?"

Tara brought out her blade. "I must be insane." Lightning flashed, reflecting from their blades.

They trotted into the forest, as Andrea explained a simple plan. They'd draw the Hunter's deep into the forest to terrain broken by draws and gullies. They needed a series of natural hunting blinds, and Tara knew such a place: a stand of large quartzite rocks—one of nature's curios well known among the young clones as a place for quiet meditation on their artificial memories.

They ran up a broad path, leaving abundant tracks for the Hunters to follow. They walked among the rocks, shards of dappled white, some no bigger than a stool, others as tall as a two-story house. The heavy rain collected into rills running between the stones, flattening ferns, and swelling dried moss. Absent the storm, the place might seem serene. Bulbous patches of green covered tree trunks that rose like cathedral pillars. The milk white stones stood like unhewn side altars.

Tonight these rocks would see sacrifice. Andrea planned her work. She'd separate the Hunters and ambush them one at a time: use her knife on the first couple, use captured pistols on the rest.

They circled back to the main path, where they lay in a thicket and waited. The hard rain seemed to pound her deeper into the sodden ground, which heaved with each clap of thunder. Her heartbeat and the rumbling merged. Her belly, arms, and legs sank into the sponge of moss and cedar needles, and she felt herself seduced by the comfort of the soft soil. She removed her night goggles to regain her focus. "These affect my depth perception and my peripheral vision. I don't need to see their faces, I just need to know when they're within reach of my blade. You keep yours on and give us early warning." She pulled out her earplugs and endured the discomfort of the booming thunder. She would need all her senses just as she'd trained with them, neither augmented nor diminished.

They lay in cold water, shivering for a long half-hour. Then, a solitary figure, a dim hunched-over shadow, inched cautiously up the main path studying the eroded footprints. He wore a heavy cloak, not black as Andrea had presumed, but a mottled blend of hues. She could see neither hands nor face, but he carried a weapon: some kind of metallic staff with a crook at the top. A pistol glistened from a holster. Her pulse quickened; she grabbed Tara's arm and whispered into her ear, "Remember. We don't move until all have passed."

Tara started to reply, but Andrea clamped a hand over Tara's mouth and signaled her to silence. The stalkers had come within hearing distance, and human voice is as distinct as a gunshot in a forest. She'd heard a hushed command from farther up the trail; they could just as well hear Tara, especially since Tara, with earplugs, didn't know to modulate her voice.

A second and third cloaked figure passed. They walked at the side of the path, carbines raised, providing flank security. Another pair followed, spread even farther to the flanks, and up the path she saw a loose column of soldiers at least platoon strength: conventional small unit tactics, excellent discipline in spacing, and far too many. A flash of lightning lit the hooded faces—hard, determined, alert eyes, momentarily stunned by the light. She counted them as they passed, thirty-six in all, in similar although not identical garb.

Tara peeled Andrea's hand from her mouth and whispered hoarsely, "They're not Hunters."

Hunters, Security Troops: it didn't much matter. The last hooded figure froze in his tracks and raised his head as if sniffing the air. *He'd heard!* And Andrea could barely contain her anger toward Tara. She clamped her hand over Tara's mouth again, this time with bruising force and she threatened Tara with a wild look.

The hooded figure held back, a small machine pistol drawn. He edged his way to their hiding place. He flinched at a huge lightning flash, braced for the loud boom and continued his search.

Andrea reached over with her free hand and plucked a plug from Tara's ear. She put her mouth to the ear and whispered in a bare breath of sound, "I'm going to get his machine pistol. If you so much as twitch, you'll get us both killed. Nod if you understand."

Tara nodded once.

The hooded soldier crept closer. Andrea raised to her haunches, ready to explode. She held her knife in a manner to slash. A few meters and a thin shroud of fern stood between her and her target. He took another step and paused. If he discovered her at a safe distance of three meters, she was dead for sure. Another two meters and she could drop him. Another crack of thunder shook the ground, rattled the fern, shaking away water that burdened it. The fern's movement caught the soldier's eye, and he stopped to inspect from a distance.

Closer! her mind screamed. All her training told her she could never close the gap in time if she lunged. But had she a choice? She resolved that the next flash of lightning was her best chance: her starting gun. He'd flinch; she'd pounce. The split second might be all she needed.

Flash! *Boom!* Andrea sprung from hiding. In one fluid movement, she leapt, leading with a powerful kick to the soldier's head, a solid connect—her heel, his head—that knocked him utterly unconscious. The blow drove him backward, one stiff splash as he hit the ground; he dropped his machine pistol in the mud. Andrea rolled, quickly regaining her feet. In an instant she straddled the downed soldier, her serrated blade in hand, ready to dispatch him with a thrust between his third and fourth rib.

A small but firm hand grabbed her wrist to stay the deathblow. "Stop!" Tara croaked in a forced whisper. "He's one of us." Tara folded back the hood.

Andrea recognized the face immediately. *Gerad!* She turned to Tara and growled, "What in hell is going on here?"

chapter 16

"He's out. I think you broke his jaw." Tara touched the massive swelling on Gerad's face.

Andrea's ire rose to the boiling point. "Forget him. Those thirty men were hunting someone . . ." She picked a clump of moss from the machine pistol's trigger housing.

"Not us."

"Well, pardon me if I don't take your word for that. As soon as Gerad's buddies figure we backtracked them, they'll be all over us. They look like the type that shoot first, then interrogate the wounded and dying." Andrea wrested her hand free of Tara's grip and repositioned the knife above Gerad's chest.

Tara interrupted. "You don't understand."

"You've got ten seconds to enlighten me. Else, I silence Gerad and we get out of here."

Andrea, intent on saving their skins, and the equally flummoxed Tara, failed to notice the sudden end of the storm's violence. The lightning and concomitant thunder wandered past the city off toward the mountains. The rain stopped, leaving fat drops of water to dribble from the trees and rattle the leaves. Clouds dissipated and shards of moonlight pierced the canopy of trees. Cool air spilled into the woods, giving rise to a thick mist.

Tara raised her hand as if to fend off a blow. "I tell you, we're not in danger. Gerad wears a wilderness cloak. So the others must be Brigon's men."

"Brigon? The clone child?" Andrea prompted.

"Who told you that?"

"Gerad, lying here." Andrea commanded, "What do you know about Brigon?"

"Long before I came into service, a clone woman got pregnant. How, no one knows for sure—not supposed to be possible, but with millions of clones, I suppose it is bound to happen. The woman fled to the wilderness and there joined a band of renegades."

"The father?" Andrea asked.

Tara sloughed off the question of paternity. "No one knows." Without missing a beat, she added, "The woman had a male child, Brigon. She and the renegades raised him."

Andrea raised a querulous eyebrow. "Raised him? How?"

Tara became defensive. "Some clone models are trained as domestics; they learn how to nurture an infant. I recall that Brigon's mother *was* a domestic model working in Sarhn, an important household. I'm sure she had excellent domestic skills."

"Enough!" Andrea impatiently terminated Tara's defense of the clone mother. "What about Brigon?"

"The boy grew up and became chief of the renegades, and he organized them. He recruited young renegades and now he has hundreds of warriors operating in small bands. The wilderness clones live in the rocks—"

Andrea cut her off. "Just tell me what these wilderness clones are doing here."

"A raiding party, most likely. They steal cattle from the barns, pilfer crops from the hydroponics farms. They raid the fisheries. They steal shoes and clothing; some raw materials and electronics."

Andrea glanced down at the unconscious Gerad. "They probably know just where and when to strike. And you do nothing to stop them."

Tara pursed her lips. "I don't want to. I want Brigon to flourish. The wilderness may be our last refuge. You saw the fence."

"And you figure the Ordinate won't come after you."

"They consider a renegade's run into the wilderness a kind of suicide. The wilderness is strewn with the skeletons of clones. Brigon doesn't cremate his dead like the Ordinate do. He leaves them in the open for the carrion birds. No Ordinate security patrol that went into the wilderness ever returned. If the patrol escapes the animals, Brigon kills them for sport. He strips the dead of clothes and weapons. The desert crabs pick their dead Ordinate bones clean in a couple of days. In the wilderness, clone and Ordinate skeletons look alike. The Ordinate are content to see so many skeletons. But they never see Brigon."

Andrea shook her head, "Nobody is that good. You make it sound like Brigon is invisible."

Tara smiled. "Brigon is almost invisible. Brigon's folk can disappear from any sensor made on Cor. This wilderness cloak—" Tara fingered an edge of the cloth: the nappy weave had a gritty, sandy texture—"is Brigon's own invention. Powered by body heat, the cloak absorbs and diffuses any kind of radiation: thermal, spectral, and electrical. And notice, when the cloth is perfectly still, it mimics natural light patterns—a nearly perfect camouflage."

Andrea watched. Slowly a shadow of Tara's hand seemed to show through the heavy cloth—in fact, absorbed, digitized, and displayed. Tara withdrew her hand, and the impression faded as she spoke. "We precinct clones need Brigon. He has trained people. He has weapons. At present, he refuses to ally with us. He believes ours is a lost cause because so few clones join the resistance. But someday, he'll have to choose: the Ordinate or us. He'll side with us."

"Who does Gerad here work for?" Andrea lowered her voice to a barest whisper.

Tara scowled. "Apparently, he works for Brigon."

"That might be a positive sign."

"How?" Tara asked.

Andrea rested back on her haunches. She lay the machine pistol across her knees. She explained, "Brigon is collecting intelligence on your operation—not because he fears you. My guess is that he realizes that at some point he needs you as much as you need him."

"I'd be happy to feed him information. Soon he'd understand the NewGen threat. He'd realize that in another ten years no more renegades will come to replenish his ranks. He'd figure out that the Ordinate will dump battalions of NewGens into the wilderness to hunt him. When he realizes his situation is as desperate as ours, he'll join us."

Andrea mused, "What I'd like to know is whether Brigon came tonight to gather intelligence or just engage in some thieving?" Andrea wanted to see if she could raise any antipathy toward this erstwhile ally.

Tara pointed to Gerad, who breathed shallow wheezes. "We'd ask him if we could."

Then, an unfamiliar voice, close by, spoke, "Why not ask me?"

Andrea swung around toward the sound. She held the machine pistol at her hip, her finger wrapped around the trigger. She turned circles and sought in vain for a target; she saw nothing. *But she heard the voice!* It had been so close; not less than twenty yards away—behind a tree perhaps.

The pleasant tenor spoke again. "Put down your weapon."

Tara echoed, "Andrea! Put down your weapon! They won't hurt us."

Andrea sensed a score of unseen weapons pointed at her. She lowered the muzzle of the pistol and gazed through the mist to the trees, and the occasional beam of moonlight. Then the forest moved. Tree trunks fell out of focus as dappled figures moved closer and the wilderness cloaks gave up their image. A pair of gloved hands removed a large hood to reveal a youthful, grinning face that rhetorically asked, "Why are we here? I came to meet the Earth woman, Andrea Flores. Imagine, running into you in this forest."

The other shapes morphed into view, pulling off their hoods, brandishing weapons: older men with gray beards—hard, humorless faces. They kept their silence.

"Providence or Gerad?" Andrea sniped. Water dripped down strands of hair into her face.

Brigon raised his hands to the sky. "Providence brought the storm; Gerad brought me. Tara brought you out for reconnaissance." He bowed slightly. "Always a pleasure to see you, Tara Gullwing."

Tara looked down at the unconscious Gerad. "How long has he worked for you?"

"He came to me first. I sent him to you. He's very useful, don't you think?" Brigon scratched his chin through a neatly cropped sandy beard. "Let's get him on his feet."

Tara shook her head. "I don't think that's going to be possible."

Brigon approached the two women, pausing to glance down at Gerad. His eyes widened as he saw the extent of the swelling to Gerad's face. He cocked his head with one eye on his unconscious comrade, the other on Andrea. "Did you do this?" His expression, his voice accused her of a crime, yet betrayed a note of surprise, even admiration.

"Yes." Andrea licked her lips, dry despite the rain.

Brigon stepped into Andrea's reach, daring her to assault him. She felt his warm breath against her face. His clear, dark eyes sparked with deadly mirth as he stared into hers, challenging her, attempting to divine her secrets. "You must have meant to kill him with that blow to the head."

"I would have been satisfied with that result."

"Then I shall be careful around you, Andrea Flores." Brigon placed a hand on Andrea's shoulder, further encroaching her space, apparently not taking his own advice.

Andrea knew the drill—two captains staring each other down, taking the measure of the other, whether adversary or ally. In either case, the data was the same. She did not avert her eyes or recoil her shoulder. Instead, she mirrored his move and put her hand on his shoulder. She thought: *He's an arrogant man. It's a wonder he hasn't got himself killed.*

She used the brief contact to study Brigon. He was lean and sinewy to the touch; well exercised and modestly fed. While keeping her eyes fixed on his, she recalled what she'd seen. He wore heavy boots to protect against the hot sand and jagged rocks. He and his men wore thick leggings and elbow-length gloves to stop fangs. The cloak sheltered them from sun and rain, and hid them from predators—especially Ordinate Hunters.

Beneath the cloak, Brigon's uniform was a simple clone work uniform, certainly stolen, and quiltlike from dozens of repairs. The collar was frayed. Yet despite these raggedy clothes, Brigon stood with the casual dignity of a potentate.

She thought back to her research on the starcruiser and the description of clone progeny—an abomination, a freak of nature. How completely off the mark! Brigon was so much more than technology's inevitable mean time between failure. Brigon, the clone child, raised in the Cor wilderness, was in fact Nature's rebellion against Ordinate biotechnology. Andrea saw a roiling anger in Brigon's eyes. This outwardly serene master of his environment had not mastered himself. Or was she merely transferring a part of herself to him?

Brigon removed his hand from Andrea's shoulder. With a couple of crisp hand signals, he summoned two of the old ones to help Gerad. Andrea watched as one reached into a pouch, removing a handful of succulent stalks. He crushed them between his fingers, releasing a pungent odor. Gerad's eyes fluttered and he sputtered awake and stifled a pitiful cry of pain. The old herbalist pried open a small tin and slathered a milky paste onto Gerad's chest. Almost instantly, Gerad slumped into a narcotic sleep. They fashioned a litter with two walking staves and Gerad's cloak.

* * *

Brigon spoke over his shoulder, "Set up a perimeter and wait for us. I will speak with the Gullwing and Andrea Flores alone."

The three retreated to a quiet place among the white stones. Tara led them to a circle of stone benches worn smooth. Tara wrapped herself tightly in her poncho. Even so, she shivered in the cold night air. Andrea sat stiffly, her wet hair matted as a black cap on her head, wisps of steam rising from wet clothes that stuck to her skin.

Brigon's cursory gaze displayed a nagging contempt for Tara's shivering. Likewise he was curious about the Earth woman's resistance to the chill in the air. He removed his cloak and laid it on the bench within Andrea's reach—a tease—and he smugly watched to see if Andrea, whose skin rippled with gooseflesh, would take it, ask to borrow it, or leave it unused on the bench.

Andrea refused to play his game. Instead, she improved her posture and purposefully ignored the warm cloak and her discomfort. She warmed her blood with a sudden dislike of Brigon. She did not like the way this man looked at her. Thus far, she saw nothing in his character but thug.

Brigon kept a steady gaze on Andrea. "I have heard of Earth. What's your business here?" He laced his voice with casual indifference, but Andrea was not fooled for a second. Brigon had made a dangerous trip through the wilderness to get the answer to that question.

"Hasn't Gerad already told you?" Andrea played coy to mock his disingenuous indifference.

Brigon smiled. His teeth looked white, a stark contrast to his dense tawny beard. He folded his hands in his lap and said, "I'd like to hear your story from your own lips."

Andrea gave him the barest account of her mission: find evidence of the NewGen threat; bring Tara to Jod.

"So you believe Eric and Tara's tales about the invincible NewGen clones?"

She answered cryptically. "I believe what I see. More importantly, what do you think about the NewGens?" Andrea tossed the better part of his question back at him.

"Well, I haven't seen any yet—in person, that is. Tara tells me they're invincible." He flourished with his hands.

Tara spoke from the periphery. Her voice quivered from the cold as she punctuated hard reality. "When you see them in person, Brigon, it will be too late."

"You overrate them." Brigon spoke directly to Andrea, while answering Tara. He raised his dark eyebrows mockingly. "They'll still raise cattle, which is important to me. Although they may be a better design, they're clones nevertheless." He gave Tara a patronizing glance.

Andrea weighed Brigon's cynicism before she spoke. "That fact is, Brigon, you need the precinct clones more than they need you."

He guffawed, and his short laugh echoed among the rocks. "I was here before any of the precinct clones in service today; I'll be here long after they're retired."

"And there lies your problem." Andrea snared him with his own words and she tightened the noose. "When the Ordinate eradicate the old-order clones, the NewGens will not tolerate your thieving. The Ordinate will send their new drudges into the wilderness after you and care nothing of the cost."

"They'll never find me. Their clones will die uselessly."

"I'm sure you're right." Then Andrea edged her voice with sarcasm. "You and your band of merry men will spend the next thirty years hiding, eating roots and rabbits. In time, these old men of yours will die, and you'll spend the last thirty years of your life alone. The NewGen clones will provide no new recruits for your tribe. If you survive to the rigors of old age, you'll finally die alone—irrelevant and forgotten."

Brigon started to retort, but fell silent. Andrea thrust another barb at him. "Actually, I'm wrong on one point. You won't die of old age. You'll die from boredom."

Brigon waved a hand as if batting a gnat. "If Tara's reports about the NewGen are correct—"

Tara's voice interjected, "And they are."

"Then, our extinction is inevitable. I'll make the best life I can."

"Make the best of the inevitable?" Tara pointed an accusing finger, punctuating each word as she said, "Now, you sound like a typical precinct clone."

Brigon stood abruptly, raised a threatening hand, but checked his quick temper. Andrea jumped to her feet and put herself between the two. Brigon tried to dismiss her, saying, "Go back to Earth. I think you came here just to make trouble."

How true. Let's make some trouble! Andrea's dislike for Brigon began to swell, but she suppressed her feelings. Brigon could still be useful.

Tara rose, shedding her poncho like an old chrysalis husk. She stood like a specter in a patch of moonlight. She announced, "I am going to lead the Underground in an attack against the Clone Welfare Institute."

Surprised, Brigon forgot his temper and laughed at her. "Oh, that's funny!"

But Tara didn't flinch. "Brigon, we need you. We

need your men and your weapons. I can get us in the city. Your men can stop the security forces long enough for us to cripple the hatchery."

Andrea spoke to Brigon. "If you and Tara can buy yourselves another year before the NewGens come on line, I can bring offworld help. Self-interest will force the Jod to intervene."

Brigon pulled at his beard. "It won't work. A frontal assault against the institute and a garrison of their best troops? That's suicide." He turned to speak directly to Tara. "This Earth woman has filled your head with desperate thoughts. Perhaps you ought to find out why." He bent down and snatched his cloak into the crook of his arm. He added, "You'll just get yourself and all your people killed following her fool advice."

Tara stepped into a shadow. "Perhaps. One way or the other we'll write our own future."

"Well then," Brigon turned to leave, "it's been nice knowing you."

As he stepped away, Andrea hurled one last bolt. "Then, you are worse than the weakest precinct clone!" Brigon stopped but did not turn to face his accuser. Andrea continued. "You'll sit on your hands and let the weak fight to secure your freedom."

Without a word, Brigon threw on his cloak and disappeared into the forest.

chapter 17

With Gerad gone, Tara gave Andrea a new escort, the clone Coop, her adjutant, the one who'd effected her capture, then argued unsuccessfully to kill her outright. Tara also let Coop know that he would lead the assault on the Sarhn barracks. Pinning the Security Troops in their barracks was the key to the whole operation. They needed unfettered access to the institute, and later access to the spaceport. At first, the big CPP withered at the news; he accepted his commission like a death sentence. "You know, Tara, we cannot defeat the Ordinate security forces. We lack fighters and weapons."

"You don't need to defeat them. You just need to block them while Andrea and I destroy the NewGen crop. Thirty minutes—all I'm asking for is thirty minutes."

Coop shook his head slightly. "Thirty minutes is a long fight."

Andrea stepped in. "Yes, it is. And it will be even longer for the Ordinate. Time stands still when you're caught in crossfire. Trust me on this. I'll teach you how to set an ambush."

Coop quickly seized this opportunity to shift some of the responsibility that Tara put on his shoulders. "We'll follow your plan."

She rebuked him. "No—not my plan; your plan. I'll teach you, but you must lead your own warriors by your own plan. And your first lesson is this: if your people see you walking around with a long face, they'll lose heart. You must talk victory and act like a conqueror. They must see you out and about, active. Your people will draw some of their energy from you. You owe them at least a week's worth of encouragement if you want them to join you for thirty minutes of mayhem."

"Okay." Coop looked down at Andrea and grinned ruefully, "You would have such a sweet face if you weren't such a dangerous woman."

Andrea ignored Coop's irrelevant observation. "We'll spend our days with your people, watch their work, share meals; then we'll make our plans in the evening."

Drawn by the groans and grunts of heavy machinery, Andrea stood at the periphery of the precinct and watched heavy earth moving equipment cut a ditch: a triangular cut, the deep side out. Other crews dug deep postholes, laying a line of concrete posts curved at the top like giant shepherd's crooks.

At intervals of a thousand feet, crews operated a crane to build crude towers, stacking sections of pipe end on end. On the outside of these prefabricated sections were a set of iron ladder rungs. Manufacturing the tower took less than three hours: each section had a flange that fit snugly into the one below, forcing the ladder rungs to line up. One scrawny workman simply slathered mortar on the lower section as the next piece hung from straps overhead. Any slip would spell an instant crushing death of the expendable workman below. Atop the cylinders they put a round cement slab, harder to maneuver; then a pallet of block, which the men mortared into a hexagonal set of walls with one door and five small windows. Finally, a second round cement slab sandwiched the walls.

"Do any of those people belong to you?" Andrea asked Coop.

"No, they come from another precinct—mostly young, inexperienced masons. I have a man working on a similar crew putting up a similar security fence at a different precinct. The steel plant in Precinct 22 manufactures the stainless steel web to string between the cement posts. The work is sloppy." He spoke as a skilled mason. "Won't last five years."

"You won't be here in five years to watch it fall down. You're being penned in like sheep." She turned to face Coop, her disgust with the fence written on her face.

Coop looked at her with angry eyes. "I know." He composed himself and said rather matter-of-factly, "The Ordinate Ministry of Internal Affairs has already broadcast messages throughout the clone precincts explaining these fences." His voice changed to a bland false warmth as he quoted: "To secure a harmonious life for all inhabitants of the precincts, the Ordinate has authorized an ambitious capital improvement—the Precinct Security Project."

Andrea pointed at the fence and said, "You should use this fence as the catalyst to harden support for your cause. Bring the uncommitted people up to see the fence. They cannot deny what they see with their own eyes. The old-order clones are being contained. As soon as the NewGen hatch, those empty guard towers will have armed occupants. As soon as the Ordinate can replace you with NewGen laborers, you're through—early retirement."

Coop glanced sideways, a look that said, *How naive.* He shook his head slightly, frustrated that he should have to say the obvious. "Everybody sees the fence go up. The fence is obvious, but they see the fence through eyes dimmed by neural imprints. The young clones cheer the progress of this great capital improvement. Many people in our precinct are, in fact, building fences in other precincts. They've made a race of it: we can build your fence faster than you can build ours. . . makes me sick. They say, *The Ordinate has got their big wall and sound barrier. It's about time we got our fence!*

Andrea argued vainly. "Show them the shape of the ditch. It's designed to stop vehicles trying to bust out—not in. And the bend at the top of the fence, it's bent inward, to keep you from climbing out."

"I know. We point to the obvious and ask them: *Why do you suppose they're fencing us in? Why have they stopped manufacturing clones?* Confronted with hard facts that any hatchling can see, they call us liars. Rather than believe their own eyes, they tell the government that we're troublemakers. We can't afford that kind of attention, especially now."

"Must be in the gene pool." *The sheep gene.* Andrea turned her back on the construction. "Let's get out of here."

When she finished her day shift at the institute, Tara returned for a quick meal, a couple hours of sleep, and planning sessions. She provided detailed descriptions of the Clone Welfare Institute—commissioning Coop to build a clay model of the institute buildings, highlighting active and passive security measures. The clay model showed the layout of the garrison and the narrow streets winding around this ancient end of Sarhn City. Andrea asked Coop to add the spaceport, complete with security points and scaled models of aircraft.

Tara found a faded schematic of the institute, which she plastered on the wall. The tattered schematic showed the miles of pipes that brought the raw materials: food and cryogenic oxygen. Color-coded lines showed waste lines leading to sewers, the power grid, and ventilation.

With an odd sense of pride, Tara explained the technical marvels in the institute. "In terms of process, the institute is completely self-sufficient." She used a thin iron rod to point to a corner of the schematic. "Here is our cryogenics plant where we manufacture oxygen. We store a five hundred-hour supply of liquid oxygen in these tanks. Pipes carry the liquid oxygen to processing central. She dragged her finger across the paper, following the spaghetti of lines toward the heart of the building. The oxygen serves two purposes: We use oxygen as our main antibacterial agent, sterilizing the liquids in which we suspend the developing clones. Also, the larva breathe the super-oxygenated liquid just as we breathe air."

"Amphibians . . ." Andrea muttered.

"Not precisely." Tara corrected her.

"How long can the larva survive if you cut off the oxygen?"

"Not long. Five minutes, maybe. Toxins build quickly. If the toxins get them, they die miserably.

Otherwise they asphyxiate, fall painlessly into hypoxic sleep. That's why we keep the five hundred-hour backup supply. We've never had an interruption of the source; however, we lose a couple from every crop due to crimped or clogged lines. It's hard to watch the larva die that way."

She's worried if these things die painlessly or not. Andrea didn't understand this woman. She steered Tara back to technical matters. "So oxygen is critical."

"Extremely critical."

"And, therefore, the weak link to the system."

"Yes. But you just can't turn off the supply. It's all automated with backup after backup, and I don't know of a shut-off valve." Tara used the iron rod to point to the multiple pumps.

Andrea smiled cryptically. "We'll just put a big crimp in the line."

Andrea had learned what she wanted to know and she let her mind wander as Tara finished her briefing. Tara described the nutrient vats where they brewed a thick mash of grains. The schematic showed a series of squat cylinders. "To the malted grain extracts, we synthesize and add various organic materials, plants mostly, ranging from legumes to cotton fiber to make the nutrient syrup. We add calcium and other minerals."

She speculated that the Ordinate even extracted materials from the clones they retired in an adjacent part of the factory. All she knew for fact was that clones went in for a final physical exam and disappeared without trace.

Tara pointed out the genetic research laboratory, and she described the computers that provided the growing clones a virtual past, training them for their limited tasks. Tara finished her paper tour by pointing to the complex of nurseries surrounding the processing plant. Andrea watched the points of access and egress—she'd already synthesized her mission: get in, blow the oxygen lines, get out.

In most tactical matters, Tara deferred to Andrea—save one. Andrea wanted to involve Tara's sister organizations in the other precincts to create diversions or otherwise raise hell. "Perhaps we can draw down the Ordinate garrison, disperse them miles away."

Tara adamantly quashed Andrea's suggestion—her conviction surprised Andrea: "Absolute secrecy! If the Ordinate knows we're coming, we're dead before we start."

"Then, just how many of your troops do you trust?"

"Forty-one, counting you and me."

Andrea tried hard to hide her misgivings about Tara's elite cadre—small, untested, poorly trained—but seemingly motivated. "And how many Security Troops do the Ordinate have on station?"

"They keep twenty-four on roving patrols around the institute, another four hundred on call in the garrison, and reserves of one thousand on a three-hour recall."

"And you have forty-one."

Tara shrank at the lopsidedness of the opposing forces, but held firm to her conviction. "We need only hit and run." She braced for more criticism.

But Andrea grinned broadly at Tara's pluck. "Sounds like not a lot of hit, and one helluva lot of run. Okay, I'll plan the mission for forty-one. What kind of explosives do you have?"

Again Tara's face fell. "We don't have that kind of firepower." She took Andrea to a small stone bunker deep in the labyrinth and showed Andrea the contents. The precinct clones had a few purloined explosives: antiquated, leaking sticks of dynamite, and scores of timing caps. Andrea held up one of the sticks. "Is this it?"

"As you can imagine, explosives are a highly controlled substance."

"This isn't enough. Can you steal some more explosives?" Andrea looked at a length of detonator cord.

"The theft would trigger a security crackdown."

"Then forget that suggestion." Andrea examined a wooden box filled with small caps packed in plastic. "At least you've got blasting caps. Is anyone in your circle good in a lab?"

Within a day, Tara produced a wide-eyed clone, an ARC model called Ariko, who worked days in the institute mixing the nutrient syrup to feed the thousands of larva. Andrea took him aside and they set up a crude lab of large crucibles, and the most accurate thermometers that a clone might acquire. They scoured the precincts and bartered for formaldehyde and ammonia, which they slowly nitrated with nitric acid. Andrea found the fledgling chemist pulverizing a yellow powder with an ancient pestle and mortar. She explained the rudiments of manufacturing the explosive, cautioning him to watch the temperature carefully: *Take your time or be blown to bits.* She left him for days, her teeth always grit, anticipating a violent explosion. Instead, he emerged, ecstatic, with a bucket of white powder. He presented it to Andrea, who praised him roundly, and they mixed the powder with heavy machine grease into a gray substance—a crude form of plastique.

Tara joined them for a test. Andrea handed Ariko two ounces of plastique and a cap. With unmitigated glee, he sculpted the plastique into a snakelike band and wrapped it around an out-of-service iron pipe. He set the timer for one minute; they scattered around a corner away from any spalding and waited. Andrea found herself more interested in Ariko's giddy countdown to the explosion. In fact, she thought the successful explosion a bit of an anticlimax.

The plastique cut the pipe in two, driving splinters of iron into the nearby walls. Andrea and Tara congratulated Ariko, who gathered the shrapnel for souvenirs. Andrea said, "We have about twenty pounds of plastique—not enough to blow up the institute, but I think we can break a few key pipes."

Coop took Andrea to inspect his training. They walked briskly through the tunnels until Coop stopped abruptly to prepare her for a disappointment. "I remember what you told me about realism: we've got to train the way we fight." He lowered his eyes. "We must train in an underground quarry with artificial light. I can't spare ammunition. We barely have enough for the mission. We don't have enough time. We—"

Andrea interrupted. "Show me what you have done."

They rounded a corner to find two guards flanking a crawl space. They welcomed Coop and Andrea without any military courtesies, and simply got out of their way. The cavern was dimly lit with a pale gray and rose light that originated behind them, reflected from the ceiling, casting no shadows. As Andrea's eyes grew accustomed to the obscure light, she saw a squad of dark figures huddled at the far end of the quarried cavern. "Can they see what they're doing?"

Coop replied, "We attack before dawn, so we rigged the lights to simulate twilight."

Andrea looked at Coop. All she saw was his dark silhouette and his long face. "Good idea."

Coop didn't smile. "Watch your step. The floor is wet." He took Andrea to meet the clones, seven middle-aged men and three wiry women, seemingly anonymous in this artificial twilight. None spoke. Each carried a weapon: a large bore rifle with a shorter military style barrel. They had old fashioned iron sights. Beneath the barrel of each weapon was an eighteen-inch copper-colored tube fastened with homemade brackets and wired to a fat battery, taped to the stock.

Coop handed Andrea one of the jerry-rigged weapons, then took her aside. "We put a particle accelerator on each weapon." He pointed down a hallway in the rock to a wall. "We painted a picture of the street coming from the security barracks in Sarhn."

Andrea strained her eyes and saw a crude attempt at perspective, the masonry walls of buildings on either side of the street tapering. Caught in the middle were shadowy figures, black uniformed Security Troops. For some reason the eyes glowed amber. They looked like a phalanx of demons. She turned to Coop, who explained, "We've got to get used to killing the shapes of the Ordinate. For most of us clones, killing an Ordinate is something like killing a family member."

Patricide. Andrea thought: *Even when the neural imprints faded, the clones know that they were genetically linked to the same Ordinate that now enslaved them.* Andrea knew from studying war that it is myth that killing is second nature to humans—for the depraved individual, yes; for mobs, yes. But not for persons. She was not surprised that clones, like humans, had to learn how to kill. So Coop concentrated his efforts on the discipline of killing the likeness of the

Ordinate to release their rational minds so that they might kill Ordinate with abandon. Adding the demonic eyes was a nice touch.

With his voice low, Coop muttered. "I've got time to teach them to aim, fire: to stand and fire again and again. And I've got to give them the confidence that they can hit something."

The silhouettes appeared a hundred feet down the painted avenue. On each silhouette, Coop's technicians had glued tile that luminesced when struck by a particle beam. Coop invited Andrea. "Go ahead and try it."

Andrea raised the rifle to her shoulder and lined up the iron sights on one of the shadows and squeezed the trigger. Click. The hammer fell. No kick. But at the end of the street, her target showed its luminescent wound, a pale blue green. She watched the pale light fade as if the wound closed and stopped the issue of this unnatural blood. In some way these specters with yellow eyes and self-healing wounds seemed more terrifying than Ordinate flesh and blood. If they could face these undying demons, they might stand well against the Ordinate. She glanced sideways at Coop.

He said, "You don't like it."

She whispered, "Coop, it's brilliant. I could kiss you."

Andrea visited Coop's training every day thereafter. She watched Coop with growing respect. Ingenious simplicity compensated for otherwise inadequate resources. Coop drilled his recruits on the simulators. He organized them into squads of ten and trained them to select targets from the crowd of silhouettes efficiently so that each volley might kill as many Ordinate as possible. He brusquely answered all the *what-ifs* with his simple standing order: "Kill anybody not dressed like us and go where I tell you."

Andrea watched these recruits immerse themselves in their imaginary war, firing imaginary bullets at imaginary foe. It all might have seemed a child's game, but Coop's people were on the other side of middle age: men and women with gray streaks in their hair. Yet they were physically tough. Aching muscles merely chastised them to work harder. There were still many years of good work left in these mature clones. Their gaunt faces recorded years of hard work and poor diet, but their eyes showed a sense of awakening. It seemed that as the neural imprints faded, their eyes cleared.

Then it dawned on Andrea—why the Ordinate kept their clones for twenty-year service followed by quick termination. Termination had little to do with preventing physical atrophy and lost productivity. Termination prevented intellectual awakening. The irony was complete: the hatchling feared death and so cooperated with the executioner. The renegades cherished life and risked it to thwart the executioner. More than ever, Andrea wanted these old renegades to win.

Coop knew his limitations and the shortcomings of his troops: none were battle tested. During the brief revolt staged by Eric, he'd seen a handful of disciplined Hunters send a thousand precinct clones into panicked flight. The Hunters slaughtered hundreds of clones as they cowered against walls and behind bushes—their frightened eyes speaking their one forlorn hope, that the Hunter's gun might jam. No one doubted that the Hunter would pull the trigger: Hunter discipline was more reliable than technology.

And so it must be for Coop's soldiers. Discipline. With simple repetitive drills, Coop inculcated the discipline he'd seen in the Hunters, a discipline to remove hesitation, a discipline to transcend fear. At last, Andrea told Coop, "Your people will stand and fight. I'm sure of it. They'll fight as long as you stand up front with them. So you've got to stay in the fight and not get yourself killed."

Coop took a deep breath. "I suppose that's the trick."

Tensions rose as the day for the assault approached. Coop's soldiers began to chafe at the *make-believe*, making rash pronouncements how they looked forward to the real action. Coop growled that he would not disappoint them—they'd better not disappoint him.

Andrea organized a leaders' recon. They could not wait for a storm to cover their movement, so she and Tara, joined by Coop and his platoon leaders, donned the garb of day laborers. They masqueraded as a work party clearing brush, hacking their way along the sonic barrier as they studied the wall.

Andrea felt the low hum of the barrier and she kept a safe distance from the invisible killer. Tara reached into her pocket and pulled out a pulpy fruit that looked like a purple mango. "Watch this."

She rolled the fruit about twenty feet into the barrier. Even as the oblong fruit tumbled to a resting place, it skittered and popped like a drop of water on a hot skillet. The purple skin ruptured and out spilled puréed mush that turned to cold steam. A moment later, the bulbous fruit had withered to a leathery skin clinging to a fat pit. Tara remarked, "They'll never expect us to come through here."

"I can imagine why not." Andrea said as she studied the desiccated fruit. "How?"

Tara raised an eyebrow and spoke through a thin smile. "I hacked my way into the barrier's computer system. I wrote a subroutine that sets up a harmonic and effectively creates a hole for us to walk through."

"Nice." Andrea acknowledged her spark of genius with a small bow. "Can they plug the hole?"

"It would take them a day to find my splice in their code and turn it around." She smirked. "However, the hole will trigger sensors that monitor the barrier's continuity. So we have to move as soon as the harmonic breaches the barrier. Coop, you can expect the garrison to send a small security detail to investigate the breach within two minutes. Even then, they'll just suspect a malfunction. They'll never expect an armed assault. No clone has ever dared to bring violence to Sarhn."

Andrea added, "Your masters have come to overrely on you. That may be their epitaph."

Coop agreed. "They rely on us to roll over and play dead. Are they in for a bunch of surprises: first they find that their barrier has a hole in it, then they meet some precinct folk who fight back."

Mindful of fleeting time, Tara interrupted this exchange of bravado. She pointed to the looming wall on the other side of the barren stretch that marked the sonic barrier. "See the old gate?"

They strained to see a small rusted cover, half as high as a man, not much bigger than one of the stones at the base. Tara turned her back to the wall as she spoke. "Unattended for years, used only by maintenance crews. A couple of our people took the pins out of the hinges. One good shove and it falls open." Again, Andrea, Coop, and company muttered accolades.

"Through that gate, Coop takes his force east to contain the Ordinate Security Troops." Tara looked at Andrea. "You and I split from the group and go west to the institute to kill the crop."

Everyone nodded.

"As soon as Andrea and I clear the institute, we work our way behind your position toward the spaceport. Coop—you pull back through the barrier. They'll pursue, giving us a chance to sneak into the spaceport maintenance sheds. We'll force our way onto a starcruiser or whatever we find that has some range."

Coop added a postscript. "You'll bring back Eric and the Jod Fleet."

"That's the plan." Tara motioned the small party back into the forest. "Tomorrow then. Two hours before dawn, we take positions in these trees. We'll rehearse one last time over the model, eat a good supper, and try to get a good night's sleep."

Andrea ate heartily. Tara stared at her plate of rice and lentils, periodically using her spoon to shove small piles of food around. Her cup of tea sat stone cold in the same spot she'd poured it. "I can't eat."

"You're excited." Andrea told her. "That's normal. This time tomorrow, you and I will be on a spaceship going faster than the speed of light on a trajectory toward Jod, toward Eric. You will have started a rebellion to save your people. You have every reason to be excited."

Tara looked up. "I feel sick. What if we fail?"

Andrea swallowed a mouthful of coarse bread and shrugged. "We'll be dead, so coping with failure won't be our problem, will it?"

Tara gave Andrea a look of disgust as she pushed

her plate away. "I'm going to pack and then try to get some sleep."

"Pack?" Andrea was surprised. "Pack what?"

A bit defensive, Tara answered. "I have stuff—stuff I want to take." She left the small table and went to her cot. There she laid out a bleach-stained cloth frayed badly at one end. She pulled a handful of treasures from under her mattress and deposited them in the center of the cloth.

Intrigued, Andrea edged around the table to spy on Tara's packing job. She asked with girlish curiosity, "What are you taking?"

"Mementos." Tara used her body to shield her few private belongings from such a crass inspection.

Andrea sidled over. "I still have an old wooden cigar box that my father gave me when I was a little girl."

"What's a cigar box?"

"Just a box that they sell cigars in—don't ask me to explain cigars." Andrea sized the box with her hands. "In it I keep my most precious memories: my first-place ribbon at the sixth grade science fair; a couple old coins, some letters, pictures . . ."

"I've got a picture." Tara pulled a yellowed scrap of paper from her cloth. She handed it to Andrea, saying, "A picture of Eric."

The yellow paper hung limp in Andrea's fingers. Carefully, she laid the scrap in the palm of her hand and looked among the creases, using her imagination to fill the gaps where image had flaked away. As she looked, her eyes aged, her lip quivered; her hands shook, nearly causing her to drop the precious scrap of paper.

"What's the matter?"

Andrea didn't hear. She stared at the face in the picture, the wide-set eyes framed between thick arched brows and high cheekbones. She knew this hairline and thick wave of jet-black hair. She knew this straight nose that had nuzzled her neck and the serious lips that burst into wreaths of smiles and so often kissed her. Andrea stroked the picture with her finger.

"Is something wrong?" Tara asked.

Andrea set her jaw and handed the paper back to Tara, repairing a crack in her voice as she said, "This picture looks just like my husband, Steve."

Tara put the offending picture away and stumbled through a clumsy effort to console, "You told me Hunters killed your husband. I'm so sorry."

The facts slammed together in Andrea's brain. She looked up at Tara, her mouth slack in disbelief, yet she knew the data fit. "The Hunters who killed Steve were looking for Eric." Andrea's face turned crimson.

Tara's face turned pale.

As she went to her cubicle to sleep, Andrea got a last-minute report on the weather: a soft rain followed by morning fog. Excellent. The fog would keep the Ordinate aircraft on the ground until it was too late. Andrea lay on her cot and struggled to erase the picture of Eric from her busy mind. She longed for the next day, when the tactical situation would consume her and trap her in the present, freeing her from the past or future. How she'd come to hate quiet nights.

She dreamed she was walking in the woods outside the Sarhn barrier. All along the granite wall, the Ordinate stands with weapons raised, prepared to repel any attack. Behind her she has an army of old-order clones: thousands poised to attack, confident of success, but completely aware that most would die in the struggle.

One man approaches from the mist—*Steve!* His face is pained; he brings bad news. She wants to run to him, but she can only walk, slowly. He stops a few yards away and holds out his arm, not to greet her but to warn her.

"What's wrong?" She reaches out to him but he does not take her hand.

He says, "Do not join this fight."

She replies, "I am committed."

Steve hangs his head and pleads again, "This is not your fight. Don't . . ."

"I must." Her breathing is difficult. She reaches out but can't touch him. She is powerless to move in his direction.

"I cannot stay to watch." He turns to leave. He is uncharacteristically sad.

"Don't go!" She cries. Tears fall down her cheeks. As he disappears, she cries again, "Steve! Don't leave me here. Don't go!"

"Time to go. Wake up." Andrea felt a delicate hand shaking her. She looked up and saw Tara looking back sympathetically. "Bad dream?"

chapter 18

The scent of predawn is most pungent before a battle. In the visual monotony of the dark, the handful of clones discovered with awe their heightened sense of smell. As they lay watching, their body weight bruised the bed of cedar needles, raising a pleasant odor. They smelled the new mushrooms bulging up—some right before their eyes. Occasionally the methane smell of a rotting log or termite mound wafted by. In the still air, they smelled their own sweat, their own breath. And with the battle looming, their imaginations anticipated the smell of gunpowder, laser canon ozone, and death: in these last quiet moments they savored every scent.

Ground fog settled into the vales and among the trees. In the distance, the Sarhn city spires, illuminated by artificial light, poked through the gray slump-shouldered shroud. Nearer, the institute glowed brightly despite the fog—an inviting, cheerful, yet antiseptic light. The high granite wall skirted the institute, an eerie sight of formidable stone, cast pale gray by a backwash of light. Nearer still, the ubiquitous fog marked the location of the sonic barrier as the heavy moisture roiled within the disrupting sound waves.

They watched for the opening. At the preprogrammed time, the Clone Welfare Institute's computers opened a harmonic tunnel—twenty feet wide—through the barrier. "There!" An anonymous whisper alerted the group. A section of the barrier had gone still, back to the shapeless gray of still fog.

Tara gave a hand signal. Coop shimmied over. Andrea gave him a communicator disk and warned him, "Do not use the communicator until the enemy knows your presence. We'll know soon enough how fast their security force reacts to a hole in the barrier."

"Understood." Coop checked the safety switch on the small silver disk and dropped it into his breast pocket.

"Chances are, Andrea and I will make first contact and break silence. With any luck, you won't hear from us until we set the charges and give the signal to pull out."

Coop gave a somber nod. He didn't expect all to go well, and Andrea sensed his anxiety; a dangerous lack of confidence. As he turned to leave, she grabbed his arm, "Coop."

"Yes?" He forced a smile.

"Just set the ambush like you planned. Make their plans the first casualty of the battle—not yours. The Ordinate can't imagine that clones can fight, so when you do fight, you'll scare half of them half to death. Make them panic. Then kill devastatingly."

Coop roused his thirty-nine fighters and they filed through the harmonic tunnel—Coop first. They disappeared to the right. Coop signaled back with a small red light: The gate had been opened as planned.

Coop's people disappeared to set their ambush outside the Security Troops' force barracks.

Tara and Andrea hoisted their heavy packs, then lumbered through the harmonic breach in the sonic barrier. They walked in a careful single file through the muddy footprints left by Coop's people. The hum grew painfully loud as they veered right or left to avoid the muck—a warning to stay centered in the harmonic tunnel. Tara looked ahead at the open gate. For the moment her thoughts were with Coop. "Maybe the Ordinate security force won't be alerted."

"Possible—but not likely." Andrea held her pistol ready. They, too, passed through the unattended gate, turned left, and skulked up a narrow set of stairs taking them to the institute's loading docks. Overhead lights carved cone-shaped beams through the fog, clearly marking the shadows. A slight breeze told Andrea that the fog would lift soon. She looked up and saw small patches of the early morning sky. They pressed along the shadows of a stone retaining wall, stopping at a corner.

Andrea heard a voice: she held her hand up to signal stop. Tara froze, then whispered, "Sentries." A pair of male voices filled the silent void with a thoughtless exchange of words—complaint and countercomplaint about boring guard duty. Andrea lay on the ground and peered around the corner. The sentries stood with their backs to the night, less than twenty feet away, their machine pistols slung over their shoulders—an easy target. She calculated the time she'd need. At worst, she could take four or five steps undetected. At best, she could breathe down their necks.

In either case, neither sentry would serve another night of guard duty.

Andrea slipped off her pack and handed it to Tara

and whispered, "Stay here." Then she unsheathed her knife. "If you hear a shot, use the comm disk and tell Coop."

She padded toward them on cat feet, picking up speed as she ran. Her confidence soared as she closed the gap. Finally, one sentry heard a crunch of gravel beneath her foot. He turned, but too late. Neither sentry had time to unsling arms. And while their hands were busy loosening straps, Andrea gutted the first, a violent rip through the diaphragm into a lung. He jumped back, stunned by his gushing wound but not dead.

The second sentry backed up while wrestling his weapon from his shoulder, but again, Andrea was on him before he could put a finger on the trigger. With an uppercut, she drove the wet blade up under his chin, nailing the man's tongue to the roof of his mouth and cramming the blade home to the brain pan. His legs failed, and for a moment she supported his weight with her knife run into his skull. He shook with uncontrolled spasms as she pulled the blade back and let him crumble onto the concrete.

She spun around to finish the other sentry she'd mortally wounded. He sat there bathed in blood, sputtering, groping at the safety on his weapon, dizzy from blood loss. His weapon wobbled in his weak hands. He squinted as his sight dimmed. Andrea admired the effort. She threw her knife with all her force and the heavy blade struck the dying man, burying itself to the hilt in his chest. He fell backwards, and as he did he squeezed a two-round burst into the air.

Tara ran from her hiding place, hunched over by the weight of the two packs, her pistol drawn. "You're all right!"

Andrea, utterly disgusted with her performance,

replied, "Call Coop. Tell him the stuff just hit the fan." Then with some effort, she pried her knife from the dead man's body. "Hurry!"

Andrea reached into the pack and retrieved two grenades. She pulled the pins and wedged them, spoon intact, under the inert bodies of the sentries. She glanced sideways at Tara, saying "When we hear the grenades, we know we have company."

They walked briskly into the building. Andrea raised her pistol at the ready and Tara copied her. Tara directed, "Turn right."

The mustard yellow corridors seemed interminably long and naked. A bank of windows on one side opened a view to a dimly lit nursery. Andrea paused to see the racks of thousands of very young larvae, pale shadows of dark-haired infant children, each encapsulated in clear glass, suspended naked in amber liquid—all attended by machines. As far as the eye could see, row upon row of larva-filled racks, ever diminishing in perspective to the dark back wall—stunning hivelike replication, offering less humanity than one might find in a hive. Andrea felt her throat tighten, unable to swallow, unable to comprehend simultaneously both the exactness of each capsule's content and the enormity of the nursery's organization.

Each suspended elfin figure seemed so perfect, especially during the sleep cycle, yet they looked cold, prying loose feelings of sympathy. *That one! With his face pressed against the glass*— But each appeared identical to its neighbors, different only in random posture. All identical. All identical.

Andrea felt a tug on her sleeve. A harried voice beckoned, "This way!"

Andrea put the nursery out of her mind as she followed

Tara deeper into the belly of the institute. After another set of turns, they found themselves in a double-width corridor. Tara pointed to the purple eight-inch pipes bolted to the ceiling. "Hear that scraping sound? Those are the slurry pipes that move the palletized nutrients."

Ka-Rump! Tara dropped her thought. Andrea motioned back, saying, "They found the grenades. Let's move!" Almost immediately they heard a siren wail, then in the distance, a volley of gunfire.

"Fire!" Coop sprung his ambush on a column of Security Troops quick-stepping from the barracks gate. His small band of clones followed their simple but deadly instructions. From rooftop perches and street-level stair stoops, each man or woman concentrated deadly fire on his or her particular partition of the killing zone. The Security Troops found themselves pinned between building walls with not so much as a blade of grass to shield them. Half the column fell under the first hail of bullets, the others scrambled up the narrow street toward the barracks only to be shot in the back, or fall from shrapnel from the grenades tossed into the melee for good measure. The air stank of sulfur. After that long minute of chaos, the street fell silent except for the groans of the dying and the ebullient cheers from the victors.

Andrea and Tara ran down the corridor to an intersection and more pipes: fat with insulation, painted white, and labeled Liquid Oxygen. The walls hummed with the vibration of large turbine pumps, and Andrea sensed they were near the heart of the institute. She also heard the faint sound of sporadic gunfire muffled by many yards of steel and concrete. "Hurry!"

The corridor opened to a cavernous bay. Andrea paused to absorb the magnitude of this assembly of machines. One must measure the floor in acres: the sixty-foot ceiling looked low and cramped given the length and breadth of the open room. Suddenly the amount of explosives they carried on their backs seemed puny.

Into this cavern, the pipes delivered the raw materials. Here, the Ordinate manufactured the syrupy "food" in massive stainless steel vats. Thick clear plastic pipes carried the black syrup past large mechanical turn-valves through walls to the nurseries. The vats gave off an odor-laden steam, a sickeningly sweet treacle smell with a hint of rotting fruit.

In a separate quadrant, another set of tubes returned a deep amber fluid to a set of machines: a dozen centrifuges and pumps. Tara explained with an odd bit of pride, "Here, we exchanged the waste products. We remove bile, urea, and excrement. Then the centrifuges collect the sloughed cells for reconstitution into the next batch of syrup. We disinfect the amniotic fluid in an oxygen bath."

"Amniotic fluid?" Irrelevant, but Andrea couldn't help but ask.

"Yes. The clone larvae produce the fluid from their kidneys. There is no better synthetic. We just keep the fluid sterile and oxygenated to the point where they can breathe the fluid."

"Where's the oxygen that goes to the clone larvae?"

Tara pointed. "Look. The filtered, amniotic fluid comes out clear as rainwater and goes to the oxygenation tanks."

"Looks like a beer factory." Andrea saw the crystal-clear plastic pipes disappear into a series of pill-shaped tanks, each twenty feet long. The liquid oxygen pipes made one stop at a pair of expansion chambers. The great pressure locked the free oxygen molecules into the liquid.

A small glassed-in area housed the computers, the brains of the institute that managed the economy of clone manufacture, plus provided the sensory experience of the student larvae—the neural imprints. Transformers at the opposite end of the man-made cavern distributed electric power to the hundreds of turbine pumps, heating kettles, computers, banks of ultraviolet lights. A marvel to behold, this factory was almost an organism in its own right—almost. Yet for all its size and complexity, this factory was less a marvel than a single cell, and in many ways more fragile.

Andrea riffled through her backpack as she reviewed her options. Tara suggested, "If we blow up the transformers, the pumps stop, and the larvae die from oxygen starvation."

"Yes, but the factory stands. After they squeegee the mess from the nurseries, they just . . ." Andrea didn't have the chance to finish her thought.

All around, heavy metal doors slammed down, sealing the room. The metal-to-metal clangs echoed throughout the factory, momentarily drowning out the whining drone of the turbine pumps. One oversized cargo door remained open and through it six Cor Hunters in full battle dress ran in, then broke into teams of two. One pair stayed at the open door; the others began patrolling the factory. Tara said plainly, "We're trapped." She checked her pistol to make doubly sure she had a round chambered, then added, "They're coming down."

Andrea pulled Tara out of sight. "Let's not wait around. We can't outlast them in a static defense."

"So what now?"

"I have an idea." Andrea pulled a quarter-pound wad of plastique from her backpack and pressed the pale green glob against the wall. She inserted a timing cap and set it for four minutes, marking her chronometer to be in sync with the charge.

"What are you doing?" Tara backed away from the live charge.

"A diversion. Take us down to the vats and the oxygen-expansion chambers."

Tara obeyed. They crouched behind pipes, ran when they could, duckwalked when they had to, all the while blind as to the movements of the Hunters. Andrea paused and set another small charge, checking her chronometer and setting the timing cap for two minutes thirty seconds. She whispered, "Go! This charge blows first."

"Why?" Tara asked on the run.

Breathing heavy, more from excitement than exertion, Andrea replied, "They will be drawn to the sequence of explosions—away from us."

"Are you sure?"

They paused for a moment before an open space, their backs against a stainless steel tank of the syrup. Tara looked around the left side, Andrea the right. Speaking as the veteran, she said, "A disciplined unit would not be drawn to the explosions but continue to sweep search, but disciplined units are rare." She counted backward ending, "Hold your ears."

Boom! The concussion rattled the floor and every thing upon it. In the distance a machine pistol spit a short burst till a command voice bellowed, "Hold your fire!"

Bits of wall plaster rained down; then dead silence. Andrea gave Tara a worried look. "I think these people are disciplined."

The next charge detonated two hundred feet farther away. Andrea crouched and listened. No reaction. The plaster dust settled; still nothing. No return fire. No hurried movements. No shouts. *These guys are good.* Her pulse quickened. "Tara," she whispered. "They're wearing body armor—aim for the face shield, or use your knife."

They waited. Andrea knew that in this deadly game, predator and prey would likely see each other at exactly the same instant. She must get the first shot and hit her mark. She heard the faint footfall, a boot crushing the specks of plaster. Then she saw a red dot from a laser gun sight shine off the wall behind her. Judging from the red dot's small jerky movements, she figured the Hunter was within thirty feet, moving with great caution, weapon raised and ready to fire. But foreknowledge is advantage.

Then a second dot shimmered from the wall on Tara's side of the silver vat. Near panic seized her—she might get one, but never two. And Tara was no match for a trained Hunter. Andrea grabbed Tara's sleeve and motioned silence, pointing to the red laser dots. Then she quickly pressed a quarter-pound glob of plastique on the steel vat and set the timing cap for three seconds. With hand signals she communicated that Tara must follow her, on her signal—*fast!*

A shadow. The Hunter on Andrea's side was the closer of the pair, and three steps would bring him into view. One . . . anxiety amplified the sound of the footstep . . . two . . .

Andrea pressed the button on the timing cap. With her pistol raised to eye level, she rounded the tank, squeezing the trigger as she ran. Her first shot smashed into the Hunter's body armor, knocking him back a step. The

Hunter, a head taller than Andrea, answered with a burst from his machine pistol, but off-balance, he fired over their heads. Andrea's second shot drilled the man through his faceplate, killing him. Andrea and Tara didn't break stride, but lunged past the fallen Hunter.

At the same instant, the second Hunter rounded the vat just in time to be cut in half by the charge. The vat ruptured, splattering black syrup over an acre of machines. The stainless steel casing and the several tons of liquid shielded Andrea and Tara from the direct effect of the explosion, but pea-size globs pelted them as they ran from the blast. The thick black sludge sloshed over the floor like lava.

Out of immediate danger, they paused to catch their breath. Yet breathing was uncomfortable because the smell of the syrup threatened to overpower them. Nevertheless, Andrea dipped her finger in some of the black sludge and put it to her tongue. Tara squinted in revulsion.

"Just as I thought, this stuff is almost pure carbon." Andrea spit. "This stuff will burn. The syrup, calcium, plastic pipes, machine solvents, the palletized protein: they'll all burn." Andrea looked around. A thin smile crept over her face.

Catching her breath, Tara pointed to the ceiling, "But the fire extinguishers . . ."

"Not a problem. We add pure oxygen—raise the temperature to four thousand degrees centigrade. At that temperature, aluminum burns; steel boils. Water, chemicals—nothing can stop such a fire. Only problems is, we better have a fast way out of the oven."

"Attack air!" Coop pointed to the low morning clouds where a pair of swept-wing planes flew in low and fast. "Get off the roofs!"

No sooner had he said the words but they saw the bright flashes from the leading edge of the wings. All around them, large caliber bullets chewed handfuls of masonry from the buildings. "Get down! Get down!" One clone stood to fire his pistol at the oncoming slaughter, but before he could fire three rounds, one of the strafing bullets smashed a hole through his chest, knocking him off his feet.

The two aircraft swooped past and banked a hard turn for another run. As Coop hustled his people onto the street, the barracks gates reopened and out poured two armored cars and infantry. The cars fired laser cannon from a flat turret mounted on a body of oblique glacis plates. With six wheels and a black lacquer finish, the armored cars looked like two large insects.

Coop jumped to the street and ran around the corner just in time to see a crimson beam cut a female clone in two at the torso. Her face registered more surprise than pain as she flopped to the ground. Coop turned and saw his people fleeing down the street. Many fired their pistols blindly behind them, as if throwing a chair to impede a charging tiger. To get out of the cross fire, Coop pressed himself into a doorway.

The armored car, in hot pursuit, outran all but three of the Ordinate infantrymen. Coop prepared two grenades and waited for the armored car to roll by. He pulled the pin, dropped the spoon and waited a dangerous two seconds before lobbing it at the feet of the three soldiers panting to keep pace with the armored car. The explosion shredded their legs and they fell clutching their mortal wounds.

Coop sprinted after the armored car, jumped on the alloy deck and stuffed the second grenade down the commander's hatch. The muffled explosion sent the machine into a spasm. It lurched to the right and drove into the building wall where it stalled. He yelled after his people, "Come back here and fight!"

Then, he climbed inside the machine, sloppy with blood and entrails. He poured the gunner from her seat and took the controls, turning the wicked laser beam against the Ordinate infantry. And he slaughtered them without pity: the smell of burnt flesh wafted back as a testimony to his deadly work.

Andrea stood with her back to a large stainless steel vat. "We don't have much time. They'll call for reinforcements now."

The two Hunters gave up their post at the cargo door. Before they scrambled down the metal stairs to join the fight, they sealed the cargo door with a loud slam. On the ground floor, they split up: one ran toward the computer room, the other toward the transformers.

"What's on the other side of that wall?"

"The cocoon room."

"Good. We're going through there."

"But it's hermetically sealed, a sterile environment."

Andrea just looked down her nose and shook her head slightly in a mild rebuke. "We're going to unseal it." She reached into her pack and pulled out a rope of plastique, fashioning it into a lazy *Z* shape on the wall. She added the timing cap and set it for three minutes.

Andrea spoke quickly. "We're going to split up for just two minutes. Put your charges on all the syrup tanks, the slurry pipes—just empty your bag. Stagger your timers between five and six minutes. I'll try to draw the Hunters to me with some minor explosions of my own."

"What about their discipline?"

"I think they're past that now—aren't you?"

Tara gave a short, nervous laugh at this gallows humor. "Yes."

Andrea continued, "I'm going to blow the liquid oxygen chambers and flood the area with pure oxygen. Your explosions will set fires that will become intense and spread rapidly. Make sure you get through the wall. Don't wait for me." She patted Tara on the shoulder. "I'll be right behind you."

Andrea grabbed her pack and ran between the pumps and pipes toward the pair of expansion chambers. She stopped to set small quarter-pound charges as she went, set for thirty seconds—they blew, adding to the chaos.

She reached the liquid oxygen pipes and followed them to the chambers. There, she tapped the casing lightly and as she suspected, the chamber was built of seamless steel at least four-inches thick. She pulled half her explosives—almost eight pounds—from the pack and molded it into a cone shape. It looked like an abalone stuck to the metal. She fixed a firing cap and ran a length of det-cord to the second chamber, where she fashioned another shape charge. In this second charge she placed a timing cap set for two minutes.

She took a deep breath and pressed the button. *Two minutes till hell.* As she did, she heard the *ping! ping!* of ricochets. Bullets splashed off the chamber walls. A splinter of steel stung her arm. Andrea dove to the floor behind a cement footing. She ignored the pain in her right arm—hot like a bee sting, the sensation of swelling was actually blood flowing. She examined the marks on the chamber to extrapolate the whereabouts of the shooter. She slid on her belly backwards: she needed room to get up and run.

Blam! The large Z-shaped wall charge blew a hole to the cocoon room, creating a cloud of debris and smoke. Then she heard a nearby voice cry, "They set a bomb on the oxygen!"

The other from a distance cried, "Quick! Pull the cap!"

The nearby Hunter ran with utter disregard for his safety to the shape charge. He ran past Andrea, nearly stepping on her, but he had no thought except to disarm that charge. Andrea stood from her hiding place, raised her pistol, and fired point-blank into the Hunter's back. The body armor failed to stop the round at such close range. The Hunter staggered forward toward the charge. She fired again. He fell to one knee but struggled back to his feet, only an arm's reach from the timing cap. Again, she fired, and this bullet ripped out a vertebra from the Hunter's neck and dropped him facedown. He was now a supplicant to Andrea's explosives.

Ten seconds. She didn't see the other Hunter. Would he attempt to undo the cap? Eight. Should she save herself? Stay back and guarantee the explosion? Seven. She heard her name. "Andrea!" *At least Tara made it through the wall.* Six. She started backing up, her pistol raised ready to fire on anyone approaching the oxygen chambers. Five. Her right arm began to ache. Four. She saw no one. *Where is the second Hunter?* Three. Andrea turned and ran toward the hole in the wall some thirty yards away.

The two shape charges blew with devastating force, ripping the chambers up from their steel-reinforced roots. The floor jerked itself out from under Andrea's feet, knocking her flat on her face. Chunks of metal rained down about her, striking her, bruising her. The hot breath of the explosion blew past, followed immediately by the icy breath of the super cool oxygen.

She struggled to her feet, scrambling on all fours like an animal toward the hole in the wall. Tara's charges blew. A pillar of white flame rose to the ceiling—no smoke. The pure oxygen had hit the fire; the combustion was complete and ungodly hot. Andrea lunged for the opening, for she was in a race with hell's own fire.

Coop's people rallied to his position, and there they fought with cold resolve. The streets were littered with the Ordinate dead and dying, yet the black-uniformed troops continued to press from all sides. Confused by active clone resistance, the Ordinate tactics dissolved into an orgy of violence. Their infantry swarmed up the street, in front of their armor.

The enraged clones answered in kind, leaving whatever cover they'd found and joined the Ordinate infantry in close combat. The narrowness of the street helped offset the numerical superiority of the Ordinate force.

The clones fought as if drugged by chaos, they sloughed off wounds and slashed back with their knives. They fired their pistols until they exhausted their ammunition, then used their pistols as clubs, splattering brains. They plucked weapons from the fallen enemy and sprayed bullets, indifferent to the casualities.

One by one, the clones fell with nobody to replace them. The rest, bleeding from fatal wounds, fought till dizziness robbed their sight, and thus blurred, they could not evade or defend against the final shot or cut. Coop fared little better than the others, as he was gut shot. He considered himself already dead.

A voice, heavily buried in static, came across Coop's comm-disk, "The institute's on fire! Fall back!"

He turned to see a column of gray smoke rising

above the crystal ziggurat, forming a fat cloud. Klaxons screamed for fire fighters. The chaos was delicious! The institute was doomed. Coop felt satisfied, as if he'd shared a great meal with his friends. *His friends . . .* With fewer than a dozen of his forty clones still standing, Coop bellowed: "Go back! Fight your way out!"

"Coop, you come too—"

"Fall back—damn you—don't question my orders!"

They obeyed and began hacking and shooting their way to the rear. Coop stayed behind. With a machine pistol in one hand, he fired into the Ordinate crowd. He slaughtered the Ordinate as they turned the brunt of their attack toward him. He emptied one pistol and picked up another from one of the many dead. With the other hand he slashed with his blade. A bullet struck him in the chest and he felt his lung collapse. He fought savagely. As his lung sucked air through his chest, he knew his agony would be short lived.

Soon, his world began to spin. His sight dimmed. And now he fought with shadows. He fired in the enemy's direction, killing another Ordinate. He felt a large blade dig deep into his side. He tried to pull the trigger on his weapon but he was too weak—his hand would no longer do his will.

Andrea put the comm disk back into her pocket as she and Tara ran away from the heat between a row of adult cocoons. The conflagration in the factory grew, pulling air from the cocoon room. Andrea stood in the draft, which felt refreshing against her sweat- and blood-soaked clothes.

Tara whispered reverently, "They're dying."

"So be it." Andrea looked at a row of cocoons. Everywhere, small green lights flickered to red as the toxin levels rose and the oxygen levels fell. Each eight-foot tube held seventy cubic feet of opaque amniotic fluid, and one NewGen clone. An ocular mask covered the eyes. A small flexible tube ran down the left nostril—delivering or extracting, she couldn't tell. All flow had stopped. A few free bubbles let go of the glass and shimmied up. Small tubes extended from the femoral arteries, and a silver cord entered the back of the neck at the spinal cortex.

They looked like underfed cattle. Skin-draped pelvic bones and ribs showed. Exaggerated shoulder blades protruded like small wings. The little bit of muscle mass was hard. And even as she watched, the skin turned from milk white to crimson blue. Some went slack, suspended in the liquid. Others clawed at their glass encasement. Were they responding to the stimuli pumped into their minds or did they sense imminent death?

"Let's get out of here." Andrea had had enough.

Then a loud cough caught their attention. Looking back to the hole, they saw a Hunter, his uniform smoldering. The man howled as he peeled off his body armor, and with it large patches of burnt skin. He threw down his face shield, now just a warped sheet of plastic. His hair was charred stubble; half his face was blistered and raw.

Andrea retrieved her pistol, crouched, took aim, and fired. But at a range of two hundred feet she missed. "Damn!"

Alerted by the shot, the Hunter dove for cover and disappeared. Andrea pulled Tara down for a brief consultation. "How far is the exit?"

"Two hundred meters."

"We can't just run for it—he'll cut us down. We can't wait here—the fire will engulf this room next."

"Then what do we do?" Tara had her pistol out.

"He's coming after us. We'll work our way toward the exit—we'll run down different rows. Maybe we can catch him in a cross fire. Shoot at anything that moves."

Tara nodded and stepped between two glass cocoons to another row. Andrea stepped briskly from cocoon to cocoon, using them as cover. Her eyes scanned the gaps looking for the Hunter—it all looked illusory: the rows and columns of squirming NewGens in their glistening cases created a blur of movement. *Where is he?*

The Hunter answered with a single shot—*pow!* The round missed her head by six inches and punctured a cocoon, striking a dying NewGen. The NewGen jerked and thrashed, stirring the claret stream from his side into a pink bath. Andrea crouched and ran six paces, then raised her head to look for her adversary.

Movement. Several rows back. She fired and missed. The sound of breaking glass rattled back. *Shoot and move!* She ran a couple steps: a burst of machine gun fire followed her, shattering the row of cocoons. Several thousand gallons of slippery fluids doused her: the force washing her back. The dying NewGen spilled from their glass coffins, collapsing to the floor tangled in their tubes, twitching like stunned fish. One fell on top of Andrea and although sightless, the NewGen reflexively grabbed her arm with a warm waterlogged hand. "Whaooh! Oooh, oh! Sheee-yit!" Andrea wrenched her arm free, then backpedaled, kicking the slithering corpses aside.

Tara shrieked, "Are you all right?"

Tara's desperate question was answered immediately by gunfire. The Hunter's machine pistol cut down another half dozen cocoons, as if they were nothing but shrubs in the way. More of the amber liquid sloshed to the floor, more NewGens fell among them.

Tara stood knee-deep in NewGen bodies and fired at the moving shadows—hitting nothing.

A spray of bullets returned. She fired again, and again.

"Get down! You fool!" Andrea barked.

Tara dropped to her knees and whispered hoarsely, "I'm out of bullets."

"Well that's just great!" Andrea wrestled herself from the NewGen clone and yelled, "We're getting out of here!" She poked her pistol above the jagged glass and fired a few blind rounds just to force the Hunter to put his head down and as she did, she crawled to dry ground, and another rack of cocoons to hide behind. She fired again: *Bam! Bam!* Click . . .

"Now we *are* screwed," Andrea growled, "Run! Run for the door." They jumped to their feet and ran. No bullets followed. *Perhaps the Hunter is out of bullets as well. Speed!* The forest of glass casings refracted the light, casting doubt as to which image was flesh and blood. She saw the sign for the door: ahead and several rows away.

They slid to a stop at the end of the long line of limp NewGen clones. For a brief second they huddled. Tara was gasping for breath. Andrea pulled out her knife and said, "I'll go first. You follow."

Peering around, they saw the door—and it was open! She ran forward and ten paces behind Tara followed. But before she reached the door, out stepped the Hunter, weapon raised in one hand, a utility knife in the other. Tara skidded to a stop at Andrea's right.

"Well, well, well. From what I hear, you're out of

ammunition." The Hunter grinned through intense pain. His oozing burns were beginning to crust. "Fortunately, I still have a bullet. So, one of you I will kill quickly; the other slowly." He aimed the gun first at Tara, then Andrea—back and forth. "Don't be coy. Which of you wants the bullet?"

Tara and Andrea stood silent. He goaded them, "Oh, talk it over if you like. I'll give you a moment to reflect."

Tara bravely said, "Shoot me."

Andrea did not contradict her, somewhat to Tara's surprise. But Andrea could slay this man in a knife fight. The Hunter could carve Tara at his leisure. So as a matter of tactics, Tara had unwittingly but nobly chosen the better course of action.

"Thanks for your input." The Hunter slowly turned the gun toward Andrea and raised the rear sights to eye level. Andrea watched as he gently squeezed the trigger. If she could judge the play in the trigger, she might at the last split second jump and dodge the bullet.

Blam! She winced, embarrassed for the moment that her eyes closed involuntarily from the sound and that her feet remained glued to the floor. She mentally surveyed her body for the wound. *What?* She opened her eyes and saw. The Hunter slowly fell—his mouth twisted, stuck on an unfinished thought; indignant wide eyes transfixed on some outrage—the top of his head exploded like a fleshy melon. The Hunter fell like a curtain, and behind him stood Brigon, obscured in his wilderness cloak, smoke curling from his pistol barrel still held in firing position.

chapter 19

Brigon stooped down to pick up the Hunter's pistol. He reloaded it with a fresh clip and handed it to Andrea. "You two certainly know how to have a good time." He wrestled with his cloak against the strong draft.

Glancing at the partially decapitated Hunter, Andrea struggled for words. She looked back at Brigon, the shock still plain on her face. She tucked the pistol into her belt. "Thank you," she said softly, almost inaudible through the cacophony of wind and battle.

As the white-hot fire in the belly of the ziggurat grew, so did the stiff draft. Latches gave way and doors flew open to let strong gusts through to fan the flames. Through the rush of wind, they heard remnants of gunfire and a rising pitch of sirens. Brigon and his two companions pulled Tara and Andrea, still slippery from a douse of amniotic fluid, through the doorway. "Follow me," Brigon ordered.

As they struggled down the corridor, Tara asked, "Why did you come back? How did you know where to find us?"

Brigon paused to glance down a long corridor, waving them forward in a single file. He spoke in a matter-of-fact tone, but his voice raised an air of untrammeled jubilance. "I was curious to see how you amateurs might do."

The wind caught Brigon's cloak and knocked him to one knee. Andrea grabbed a fistful of his garment and helped him up. He grunted a thank you, then continued. "We watched you go in through the sound barrier. We heard a short gun fight; then silence."

An explosion signaled the death of a large transformer and the overhead lights went black. Andrea felt a hand grab her shoulder from behind; Brigon grabbed her wrist from the front to prevent a break in contact during this moment of blindness. *Trained instinct.* Andrea approved.

Dim amber emergency lights flickered on. Brigon nodded to one of his men to walk point. He spoke loudly to be heard over the wind. "We assumed the Ordinate forces had eradicated you in two minutes, so we started our march home. Then the gunfire started again. I stopped the column. I thought, *Perhaps the Ordinate were simply finishing the wounded*—then we heard laser cannon. And voices—defiant clone voices. I didn't even have to give orders—my troops turned and ran back as fast as they could through the barrier, toward the noise."

The point man came to an intersection in the long hall and raised a clenched fist to signal a halt. Brigon signaled a question with hand gestures. The point responded by holding up eight fingers, putting the palm of one hand on his head, then pointing to the left. Brigon translated in a whisper, "Eight, full battle gear, moving away." Then he finished his story in a quick staccato of phrases: "We ran into the remnant of your force. We laid down protective fire. The Ordinate retreated. The street was littered with dead—a festival of butchery. Breathtaking. One of your survivors told me where to find you in the institute."

Tara leaned in to catch the end of Brigon's story. "A survivor? How many casualties?"

Before Brigon could answer, the point man signaled them to advance. "Let's go. Be ready."

They turned right, staying a hundred feet behind the point man. Again, he alerted them to a group of hostiles running though the corridors: armed forces, fire fighters, and litter bearers. Tara tapped Brigon on the shoulder lightly and whispered, "We're almost outside. Just a couple hundred feet."

The point man suddenly crouched low, raised two fists in the air and crossed them over his head; then instantly buried himself in his wilderness cloak. Brigon barked, "Cloak! Josh—you cover Tara." Then he grabbed Andrea by the waist and pulled her toward him roughly, bending her over and pressing her toward the floor and against the wall. He pulled his cloak over them, sealing out the last remnant of light. His mouth was next to her ear as he whispered, "Don't even breathe."

His grip was unyielding. Andrea felt his fingers and thumb dig into her ribs, as if he might keep her from breathing. She felt his pulse from his arm wrapped around her, and his beard and warm breath against her neck as he pinned her against the wall. This rough handling opened the wound in her shoulder and sent shards of pain down her back. Crouched over, she felt the machine pistol barrel digging into her thigh. Seconds seemed like hours. She listened. *Heavy foot-*

steps. Boots. Twenty, maybe thirty men, running single file down the corridor just inches from them. And what if one should trip over an invisible obstruction? Andrea held her breath and tried to meld into the wall.

The sound of boots faded quickly. Brigon threw off the cloak, pulled Andrea to her feet, and said, "Let's go." He saw the fresh blood ooze through the torn fabric on her shoulder and gently but quickly probed the wound with his finger. "It's a small wound."

They picked their way through the rest of the institute and left by a side exit. From all directions, men and women in white and pale green lab coats swarmed about the building. Helmeted men, buglike in appearance, axed doors. Frantic technicians rushed into the building bearing litters in an effort to save some remnant of their first crop of NewGen clones. They brought back a cargo of waterlogged and singed flesh and lay the naked bodies on the lawn. In that small formal garden, medical personnel fought to revive a handful of limp clones—restoring some warmth to a few of the ghastly blue figures—abandoning many more as rubbish. They cursed the litter bearers. "Stop bringing us dead ones! You idiots! Be more selective."

Overhead, the cloud of smoke fairly blocked the sunlight. Aircraft hovered high above the ziggurat, dropping what amounted to thimbles of red fire retardant on the expanding blaze. The intense heat blew away their pusillanimous efforts back into their faces, so powerful was the updraft. Nearby, sporadic gunfire and smoke from smaller fires added to the general chaos.

So complete was the bedlam, that Brigon and company skirted the crowd unmolested. They scampered up a set of stairs onto the great granite wall. There they enjoyed cover, excellent fields of observation, and a direct route to their comrades who controlled the gate near their egress through the sonic barrier.

Andrea took genuine delight in watching the futility of the Ordinates' efforts. She especially noticed with pleasure the dull panic on the faces of the supervisors—the manager class. They knew what the technicians were too busy to contemplate: the gun battle and the fire were not just a disaster to be managed, but the end of a way of life.

Tara seized the lull to ask her question again. "How many casualties?"

Brigon set his jaw to deliver the hard news. "We found only six of your troop still standing, and all of them wounded one way or the other. My people have them within a defensive perimeter at the wall; we'll meet them there, then go through the sonic barrier."

Stunned by the extent of the losses, Tara stammered, "Coop?"

"Dead. He held the rear while his people fell back. It looked like he'd been building a tomb, using the Ordinate dead as bricks—all stacked around him. Impressive sight: Coop lying on a heap with his blade still in his hand. I even thought of fighting our way back to recover his body . . ." Brigon hesitated, uncomfortable with his narrative.

"Why didn't you?" Andrea asked. She hadn't thought such sentiments possible for the cynical Brigon.

Brigon gave Andrea a cold look. "Such a foray would have been to enhance my reputation, not Coop's."

Andrea blushed at Brigon's candid response to her rude question. She turned her face toward the rising shroud of smoke.

As if the possibility had never entered her mind, Tara muttered, "Coop gone?" She said the word *gone* as if Coop might come back, as people are wont to speak in euphemisms about the dead. Tara wrestled with the finality. She turned to Andrea and said, "I can't go to Jod with you now."

This change in plans startled Andrea. "What do you mean?"

"With Coop dead, there's no one to lead the Underground. After today, the Ordinate will crack down on the old-order clones. They'll hurry the fences, quarantine us where we'll wait for extermination. They'll slaughter us like cattle, unless the precinct clones use their numbers to resist. I've got to make them see. I can't leave them here leaderless."

Andrea reached forward and grabbed Brigon's arm to pull him into this conversation. "Brigon can lead the precinct clones."

Bullets from sporadic gunfire whistled overhead. Josh ducked. Brigon merely paused and looked down from the wall to locate the source of the spent rounds. Then he raised his hand to fend off Andrea's suggestion.

Andrea pressed. "Brigon, you own the wilderness. You can hide thousands in that wasteland. You can train them to fight. You know weapons; tactics. Already, you take old or injured precinct clones and turn them into fighters."

"They seek me: I don't recruit them."

"And now the entire clone population is marked for death, maybe not today, but in a matter of a few short years. They'll seek you soon enough. Are you going to turn them away?"

Brigon tried to change the subject. "We'd better keep moving."

Andrea stood in his way and whispered, "You must lead the precinct clones: you can't refuse."

"Really? Why?" He looked past her, trying to ignore her.

Andrea smiled wryly. She painted the chaos below with a sweeping gesture. "Because you love the fight. That's why you came back."

He whispered in kind. "What I *love* is not relevant. And your clone friends are doomed. All of this"—Brigon stood, arms folded, looking past Andrea at the carnage and wreckage around him—"is vain. The Ordinate will rebuild. And as you well know, they will rebuild on the backs of precinct clone labor. So in a sense, you are asking me to fight the precinct clones and the Ordinate at the same time." Brigon nudged her to pick up the pace.

"Haven't you been fighting both sides all your life?"

"I've just been trying to survive. Open war against the Ordinate is pointless. In the end, you can't win." Brigon raised his hand to signal his men to stop.

"We can win." Andrea raised her voice. "If you stay here and lead the Underground, I can take Tara back to the Jod. With Hal K'Rin's help, she and Eric can convince the Council of the NewGen threat. The Jod will send their fleet—the largest and best in the galaxy—to your aid."

Brigon paused in thought. He studied the light in Andrea's eyes. An explosion above the ziggurat raised a fireball, but did not break his concentration. The rising pitch of the gun battle at the wall seemed a bare nuisance. "I can't."

Tara grabbed Brigon by the arm and turned him around. "We don't want to talk you into something you don't want to do."

Both Brigon and Andrea gave Tara a harsh look, each for different reasons. Then Brigon softened as he addressed Tara. "Your people fought well. With a thousand like them, I could burn Sarhn to the ground." Then he turned to speak with Andrea and sounded like a judge pronouncing his own sentence. "All right. I'll take charge of Tara's forces on this condition—that you return before the next summer, with or without the Jod fleet."

Andrea looked into his dark eyes as she said, "I promise. I'll bring what help I can, or come alone."

"I believe you." Brigon gently took a handful of Andrea's sticky hair at the nape of her neck, then let go.

Andrea felt a chill. *Good. Done. I can complete my mission.* Andrea solved the problem of prying Tara loose, but on a different level, she was bothered by Brigon's simple trust: *I believe you.* But what did Brigon's motives matter to her? She'd solved the immediate problem: Brigon would stay; Tara would accompany her back to Jod. The rest was out of her hands—except that she'd made a promise. She'd worry about that if she got off Cor in one piece.

Get off Cor. Andrea looked over the buildings and saw Ordinate troops securing the streets. Aerial transports brought troops from the far end of the city. "Tara, we're going to have a hard time getting to the spaceport. The streets are filling up with soldiers. They'll shoot anything that moves now."

Brigon called to his lieutenant, "Josh—give Tara your wilderness cloak." At the same time he unfastened a neck clasp and in one fluid movement handed his cloak to Andrea. "These will help you get into a ship. Remember, stay perfectly still for six seconds and you blend into your surroundings. When you move, try to stay against a patterned or monochrome background—even then, move, halt; move, halt."

Andrea did not argue, but wrapped herself in the cloak. She noticed the weight of the dense cloth and the odor of Brigon's sweat. Still tacky from her bath in amniotic fluid, speckled with dollops of nutrient syrup, blood, and smoke, she felt far from fresh.

On the move again, they traversed the wall and found the Ordinate security forces massing everything they had against the clone's defensive perimeter. The Ordinate, in body armor, skittered from their hiding places, dodging snipers. They set up laser cannon on tripods.

From his perch above the wall, Brigon pointed to the enemy positions. "We're well protected by the stone wall. They can't get a good shot at us. So, they're setting up to contain us. Look—" He spoke directly to his two men as calmly as if this were just another training exercise. "Their line of fire makes a killing zone in *front* of our position. Odd, don't you think? And note the large formation of troops huddled behind the buildings. What do you suppose they're planning?"

The wilderness clone, Josh, answered, "They're going to try to flush us out of our position from behind and force us into their killing zone. Also, if we break contact and make a run for the woods, they're set to pursue."

"Correct." Brigon fished a small set of binoculars from his pouch and looked over the forest. In the distance he saw aircraft on the ground disgorging troops. "I see 'em: five or six units. They're trying to envelop us. They have a forty-minute march to take positions behind us. So, we've got to get out of here, and fast. I don't much like the idea of being caught in the middle. We'll move our people through the barrier and into the forest. There we can make a run for it. Quick, put a line over the wall."

Tara interrupted. "I made the breach in the sonic barrier; I can close it."

Brigon's smile masked the strain. "That's good news. I can handle my front if you cover my back. I was beginning to think my promotion to precinct clone commander was going to be short lived."

"I need to reach my computer terminal tied to the security protocols." Tara pointed back to outbuildings illuminated by the white flames lapping the institute. "I can watch your progress through the breach. Give me a signal and I'll shut it down."

"I'll signal you with . . ." Brigon checked a small canister clipped to his utility belt ". . . green smoke."

While Brigon and Tara laid plans to close the breach in the sonic barrier, the silent wilderness clone took a nylon cord and metal piton from his cloak. He tapped the metal sliver into a crack in a large chunk of granite, fastened the quarter-inch cord to a small ring, and tossed the cord over the sixty-foot drop. Then as if to demonstrate confidence in his work, he grabbed the line, curled his cloak into the crook of his arm, and climbed over the wall. He looked like a spider dangling at the end of a thread, sliding down to the moss-covered ground. Josh followed, then Brigon took the line in his hand. He said, "See you next summer . . . I want my cloak back." Brigon slid down the line and did not look back.

Andrea didn't nod or wave. She didn't speak. She merely looked over the wall and watched as Brigon let go of the cord and hit the ground running. She jerked the piton from the crevice and tossed it over the wall. "Okay, Tara, take us back into this bar fight."

* * *

Brigon whistled, a loud shrill summons. His lieutenants hustled to his side, relieved at once to see him, then momentarily crestfallen to learn that they were about to be surrounded. They brightened just as fast when Brigon told them Tara would close the breach in the sonic barrier and thereby guard their rear. With a few brisk orders, Brigon set a tactical withdrawal into motion. One-third of his troops left their positions and scampered through the breach into the wood line, taking up positions to provide covering fire. In this way the last third would withdraw under the protection of a blanket of blistering small arms fire.

Wearing the wilderness cloaks, Tara and Andrea ran as a blur through the crowds. The Ordinate fire fighters and technicians were reduced to gawking at the flames that shot skyward like a bright geyser. The Security Troops had quit the institute to concentrate on the military operation forming at the gate.

Tara ducked into the outlying administration building and ran up flights of metal stairs—Andrea close on her heels—and through a deserted warren of cubicles to her twelve-square-feet of work space.

She lunged at the console on her desk and after a deft peck or two at the control panel, she announced, "The security systems are still up." She rubbed her hands on her pants to remove some of the surface grime from her fingers.

"Thank God." Andrea ran to the window and peeled back the vertical blinds. "Brigon's men are passing through the breach now. The Ordinate forces are keeping their heads down, but they're assembling to pursue."

Tara's fingers danced across the console, hauling

data to the amber screen. "I've got the file that defines the breach. All I have to do now is hit the *execute* key. Is Brigon through?"

"Not yet." Andrea watched Brigon's disciplined withdrawal. The clones in the tree line effectively stalled the Ordinate with heavy suppressing fire, but she knew that as soon as they broke contact to flee into the woods, the Ordinate would swarm after them. A wicked smile crossed her face. "Tara, I've got an idea."

"Not now." Tara was annoyed by this distraction.

Andrea chortled. "I'm going to teach you the concept of *payback.*"

"What?"

"Trade places with me quickly." Andrea skipped over to the console. "Show me the *execute* key."

"There." To the right of a panel of one hundred twenty-eight keys lay a single yellow disk with a dark blue border. "Touch the yellow to execute."

Andrea waved Tara away. "Now go to the window and tell me when you see the green smoke."

Tara obeyed. There was no time to argue. "The last of them are running at twenty-foot intervals through the breach. Okay, they're through! I see Brigon on the far side. The green smoke! Hit the execute button!" She turned to find Andrea smiling. "Hit the button!"

"Patience, Tara. Tell me what you see."

"Brigon's troops just disappeared into the woods. Hit the button!"

"Good. What are the Ordinate doing?"

"They're running through the gate, of course. Toward the breach. Hit the button before it's too late!" The Ordinate regulars poured down the embankment, weapons raised, firing blindly into the trees.

"Oh, but it's too early," Andrea cooed. "Tell me when

the breach is full of Ordinate troops. Don't worry if a couple zealots get through."

Tara understood completely now, and her hands shook as the chill of this cold-blooded deed grabbed her. With no emotion she reported, "The breach is full. *Now.*"

Andrea hit the button, then ran to the window to inspect her handiwork. Agony. The men caught in the sonic barrier stiffened as if jolted by a lethal surge of electricity. Their spines arched—an exaggeration of human anatomy, followed almost as quickly by a tuck into a fetal position. All of them grabbed their heads with their hands, clawing their own eyes and ears as they reflexively kicked their feet. Their comrades stood and watched in horror as the men in the grips of the Ordinate security barrier screamed their last. Then the bodies swelled as the ultrasound changed body fluids to vapor: uniforms ripped, exposing purplish lesions on the bloated torsos.

"It's awful." Tara shook her head.

"Yes, but it is justice."

chapter 20

Again, the bedlam and the wilderness cloaks combined to provide good cover. Tara and Andrea walked past scenes of destruction where Coop's small band scarred the city: medical personnel—including precinct clones—sifted through the Ordinate dead and wounded. Fire fighters sprayed chemicals on the burning hulks of two armored cars. Tara paused to watch a fire-damaged building collapse under its own weight, scattering workers to a safer distance. Sirens wailed, voices shouted instructions, but for the moment the air lacked the sound of gunfire.

They skirted the worst of the damage and arrived at the spaceport. The small hangars were devoid of tactical aircraft. Ground crews hustled about gathering supplies, anticipating the aircrafts' return. Two sleek intermediate star cruisers sat at the end of the blue launchpad, one in a temporary maintenance bubble. Agitated technicians approached, wheeling a sensor array before them, agreeing with each other: *We should just kill them all! Yes, just get it over with.*

Andrea tightened her wilderness cloak about her

and stood as still as a corpse. Her back against the wall, she felt exposed. Every instinct lashed her to dispatch these two technicians: *How can they not see me? They're looking right at me!* But the technicians saw nothing but inanimate brick and mortar, the illusion projected by the wilderness cloak. The two technicians passed within feet of her: she smelled cleaning solvents on their clothes.

Her heart pounded. Andrea did not trust the cloaks yet. She cut her eyes across the thin observation slit in the cloth to see how Tara managed this close encounter. She saw nothing but the blue tile of the pad, red brick, and smoke slipping behind buildings across the horizon. "Tara!" she tried to project her voice no further than necessary.

"Yes." Tara shifted position and a stretch of red masonry blurred. She lowered her face covering—the gold flecks in her hazel eyes caught the morning light. She looked in Andrea's general direction, and whispered, "These cloaks take some getting used to."

Andrea suggested the long route around the peripheral wall toward the starcruisers. The circuitous route kept them far away from ground traffic and security patrols. Tara walked point and by agreement, Andrea stayed two arms' lengths behind Tara's left shoulder. Andrea kept her pistol drawn but concealed in the cloak. They plodded with deliberate, glacial sloth, pausing every couple of steps to let the cloaks settle on a new pattern. Suspecting an occasional glance in their direction, Andrea emitted a hushed order, "Freeze!"

The lack of motion wore them down more than the rest of the day's exertions. At last they stood within a stone's throw of the two starships and Andrea said, "Let's sit here a moment and decide our next move."

They slouched down on the blue ceramic launchpad, disappearing. They watched and spoke in whispers. Andrea focused on the closer ship, an armed freighter. The boarding ramp was down, inviting Andrea and Tara aboard. A woman in a tan jumpsuit exited with a toolbox and walked over to the sister starcruiser cased in the maintenance bubble. Andrea whispered, "Looks like everybody's pulling maintenance on the other ship."

"That happens."

"How many crew will they leave on board?"

Tara held up two fingers. "As few as two; as many as a dozen—I guess after this morning, most are busy elsewhere."

Andrea pointed at the sleek star freighter. "You don't know how to fly one of these, do you?"

"I can work the computers—probably help with the guidance systems, but I don't know hardware. I figured you knew how to pilot a ship."

"Hmmm. These can't be too different from a Jod model. Physics is physics, right?"

"I suppose." Tara squirmed.

"Well, one of us has to fly this bird, the other must neutralize any remaining crew. And you can't fly—"

"Neutralize? You mean kill them." Tara's eyes narrowed.

"You don't have to stop and take their pulse if you don't want to." Andrea's voice iced over. "Do you want to get off this rock or don't you?"

Tara answered with silence.

"Good." Andrea laid out her plan. "I'll go straight to the bridge. You work the corridor back to engineering—one long corridor down the spine of the ship. Seal the cargo hatches manually." Andrea poked her hands from her cloak and demonstrated jerking a wheel a half-turn clockwise. "Meanwhile, I'll take us up and out as fast as possible. As soon as we leave the gravity well, we'll make the jump to the Jod system. You can bet the Ordinate will be hot on our tail."

They edged their way tediously to the boarding ramp, then briskly ran aboard. Andrea directed Tara toward the back of the ship while she moved forward.

As she approached the bridge, the doors automatically hissed open. She saw a young man, wearing the unadorned cadet's uniform, studying the communications panel and a tactical display of their troop deployments around the clone precincts. He didn't look up, but said, "Come take a look at this, Phil." Boyish excitement, urgent concentration filled his voice—a cadet intern left aboard while the rest of the crew joined the melee outside. Andrea silently pulled back the hood of the cloak and crept up behind the adolescent, her pistol in her hand.

"Phil, is that you?" He spun around in his chair and found Andrea standing over him. His eyes flashed from repulsion to fear, then to despair as he reached for his belt and found that he was unarmed. Had she seen herself in a mirror, she might have appreciated the young man's gut reaction. Her shoulder was bathed in her own blood. She'd been drenched in amniotic fluids turned sticky from evaporation and crusting to a yellow chalk. Smoke and ash clung to her hair matted into short, gnarled strands. Flecks of red—leftovers from the Hunter's head wound—peppered her neck and face. She was the picture of death in search of her own kind.

Andrea watched the youth's face turn crimson, then pale. "Get up." She motioned with the barrel of the pistol. She read his eyes and added, "Don't try to be the hero. Your officers shouldn't have left you here alone. This is not your fault."

She motioned him to the door, stepping behind him, and led him to the main hatch and boarding ramp. Tara approached from the back end of the ship. "It's empty."

Andrea acknowledged with a nod, motioning Tara to leave—a silent rebuke: *Go to the bridge.* But Tara didn't move. For all the day's killing, it came down to this insignificant cadet—one last obstacle and they would be on their way out of this hell. One spent bullet, and they could consign this awful day to history. Tara watched as if her fate were joined somehow to the cadet's.

Andrea poked the pistol barrel between the youth's shoulder blades, prodding him to the open hatch. In blew a breeze tainted with the smell of smoke. Andrea raised her pistol and clubbed the young man over the head, a blow that opened a small scalp wound, and with a shove, she dumped him into unconsciousness. The cadet's body rolled down the ramp to the blue launchpad below.

Tara tried to find her voice; instead, she issued a single syllable, *Oh!*—a stifled exclamation that mixed a groan with surprise. "You spared him."

"If you think so—fine." Andrea hit the control that raised the ramp and sealed the hull hatch. She ran past Tara to the bridge, jumped into the pilot's seat, and toggled a line of switches, firing the engines. The starcruiser shuddered. "Navigator sits there." Andrea directed Tara to a chair overlooking a seventy-two-inch screen, presently showing the star chart for the Cor System.

Tara took her seat and quickly taught herself how to

enter coordinates and plot a course. She placed an audio plug into her left ear. "Look at the rearview screen, Andrea."

The cadet staggered into the camera's field of view, holding his head, yelling for help. Ground crew from the adjacent starcruiser ran to his aid. After some arm waving and pointing, a uniformed supervisor raised a comm disk to his face.

Andrea slapped the console. "Didn't hit him hard enough. They know we're here." Andrea pressed the throttle, increasing thrust, gently lifting all the weight from the landing gear, "But they're too late." Andrea keyed an ascent angle into the computer, raising the nose of the freighter skyward; then she accelerated as fast as she dared in atmosphere.

Tara pulled at her matted hair. "I'm glad you spared his life."

"Why? Do you know him?" Andrea asked sarcastically.

"Why did you spare him?"

Andrea bristled at this critique, but she sloughed it off with a casual admission, "I was tired; I got sloppy. Satisfied?"

Weariness marred Tara's face, but her eyes remained alert. "I was beginning to worry that you enjoyed your work too much."

Andrea silenced Tara with a look, adding, "Listen, Tara. You don't know me." She tapped herself over her breast. "You can't begin to know what I feel. Why don't you just plot us a solution out of here: we'll have time for a nice long chat later." She bit her tongue to keep from tossing the epithet, *Presumptuous clone!*

Tara sat tight-lipped in front of the navigational screen.

Moments later, the main screen showed them the black void of space ahead, and behind them the bright tan and blue planet. The raging fire in the city of Sarhn sent a column of gray smoke visible from space: a tube of smoke bent by the wind, flattened by a pressured layer in the atmosphere. Tara pressed her face closer to the screen. She magnified the image fifty times to study the destruction she'd caused. She'd destroyed the institute, the temple, and for many clones, heaven itself. Through the haze, she saw small flashes of light, explosions caused by the spreading conflagration. She heard the thousands of souls cry out in pain, blaming her. She muttered, "I'm sorry . . ."

Andrea overheard and presumed the apology was directed her way. "Sorry for what?"

Tara turned and said, "I wasn't talking to you." She switched off the rear screen and returned to her navigational work. Then her audio plug interrupted her. Tara reported, "I'm picking up radio traffic directed to all Cor ships within the system." Tara switched the audio to broadcast. . . . *any means available. Repeat. An enemy has seized the Starfreighter Benwoi. Engage. Destroy by any means available. Repeat . . .*

"Switch it off." Andrea steered her renegade ship toward open space as she looked at her tactical display. "I just picked up a pair of battle cruisers accelerating to intercept us."

Tara killed the audio. "I've got a solution for the jump to the Jod System. You can engage at will."

"Hang on to something." Andrea grabbed the lever to engage the FTL drive. Then she spoke to the black ether, "H'Roo, you'd better be waiting on the other side: I'm bringing bad company." She pushed the lever forward and punched the button, then instantly felt the surge as they jumped to FTL speed. The view screens automatically blanked; then returned with on-board computer simulation, displaying from memory what the sensors could not see at this speed.

"We're safe for now." Andrea wiped the nervous perspiration from her forehead and turned from her console. She took a long look at Tara, who seemed lost in recollections of the day. Tara wiped a tear with the back of her hand, revealing a small circle of pale skin on her otherwise dirty cheek.

Andrea demanded, "What's the matter with you now?"

Tara wiped another tear. "Everything. Coop's dead. My friends, they're all dead or they'll soon be dead. I'll probably never see them again. I shouldn't be here safe. I should be with them." She covered her face and cried.

At least she waited until the work was done. Andrea shook her head. *At least she waited . . .* She envied Tara, who could indulge herself in such a blessed release, these free-flowing tears. How was it then that years ago Andrea cried for days, howled like a beast, bereft of husband and child—and she got no healing, no cleansing? She ran out of tears long before she ran out of pain. She ran out of tears and replaced them with rage—a rage that served her adequately, didn't heal her wounds but bandaged them well enough. And today? Had she finally run dry on rage? Why had she let the cadet live? Was she really that tired? *Fatigue does make cowards of us all . . .*

Finally out of immediate danger, exhaustion numbed every sense and feeling. Softly, Andrea told Tara, "You'll have to cry for both of us. I am going to take a shower."

Andrea commandeered the captain's cabin and

started a roaring hot shower. She rifled the drawers and found a set of toiletries: body lotion, hair gel. After carefully draping the wilderness cloak over a chair, she shed her soiled clothes like an old skin. Then with physical rapture, she stepped into the cascade of hot water. The crusted collage of stains and dried blood loosened and eroded from her skin in streaks, collecting in a murky swirl at the drain by her feet. She lathered her skin, cleansing the oozing wound on her shoulder that turned the lather pink. Today's swollen flesh surrounding the splinter of lead dwarfed yesterday's scar that she carried from the Harbor Massacre. She washed and rewashed her hair, rinsing away grit and salt from her scalp, tilting her head back to lavish her face with sweet water. She took a small brush to her fingernails to scrub the dirt stubbornly rooted there. Fatigue rinsed away with the lather.

And after she had scrubbed herself pink, she stood under the water and let it pummel the back of her neck and shoulders. How often as a young girl she pondered her future standing in a shower in the safety of her father's house, draining the heat from the solar collectors and leaving him to a short, cold splash. The thought brought an impish grin to her face.

As if following an instinct, Andrea's mind wandered to the future. So many important issues remained out of her hands. K'Rin must still convince the Jod council to mobilize against the Cor Ordinate. Plus her oath to Brigon: she made the oath as an expedient. Was her promise worth anything? Perhaps she could bring Eric and Tara back with her in the summer. They might set up a fifth column on Cor. *Too many details.* She tried to put her busy mind to rest.

And Eric—Steve's double—I will learn the connection—

if one exists. Eric lives under K'Rin's protection. The Ordinate Hunters murdered Steve. K'Rin invites me into his household. He knows something he won't tell me. I can't solve that puzzle now. She put her head under the shower, and Andrea's mind shut down as she abandoned herself to the hot pounding water.

Two hours later, Andrea stepped back onto the bridge. She wore a long green robe, her skin still glowing from the hot shower. Her slicked-back hair glistened in the soft artificial light. In either hand, she carried a large glass tumbler of aromatic tea. She found Tara doggedly working the navigational console, learning the ship's systems as if she did not know what else to do.

Andrea offered the steaming tea to Tara and said, "Take the rest of the day off."

Continued in Book II of The Tenebrea Trilogy:

Tenebrea's Hope.